TRIPMASTER
MONKEY

ALSO BY MAXINE HONG KINGSTON

The Woman Warrior   (1976)

China Men   (1980)

Hawai'i One Summer   (1987)

TRIPMASTER
MONKEY

His Fake Book

Maxine
Hong
Kingston

 ALFRED A. KNOPF   NEW YORK   1989

THIS IS A BORZOI BOOK

PUBLISHED BY ALFRED A. KNOPF, INC.

Copyright © 1987, 1988, 1989 by Maxine Hong Kingston
All rights reserved under International
and Pan-American Copyright Conventions.
Published in the United States
by Alfred A. Knopf, Inc., New York,
and simultaneously in Canada by Random House
of Canada Limited, Toronto.
Distributed by Random House, Inc., New York.

Owing to limitations of space,
permission to reprint previously published
material may be found on page 343.

Library of Congress Cataloging-in-Publication Data
Kingston, Maxine Hong.
Tripmaster monkey : his fake book /
Maxine Hong Kingston.—1st ed.
p.   cm.
ISBN 0-394-56831-1
I. Title.
813'.54—dc19   88-45762   CIP

Manufactured in the United States of America
First Edition

TO EARLL

This fiction is set in the 1960s, a time when some events appeared to occur months or even years anachronistically.

CONTENTS

TRIPMASTER
MONKEY

TRIPPERS AND ASKERS

 MAYBE IT COMES from living in San Francisco, city of clammy humors and foghorns that warn and warn— omen, o-o-men, o dolorous omen, o dolors of omens—and not enough sun, but Wittman Ah Sing considered suicide every day. Entertained it. There slid beside his right eye a black gun. He looked side-eyed for it. Here it comes. He actually crooked his trigger finger and—bang!—his head breaks into pieces that fly far apart in the scattered universe. Then blood, meat, disgusting brains, mind guts, but he would be dead already and not see the garbage. The mouth part of his head would remain attached. He groaned. Hemingway had done it in the mouth. Wittman was not el pachuco loco. Proof: he could tell a figment from a table. Or a tree. Being outdoors, in Golden Gate Park, he stepped over to a tree and knock-knocked on it, struck a match on it. Lit a cigarette. Whose mind is it that doesn't suffer a loud takeover once in a while? He was aware of the run of his mind, that's all. He was not making plans to do himself in, and no more willed these seppuku movies—no more conjured up that gun—than built this city. His cowboy boots, old brown Wellingtons, hit its pavements hard. Anybody serious about killing himself does the big leap off the Golden Gate. The wind or shock knocks you out before impact. Oh, long before impact. So far, two hundred and thirty-five people, while taking a walk alone on the bridge—a mere net between you and the grabby ocean—had heard a voice out of the windy sky— Laurence Olivier asking them something: "To be or not to be?" And they'd answered, "Not to be," and climbed on top of the railing, fingers and toes

roosting on the cinnabarine steel. They take the side of the bridge that faces land. And the City. The last city. Feet first. Coit Tower giving you the finger all the way down. Wittman would face the sea. And the setting sun. Dive. But he was not going to do that. Strange. These gun pictures were what was left of his childhood ability to see galaxies. Glass cosmospheres there had once been, and planets with creatures, such doings, such colors. None abiding. In the *Chronicle*, a husband and wife, past eighty, too old to live, had shot each other with a weak gun, and had had to go to a doctor to have the bullets prized out of their ears. And a Buddhist had set fire to himself and burned to death on purpose; his name was Quang Duc. Quang Duc. Remember. In the cremations along the Ganges, the mourners stay with the burning body until its head pops. Pop.

Today Wittman was taking a walk on a path that will lead into the underpass beneath the gnarly trees. In fact, the park didn't look half bad in the fog beginning to fall, dimming the hillocks that domed like green-grey moons rising or setting. He pulled the collar of his pea coat higher and dragged on his cigarette. He had walked this far into the park hardly seeing it. He ought to let it come in, he decided. He would let it all come in. An old white woman was sitting on a bench selling trivets "@ $\frac{1}{2}$ dollar ea.," which a ducky and a bunny pointed out with gloved fingers. She lifted her head and turned her face toward Wittman's; her hands were working one more trivet out of yarn and bottlecaps. Not eyelids exactly but like skin flaps or membranes covered her eye sockets and quivered from the empty air in the holes or with efforts to see. Sockets wide open. He looked at her thick feet chapped and dirty in zoris. Their sorry feet is how you can tell crazy people who have no place to go and walk everywhere.

Wittman turned his head, and there on the ground were a pigeon and a squatting man, both puking. He looked away so that he would not himself get nauseated. Pigeons have milk sacs in their throats. Maybe this one was disgorging milk because last night a wind had blown in from the ocean and blown its squabs out of their nest, and it was milking itself. Or does that happen in the spring? But in California in the fall as well? The man was only a vomiting drunk. This walk was turning out to be a Malte Laurids Brigge walk. There was no helping that. There is no helping what you see when you let it all come in; he hadn't been in on building any city. It was already cold, soon the downside of the year. He walked into the tunnel.

Heading toward him from the other end came a Chinese dude from China, hands clasped behind, bow-legged, loose-seated, out on a stroll—

that walk they do in kung fu movies when they are full of contentment on a sunny day. As luck would have it, although there was plenty of room, this dude and Wittman tried to pass each other both on the same side, then both on the other, sidestepping like a couple of basketball stars. Wittman stopped dead in his tracks, and shot the dude a direct stink-eye. The F.O.B. stepped aside. Following, straggling, came the poor guy's wife. She was coaxing their kid with sunflower seeds, which she cracked with her gold tooth and held out to him. "Ho sick, la. Ho sick," she said. "Good eating. Good eats." Her voice sang, rang, banged in the echo-chamber tunnel. Mom and shamble-legged kid were each stuffed inside of about ten homemade sweaters. Their arms stuck out fatly. The mom had on a nylon or rayon pantsuit. ("Ny-lon ge. Mm lon doc." "Nylon-made. Lasts forever.") "No!" said the kid. Echoes of "No!" Next there came scrabbling an old lady with a cane. She also wore one of those do-it-yourself pantsuit outfits. On Granny's head was a cap with a pompon that matched everybody's sweaters. The whole family taking a cheap outing on their day offu. Immigrants. Fresh Off the Boats out in public. Didn't know how to walk together. Spitting seeds. So uncool. You wouldn't mislike them on sight if their pants weren't so highwater, gym socks white and noticeable. F.O.B. fashions—highwaters or puddlecuffs. Can't get it right. Uncool. Uncool. The tunnel smelled of mothballs—F.O.B. perfume.

On the tunnel ceiling, some tall paint-head had sprayed, "I love my skull." And somebody else had answered, "But oh you kidney!" This straighter person had prime-coated in bone-white a precise oval on the slope of the wall, and lettered in neat black, "But oh you kidney!"

He would avoid the Academy of Sciences, especially the North American Hall. Coyotes and bobcats dead behind glass forever. Stuffed birds stuffed inside their pried-open mouths. He was never going to go in there again. Claustro. Dark except for the glow of fake suns on the "scenes." Funeral-parlor smell seeping through the sealant.

Don't go into the Steinhart Aquarium either. Remember *The Lady from Shanghai*? The seasick cameras shoot through and around the fish-tanks at Orson Welles and Rita Hayworth saying goodbye. The fish are moving, unctuously moving.

No Oriental Tea Garden either. "Oriental." Shit.

On the paths where no other human being was wending, he stepped over and between fallen trees into sudden fens of ferns and banana trees with no bananas. A wild strawberry—someone had been wounded and bled a drop here—said, "Eat me," but he didn't obey, maybe poison. How come ripe when it isn't even spring? There were no flowers in the Shakespeare Garden, its plants gone indistinguishably to leaf and twig.

Long before Ocean Beach and the Great Highway, he turned back into the woods. Eucalyptus, pine, and black oak—those three trees together is how you tell that you're in Northern California and not Los Angeles. The last time he had walked along the ocean, he ended up at the zoo. Aquarium and dank zoo on the same day. "Fu-li-sah-kah Soo." He said "Fleishhacker Zoo" to himself in Chinatown language, just to keep a hand in, so to speak, to remember and so to keep awhile longer words spoken by the people of his brief and dying culture. At Fu-li-sah-kah Soo, he once saw a monkey catch a flying pigeon and tear it up. In another cage, a tiger backed up to its wading pool and took a dump in it. The stained polar bears make you want to throw things at them and to bite into an eraser.

If it were Sunday, football roars would be rising out of Kezar Stadium, and everywhere you walk, in the woods, along the Chain of Lakes, at the paddock of buffaloes, you'd hear the united voice of the crowd, and the separate loudspeaker voice of the announcer doing the play-by-play. Football season. Good thing that when he was in school, an American of Japanese Ancestry had played on the Cal football team, and there had been a couple of A.J.A. pompon girls too. Otherwise, his manhood would have been even more totally destroyed than it was.

Having lost track of his whereabouts, Wittman was surprised by a snowy glass palace—the Conservatory—that coalesced out of the fog. A piece had sharded off and was floating to the right of the spire on top of the cupola— the day moon. Up the stairs to this fancy hothouse (built with Crocker money), where unlikely roses and cacti grow, climbed a man and a dog. They were the same color and leanness, the dog a Doberman pinscher. "Bitch. You fucking bitch." The man was scolding the dog, the two of them walking fast, the dog pulling forward and the man pulling the short new chain taut. "Who do you think you are, bitch? Huh, bitch? You listening to me? Who the fuck do you think you are?" The man had plucked his eyebrows into the shapes of tadpoles, the same definition as the dog's, which were light tan. The dog wore a shame look on its face, and its legs were bending with straint. "Bitch animal," said the man, who looked nowhere but at his dog. "How could you, huh, bitch? Huh? You listening to me?" A yank on the choke-chain. "You hear me? You cuntless bitch."

Along a side path came another Black man, this one pushing a shopping cart transporting one red apple and a red bull from Tijuana. It was time, Wittman thought, to stop letting it all come in.

"Newspaper, sir?" said the man with the red bull. "Newspaper. Ten cents." He was holding out a folded page of newspaper. He was embracing an armload of these folios and quartos. Wittman had dimes in his pocket, so bought one. The man thanked him, and specially gave him a color insert from last Sunday's paper. He must be illiterate and not know that newspapers come out new every day.

Some children were climbing rocks. A little girl, who was at the top of the pile, jumped off, saying, "Don't tell *me* your personal problems." She talked like that because she copied women. "I got problems of my *own*," she said. The kid was ruined already. A shot of hate went from him to her that ought to have felled her, but up she climbed again. Wittman tossed his smoke and headed for an exit from the park.

Under a bush was a rag that had been squirted with blue paint. That rag had sucked a boy's breath and eaten up his brain cells. His traitorous hand that should have torn the rag away had pressed it against his face, smeared him blue, and made him drag in the fumes.

Wittman stood at the bus stop on the corner of Arguello and Fulton. He was avoiding the corner where the grizzly bear on one rock and the mountain lion with tensed shoulders on the opposite rock look down at you. The Muni bus came along on the cables not too much later. Continue. "I can't go on, I go on." "I can't go on comma I go on." Wow.

On the ride downtown, for quite a while—the spires of St. Ignatius to the left and the dome of City Hall straight ahead as if rising out of the center of the street—San Francisco seemed to be a city in a good dream. Past the gilded gates of the Opera House and Civic Auditorium. Past the Orpheum, once "the best vaudeville house in the West"; on the evening of the day of the Earthquake and Fire, its actors went to the park and sang an act from *Carmen*. In 1911, Count Ilya Tolstoy, *the* Tolstoy's son, lectured in the Orpheum on "Universal Peace." Wittman had heard the orotund voice of Lowell Thomas intone, "THIS IS CINERAMA!" The Embassy, the Golden Gate, U. A. Cinema, the Paramount, the Warfield, the St. Francis, the Esquire. Then the neighborhood of the Curran, the Geary, and the Marines Memorial, where he had seen the Actor's Workshop do *King Lear* with Michael O'Sullivan as Lear—"Blow, winds, and crack your cheeks." Out the bus window, he kept spotting people who offended him in their postures and gestures, their walks, their nose-blowing, their clothes, their facial expressions. Normal humanity, mean and wrong. He was a convict on a locked bus staring at the sights on the way from county jail to San Quentin. Breathe shallow so as not to smell the other passengers. It's true, isn't it, that molecules break off and float about, and go up your nose, and that's how you smell? Always some freak riding the Muni. And making eye contact. Wittman was the only passenger sitting on a crosswise seat in front; the other passengers, facing forward, were looking at him. Had he spoken aloud? They're about to make sudden faces, like in *El. Who, if I cried out, would hear me among the angels' hierarchies?* All right, then, all right. Out of a pocket, he took his Rilke. For such gone days, he carried *The Notebooks of Malte Laurids Brigge* in his pea coat—and read out loud to his fellow riders: " 'My father had taken me with him to Urnekloster. . . . There remains whole in my heart, so it seems to me, only that large hall in which we used to gather for dinner every evening at seven o'clock. I never saw this room by day; I do not even remember whether it had windows or on what they looked out; always, whenever the family entered, the candles were burning in the ponderous branched candlesticks, and in a few minutes one forgot the time of day and all that one had seen outside. This lofty and, as I suspect, vaulted chamber was stronger than everything else. With its darkening height, with its never quite clarified corners, it sucked all images out of one without giving one any definite substitute for them. One sat there as if dissolved; entirely without will, without consciousness, without desire, without defence. One was like a vacant spot. I remember that at first this annihilating state almost caused me nausea; it brought on a kind of sea-sickness which I only overcame by stretching out my leg until I touched with my foot the knee of my father who sat opposite me. It did not strike me until afterwards that he seemed to understand, or at least to tolerate, this singular behavior, although there existed between us an almost cool relationship which would not account for such a gesture. Nevertheless it was this slight contact that gave me strength to support the long repasts. And after a few weeks of spasmodic endurance, I became, with the almost boundless adaptability of a child, so inured to the eeriness of these gatherings, that it no longer cost me effort to sit at table for two hours; now these hours passed comparatively swiftly, for I occupied myself in observing those present.' " Some of those present on the Muni were looking at the reader, some had closed their eyes, some looked out the window, everyone perhaps listening.

" 'My grandfather called them "the family," and I also heard the others use the same term, which was entirely arbitrary.' " Wittman read on, reading the descriptions of the four persons at table. The bus driver did not tell

him to shut up, and he got to the good part: " 'The meal dragged along as usual, and we had just reached the dessert when my eye was caught and carried along by a movement going on, in the half-darkness, at the back of the room. In that quarter a door which I had been told led to the mezzanine floor, had opened little by little, and now, as I looked on with a feeling entirely new to me of curiosity and consternation, there stepped into the darkness of the doorway a slender lady in a light-colored dress, who came slowly toward us. I do not know whether I made any movement or any sound; the noise of a chair being overturned forced me to tear my eyes from that strange figure, and I caught sight of my father, who had jumped up now, his face pale as death, his hands clenched by his sides, going toward the lady. She, meantime, quite untouched by this scene, moved toward us, step by step, and was already not far from the Count's place, when he rose brusquely and, seizing my father by the arm, drew him back to the table and held him fast, while the strange lady, slowly and indifferently, traversed the space now left clear, step by step, through an indescribable stillness in which only a glass clinked trembling somewhere, and disappeared through a door in the opposite wall of the dining-hall.' "

None of the passengers was telling Wittman to cool it. It was pleasant, then, for them to ride the bus while Rilke shaded and polished the City's greys and golds. Here we are, Walt Whitman's "classless society" of "everyone who could read or be read to." Will one of these listening passengers please write to the City Council and suggest that there always be a reader on this route? Wittman has begun a someday tradition that may lead to a job as a reader riding the railroads throughout the West. On the train through Fresno—Saroyan; through the Salinas Valley—Steinbeck; through Monterey—*Cannery Row*; along the Big Sur ocean—Jack Kerouac; on the way to Weed—*Of Mice and Men*; in the Mother Lode—Mark Twain and Robert Louis Stevenson, who went on a honeymoon in *The Silverado Squatters*; *Roughing It* through Calaveras County and the Sacramento Valley; through the redwoods—John Muir; up into the Rockies—*The Big Rock Candy Mountain* by Wallace Stegner. Hollywood and San Elmo with John Fante. And all of the Central Valley on the Southern Pacific with migrant Carlos Bulosan, *America Is in the Heart*. What a repertoire. A lifetime reading job. And he had yet to check out Gertrude Atherton, and Jack London of Oakland, and Ambrose Bierce of San Francisco. And to find "Relocation" Camp diaries to read in his fierce voice when the train goes through Elk Grove and other places where the land once belonged to the A.J.A.s. He will refuse to be a reader of racist Frank Norris. He won't read Bret

Harte either, in revenge for that Ah Sin thing. Nor *Ramona* by Helen
Hunt Jackson, in case it turned out to be like *Gone with the Wind*. Travelers
will go to the reading car to hear the long novels of the country they were
riding through for hours and for days. A fool for literature, the railroad
reader of the S.P. is getting his start busting through reader's block on
the Muni. Wittman's talent was that he could read while riding without
getting carsick.

The ghost of Christine Brahe for the third and last time walked through
the dining hall. The Count and Malte's father raised their heavy wineglasses "to the left of the huge silver swan filled with narcissus," Rilke's ancestral tale came to a close, and the bus came to the place for Wittman to
get off. He walked through the Stockton Street tunnel—beneath the Tunnel Top Bar on Bush and Burill, where Sam Spade's partner, Miles Archer,
was done in by Brigid O'Shaughnessy—and emerged in Chinatown. At a
payphone—this was not the phone booth with the chinky-chinaman corny
horny roof—he thought about whether he needed to make any calls. He
had a couple more dimes. What the hell. He dropped one into the slot
and dialed information for the number of the most ungettable girl of his
acquaintance.

So, that very afternoon it happened that: It was September again, which
used to be the beginning of the year, and Wittman Ah Sing, though not a
student anymore, nevertheless was having cappuccino in North Beach with
a new pretty girl. The utter last of summer's air lifted the Cinzano scallops
of the table umbrella, and sun kept hitting beautiful Nanci Lee in the hair
and eyes. In shade, Wittman leaned back and glowered at her. He sucked
shallow on his cigarette and the smoke clouded out thick over his face, made
his eyes squint. He also had the advantage of the backlighting, his hair all
haloed, any zits and pores shadowed. She, on her side, got to watch the sun
go down. A summer and a year had gone by since graduation from Berkeley. Somebody's favorite tune was "Moscow Nights," and balalaikas kept
trembling out of the jukebox.

"You," he said. "You're from L.A., aren't you? Why didn't you go back
there?" Well, the place that a Chinese holds among other Chinese—in a
community somewhere—matters. It was a very personal question he was
asking her. It would pain a true Chinese to admit that he or she did not have
a community, or belonged at the bottom or the margin.

People who have gone to college—people their age with their at-
tee-tood—well, there are reasons—people who wear black turtleneck

sweaters have no place. You don't easily come home, come back to Chinatown, where they give you stink-eye and call you a saang-hsü lo, a whisker-growing man, Beatnik.

Nanci brought her coffee cup up to her mouth, bouging to catch the rim, and looked warily, he hoped, at him over it. Beautiful and shy, what a turn-on she is. She took a cigarette out of her purse, and held it in front of that mouth until he lit it. "Yes, I'm from Los Angeles," she said, answering one of his questions. Pause. Take a beat. "I'm going back down there soon. To audition. I'm on my way." Pause yet another beat or two. "Why don't you go back to Sacramento?"

Unfair. No fair. L.A. is wide, flat, new. Go through the flashing arch, and there you are: Chinatownland. Nothing *to* going back to L.A. Cecil B. DeMille rebuilds it new ahead of you as you approach it and approach it on the freeway, whether 101 or over the grapevine. But, say, you stake a claim to San Francisco as your home place. . . .

"Golden Gate Park was wild today. I fought my way out. Lucky." He blew smoke hard between clenched teeth. "The paint-heads were cutting loose out of their minds, and messing with my head. Through the pines and eucalyptus, I could smell the natural-history museum. They may have let those trees grow to hide the funeral-parlor smell, which seeps through the sealant. You got claustro, you got fear of the dark, you keep out of museums of natural history; every kind of phobia lets you have it. It's too quiet, the ursus horribilus propped up on its hind legs; his maw is open but no roar. I don't like walking in the dark with fake suns glowing on the 'scenes.' Pairs of cat-eye marbles look at you from bobcat heads and coyote heads. Freak me out. The male animals are set in hunting poses, and the female ones in nursing poses. Dead babies. There's a lizard coming out of a dinosaur's tail. Stiffs. Dead behind glass forever. Stuffed birds stuffed inside pried-open mouths. 'Taxidermy' means the ordering of skin. Skin arrangements. If you're at my bedside when I die, Nanci, please, don't embalm me. I don't want some mortician who's never met me to push my face into a serene smile. They try to make the buffaloes and deer more natural by balding a patch of hair, omitting a toenail, breaking a horn. I paid my way out of the park. I saw the pattern: twice, there were people refashioning and selling castoffs. Flotsam and jetsam selling flotsam and jetsam. I bought this insert from last Sunday's paper."

Nanci took the paper from him, and folded it into a hat. She put it on Wittman's head. She was not squeamish to touch what a dirty stranger had touched, nor to touch this hairy head before her. He was at a party. He took off the hat, and with a few changes of folds, origamied it into a popgun. He whopped it through the air, it popped good.

"In Sacramento, I don't belong. Don't you wonder how I have information about you and L.A., your town? And how come you have information about me? You have committed to memory that I have family in Sacramento." And, yes, a wondering—a wonderfulness—did play in her eyes and on her face. Two invisible star points dinted her cheeks with dimples; an invisible kung fu knight was poking her cheeks with the points of a silver shuriken. "And I bet you know what I studied. And whether I'm rich boy or poor boy. What my family is—Lodi grocery or Watsonville farmer, Castroville artichoke or Oakland restaurant or L.A. rich." Smart was what he was. Scholarship smart.

"No," she said. "I don't know much about you."

No, she wouldn't. She was no China Man the way he was China Man. A good-looking chick like her floats above it all. He, out of it, knows ugly and knows Black, and also knows fat, and funny-looking. Yeah, he knows fat too, though he's tall and skinny. She's maybe only part Chinese—Lee could be Black or white Southern, Korean, Scotsman, anything—and also rich. Nanci Lee and her highborn kin, rich Chinese-Americans of Orange County, where the most Chinese thing they do is throw the headdress ball. No, he hadn't exactly captured her fancy and broken her heart. When the rest of them shot the shit about him, she hadn't paid attention. Though she should have; he was more interesting than most, stood out, tall for one thing, long hair for another, dressed in Hamlet's night colors for another. Sly-eyed, he checked himself out in the plate-glass window. The ends of his moustache fell below his bearded jawbone. He had tied his hair back, braided loose, almost a queue but not a slave queue, very hip, like a samurai whose hair has gotten slightly undone in battle. Like Kyuzu, terse swordsman in *Seven Samurai*. A head of his time, ha ha. He was combat-ready, a sayonara soldier sitting on his red carpet beside the palace moat and digging the cherry blossoms in their significant short bloom.

"You must not have been in on the Chinese gossip," he said, counting on what would hurt her, that at school she had been left out by the main Chinese. (They left everybody out.)

"Let me tell you about where I was born," he said. She was, in a way, asking for the story of his life, wasn't she? Yeah, she was picking up okay.

"Chinatown?" she guessed. Is that a sneer on her face? In her voice? Is she stereotypecasting him? Is she showing him the interest of an anthropologist, or a tourist? No, guess not.

"Yes. Yes, wherever I appear, there, there it's Chinatown. But not that Chinatown." He chinned in its direction. "I was born backstage in vaudeville. Yeah, I really was. No kidding. They kept me in an actual theatrical trunk—wallpaper lining, greasepaint, and mothball smells, paste smell. The lid they braced with a cane. My mother was a Flora Dora girl. To this day, they call her Ruby Long Legs, all alliteration the way they say it."

Yes, when she came near the trunk, a rubescence had filled the light and air, and he'd tasted strawberry jam and smelled and seen clouds of cotton candy. Wittman really does have show business in his blood. He wasn't lying to impress Nanci. He was taking credit for the circumstances of his birth, such as his parents. Parents are gifts; they're part of the life-which-happens-to-one. He hadn't yet done enough of the life-which-one-has-to-make. Commit more experience, Wittman. *It is true you were an actor's child, and when your people played they wanted to be seen. . . .*

"She did the blackbottom and the Charleston in this act, Doctor Ng and the Flora Dora Girls. Only, after a couple of cities, Doctor Ng changed it to Doctor Woo and the Chinese Flora Dora Girls so that the low fawn gwai would have no problem reading the flyers. 'Woo' easier in the Caucasian mouth. Not broke the mouth, grunting and gutturating and hitting the tones. 'Woo' sounds more classy anyway, the dialect of a better-class village. 'Woo' good for white ear. A class act. You know?" Of course, she did not know; he rubbed it in, how much she did not know about her own. "Doctor Woo's Chinese Flora Dora Jitter and June Bug Girls were boogie-woogying and saluting right through World War II. Yeah, within our lifetimes."

"What *was* the blackbottom?" she asked.

For her, he danced his forefingers like little legs across the tabletop. (Like Charlie Chaplin doing the Oceana Roll with dinner rolls on forks in *The Gold Rush.*) " 'Hop down front and then you doodle back. Mooch to your left and then you mooch to your right. Hands on your hips and do the mess around. Break a leg and buckle near the ground. Now that's the Old Black Bottom.' " She laughed to see one finger-leg buckle and kick, buckle and kick, then straighten up, and the other finger-leg buckle and kick all the way across and off the table. Knuckle-knees.

O Someday Girl, find him and admire him for his interests. And dig his allusions. And laugh sincerely at his jokes. And were he to take up dandy ways, for example, why, remark on his comeliness in a cravat. Say "He's beau," without his having to point out the cravat.

But at the moment, this Nanci was smiling one of those Anne Bancroft–Tuesday Weld sneer-smiles, and he went on talking. In case she turns out to be the one he ends up with, he better tell her his life from the beginning. "You have to imagine Doctor Woo in white tie, top hat, tails—his Dignity. He called that outfit his Dignity. 'What shall I wear? I shall wear my Dignity,' he used to say, and put on his tux. 'I'm attending that affair dressed in my Dignity.' 'My Dignity is at the cleaner's.' 'My Dignity will see me out,' which means he'll be buried in it. Doctor Woo did sleight of hand, and he did patter song. He also did an oriental turn. Do you want to hear a Doctor Woo joke? No, wait. Wait. Never mind. Some other time. Later. It'd bring you down. He rip-rapped about sweet-and-sour eyes and chop-suey dis and dat, and white people all alikee. Yeah, old Doc Woo did a racist turn." (What Wittman wanted to say was, "Old Doc Woo milked the tit of stereotype," but he went shy.) "The audience loved it. Not one showgirl caught him up on it." Wittman made lemon eyes, and quince mouth, and Nanci laughed. He scooped up shreds of nervous paper napkins, his and hers, wadded them into a ball—held it like a delicate egg between thumb and forefinger—palm empty—see?—and out of the fist, he tugged and pulled a clean, whole napkin—opened the hand, no scraps. Come quick, your majesty. Simple Simon is making the princess laugh; she will have to marry him. "During intermissions and after the show, we sold Doctor Woo's Wishes Come True Medicine. The old healing-powers-and-aphrodisiacs-of-the-East scam. I'm dressed as a monkey. I'm running around in the crowd handing up jars and bottles and taking in the money. Overhead Doc Woo is giving the pitch and jam: 'You hurt? You tired? Ah, tuckered out? Where you ache? This medicine for you. Ease you sprain, ease you pain. What you wish? You earn enough prosperity? Rub over here. Tired be gone. Hurt no more. Guarantee! Also protect against accidental bodily harm. And the Law. Smell. Breathe in deep. Free whiff. Drop three drops—four too muchee, I warn you—into you lady's goblet, and she be you own lady. Make who you love love you back. Hold you true love true to you. Guarantee! Guarantee!' We sold a line of products: those pretty silver beebees—remember them?—for when you have a tummy ache?—and Tiger Balm, which he bought in Chinatown and sold at a markup—cheaper for Chinese customers, of course. The Deet Dah Jow, we mixed ourselves. I use it quite often." "Deet Dah Jow" means "Fall Down and Beaten Up

Alcohol." Medicine for the Fallen Down and Beaten Up. Felled and
Beaten.

"When I smell Mahn Gum Yow," said Nanci, saying "Ten Thousand
Gold Pieces Oil" very prettily, high-noting "gum," "I remember being sick
in bed with the t.v. on. I got to play treasure trove with the red tins. I liked
having a collection of gold tigers—they used to be raised, embossed—
they're flat now—with emerald eyes and red tongues. I thought Tiger Balm
was like Little Black Sambo's tiger butter. That in India the tigers chase
around the palm tree until they churn into butter. And here they churn into
ointment."

May this time be the first and only time she charms with this tale, and
he its inspiration. "Yeah," he said. "Yeah. Yeah."

He continued. Onward. "Backstage old Doc Woo used to peptalk the
Flora Dora girls about how they weren't just entertaining but doing public
service like Ng Poon Chew and Wellington Koo, credits to our race. Show
the bok gwai that Chinese-Ah-mei-li-cans are human jess likee anybody
elsoo, dancing, dressed civilized, telling jokes, getting boffo laffs. We got
rhythm. We got humor." Oh, god, he was so glad. He had not lost it, then
—the mouth—to send the day high.

Nanci said, "You aren't making this up, are you?"

"Hey, you don't believe me? I haven't given you anything but facts. So
I don't have an imagination. It's some kind of retardation. So I am incapable
of making things up. My mother's name is Ruby, and my father is Zeppelin
Ah Sing. He was a Stagedoor Johnny, then a backstage electrician, then
emcee on stage. To get Mom to marry him, he bought out the front row of
seats for entire runs. He loved her the best when she was on stage as Ruby
Long Legs; and she loved him best leading his Army buddies in applause.
They got married in Carson City, which is open for weddings twenty-four
hours a day.

"To this day, whenever they go gambling at State Line, they start divorce proceedings. To keep up the romance. My parents are free spirits—
I'm a descendant of free spirits. He left her and me for World War II. My
aunties, the showgirls, said I was a mad baby from the start. Yeah. Mad baby
and mad man." Come on, Nanci. The stars in a white girl's eyes would be
glittering and popping by now.

"Uh-huh. Uh-huh," she said. "Uh-huh."

"You should have seen me in my Baby Uncle Sam outfit. The striped
pants had an open seam in the back, so if I could grow a tail, it would come

out of there. Sure, the costume came off of a circus monkey or a street-dancing monkey. You want details? I can impart details to you." She wasn't bored out of her mind anyway. Please be patient. Are you the one I can tell my whole life to? From the beginning to this moment? Using words that one reads and thinks but never gets to hear and say? "Think back as far as you can," he said. "First it's dark, right? But a warm, close dark, not a cold outer-space dark." A stupid girl would think he knew her personal mind. "Then you made out a slit of light, and another, and another—a zoetrope —faster and faster, until all the lights combined. And you had: consciousness. Most people's lights turn on by degrees like that. (When you come across 'lights' in books, like the Donner Party *ate* lights, do you think 'lights' means the eyes or the brains?) I got zapped all at once. That may account for why I'm uncommon. I saw: all of a sudden, curtains that rose and rose, and on the other side of them, lights, footlights and overheads, and behind them, the dark, but different from the previous dark. Rows of lights, like teeth, uppers and lowers, and the mouth wide open laughing—and either I was inside it standing on the tongue, or I was outside, looking into a mouth, and inside the mouth were many, many strangers. All looking at me. *For a while they looked at me, wondering at my littleness.* And pointing at me and saying, 'Aaah.' Which is my name, do you see? Then one big light blasted me. It was a spotlight or a floodlight, and I thought that it had dissolved me into light, but it hadn't, of course. I made out people breathing—expecting something. They wanted an important thing to happen. If I opened my mouth, whatever it was that was pouring into my ears and eyes and my skin would shout out of my mouth. I opened my mouth for it to happen. But somebody swooped me up—arms caught me—and carried me back into the wings. Sheepcrooked m'act." . . . *a door had swung open before you, and now you were among the alembics in the firelight. . . . Your theater came into being.*

Yes, this flight, this rush, the oncoming high. He had talked his way— here—once more. Good and bad, the world was exactly as it should be. The sidewalk trees were afire in leaf-flames. And the most beyond girl in the world was listening to him. The air which contained all this pleasure was as clear as mescaline and he was straight. The sun was out which shines golden like this but three times a San Francisco autumn.

"When I was a child," said Nanci—*her* turn to talk about *her* kiddie-hood—"I had a magic act too. But it wasn't an act. I didn't have an audience; it was secret. I believed I could make things appear and disappear by taking every step I had seen the magician take at my birthday party. I sprinkled salt on a hanky to make a dime appear." She opened a paper napkin, and shook salt into it. What's this? She doing geisha shtick for me? "I tied the corners together and said my magic words. Then undid the knot, and blew the salt." She made kiss-me lips, and blew. The wind is driving snow off of a silver pond. The wind is driving a snowcloud across the full moon. "I didn't find a dime then either. What step did I do wrong—not enough salt, too much salt? Didn't I tie the knot right? It has to be a seventh birthday?" She giggled, looked at him to help her out, to sympathize with her gullibility or to laugh at her joking. Doesn't she know that all magic acts you have to cheat, the missing step is cheating? You're not the only one, Wittman, who fooled with magic, and not the only one who refuses to work for money. And also not the only one to talk. She had to talk too, make this a conversation. In those days, women did not speak as much as men. Even among the educated and Bohemian, a man talked out his dreams and plans while a girl thought whether she would be able to adapt herself to them. Girls gave one another critiques on how adaptable they were. The artistic girls had dead-white lips and aborigine eyes, and they wore mourning colors. There were two wake-robins, Diane Wakoski and Lenore Kandell; the latter wailed out sex-challenge poems larger and louder than the men, who were still into cool.

"Why did you ask me out?" asked Nanci.

Because you're beautiful, he thought, and maybe I love you; I need to get it on with a Chinese-American chick. He said, "I wanted to find out if the most beautiful girl of all my school days would come to me." There. Said. Would come to me. Intimate. He let her know that he used to be— and still was—in her thrall. "I'm calling you up," he had said on the phone, "to celebrate the first anniversary of our graduation. Come tell me, have you found out, 'Is there life after Berkeley?' " "I told you—we're having a reunion, a party for me."

"Shouldn't we be at Homecoming, then, with everyone else?"

What? Buy her a lion-head chrysanthemum, pin it on her tweed lapel? Do the two of us have to walk again past the fraternities on College Avenue, and admire their jungle-bunny house decorations? The Jew Guais too with Greek letters—Sammies—and Yom Kippur banners. Yeah, there were a Chinese fraternity and sorority, but if you were bone-proud, you didn't have anything to do with SOP sisters and the Pineapple Pies. Nor the Christian house, which let anybody in. The crowd let the city and county sawhorses route them, governments too co-operating with football. He was always walking alone in the opposite direction but ending up at Strawberry

Canyon—the smell of eucalyptus in the cold air breaks your heart—among the group looking down into the stadium for free. Only he was up here for the walk, awaiting a poem to land on him, to choose him, walking to pace the words to the rhythm of his own stride. And there was all this football interference. The Cal Marching Band, the drum booming, and the pompon girls kneeling and rotating an arm with pompons in the air, and the teams running toward each other with the crowd going oo-oo-OO-OH! How do all those people know you're supposed to stand and yell that yell at kickoff? The reason he didn't like going to football games was the same reason he didn't like going to theater: he wanted to be playing. Does his inability at cheers have to do with being Chinese? He ought to be in Paris, where everything is dark and chic.

"The Big Game soon," she said.

"Weren't you an Oski Doll? You were an Oski Doll, weren't you?"

"Come on. It was an honor to be an Oski Doll. It's based on scholarship too, you know? It's a good reference. Some of us Oski Dolls helped integrate the rooting section from you boys."

" 'Here we go, Bears, here we go.' 'We smell roses.' 'All hail Blue and Gold; thy colors unfold.' 'Block that kick, hey.' 'Hold that line, hey.' 'The Golden Bear is ever watching.' "

"See? You did participate."

"Well, yeah, I went to the Big Game once. Stanford won." But most of the time I was participating in the big dread. "Those songs and cheers will stick in the head forever, huh?"

"I know your motive for wanting to see me," she said. "You want to know how you were seen. What your reputation was. What people thought of you. You care what people think of you. You're interested in my telling you."

He looked at the bitten nails of the fingers that held her cigarette and of her other fingers, both hands; they put him at ease. "Yes, if you want to tell me, go ahead."

"Well, let me think back," she said, as if school had been long ago and not interesting anymore. "It seems to me you were a conservative."

No. No. No. He had been wild. Maybe she thought it flattered a Chinese man to be called temperate? Safe. What about his white girlfriends? What about his Black girlfriend? His play-in-progress? That he read aloud on afternoons on the Terrace and at the Mediterraneum (called The Piccolo by those hip to the earlier Avenue scene). There had been no other playwright. Of whatever color. He was the only one. She hadn't cared for his poem in *The Occident*?

"Conservative like F.O.B.? Like Fresh Off the Boat?" He insulted her with translation; she was so banana, she needed a translation. "Conservative like engineering major from Fresno with a slide rule on his belt? Like dental student from Stockton? Like pre-optometry majors from Gilroy and Vallejo and Lodi?" But I'm an artist, an artist of all the Far Out West. "Feh-see-no. Soo-dock-dun," he said, like an old Chinese guy bopping out a list poem. "Gi-loy. Wah-lay-ho. Lo-di." But hadn't he already done for her a catalog of places? Repeating himself already. One of his rules for maintaining sincerity used to be: Never tell the same story twice. He changed that to: Don't say the same thing in the same way to the same person twice. Better to be dead than boring.

"I mean quiet," she said and did not elaborate, poured more espresso out of her individual carafe, sipped it, smoked. She wasn't deigning to go on. No examples. He had talked for four years, building worlds, inventing selves, and she had not heard. The gold went out of the day. He came crashing down. He must have been feeling good only because the sun was out amid grey weeks. (In the plague year, according to Defoe, the people's moods were much affected by the weather.)

"Well?" she said, pushing away from the table, her shoulders up, like a forties movie girl being hugged. "I have an appointment at three-thirty." As if she had come to the City for that important appointment and incidentally might as well have met with him too, a former classmate, after all. But there was no guile on her face, which seemed always uplifted. Was she joyful, or was that curve the way her mouth naturally grew? The way some cats and dogs have smile markings. Yeah, it was not a smile but a smile marking.

"Hey, wait a minute," he said, and grabbed her hand, held hands with her, a sudden endearment achieved right smack through force fields. "Let's go for a walk. Come for a walk with me. I live near here. Yeah, I do. Let me show you where I live."

Since she, in truth, did not have an appointment, she agreed to go with him. Finding digs, having digs, arranging them interested each of them very much. *God's solitaries in their caves and bare retreats.*

"Let's walk," he said, stubbing out his cigarette. Let's amble the blue North Beach streets as the evening sun goes down into the far grey water.

Though they walked through the land of the wasted, no Malte sights popped out to hurt him, she dispelling them. By day, the neon was not coursing through its glass veins. The dancing girl in spangles and feathers had flown out of her cage, which hung empty over the street. Nobody barked and hustled at the doorways to acts and shows. The day-folks, wheeling babies, wheeling grandpas, holding children by the hand, were shopping for dinner at the grocery stores and the bakery, dropping by the shoe repair. Oh, the smell of the focaccia ovens—O Home. A florist with white moustachios jaywalked through traffic with armsful of leonine football chrysanthemums. Behind glass, at the all-day-all-night place on the pie-wedge corner, poets, one to a table, were eating breakfast. The Co-Existence Bagel Shop was gone. The old guys, *Seventh Seal* knights, had played chess with Death and lost. The Bagel Shop, Miss Smith's Tea Room, Blabbermouth Night at The Place—all of a gone time. Out from the open door of La Bodega, a folksy guitar sweetened the air. The guitar was being passed around, and each played the tune he knew. You should have been there the night Segovia dropped by and played flamenco. Wittman musefully sang as if to himself a Mose Allison riff.

> A *young ma-a-an*
> *ain't nothin' in this world today.*
> *Because the ol' men's*
> *got all the money.*

The air of the City is so filled with poems, you have to fight becoming imbued with the general romanza. Nanci's long black hair and long black skirt skirled with the afternoon breezes. The leather of her shoulder bag strapped a breast. Her arms and outstretching legs were also long and black; she wore a leotard and tights like an old-fashioned Beat chick but, honestly, a dancer, dance togs for a good reason. Here he was: Wittman Ah Sing profiling down the street with a beautiful almost-girlfriend, clipping along, alongside, keeping up with him, the two of them making the scene on the Beach, like cruising in the gone Kerouac time of yore.

He ducked into the bookstore. She followed right on in. She stood beside him, browsing the rack of quarterlies, quite a few brave Volume I Number Ones. There were homemade books too, mimeo jobs, stencils, and small-press poetry that fit neat in the hand. On the top rack—right inside the door at eye level for all to see coming in or going out—was: an artistic avant-garde far-out new magazine that had published—in print—a scene from his play-in-progress—the lead-off piece—with his byline—right inside the front cover. He could reach over and hand it to her, but it would be more perfect if she happened to pick it out herself, come upon his premiere on her own, and be impressed. (F. Scott Fitzgerald, trying to impress Shei-lah Graham, had driven to every bookstore in L.A., but could not find a copy of any of his books.)

Wittman went downstairs to the cool basement, where among the bookshelves were chairs and tables with ashtrays. He had first come to this place when he was a high-school kid on one of his escapes from Sacra-mento, Second City to Big City. No *No Free Reading* sign. No *No Smok-ing*. You didn't have to buy a book; you could read for nothing. You had a hangout where you didn't have to spend money. Quiet. All the radios in Chinatown blaring out the ball game, but here, we don't care about the World Series. He hadn't known the City Lights Pocket Book Shop was famous until the *Howl* trial, which he had cut school to attend. "Shig" Shi-geyoshi Murao was the one charged with selling an obscene book. The muster of famous poets had blown Wittman away—everybody friends with everybody else, a gang of poets. He, poor monkey, was yet looking for others of his kind.

There had been a Chinese-American guy who rode with Jack and Neal. His name was Victor Wong, and he was a painter and an actor. Wittman had maybe seen him, or someone Chinese with the asymmetrical face of a character actor; he wore a white t-shirt with paint streaks and "hand-tooled leather shoes." Victor Wong, who went to the cabin in Bixby Canyon with Jack Duluoz and Neal/Cody. All this written up in *Big Sur*, where Jack calls Victor Wong Arthur Ma ("Little Chinese buddy Arthur Ma." Shit.), and flips out of his gourd walking in the moonless night above the wild ocean that rants for his life. Jack hangs on to the side of the mountain and listens and shouts back and sings. "Mien Mo Big Sur killer mountain for singing madly in." It would have been better if Victor/Arthur had been a writing man like the rest of them, but anyway he talked a lot and was good at hallu-cinations. "Little Arthur Ma [yet again "little"!] who never goes anywhere without his drawing paper and his Yellowjacket felt tips of all colors, red, blue, yellow, green, black, he draws marvelous subconscious glurbs and can also do excellent objective scenes or anything he wants on to cartoons—." They stay up all night, and Arthur Ma keeps making it up; he's not one of those storytellers who has to rehearse in the bathroom. Wittman had not gone up to the man with the character actor's face—one eye big, one eye small—and grabbed him by the arm and introduced himself. The poets at

Big Sur fall asleep but not Arthur, who stays awake with Jack, the two of them yelling till dawn. ". . . and Arthur Ma suddenly yells: 'Hold still you buncha bastards, I got a hole in my eye.' "

It would be nice were Nanci to walk down the pine-slab steps and say, "Oh, you're published. Why didn't you tell me? Will you autograph a copy for me?" Holding his words to her bosom.

Girls in my native land. May the loveliest of you on an afternoon in summer in the darkened library find herself the little book that Jan des Tournes printed in 1556. May she take the cooling, glossy volume out with her into the murmurous orchard, or yonder to the phlox, in whose oversweet fragrance there lies a sediment of sheer sweetness.

She was two aisles away browsing through the French and German shelves. The Europeans made books with creme linen paper; the soft covers were not illustrated except for a sharp line of vermillion trim. When you slice the pages open with your paperknife, the book will have flossy raggedy edges. You feel like owning books like that. Remember Phoebe Weatherfield Caulfield asking Holden to name one thing he liked a lot? "Name one thing." "One thing I like a lot, or one thing I just like?" "You like a lot." Wittman liked a lot this poky hole in the San Francisco underground earth. He will not point out to Nanci what's so good about it. Spoil it to make a big deal. She had to take a liking of her own accord. He took his own sweet time, testing her scanning and skimming of foreign lit.

But the next time he looked her way, she was talking to a couple of Black guys, laughing, carrying on in French. Maybe they had met before, or maybe she let herself be picked up. There was something Black about her too, come to think of it; it was in a fullness of the mouth, and a wildness in her clothes, and something about her dry hair. "Très joli. Ahh, très joli. Oo-la-la, très joli." So, people really do say "Oo-la-la." She and they were mutually delighting in something. These black French must have lately arrived from one of those colonial places. Their faces were not chary and wary; they were not "friendly," or "bad," or "loose." Their long hands and fingers wafted through a gentler atmosphere. Give them a few more weeks among the Amerikans; we'll show them how far très joli manners get them, and how much respect with *Saturday Review* tucked under the arm. They'll tighten up their act. Turn complicated. He squeezed past them; they easily stepped aside, gave him no trouble. Let's go already, Nanci. Wittman gave a jerk of his head—¡Vamos! ¡Andalay!—and, surprisingly, she said her adieux and followed him up the stairs. You would think only homely girls obey like that.

script says—The Girl. Not The White Girl. The Girl. She's just a girl in New York on her own. No family from the old country camping in her apartment."

"I hate *The Seven Year Itch*. I loathe it."

"Just testing. I was testing you. You passed." Therefore, thou art mine, sought and found.

"But you're right. She could very well look like me. There isn't any reason why she shouldn't look like me. Wittman?" She had his sleeve in her fingers, and pulled at it for them to stop walking so fast. "I was thinking of *Krapp's Last Tape*. I could do it by myself, no other face up there to compare mine to. A director doesn't have to match me. My lost love who's beside me in the boat could be a male nurse. 'We lay there without moving but under us all moved, and moved us, gently, up and down, and from side to side.' When Krapp says, 'Let me in,' I, a woman, could mean: Open your eyes, and let me into your eyes."

Why hadn't he thought of that? She must think him ill-read and a dried-up intellectual not to have seen the sensuality in Beckett. "You're resorting to Krapp, Nanci, because of being left out of the Hogan Tyrone Loman Big Daddy family. And whatever the names of those families were in *Seven Brides for Seven Brothers*. Seven white brides for seven white brothers. They took a perfectly good pro-miscegenation legend and wrote fourteen principal parts for Caucasians. I know legends about seven Chinese brothers named Juan; they were part of a nation of one hundred and eight heroes and heroines. What I'm going to do, I've got to wrest the theater back for you. Those Juans were hermanos chinos.

"I understand your agony, Nanci," he said. "The most important tradition in my high school was the senior play. My year they did *The Barretts of Wimpole Street*. The student who won the most Willie Awards was supposed to play the lead. In the U.K., 'willie' means 'weenie'; in Sacramento, it means 'talent.' I was the man of a thousand faces and got my Willies for winning talent shows. Robert Browning, tall, thin, sensitive, dark, melancholy—that's me, let me count the ways. But the drama coach held auditions. Then he told me, I'm the emcee for the evening, the 'host'; I warm up the audience, talk to them entr'acte, do my stand-up shtick, whatever I like, do my magic act, my ventriloquist act, throw my voice, 'Help. Help. Let me out.' I'd be featured. Very special, my spot. The way they staged *The Barretts of Wimpole Street* was Wilderesque, with an important *Our Town* stage manager character played by me. I look like Frank Craven, who had Chinese eyes and a viewpoint from the outskirts of Grover's

Corners, U.S.A. I did my medley of soliloquies, Hamlet, Richard III, Macbeth, Romeo. No Juliet. I did my bearded Americans, Walt Whitman and John Muir, guys with a lot of facial hair to cover up my face and my race. Mark Twain: '. . . a white to make a body sick, a white to make a body's flesh crawl—a tree-toad white, a fish-belly white.' Between *Barretts*, I also did great movie lines. 'Philip. Give me the letter, Philip.' 'Last night I dreamt I went to Manderley again.' 'As God is my witness, I'll never be hungry again. Chomp chomp.' 'The calla lilies are in bloom. Such a strange flowah.' "

Nanci guessed the actress whom each of those lines belonged to. " 'Maybe you found someone you like betta,' " she said. "Mae Clarke before James Cagney shoves the grapefruit in her kisser. 'I'd rather have his one arm around me than be in the two arms of another man.' "

"I know. I know. That movie where Linda Darnell and the British flyer and Tab Hunter are marooned on an island of desire. The British flyer has one arm, and Tab Hunter has the two arms but doesn't get the girl."

"No. Thelma Ritter says it to Marilyn Monroe in *The Misfits*."

"Nanci, I think we're on to something. That line is so meaningful, they've used it in two movies. It's what you call a perennial favorite. Women have all the good lines. I almost turned into a Mei Lan Fan androgyne doing those lines single-handed. I'm ruined for ensemble work. I haven't been on the stage since."

Grant Avenue, or Du Pont Gai—they/we call it Du Pont Gai—changed from North Beach to Chinatown. That factory which baked the Beatnik fortune cookies for the Actor's Workshop benefit should be situated at this border. You can't pick out just exactly which Italian store or Chinese store or red or red-white-and-green festooning it is that demarcates the change, but suddenly or gradually—depending on how closely you're keeping a lookout—you are in the flak and flash of Chinatown. Autumn was here: A red banner strung above the street announced the Double Ten parade and its sponsors, the Chinese-American Anti-Communist League and the Six Companies. They'll leave the banner up there all this month before Double Ten and afterwards into winter. To show Immigration and HUAC that we Chinese-Americans, super Americans, we too better dead than red-hot communists. Neither Wittman nor Nanci had plans to observe Double Ten. They had no idea how you go about doing that since nobody they knew showed much interest. It seemed like a fake holiday. A woody station wagon with Ohio plates drove slowly by. Painted across it was: "North

Beach or Bust." Poor bastards. Too late. They had crossed the country to join the Beatniks.

"I'm writing a play for you, Nanci," said Wittman. Wait for me while I write for you a theater; I will plant and grow for you a pear garden. Then she did look at him—he's wonderful. She stopped in her tracks to look up at him. She took his upper arm with her two hands. "I'll write you a part," he said, "where the audience learns to fall in love with you for your ochery skin and round nose and flat profile and slanty eyes, and your bit of an accent."

She made a pouty mouth. They walked on, she still holding his arm with both hands. Nanci, as a matter of fact, had a pointy nose with a bridge, where her dark glasses had a place to sit. Even Marilyn Monroe, blonde, dead, had not been able to get away with a round nose. Rhinoplasty. Nanci looked good. When the directors tell her, "You don't look Chinese," they mean: too pretty for a Chinese. She had represented Cal at the intercollegiate (Chinese) beauty-personality-good-grades contest at U.C.L.A.

What theater do we have besides beauty contests? Do we have a culture that's not these knickknacks we sell to the bok gwai? If Chinese-American culture is not knickknackatory—look at it—backscratcher swizzle sticks, pointed chopsticks for the hair, Jade East aftershave in a Buddha-shape bottle, the head screws off and you pour lotion out of its neck—then what is it? No other people sell out their streets like this. Tourists can't buy up J-town. Wait a goddamn minute. *We* don't make Jade East. It's one of your hakujin products by Swank. Would we do that to you? Make Jesus-on-the-cross bottles, so every morning, all over the country, hairy men twist his head off, and pour this green stuff out of his neck? So what do we have in the way of a culture besides Chinese hand laundries? You might make a joke on that— something about 'What's the difference between a Chinese hand laundry and a French laundry?' Where's our jazz? Where's our blues? Where's our ain't-taking-no-shit-from-nobody street-strutting language? I want so bad to be the first bad-jazz China Man bluesman of America. Of all the music on the airwaves, there's one syllable that sounds like ours. It's in that song by the Coasters. "It'll take an ocean of calamine lotion. Poison iv-ee-eeee-ee." No, not the ivy part. It's where they sing, "Aro-ou-ound-aaaaa-ah." Right there, that's a Chinese opera run. A Coaster must have been among those Black guys you see at the Chinese movies and at dojos seeking kung fu power.

Wittman and Nanci toned down any show-off in their walks. Chinese like for young people to look soo-mun or see-mun. Proper. Well turned out. Decorous. Kempt. The Ivy League look is soo-mun. Clean-cut all-American. For girls: sprayed, fixed hair—hair helmet—and they should have a jade heart at their throat always. Wittman was glad Nanci was wearing a defiant black leotard. If they were Japanese and walking through J-town in their grubbies, the Issei, who have a word for every social condition, would call them "yogore." (Zato-Ichi the Blind Swordsman, who flicked his snot into the haw-haw-haw mouth of a villain, is yogore. He'd be rolling the snotball all the time he's pretending to be putting up with their taunts.) Wittman went up Jackson Street (Dik-son Gai), sort of herding Nanci, turned her at the corner, guided her across the street by leaning toward her or leading away. Strange the way a man has to walk with a woman. She follows his lead like they're dancing, she wasn't even a wife or girlfriend. Did you hear what Jack Kennedy said to his media advisers, who told him that in pictures Jackie isn't walking beside him enough? He said, "She will just have to walk faster." (It is not a Chinese custom for women to walk behind men. That's a base stereotype.) No, Wittman didn't want to slow down for anybody either, become an inclining, compliant owned man. Husbands walk differently from single guys. He unlocked the door of his building, having to reach in through the security bars for a somewhat hidden lock. Nanci went right on in. They climbed the many steps and landings, she ahead, and he behind thinking, "Pomegranates." They didn't run into anybody in the hallways, all decent people at work, their doors shut, rows of jailhouse-green doors.

"My ah-pok-mun," he said, opening the door wide to his roomland, switching on the overhead light, which also switched on the desk lamp. "Come in. Come in," turning his desk chair around for his guest. "Welcome to my pok-mun. Sit. Sit." He dumped the fullness of his ashtray into the trash and set the ashtray next to his mattress on the floor. "For sitting furniture, I don't have but the one chair." She hung her suede jacket over the back of it, and sat down. Sweeping open his invisible magician's cape, he presented: his roomland, his boxes of papers, his table, which was desk and dining table, his hotplate on a crate, which was a cupboard for foodstuffs such as instant coffee and Campbell's Soup, edible out of the can. (Cook like a Mexicano: Put the tortilla directly on the burner, flipflop, ready to eat. So you get burner rings on your tortilla, but fast and nongreasy.) He quoted to her some Beat advice: " 'How many things do you own?' 'Fifteen.' 'Too many.' " No rug here. No sofa here. Never own a rug or a sofa. And thus be free. " 'What's the use of living if I can't make paradise in my own roomland?' " Peter Orlovsky was another one good at how to live. She laughed but did not give him the next lines, which are: "For this drop of time upon my eyes / like the endurance of a red star on a cigarette / makes me feel life splits faster than scissors."

Good thing the typewriter crouched, ready, on the table—his grand piano—that faces the window, where you look out at another pok-mun. If he was going to bring people up here, he ought to have been a painter. Painters have something to show for their work—an easel with the painting they're working on like a billboard all sunny under the skylight, their food composed into still-lifes, their favorite colors everywhere. They get to wear their palette on their grey sweatshirts, and spatters and swipes on their blue jeans. He sat down on the mattress, straightened out his sleeping bag, bed made.

"So this is where you live," Nanci said, looking down into one of his cartons, not touching the poems, just looking.

"See that trunk over there?" He pointed at it with the toe of his boot. Books, papers, his coffee cup sat on its lid; a person could sit on it too, and it become a second chair.

"That's the trunk I told you about. Proof, huh? Evidence. It exists. It *became* a theatrical trunk; it used to be a Gold Mountain trunk." It was big enough for crossing oceans, all right. It would take a huge man to hoist it onto his back. The hasps and clasps were rusty (with salt sea air), and the leather straps were worn. Big enough to carry all you own to a new land and never come back, enough stuff to settle the Far West with. And big enough to hold all the costumes for the seventy-two transformations of the King of the Monkeys in a long run of *The Journey to the West* in its entirety. "My great-great-grandfather came to America with that trunk."

"Yes," said Nanci, "I recognize it." Every family has a Gold Mountain trunk in their attic or basement.

"I can't die until I fill it with poems and play-acts," said Wittman.

"Would you like to read me a poem?" asked Nanci.

Oh, yes. Yes, I would. My name is Wittman Ah Sing, but you may call me Bold. When you get to know me better, you may call me Bolder, and I'll show you like Emily Dickinson secret poems in the false bottom of my Gold Mountain theater trunk. Oh, too guest-happy.

He rummaged through a carton for a poem that had made him feel like a genius when he made it. "New poems. New green poems. Haven't gone over this batch. Too green. Need one or two more drafts, make fair copies." Oh, shut up. Take one up at random. Any old poem.

Remember when everyone you fell in love with read poems and listened to poems? Love poetry has gone. And thou? Where went thou?

He put on his intellectual's glasses with the heavy black rims, scowled, made no eye contact. Oh, no—a poem—nah, a paragraph—that had been forced on speed, and coffee jacking the bennies up higher, then grass to smooth out the jaw-grinding jangles—does it show? A poem on beanie weenies, when he was a frijoles head—from his Making a Living series, a cycle of useful poetry—well, prose poems, actually—Gig Poems. Wishing he had a chance to re-do it, explain, he read aloud to Nanci something like this: Should a window-washing poet climb over the edge of a skyscraper, one leg at a time, onto his swing, and unclutch the ropes, may the tilted City hold still. Don't look down those paned streets. In view of the typing pools, he makes a noose, and tests the slide of it, and the dingle dangle of it. Yes? Yes? No? No? Yes? No? Hey, look—sky doggies. Up here—a stampede of longhorns. Point the rope like a wand, whirl a Möbius strip, outline a buffalo. Shoot la riata sideways over the street, overhead at the helicopters, jump in and out of it, and lassoo one of those steers. It drags the poet right off the plank—but the harness holds! Hey, you pretty girls of the typing pool, give me a big pantomime hand. Can't hear the clap-clap, but it's applause, and it's mine. Kisses blow through glass. Their impact knocks me off again, falling far down, and down as the pulley runs, and brakes. I vow: I will make of my scaffold, a stage.

The poet—the one in real life, not the one in the poem—wouldn't mind, when the poem ends, if his listening lady were to pay him a compliment. Such as agreeing, yes, let's transfigure every surface of the City with theater. Such as saying, "Did you on purpose make the line that tells about the tilted City bevel upsettingly—the verb fulcrumming a lot more phrases on one end than the other?" He'd love her for such particular appreciation. At least, praise him on the utilitarian level. From out of my head into the world. The window-washer was using newspapers and water, the chemicals in newsprint as good as Windex spray. Also, you can get rich by contracting with the owners of buildings for window-washing services a year in advance. Charge thousands, but pay the window-washers minimum wage by the hour. The kind of men you hire, whatever you pay them, they think it's a lot.

Nanci made no move to show that she heard that the poem was over. Give her a love story, Wittman. He ought to have read her the one about how this broken-hearted guy had long ago stashed in his *Physicians' Desk*

Reference the last letter, unread, from the ex–love of his life, written upon taking her leave of him. A lifetime later, an envelope falls out of the *P.D.R.* . . . (No, he wasn't a doctor. Each head had his own *P.D.R.* to identify street pills, and their effects and side effects, that is, trips and side trips.)

"Want to hear another one?" he asked.

"Okay," she said.

He reached into the poem box beside the black curve of her calf. His arm could graze its black length. But a true poet can't love up a woman who doesn't get that he's a poet. He can't touch her until she feels his poetry. Japanese have a custom where the host leaves a piece of art about, and the guest may notice it. The carton was labeled The International Nut Corporation, 100 Phoenix Ave., Lowell, Mass. His soul chick would notice it, and say, "Did you make a pilgrimage to Kerouac's town and his city?" Then he grabs her leg.

"What do you want to hear? How about one of my railroad cantos? A land chantey, the worker-poet as chanteyman? How's about a dueling sequence? 'The Dueling Mammy,' ha ha. Loss poems? You need a revenge sonnet? I've got twenty-eight sonnets now. I have one hundred and twenty-six sonnets to go to catch up with Shakespeare, who finished everything at the age of forty-five. I'm twenty-three. You too, right?"

She nodded, crossing one of those legs over the other. She folded her arms under her breasts.

He read to her about the ineluctable goingness of railroad tracks. Then he gave her the poet's intense stare, holding her eyes until she spoke. "Lovely," she said. "Sweet."

But he did not want to be sweet and lovely.

He dug deeper into the poem box, letting the ashes of his cigarette fall right on in. He took hold of a bane poem. Standing up, as if on platform, he read to her about mongoloids. " 'What's wrong with the baby, doctor?!' 'Is it deformed!?' 'Is it Chinese?!' Interbang?! Interbang!? 'But *we're* Chinese.' 'He's *supposed* to look like that!?' 'How can you tell if it's defective or if it's Chinese?!' 'Look at its little eyes.' 'Its tongue's too long.' 'Yellow skin *and* yellow jaundice?!' 'It's mongoloid?!' 'It's mongoloid!' 'It's an idiot?!' 'It's a mongolian idiot!' 'They're affectionate.' 'No, they bite.' 'Do they drool?!' 'All babies drool.' 'Can they be house-broken?!' 'Let's put it in a home.' The chorus goes like this: 'Gabble gobble. One of us. One of us.' " Wittman opened his eyes as wide as they got and looked into Nanci's— epicanthic eyes meeting epicanthic eyes. Fingers wiggling to communicate.

" 'Look at it cry!' 'Is that a cleft palate in there? And a giraffe tongue?!' 'It's got a wee penis.' 'All babies have a small penis.' 'Unlike apes, mongoloids do not turn dangerous to their keepers at puberty.' " Wittman played like he was sitting with the other mongoloid children on the go-around in the playground at the home. Their arms and chins hang over the top railing, a head lolls. A club foot gives the earth a kick, and they go around and around and around. Reading in the manner of Charles Laughton as the Hunchback of Notre Dame (who grunted and snorted in some scenes, and in others discoursed fluently on the nature of man) and like Helen Keller, he stuttered out, " 'Wa-wa-wa-water? Gabble gobble, one of us.' "

No coward, Wittman asked Nanci, "How do you like my work?" Straight out. Asking for it. I can take it.

"You sound black," she said. "I mean like a Black poet. Jive. Slang. Like LeRoi Jones. Like . . . like Black."

He slammed his hand—a fist with a poem in it—down on the desk—fistful of poem. He spit in his genuine brass China Man spittoon, and jumped up on top of the desk, squatted there, scratching. "Monkey see, monkey do?" he said. "Huh? Monkey see, monkey do?" Which sounds much uglier if you know Chinese. "Monkey shit, monkey belly." "A lot you know," he said. "A lot you know about us monkeys." She got up and stood behind her chair. He sprang from the desk onto the chair, and from the chair to the mattress, and from the mattress up to the desk again, dragging his long arms and heavy knuckles. His head turned from side to side like a quick questioning monkey, then slower, like an Indian in a squat, waggling his head meaning yes-and-no. He picked a flea from behind an ear—is this a flea?—or is it the magic pole in its toothpick state that the King of the Monkeys keeps hidden behind his ear? He bit it. "Monkey see. Monkey do. What you do in fleaman's pok-mun?" She didn't answer him. He picked up loose papers with one hand and looked at them, scratched his genitals with the other hand, smelled hands and pages, nibbled the pages. " 'Black?' " he hatefully imitated her. " 'Jive.' " He let drop the papers, nudged one farther with his toe, and wiped his fingers on his moustache. "That bad, huh?" He lifted a page and turned it, examined it back and front. Upside down and sideways. " 'LeRoi Jones?!' " He recoiled from it, dropped it over the edge of the desk, and leaned way over to watch it fall. Keeping an eye on it, he picked up another sheet and sniffed it. "Too Black. If you can't say something nice, don't say anything at all. That's my motto." He wadded it up and threw it over his shoulder. He jumped on top of the trunk, scrunching and scattering the whole shit pile, then pounced on a page, and returned with it to the desk. "This is it! Here's one you'll like. That is, likee. Guarantee. Ah. I mean, aiya. 'Wokking on da Waywoad. Centing da dollahs buck home to why-foo and biby. No booty-full Ah-mei-li-can gal-low fo me. Aiya. Aiya.' " He wiped his eyes with the paper, crushed it, and pitched the wad at the window, which was shut. Sorting papers into two piles, he said, "Goot po-yum. Goot. Goot. No goot. No goot. Goot. No goot." He tasted one, grimaced. "No goot." Breaking character, he said, "Now, if I were speaking in a French accent, you would think it charming. Honk-honk-ho-onk." He did the Maurice Chevalier laugh, which isn't really a laugh, is it? He started new piles. "Angry po-yum." "Sad po-yum." "Goot and angry." "Angry." "Angry." "Imitation of Blacks." He threw some to the floor. "Angry too muchee. Sad. Angry sad. No goot. Angry no goot. Sad. Sad. Sad."

"Please don't freak out," Nanci requested, standing behind the chair.

"I am not freaking out," Wittman said. "I've got to tell you the real truth. No lie. Listen, Lois. Underneath these glasses"—ripping the glasses off, wiping them on his sleeve, which he pulled out over his hand, so it looked like one hand was missing—"I am really: the present-day U.S.A. incarnation of the King of the Monkeys." He unbuttoned his blue chambray workshirt, which he wore on top of his black turtleneck. "Promise me you won't blab this all over the front page of the *Chron*. You'd like a scoop, I know, but I'm trusting you to keep our secret. For the sake of the world."

Now, if Nanci were the right girl for him, she would have said, "Dear monkey. Dear, dear old monkey. Poor monkey." She could scratch his head and under his chin, laugh at his antics, saying, "Poor dear monkey, what's to become of you?" and have him eating out of her hand. "Dear monkey. Poor poor monkey. You do have such an endearing Chinese giggle."

But who could be the right consoling girl for him? Nanci was getting into her jacket and finding her purse. How fucked up he is.

She hurried for the door, and got it open. She turned in the doorway, and said, "An actress says other people's words. I'm an actress; I know about saying other people's words. You scare me. A poet saying his own words. I don't like watching." She held up her hand, "Ciao," closed her fingers, and shut the door.

Alone, Wittman jumped off the table to the mattress, trampolined off that to the Gold Mountain trunk and onto the chair. Keep up the mood, not in liege to her. Elongating his chimp-like torso, he stretched for a look at himself in the built-in mirror on the door. He ruffled out his hair. Sao mang mang mang-key maw-lau. Skinny skinny monkey. "Bee-e-een!" he yelled, loud enough for her to hear. "Bee-e-een!" which is what Monkey yells when he changes. He whipped around and began to type like mad. Action. At work again.

And again whammed into the block question: Does he announce now that the author is—Chinese? Or, rather, Chinese-American? And be forced into autobiographical confession. Stop the music—I have to butt in and introduce myself and my race. "Dear reader, all these characters whom you've been identifying with—Bill, Brooke, and Annie—are Chinese— and I am too." The fiction is spoiled. You who read have been suckered along, identifying like hell, only to find out that you'd been getting a peculiar, colored, slanted p.o.v. "Call me Ishmael." See? You pictured a white guy, didn't you? If Ishmael were described—ochery ecru amber umber skin —you picture a *tan* white guy. Wittman wanted to spoil all those stories coming out of and set in New England Back East—to blacken and to yellow Bill, Brooke, and Annie. A new rule for the imagination: The common man has Chinese looks. From now on, whenever you read about those people with no surnames, color them with black skin or yellow skin. Wittman made an end run, evaded the block. By writing a play, he didn't need descriptions that racinated anybody. The actors will walk out on stage and their looks will be self-evident. They will speak dialects and accents, which the audience will get upon hearing. No need for an unreadable orthography such as Mark Twain's insultingly dumb dis and dat misspelling and apostrophying. Yes, the play's the thing.

It is ridiculous. Here I sit in my little room, I, Brigge, who have grown to be 28 years old and of whom no one knows. I sit here and am nothing. And nevertheless this nothing begins to think and think, five flights up, on a grey Parisian afternoon, these thoughts: . . .

A long time ago, before the blackbottom, a band of ancestors with talent left their music house, which was the largest hut in Ancient Wells, a place, and sailed a music boat a-roving the rivers of China. They beat the big drum hard, which vibrated in stomachs and diaphragms for miles around. An audience gathered on the riverbank, and saw the red swan boat come floating on strains of mandolin and flute. Between red wings, got up in the style of putting-on-a-show, rode the players. To the knocking of the wood fish drums—dok-dok-dok—the singer lifted his skylark voice over water and fields. He threw out ropes, and their audience pulled them to shore. Party time again. Let musicians rule. Play a—what kind of music?—how does it go?—and make the world spin in the palm of your hand.

Our Wittman is going to work on his play for the rest of the night. If you want to see whether he will get that play up, and how a poor monkey makes a living so he can afford to spend the weekday afternoon drinking coffee and hanging out, go on to the next chapter.

LINGUISTS AND CONTENDERS

 WITTMAN AH SING wrote into the dark of the night, through dinner time and theater time and bar time. *Here I sit in the cold night, writing . . . the recluse in his night. . . .* He followed the music boat on courses of waterways—sailing the Long River across the Earth and guided by the River of Stars in the sky—to the mouth or the ass end of China—the Pearl River Delta, where Americans come from. The Boca Tigris ejects *The Song Boat* into the bay between Macao and Hong Kong. Our singer poles it to the Typhoon Shelter. Gliding out of the glittering black of water and starry sky come other sudden lit boats. Land-people hire them for a night of eating, gambling, sleeping on the water. Here's a boat selling escargots, steaming on the stove and smelling up the air with anise and garlic and snail. "Fresh shrimp," shouts a cook, and tosses a live prawn across to a dining-table boat; it dances the Japanese shrimp dance. A trysting lover throws it back, "Ho. Ho, la. Cook it, la. Cook it with scallions." And from another boat, he orders for his veiled lady: clams steeping in black-bean sauce. And here's a boat named *Cowboy* bringing rice and kettles of jook. And here's a floating bar with the beer and wine. Order the wine of the poets, the plum rosé that inspired Tu Fu and Li Po. The lights of the city on hills make a vertical shimmer from sky straight into the water, like a backdrop, like a dream.

"What do you want to hear?" Our singer, Joang Fu, calls for requests and dedications. (His name, Joang Fu, pronounced like Joan of Arc, like a bell of Time, means Inner Truth, which was also Wittman's byname, it so happened. Named by his father at the throw of the Ching.) "Our band has traveled more than five thousand days, and found no gold, and found no eagle-feather shield, but we bring back music to our tribe." Balancing, he hands a menu of songs over to the lovers. "We've stolen spells and bells from Tigermen. I can melt snow with my voice. Listen. Listen to the peal of these tiny silver cymbals." The cymbals are no bigger than a pair of ears. "How far can you follow the rings of ringing? Do they sound longer in the crevasses and altitudes of the Himalayas or across water?" As bait, he tells bits of many stories and the most terrible customs you never did see. He makes sounds of other tongues. "Id al-Kabir. Id al-Kabir. A god asks a father to sacrifice his son. What to do? Hear the aria as he raises his knife. Hear the opera of White-Hat Muslims at the Great Festival of the Sacrifice. Hear the Passover songs of Blue-Hat Jew Guai Muslims of the northwest. We've found the lost story of Monkey and the Muslim. Hear how we were captured by the Lolos and escaped with their wild music too. Do you want to listen to me yodel-lay-hee-hoo like a Mongol cowboy wailing with the Gobi wind? Hear the songs that we sang against Genghis Khan." Then, in a softer voice, confidentially: "My parents sold me to this opera troupe, and I'm trying to save money to buy my freedom and go to Hollywood to join the movies. I ran away in a storm one night, and met a beautiful girl, alone and wet in the rain. I sang her a song. Do you want to hear it? And she sang back to me, eerily. I remember her song. Do you want to hear it? Do you think she's a real girl, or is she a snake?"

Springing up, the singer lands nimbly on the railing of the lovers' boat, where he hunkers, riding the easy sea's rise and fall. It's a rich man's boat, like a floating gazebo with its horned topside and red pillars, and veranda railings all around. He fills the shy silence for the lovers, "I myself have sailed to Bali." (Like Antonin Artaud, who also sailed there in his imagination, he could've said, but a lot had to be left out.) "There, women play gods, and men play demons and monkeys." He has given the rich man a cue to look teasingly into his lady's eyes, and to toast her, "To a goddess," and to flirt with her, "From a demon." "I stayed up chitter-chattering and chanting all night with monkey dancers, little boys in the inmost circle, me, Joang Fu, among the youths in the next circle, middle-aged men in the middle, and old men on the outside—kit-chak kit-chak kit-chak—hum hum —waves of humming in fumes of clove and cubeba cigarettes—until gods dropped out of the sky and did their dramas amidst men and monkeys— halleluia hands halleluia hands."

Joang Fu gets a good look at the dark lady's unveiled face. The other boats have slipped away, and she has had to lift her netting to eat. Their oarswoman has fallen asleep, and the little boat turns in its own world. The dark lady says something to her fella, who makes the request for a new song. That world-wandering songboatman sings Stephen Foster of the West. " 'All the world is sad and dreary, everywhere I roam. . . .' " No, wait, wait. Let's go back earlier—the world is yet newer. She asks to hear "The Gold Mountain Song." "O, Susanna, don't you cry for me. I'm going to Californyah with a banjo on my knee." "O, Susanna," the song of the Gold Rush.

The lady sees to it that our singer is paid lavishly. *The Song Boat* returns for him, and the troupe skims away, treating its audience to a skiddooing tableau vivant—a would-be king is pouring poison into the sleeping king's ear, his crown pushed aside. A juggler throws the vial into the air, where other bottles are flying; they are caught, caught, caught, though the boat is shooting fast away.

Well, it was the ass end of things, all right. As you know from San Francisco Bay, hungry birds, swirling and diving, mirror the swirls of fish below them. Fishing boats follow these whirlwinds of birds farther and farther out to sea. The smallest boats turn back soonest, empty, and then the others also have to quit. So—no more entertainment dollars. The musicians sell their instruments and sing a cappella. Then, following the unlucky fishermen, they go on land, where they become as vagabond as poets who wrote on rocks and leaves.

At the Dogs Don't Mind restaurant (which has piles of orts on top of the tables, and bones and slop buckets under the tables, but "dogs don't mind"), he strolls from table to table, like a bridegroom, and tells homesick tales about pirates; he maps their hideouts among the dangerous keys and straits. City people can't simultaneously eat and hear about torture-for-ransom; he disgusts them and wins their food. Whoever hears his sea yearnings stops feeling sorry for the people of the water and, instead, envies them their free lives. Born on the sea and never been landed, before. He'd met, so he says, Cheng I Sao, widow and lady pirate, but he can't say what she looks like because she uglifies herself with the blue-and-black make-up of a stage villain. "I sent a poem for her to finish, but she returned it rhyming in 'no' when I'd set it up for an inevitable 'yes.' Do you want to hear how it goes?"

It was a good job. All profit, no overhead except for food you have to eat regardless. And with self-discipline, he can live on what the dogs don't mind. When the beer and wine cart comes around, and the voice dries out, why, somebody's sure to buy a drink. And the friendly storyteller is likely to be invited to join in eating the rest of the dinner. You can always add one more guest to a Chinese meal; everybody eats from the mutual food in the middle. Feed the storyteller. Feed the storyteller.

Joang Fu invents and throws out generous new lines of bait: "I met a scientist who experimented in his laboratory with opium and mushrooms, and discovered how to make his sperm addictive." Oh, the listeners were laughing already in anticipation of scenes of gluttonous unending sex. Ladies undone. Gentlemen unpantsed. "How does he find out it's truly addictive? How many women have to be chasing you before you know? What happens to the economy when you market addictive sperm? Wheeling and dealing dope sperm. 'Oh, no, this sperm's been cut.' 'Does she love me for myself or for my golden sperm?' "

On moonless nights, our storyteller kindles light from the faces of listeners, and they cannot bear to leave. The gambler is turning over his hand. The executioner has raised his ax to the apex. The father is pressing his knife on the son's throat. The princess is untying her blindfold. The widow lady pirate kisses the guy with the sperm. The storyteller pauses. "Pay up. Pay up," he says. "Time to pay up." And who could stand not to know what happens next? What's money for, after all? The more money comes kerplunking down, the more flash in the swordplay, and heartfelt the lovers' vows to meet again, and aphrodisiacal the sperm. Prolong the outcome, make the story burst one more time into payoff—like two-stage fireworks— one last outburst that wipes out stars—just when they thought it was the end.

On the radio, Sweet Dick Whittington the Allnight Cat was playing King Pleasure.

> *When you see danger facing you,*
> *little boy, don't get scared.*
> *When you see danger facing you,*
> *little boy, don't you get scared.*
> *When you see danger facing you,*
> *little fellow, don't get yellow,*
> *and blu-u-e.*

Then, Cannonball Adderly, being interviewed, told about a young musician coming to New York. "He gets cut bad." He has to stop playing his tune, and change his ways to New York ways. "He becomes a better musician," says Cannonball. That can't be true. New York cant.

On the Black station, people were phoning in and arguing whether you can tell somebody's color by his voice. Back at the jazz station, Wittman heard: "Louis B. Armstrong and John Cage credit Chinese opera for inspiring their rhythms." Yes? Yes? Was Wittman's yearning giving him an hallucination of the ear? A piece he could not identify bingbanged forth and jangled his mind.

The reason he had the radio on was that whenever he stopped typing, he heard someone else nearby tapping, tapping at a typewriter, a typing through the night. Yes, it was there, steady but not mechanical. Not furnace or pipes or adding machine or teletype or timer. Not an echo. Now and again, the noise did hesitate, as if for thought, then a few word-length taps. An intelligence was coming up with words. Someone else, not a poet with pencil or fountain pen but a workhorse big-novel writer, was staying up, probably done composing already and typing out fair copy. It should be a companionable noise, a jazz challenge to which he could blow out the window his answering jazz. But, no, it's an expensive electric machine-gun typewriter aiming at him, gunning for him, to knock him off in competition. But so efficient—it had to be a girl, a clerk typist, he hoped, a secretary, he hoped. A schoolteacher cutting mimeo stencils. A cookbook writer. A guidebook-for-tourists writer. Madam Dim Sum, Madam Chinoiserie, Madam Orientalia knocking out horsey cocky locky astrology, Horatio Algiers Wong—he heard the typing leave him behind.

He picked up a ballpoint and crossed out by the line what he had written that night, every page. He had been tripping out on the wrong side of the street. The wrong side of the world. What had he to do with foreigners? With F.O.B. émigrés? Fifth-generation native Californian that he was. Great-Great-Grandfather came on the *Nootka*, as ancestral as the *Mayflower*. Go-sei. The story boat has got to light out on the Mississippi or among the houseboats on the San Joaquin Delta. It should work the yachts at Lake Tahoe. His province is America. America, his province. But story boats and story teahouses where a professional can talk are as gone at Lake Anza and the Bay as they must be gone from China. What is there beautiful and adventurous about us here? Dave Brubeck was playing "Take Five" on the radio.

Wittman took the trash down the hallway to the garbage closet. The pages made a flying noise down the chute. Pure Jack Kerouac set fire to his day's words. There used to be a furnace at 17 Adler Place—the Chinese

Historical Society of America is in that building now—where the Society of Beautiful Writing used to burn important papers. Fire up them poems. See the phoenixes and salamanders. The Society took the ashes to Baker Beach and Fort Point and scattered them in the Bay. Much purer than sitting in the garbage waiting for the truck to the dump.

It's all right. Wittman was working out what this means: After two thousand days of quest, which takes a hundred chapters to tell, and twenty-four acts, seven days to perform, Monkey and his friends, Tripitaka on the white horse, Piggy, and Mr. Sandman, arrive in the West. The Indians give them scrolls, which they load on the white horse. Partway home, Monkey, a suspicious fellow, unrolls the scrolls, and finds that they are blank scrolls. "What's this? We've been cheated. Those pig-catchers gave us nothing. Let's demand an exchange." So, he and his companions go back, and they get words, including the Heart Sutra. But the empty scrolls had been the right ones all along.

Back at his table, Wittman put his head down and groaned. He ought not to have gone ape in front of Nanci. It was the sort of episode that can back up on you anytime and make you want to shoot the embarrassment of it clean out of your head. Too late. *And one has nothing and nobody, and one travels about the world with a trunk and a case of books and really without curiosity. What sort of life is it really; without a house, without inherited things, without dogs?* With Rilke singing the sound track of my life?

A rooster crowed. It woke up in a cage stacked above and beneath other chickens, grain and shit dropping from tier to tier; the grocer must be pushing the cages out to the sidewalk. Zoning laws are different here from Union Square, I. Magnin's and the City of Paris, or else we're breaking them. The fish trucks were unloading today's catch, lobsters and catfish coming back to life in window tanks. Farm trucks were bringing vegetables and fruit from the Valley. Soon alarm clocks will ring and toilets flush. It was time to go to sleep. *I have taken action against fear. I have sat all night and written and now I am as agreeably tired as after a long walk over the fields of Ulsgaard.*

Sleeping in this part of the City was very odd. He was often awakened by dinosaur garbage-truck noises. But in daylight the garbage would still not have been picked up. Why is the air shattering like it's raining glass? *To think that I cannot give up sleeping without the window open. Electric street-cars rage ringing through my room. Automobiles run their way over me. A door slams. Somewhere a window-pane falls clattering: I hear its big splinters laugh, its little ones snicker. Then suddenly a dull, muffled noise*

from the other side within the house. Someone is climbing the stairs. Com-
ing, coming incessantly. Is there, there for a long time, then passes by. And
again the street. A girl screams: Ah tais-toi, je ne veux plus. An electric car
races up excitedly, then away, away over everything. Someone calls. People
are running, overtake each other. A dog barks. What a relief: a dog. Toward
morning a cock even crows, and that is boundless comfort. Then I suddenly
fall asleep. More than one pane of glass has fallen; an entire glass side of a
building has crashed down, but the next day, if he remembers to look, the
street will not be covered with glass. The electric cars do not run on this
street at four in the morning.

The storyboatman vaults on his pole of changing lengths. He whizzes
through lands and time. He touches down here, and he takes off and
touches down there. Over Angel Island. Over Ellis Island. Living one very
long adventurous life, thousands of years long, perhaps accomplished with
the help of reincarnations and ancestors.

The calls in Wittman's dreams came from the children of the building
going off to school. *I don't even know how it is possible for school-children*
to get up in bedrooms filled with grey-smelling cold; who encourages them,
those little precocious skeletons, to run out into the grown-up city, into the
gloomy dregs of the night, into the everlasting school day, still always small,
always full of foreboding, always late? I have no conception of the amount
of succor that is constantly used up. Bang! Bang! Bang!—that's the
grandmas smashing garlic with the flats of their cleavers. (Knights dealt
what the storytellers called garlic-banging blows.) Bang! Bang! They were
also chopping up pork for patties, and shrimp into paste. There was a
kitchen on this floor anybody could use. On its kitchen scroll, Wittman was
able to recognize three words—"Food body fire"—out of about ten, and
took Confucius to mean that the superior person, fueling up, pays no mind
to aesthetics. That humming that underscored everything was the motor
sound of sewing.

At noon, Wittman got up and walked his bathroom gear, including his
private roll of toilet paper, down the hall. He walked in on a woman, who
scolded him from her throne, "Who you think you are, haw, boy? Haw,
boy?" As he stepped out—her own fault, she hadn't locked the door—she
called him some of the many Chinese words for "crazy"—"Saw! Deen!
Moong cha cha! Ngow! Kang!" So many ways to go bananas. Kang, the
highest degree of nuts. "Too late, he's gone kang." He returned to his room
and pissed in the sink. "There comes a time in life when everybody must
take a piss in the sink—here let me paint the window black for a minute."

He brushed his teeth and washed up, plotting how he might have social-ized better with that bathroom woman. "It happens in the best of families," he might've said.

He took time combing out his moustache and beard, which were sparse but coarse. Hairs didn't just hang there, they stood out. His face was wired. Buttoning up his dark green shirt, he took a good look at his skin above the collar—yellower. Sallow like tallow. This effect of the wearing o' the green had been pointed out through the years by his mother, aunties, kid friends, make-up artists. "Don't wear green." One said it like a secret, another like a helpful hint, yet another, a sure fact that any fool knows. "Green's a bad color." For a long time he thought it had to do with bad taste or bad luck. Or his own personal complexion. "Green doesn't look good on you." Then some dorm guy said, "We look yellow in that color." It had to do with racial skin. And, of course, from that time on, he knew what color he had to wear—green, his color to wear to war. He tied his hair back in the samurai–Paul Revere–piratical braid. He had assumed his mirror face, but thought he always looked like that. Once, on drugs, on the mirror trip, this face had zoomed backward and whomped forward in time—he was a star, a tadpole, a cave baby, himself like now, then a dry old man with skull pushing against, almost protruding out of, his skin. Then he saw through skin to poor, jest-ing, once-singing Yorick. And his farflung soul returned on a starpoint of light in Yorick's eyehole.

He put on the suit that he had bought for five bucks at the Salvation Army—the Brooks Brothers three-piece navy-blue pinstripe of some dead businessman. Wittman's suited body and hairy head didn't go together. Nor did the green shirt and greener tie (with orange-and-silver covered wagons and rows of Daniel Boones with rifles) match each other or the suit. The Wembley label on the tie said, "Wear With Brown Suit," which Wittman defied. He pulled on his Wellingtons and stomped out onto the street. His appearance was an affront to anybody who looked at him, he hoped. Bee-e-en! The monkey, using one of his seventy-two transformations, was now changed into a working stiff on his way to his paying job.

Out on the street, Wittman fitted onto his mongolian cheeks his specta-cles that blurred everything, thus finding metaphors everywhere, like how a cable car looks like an animal-cracker box. Some things he couldn't tell what the fuck they were, so he'd go up to a bedevilment and have a look-see, not to miss out. Like Rimbaud, I practice having hallucinations. He had picked his hallucination glasses out of the Lions Club donation box at the bank.

What got him to take the glasses off, a brother of the streets hit him up for a light. In thanks, the street man offered a look through a toilet-paper roll tube, which he demonstrated how to use. One eye peeping, other eye squinting, he pointed that pirate spyglass viewfinder, here, there, everywhere, and said, "Wow. Oh, wow. Here, hippy, dig." I look like a hippy dippy's idea of a hippy dippy.

Wittman's turn, he saw encircled: the traffic light change to amber, and a sparrow burst out of the light can, straw straggling after it. Autumn nest. A bum-how pass wine to his fellow clochard, who drank from the bottle without first wiping its mouth. Water flow in the gutter at their feet—Lenny and George at the river. "Guys like us . . ." Tu Fu and Li Po beside the Yangtze. Pigeons. He looked for i.d.s on their red ankles. Nope, these hadn't performed in Doctor Woo's Bill and Coo act. The red flag click up in a parking meter. A hand put money into a newspaper dispenser and take two *Chronicles*. A leaf. Faces. He thanked the cinéma-vérité freak for the look-see. "Hippy, you are welcome."

At the department store where he had a job—"Are you in the English Department or the History Department?" "I'm in the Toy Department." —it was Hallowe'en month. Wittman had helped trick up the kid dummies in flat apron-like run-over-with-a-steamroller cartoon costumes. The Management Trainees had sent out a memo: Floor personnel to wear costumes of their choice on Hallowe'en, which Wittman hoped would not fall on one of his workdays, Tuesday, Thursday, Friday, 1:00 to 9:00 p.m., Open Late for Your Shopping Convenience. Another season, in the Candy Department, he had worn rabbit ears and white gloves. For revenge, he had stolen candy—white chocolate—and saved on buying groceries. Do something about your life. Find a way out before you have to set up Christmas Toyland. Transfer into Notions? Sell armpit shields and corn pads? When he was a kid, he thought he could be happy forever working in a store. The tall glass at Kress had curved around brand-new toys, each one in many copies, which the owner arranged as he pleased. Is this malcontentedness what comes with a liberal-arts education? The way they taught you to think at school was to keep asking what's really going on. What's that thing at the end of this assembly line *for*? Why merchandising? Why business? Why money? Who are the stockholders? What else have they got their fingers into? Are any of the holdings in bomb commodities? Seek out vanities and emptiness. Which way out? Which way out? One of the clerks spotted him, and left the floor—quitting time for her. No wonder he didn't know anybody. But anything's better than the Defense Department. And he wasn't a soldier. He wasn't a prison guard. He was barely employed, a casual employee.

Wittman readied his station, sized up the house. Who are these people that no matter what odd time of day or night they have the wherewithal to go shopping? Put up roadblocks, do a survey, where are they going, and what do they do for a living? Are there many people like himself, then? They're all poets taking walks? "Just browsing." "Just looking." Between customers he was supposed to staple-gun black-and-orange corrugated cardboard into walls and along counters. The toys on the demonstration table could use a tidying up. Few of them sprang into action today because the customers had wound them too tight, unsprung them, or their batteries were shot. He pressed the laying hen, and a white marble rolled out of a hole in her stomach. He turned her upside down and re-inserted the half-dozen marbles that had rolled to the little fence. So it has come to this. (Lew Welch, the Red Monk, says: now and again, stop and think, "So it has come to this.")

The other clerk, Louise—see? he remembers their names, so there's something wrong they don't remember his—Louise was standing on top of a ladder, taking down a Back to School theme sign. He pretended he didn't see her. Let her do it herself, he's not good enough for her to say hello to.

Two tourist ladies held a large toy before his critical eyes. "Would my grandson like this? What is it? How much is it?" How come people leave their brains at home when they go on vacation? "It's a basketball gun," he said. "See? It says so right here. 'Basket Shooter.' You shoot this ball with this gun into this hoop here. It's a basketball game, but it's like a cannon." No kidding. The fuckers were turning basketball into target practice. "It's the cheapest large toy we have." Any job can be human as long as there are other people working in the same room as you. Even in a hell of noise, such as an automobile plant, you can roll a tire or pass a tool to the next guy on the line, and do it with good will. There are big people in small jobs, and small people in big jobs, and big people in big jobs, and small people in small jobs. The only wrong job would be where you have to be cooped up by yourself making some evil item, such as a bomb part, and never meet anybody. So here were this grandmother and her buddy giving him a chance to make this toy job human. Humanize them, as they said in the Cal Education Department, meaning one's contacts in the teachable moments during contact hours.

"For the good of the kid, your grandson," said Wittman, "you should not buy him this thing that is really a gun."

"You said it was a basketball game," said the buddy.

"But the kid shoots the ball with this trigger, see?"

"How clever," said the grandma. "May I try it?"

"No, no. We can't take it out of its blister pack. You don't want the kid to grow up to be a killer, do you?"

"Oh, is this Basket Shooter dangerous? I don't want to buy him anything dangerous."

"We don't want him to hurt himself," the buddy agreed.

"Well, kids can't hurt one another with this basketball gun even if they aimed point-blank at any part of the body. The harm comes from their pretending to kill. They learn to like the feel of weapons. They're learning it's fun to play war."

"Are you one of those people against war toys?" "We didn't come in here to be lectured to."

"Yeah, I'm against war toys. I'm anti-war. Look, I'm looking after your grandkid better than you are if you're going to let him grow up to be a draftee."

"We don't have to listen to this." "I'm buying whatever present I want to buy for my grandson. I'll take this—this Basket Shooter." She flipped out her charge card. "How much is it?"

"Fifteen ninety-nine," said Wittman, who discovered that his anger was mightiest when he was forced to be a spokesman for an inimical position. Speak up against charge cards too, Wittman. Instead he wrote up the sale, let these women fuck over themselves and the kid.

"Where's the ladies' room?" a lady interrupted, bouncing impatiently like she was going to unload on the spot. He gave her the labyrinthine though most direct directions to the restroom, which he had never actually heard a store manager say should be kept secret and hard to find. "You stay here, honey," she said to her son. "Mommy has to go take a grunt for herself. Stay there, Bobby, stay there. Keep an eye on him, okay?" She was dumping him.

"Wait a minute," said Wittman. "No. We're not a nursery. You can't leave him here."

"I'll be right back," she said from aisles away.

The place was filling up with dumped kids. They were poking holes in cellophane boxes. One was rubbing his runny nose on the very clean white plush tummy of a Snoopy. "Stop that," said responsible Wittman. "Go away. Go that way," he suggested, pointing in the direction of the Shoe Department. "Shoo." Was that a diaper smell? He ought to get on the intercom. "We have a lost child, a lost bleeding child found unconscious, possibly dead, in the Toy Department." Don't you mothers drop your get on me.

"Sir. Sir." It was Louise coming at him with a clipboard like a P.E. coach. "Sir. What's your name again?"

"Wittman Ah Sing."

"Right. You're supposed to be hanging up the bicycles. Not those bicycles. Bring up the new ones from the stockroom, will you? I *could* bring them up myself. They're not heavy, just unwieldy." Give a man credit for muscles, why don't you?

"I'll get them," said co-operative Wittman, glad to get off the floor. Take his own sweet time.

Down in the stockroom, through his own cigarette smoke came fuming the smell of somebody smoking dope. As I live and breathe. Wittman took off his glasses to see. You know, by the time your brain recognizes the smell of reefer, you're high already. On the way, far out, gone. No innocent passersby. He followed the redolence and the loosening—or are they tightening?—vibes through the mazes of merchandise and came upon a fellow reading at a coffee table, at home as he could be. The radio was on the classical station. The man did not jump to his feet and start working; Wittman must not look boss. Crates had been stacked to block off a private room, and there were extension cords leading to a percolator and reading lamp, all new and belonging to the store. "Come in if you like," invited this man, who seemed to have it made.

Wittman entered through an opening in the barricade. "You live here?" he asked.

"No, I work here, like you. I'm stockboy." He seemed too old to be stockboy, his forehead high because balding. An ancient Chinese would have tonsured his head to get such baldness. "Have a seat," he said, passing Wittman a roach in a paper-match holder.

"No, thanks. I'll have some coffee, though." The stockboy unpacked a new cup, blew the wood shavings out of it, and poured coffee. Wittman sat down across from him. "I used to dope, I don't dope anymore. I've seen all there is to see on dope; the trips have been repeating themselves, looping like *Dead of Night*. I liked dope; I learned a lot. I felt religious. I felt communal. I believed in all sorts of things: the possibility of getting so far out that we pop through to another reality. Change one's head, change the universe. The paranoia was driving me nuts, however. Too ripped. I don't like getting wasted anymore. Nice hideout you've got here."

"Yes, I keep out of the way." He was one of those older guys, hip to the underworld, an ex-con maybe, or a Beatnik who will never sell out. "Work some, hide out some. Make accordion time." He was giving Wittman valuable, true orders.

"I'm hip," said Wittman. "I'm hip to accordion time." Like collecting garbage fast before the sun comes up, and free by morning for the day. Be a garbageman; be a mailman. This stock guy wasn't a jailhead, then, but wise to jobs, how to work from the inside. "What do you do down here with your extra time?"

"Handle consciousness."

"Hey, I do too. Me too. I want to do that too, man. How do you do it? Have you found some good ways? Lay low, right?"

"One way—I sit, I hang on to my seat." He demonstrated—looking straight ahead, arms straight down stiff, shoulders up, hands pulling up on the stool, butt pushing down. "Sit tight," he said.

"Is it better to keep your eyes open like that? Or is it better to shut them?"

"Open if no horror is . . . transpiring in the very room. Shut if they're torturing your family in front of you. Open if your mind goes places. Use your good sense. Slow the centrifugal-force machine down. However, the stopped trip is also dangerous. 'I. Can't. Take. My. Eyes. Off. Of. That. Spot. Spot. Spot. Spot.' The groove-rut is a killer." He stared at the daisy on the percolator. If he were actually stopped, his facial bones would slam into his skin, not a mind trip but an observable phenomenon. "The hell of whatever's going on goes on forever."

"Yeah. Like a short loop of film. 'When is this trip going to change?' Though the speed trip is no good either. Eschew speed."

"There's nothing to do under either circumstance but wait until you are let go. I would say, as a rule, open eyes is better, don't get so lost. Find a locus and a focus in this room, for instance, though it becomes crowded with . . . becomes crowded. I say open—and hang on to your seat."

Because our Wittman had not been brought up in a religion, he admired this man's ability to know that something starts us up and stops us and lets us move again, and that there were holy ghosts or something all around. Too much. Far out of sight, as Spenser exclaimed, ripped with amazement in *The Faerie Queene*. Two intelligent conversations in two days. Oh, yes: "Trippers and askers surround me." Crazy Jane Talks with the Bishop. Wotta Bishop.

"You have a good trip for me?" asked brave Wittman, butt-sitting. "Any

good trips?" Be careful what you hear. You set yourself up. You get imprinted with a bad trip, you're fucked for life. The words don't come true
now, they come true later in some real-life form.

"When I have friends, I take them for a ride on the coast train to Santa
Cruz. We carry archery equipment into the redwood mountains. We each
shoot an arrow straight up overhead. The red nock feathers look like a space
bird blasting off between the evergreens, going up and up clear past the tallest Kings Canyon sequoia into the nothing sky, and hangs there and hangs
there. Then the steel tip dips, flashing—it has stabbed the sun and is bringing a piece of it down to us on Earth. The arrow turns and falls. I stand my
ground. If it's going to hit me, it hits me. Last time, it went into the ground
between my toes. The friends also shoot all together—a flock of space birds
—and run when the arrows rain down. If the weather turns to rain, we put
out buckets and cans upside down among the trees, and listen to God's
rhythms."

Wittman wanted to be one of the friends to do interesting things like
that. The eidolons were dancing around the man's head and cakewalking
over to Wittman's head. Contact high one more time. Their inhalations
and exhalations stoked the ions in their halos a-hopping and a-changing.
The +'s and —'s a-winking and a-blinking like cartoon eyes.

"I had a pretty good time in the Santa Cruz Mountains myself," Wittman said, returning good trip for good trip. "I was on my way to the Monterey Jazz Festival, but ended up in those woods too. I saw two kinds of lep-
rechauns, one tall like a tree and the other round like a boulder, kneeling
with its gnomish back toward me. When I tried to study them, they went
transparent. Their clothes and bearing reminded me of friends of mine.
They didn't say anything." He had not, once back in cities, asked those
friends if they had dreamed or thought of being in a redwood forest at
that hour. This new amigo was understanding him and the anti-scientific
nature of those woods. Nobody here but us empiricals. The knucklebone
maniac of the Santa Cruz Mountains had been on the loose—a cannibal
arrested with his pockets full of hikers' knucklebones—and had skipped
them.

The stockman licked two rolling papers together and pushed some grass
into line with an eight of hearts. (Another way to handle consciousness is to
play solitaire like George in *Of Mice and Men*.) A neat and graceful roller,
he made himself a tight, dry joint, not offering his guest a hit this time.

"Where you from?" Wittman asked, something out-of-state in the way
the fellow said "the coast."

"Back East." He rubbed the back of his neck as if he were laboring in the sun. "There was a year when I was the Yale Younger Poet."

"No shit," said Wittman. "What are you doing here?" Why end up at the same place as me? Where's the glory? There ought to be ongoing glory. A Yale Younger Poet should be swirling his cape and plumes at the Mandrake and the Blind Lemon, dueling with pretender poets at Mike's Pool Hall, riding with Jim Young, and Bob Younger, Cole Younger, and the James brothers, Vaughan Williams conducting "Seventeen Come Summer" on the sound track.

"I like my job."

But what's there to like being an old stockboy? Was this a poet humbled but not from anything major like war, just the daily shit—job, friends, girlfriends, relatives, food, cleaning up—the ordinary middle-size life stuff that we're all supposed to handle, and he's gone under?

Even Wittman isn't so down that he likes his job. There's a poet's career, get your ass in gear. First, do a reading in North Beach, non-invitational, get to your feet at The Coffee Gallery or Nepenthe or The Forum, make ass. Find the open mikes, and sing. Stand in doorways of auditoriums where known poets are on platform, and hand-deliver dittos of your own outcast poetry; Richard Brautigan did that. And Bob Kaufman on megaphone in front of the St. Francis Hotel. Bring the poems back to the East Bay to read to Jack Spicer at Robbie's, the F.O.B. cafeteria men acting like they don't notice you. Then, single poems published around the country. Yale publishes the first collection. Wittman Ah Sing—the Yale Younger Poet of 1967 or 1968 or 1969. Nineteen seventy at the outermost shot. The Lamont people publish the second collection. And so on. Until you get to be Robert Frost inaugurating the President. And here's this Yale Younger stock guy getting older and going nowhere, ending up a minor poet, Wittman's never heard of him. (How is a minority poet a minor poet? You might make a joke on that.)

Ask him what he's got against the life I want. "Like Einstein said, 'It is the duty of the scientist to remain obscure.' You think it's the duty of the poet to remain obscure?"

"Einstein was feeling bad about the Bomb," said the Yale Younger Poet. "The Bomb was the penultimate. Einstein died without telling us the last thing he knew."

"What's that? Do you have a suspicion what it is?"

"It's either Nothing, or it's the malevolence of ultimate reality."

Were the two of them to sit quietly thinking, they might feel the pres-

ence on high of an evil thing that roams the sky. Mention of it brings it closing in. It is hovering over the rooftop. It's the size of Mt. Diablo. There are
probably more than one. Good thing they were in the basement.

"Have you heard the one about spacemen who flew to the end of the
universe?" said Wittman, trying to regale the down poet. "In the last wall
was a metered telescope. They dropped a dime to see what they could see.
'Oh, wow. Will you look at that?' 'What is it?' 'Nothing.' "

The Yale Younger guy nodded, smiled.

"This gig leaves your head free for poems, right?" asked Wittman.

"I quit poetry. I don't write poems anymore."

"Can you do that? You don't write it down, but you're still a poet, huh?
You *be* a poet. You don't have to *do* poetry. You be a poet, everything that
you do is poetry, right? You don't need to actually scribe. You have human
feelings, you're a poet regardless of words, which, as you know, especially
on dope, are very, very far removed from Things. I had Mark Schorer for
Twentieth Century British and American Lit. His face sad and blue like
Humphrey Bogart's, he said that Being beats Doing. He quoted George
Sand, 'He who draws noble delight from poetry is a true poet though he has
never written a line in all his life.' You draw noble delight, don't you?"

"No, I don't read poetry much."

"I don't think I'm ready for Being yet," said Wittman. "I'm going to
start a theater company. I'm naming it The Pear Garden Players of America. The Pear Garden was the cradle of civilization, where theater began on
Earth. Out among the trees, ordinary people made fools of themselves acting like kings and queens. As playwright and producer and director, I'm
casting blind. That means the actors can be any race. Each member of the
Tyrone family or the Lomans can be a different color. I'm including everything that is being left out, and everybody who has no place. My idea for the
Civil Rights Movement is that we integrate jobs, schools, buses, housing,
lunch counters, yes, and we also integrate theater and parties. The dressing
up. The dancing. The loving. The playing. Have you ever acted? Why
don't you join my theater company? I'll make a part for you."

"I don't know."

"You'd have to work for no pay. You might need to chip in for costumes
and props."

"I'll think about it."

"You don't mind if I come down here and visit once in a while, and let
you know how the play is coming along?"

"Do that."

Yes, he would. This Yale Younger guy was a real poet, all right. Amazing the creativity that came pouring out in his presence. Now that the Pear Garden in the West had been confided—and promised, twice—it will have to be made to come about.

Wittman rolled two bicycles into the freight elevator. One of these days, he'd have to go to the library and look up the Yale Series of Younger Poets, and see if his new friend looked like any face on a dustjacket. He wasn't James Agee, he knew that. Agee's vision of the malevolence of ultimate reality was that we're cattle grazing green pastures, believing that those who are rounded up go somewhere even more wonderful. A young bull escapes from Chicago and tries to warn the herd about cattle cars and stockyards and mallet guns and meathooks. Agee, another Yale Younger Poet.

Upstairs, Wittman propped one bicycle against the wall and the other on its kickstand. He rolled the ladder under the empty space on the pegboard. He picked up a bicycle by the crossbar and climbed up, but at the top saw that there were no fasteners. With its front tire turned against the board, the bike fit on the shelf okay. Leaving it balanced up there just so, he looked for hooks, which did not seem to be under the cash-register counter either. From that coign of vantage, he saw another shopper leaving her kids. No more Mr. Nice Guy. "Hey. Hey, you. Do I look like a babysitter, huh? This is not a nursery. I am not a babysitter. Don't you leave your kids here. Take those kids with you."

"I'm sorry," she said. "It won't happen again." She wasn't sorry; she's on her way out of here without kids. Don't let her get away. Escalate. "Wait a minute. I want to talk to you. You can't walk off easy." This minding so much about justice must have to do with being Chinese. "You're in the big city, ma'am." Yeah, let her have it. "I'm taking you in to see the manager." Not meaning that. Never call the cops—a Berkeley rule.

"How come these other children get to stay here?" the woman said. "My children are well behaved. I'm coming right back. I was just going out to put my packages in the car. I'm coming back for them. It's dangerous to take children across the parking lot without holding them by the hand. Look. Look at how much money I've spent in your store." Her arms were full of bags and boxes with the store's logo. "I buy here. I buy here, and you can help a customer out for once." "Backward I see in my own days," Walt Whitman said, "where I sweated through fog with linguists and contenders."

The bicycle at the top of the ladder was rolling, and when Wittman rushed up to halt it, the mother escaped. And those two pulling out boxes of model cars from the bottom of a stack were hers. Her get. "If you leave those kids here," he ought to have said, "I'm going to nail their feet to the floor. One foot each. I'm going to teach your vampire kids how to pivot." The next one, then. He would deal effectively with the next abandoning mother. It was a good thing that photographing babies for a Penny-a-Pound was a concessional job, and he would not be rotated to it.

The hooks were in the drawer with the charge slips. He climbed up with them, but now the bicycle was in the way of places for the hooks. He tried moving it aside farther along the shelf. The wheels turned, carrying his hand along, and it caught under a fender, cutting the skin, bunching a flap up. He pulled the bike the other way, and the gear sprockets and chain chewed into his tie and did not let go. A customer was nagging, "Isn't anybody around here going to wait on me?" Not me. "You. I'm talking to you." He lifted the bike connected to his tie, and carried it down the ladder without strangling himself.

His nose to the bicycle seat, good thing nobody's butt has yet sat upon it, he cut the tie with the dull scissors on a string tied to the counter. The Steppenwolf gnaws his leg free from the trap of steel, he thought.

He wrestled the bicycle up the ladder again, saw that the hooks were still not in place, and brought it down again.

Up again. Insert hooks in pegboard. Down again. Up one more time with the bike. The hooks did not meet the frame; if part of the bicycle fit on one hook, the rest of it did not fit on any of the others. Down. I have not found right livelihood; this is not my calling. Oh, what a waste of my one and only human life and now-time.

"It's time for the presentation," Louise was saying to him, the bicycle again on the verge of the shelf, maybe to topple on a customer or her. "Let's go. I don't want to be late." Though nobody else seems to be taking charge of the floor, the two of them are about to leave? He acted as if he knew exactly what she was talking about. The way to hang on to a job is to pretend you understand whatever's going on. Figure it out as you go along.

Louise, clutching a long clutch purse under an arm, handed him her wrap for him to help her into it. "Hold my shrug, please?" she said. It's probably called a shrug because it would fall off if she shrugged. She wiped her hands on her skirt. Sausage skin. She led the way to the street level and out the main entrance, letting him hold the door open, like they were on a date.

How dark it was already. Day was gone, and he had just gotten up. The fog was dropping a veiling—a star-filter—over the streetlights and head-lights, already on. Five o'clock, and most people were rushing home. They had commuted here before daylight, which shone on them on their too few days off. How fucked up they must be. Like veals that spend their lives in the dark.

"Get us a taxi. The store's paying for a taxi," Louise was saying, strad-dling the curb, finger in the air. She must be from New York. Don't you order a cab by phoning for it? A cab with no passenger came out of the fog; his hand shot up like in the movies, and—surprise—it pulled that obedient cab right over. (His being so cheaply surprised—this being new at almost every dumb thing—must also have to do with being Chinese, or will it go away with age?)

She pointedly waited for him to open the door, and slid in sideways, lady-like (not head first with butt in his face). "The Jack Tar," she told the driver. "What happened to your tie?" she asked in the intimate backseat.

"This is the new style. Don't you talk to the buyers? The short tie is going to hit the City by next week. You watch. The man in a grey flannel suit will be wearing this castration tie." A man of mode talking here. "If I were wearing a velvet tie, would you stroke it?"

"Of course I wouldn't. Why would I do that?"

"Because a womanly hand naturally likes to finger nappy velvety furry fuzzy wuzzy nap pile. I could take advantage of your instincts. But I won't. I make it a policy to tell women exactly what I'm up to from the get-go, and I expect women to be up front too. Nobody ambush anybody's instincts. Put your cards right out there on the conscious level. Don't take advantage. If you want to stroke my tie and work your way up and down to the rest of the bod, you have to tell me that that's what your intentions are, and not pretend you're interested in retailing that type of tie. Years from now, when our affair is over, or we're getting a divorce, I don't want you to say you were just interested in my necktie, and one thing led to another, and it was all my fault."

"What are you talking about?" she said.

"I am practicing on you my technique of honesty with women. Alas, women I've tried it on decide not to see me again."

"You've got motor oil or something on you. And your hand is bleed-ing." The girl of my dreams does not say that line distastefully, Louise.

"This is a workingman's hand, and this on my tie is the grease of hard labor."

She didn't answer. Neither said anything for slow blocks. Wittman smoked out the window.

"What are you doing this weekend?" she asked.

"I don't know. I haven't thought about it." The trouble with people in the workaday world is that they live for the weekends. Don't live for the weekends.

"The U.S.S. *Coral Sea* is coming in on Sunday. I know a couple of guys on it. I'm bringing my girlfriends to meet them. It's going to be a really nice weekend." Why's she telling him this? Isn't it bad manners to discuss a party that somebody's not invited to? Oh, he gets it. She's being friendly, talking about her social life with a business colleague.

So, the Navy is sailing home to San Francisco, and Louise and the wahines will be at Naval Air Station Alameda to greet them. You can count on women to have a life outside of the office. Others with outside lives: people who speak another language, criminals, people who dress differently from mannequins. Louise is not the kind of girl he's used to. The ones at school would have met ships to convert the sailors from war.

Central Casting put this influential girl beside him on this backseat taxi ride, and his next line should be: "Are you going to make the sailors go AWOL to keep them from sailing on Sasebo and Kobe and Subic and Pearl Harbor and the Gulf of Tonkin and setting up strategic hamlets and imperializing other countries?" Be a responsible citizen. "Fuck the war out of them, Louise," he said.

"What did you say? Hey, don't talk dirty. I just date them. That's all."

"As long as nice girls like you think that men look cute in uniforms, they're going to keep warring and killing."

"Men *do* look cute in uniforms. *You'd* look cute in a uniform. The ones with the best uniforms are the Marines."

What's the use, huh? Babytalk. They were on Van Ness Avenue, passing the showrooms of new cars. She pointed out the one so-and-so owned and the one she wanted once she got promoted to buyer. "Buyers go on buying trips to New York and Europe." They passed the Board of Education building. If she were smarter, he'd entertain her by telling about the City's multiple-choice test for teacher applicants. They arrived at the Jack Tar Hotel, which people were still making fun of because of its plastic red, blue, and yellow panels (the same colors as the pipes outside of walls at the new architecture building at Cal), forever modern and ugly. The searchlight that was sweeping the sky was shooting from the Jack Tar, not from a car show. The fog or clouds caught in the big beam roiled and

boiled; it seemed to be raining up there. Louise paid for the taxi. She and Wittman became part of the crowd beaconed here.

"Hi. Hello. Hi, there," Louise said left and right, stirred up by a crowd. Party time. They followed the arrows to one of the convention rooms, where there was a sign-in table at the door. His name wasn't on the rolls; he wasn't a Management Trainee anymore and should be back minding the store. But as long as he was here, he might as well stay. Gee, thanks. You're welcome too. Too bad he didn't rate a name tag, stick it on his tie to make it longer, or tape up the cut on his hand. "*One* good thing, you're tall," Louise said. What did she mean by that? So he could see above the crowd? So she could have a tall escort? His height made up for his color? A sales-man howdy-doodied her, and she peeled away from his tall side.

There was a food table with a drizzly grizzly bear made out of plastic ice, the California bear, re-usable for every occasion. Wittman loaded a tiny plate with coldcuts, deviled eggs, battered deep-fried shrimp, carrot sticks, and sheet cake. As soon as the Mexican-looking lady in the maid outfit put the shrimp down, people glommed on it, very aggressive and rude over food. Wittman ate in a corner, near an ashtray. A Pilipina-looking lady asked him what he wanted to drink. "A martini," he said. She wrote that down without asking for money. So, this was not no-host. Good.

There was no other of his ethnic kind here. Counting the house every time. Can't help it. Made racist by other people's trips. Politics and war—other people's bad trips that spoil the ad-hoc scene. What's wrong with him that he keeps ending up in Caucasian places? Like the English Depart-ment. Like Management Training. Like the Actor's Workshop audience. He didn't have a thing for bok guai. And he wasn't, as far as he knew, black-balled by Chinese. So where were the brothers? Where was fraternité? Wherever I go, I do the integrating. My very presence integrates the place.

The serving lady came back with a martini for him, and he didn't have any place to set down his paper plate and the glass and the cigarette in his mouth. So he slid down the wall to the floor, and made of the floor both chair and table.

Over a roomful of people, there spreads an invisible blanket that covers everybody. Wittman was drawing it to himself, bunching it, stuffing it into a hole in his corner (that leads to the fourth dimension). He shot back stink-eye for stink-eye. He felt satisfaction at having found an answer for how to sit wherever, and from now on he can use it in many situations, in line at the movies, for example, in line for a restaurant table, a teller's window, an airplane, and, if the world got very bad, in an Army line, in a bread

line. And when he gets to the Tuileries, where you have to pay to sit on a folding chair, he'll have a seat ready. Yes, the earth means to be benevolent, after all, and always provides a place for the weary to sit down.

Then—here they come—"orientals," all in a group. A guy and three chicks, one in a cheongsahm. He was against girls who wear cheongsahm. This oriental group were busily talking to one another; *they* didn't have trouble finding their coterie. The guy, embarrassingly short, twinkling away in his cute suit, reached up and clapped a white guy on the back, gave him the old glad hand, got patted on the back in return. Then he was introducing the chicks, every one of them pretty. Suddenly, as if a volume knob had been turned up, the oriental was no longer saying "rhubarb rhubarb rhubarb." Bouncing about on his toes out of exuberance and shortness, he distinctly said, "Wanta get your ashes overhauled, huh?" *Over*hauled? He had a Hong Kong San Francisco accent. Too bad he wasn't Japanese. Nobody laughed, so he said it again, a broader delivery, a thumb at the girls, who didn't seem to notice, or pretended they didn't. He was telling a sex joke—American guys tell sex jokes—man to man—but if it didn't go over, it could be taken as a cigarette joke, everybody standing around with long ashes. Or a car joke. Hedging his bets, the coward. If Wittman were not already on the floor, he would have slunk down now.

One of the girls—not the one in Miss Chinatown Narcissus Queen drag—turned around—her spike heels stabbed and drilled the carpet—walked over to Wittman in the corner, and said, "Get up, and quit making a fool of yourself."

"What business is it of yours?" he answered in Chinese. She went right back to her friends. She probably hadn't heard how snappy his comeback was; she probably didn't even know the most common Chinese sayings, such as, "What's it to you?" He stood up. He'll get her. "Slowly I turn, step by step, inch by inch, closer and closer." The clique left for the next part of the program.

Everybody moved into a room with a platform. A banner read, IT'S MATTEL—IT'S SWELL. Wittman took a seat by the door. An executive at the microphone welcomed "the community of retailers" to the "premiere" of new toys. "But first," he said, "let me show you the stats." A chick in net stockings held up a poster. It had a pie chart on it. "Entertainment dollar," said the man. "Family fun." In Wittman's entire life, whenever anybody—econ professor, insurance salesman, t.v. newscaster—threw one of these percentage pies at him, his mind died. For the hell of it—he had little

enough to do—he paid attention, but the next thing he knew, he was aware of not having listened for some time.

The orientals—all right, the Chinese-Americans—were sitting together near the front. They've set up the section where we're all supposed to come sit, which they'd done to the school cafeteria of every school he ever went to. At Cal, they had their own rooting section within the rooting section. Watch. One by one they're going to turn around and sneak a peek at him. See? One of the girls—a dec-art major, or a child-development major—put her elbow up on the back of her chair, profiled the room. He and she gave each other the old once-over. They both looked away; why should they greet each other? (Because your parents and grandparents would have run up yelling to one another and shouted genealogies of relatives and friends and hometowns until they connected up.) I am not going to the prom with the only Chinese girl in the class. I am not going to be the one to room with the foreign-exchange student.

The guy had a shaved neck; the girls had sheets of black hair, one bob and two pageboys. Their hair was so shiny that you could see why you call the crown of the head the crown. Buddhaheads. Is it really true that Caucasians have more of a variety of looks than other people? Grant that almost all Black people and russet people have brown eyes. Do they say they can't tell us apart because we all have brown eyes and we all have black hair? Whereas they have red hair and strawberry blonde and dishwater blonde and platinum and wisps-of-tow and auburn, and brown, and black. And they also have curly and wavy as well as straight. Ash blonde. Honey blonde. Taffy. Hey, wait just a minute. Hold everything. Are there all those kinds of blondes or are there lots of words? There are lots of words *and* all those blondes. Because of the words, and vice versa. People look at blondes with discernment. When you think about it, aren't blondes sort of washed out? Pale? But there's an interest in them. Everybody looks at them a lot. And sees distinctions, and names the shades. Those four heads were each a different black. Kettle black. Cannonball black. Bowling-ball black. Licorice. Licorice curls. Patent-leather black. Leotard black. Black sapphire. Black opal. And since when have ashes been blonde? Ashes are black and white. Ash black. And his own hair. What color was his own hair? He pulled a mess of it forward. It's brown. But he always put "black" on his i.d.s. I've got brown hair. And never knew it though combing it at the mirror daily because when you think of Chinese, Chinese have black hair. This hair is brownish, and two of the heads of hair in front are brownish too. He felt the dearness of those four people. Keep an eye out from now on. There are probably more of us with brown hair than black hair. Easy to think up words for browns. Chestnut, and more. We'll make up many, many names for dark.

"Let me have a little fun with you," said the emcee, who was telling business jokes. At least he didn't tell race jokes. A lot of people warm up meetings with race and sex jokes. "Seriously, folks," he said. "The concept of toys," he said. "Fun." "Play." "Core departments." "Meet the needs of the key customer audiences." (Where did my toys go? I've stopped having toys.)

Helpers ran up and down the aisles handing out "literature"—more pies, pictures and descriptions of toys, their stock numbers, order forms, handouts, inserts. As the executives talked—the people who introduced them were very honored by their presence—they had long titles, Western Regional this and that—you were to follow along marking up a page, then insert it among other pages. The pages were numbered like 19.B.2.a. Very scientific. Pagination. You could add to this binder forever at any point. Lots to do. Wittman hated this perversion of the classroom and books and the decimal system. All four of the other Chinese-Americans were taking information down in their notebooks like this was a difficult college lecture. "And that's true too," they wrote, which is a line in *King Lear*. Wittman had written a paper on how an actor playing Gloucester must have written it in the margin of his script.

With the nice sharp pencil they'd given out for free, Wittman drew a grid, a copy of his time sheet, and marked the days he'd cut out from work. The regular workers accumulated one day of sick leave per month. He had used up his accrued days. Now that he'd been demoted, was he accruing a half-day per month? It seemed that he was six days overdrawn. When would be a good day to cut out again? You don't want a conspicuous pattern of absences. It was time to call in sick on a Tuesday again. An absence is more enjoyable when you can anticipate it for days in advance. Taking a long weekend is suspect, of course. Taking off on Wednesdays is good— breaks the back of the week. But he didn't work Wednesdays anymore.

Is it time yet to speak up and give this meeting some life? Well, to tell the truth, the reason he was no longer in Management Training was that he had treated it like school. It wasn't a school? He had raised his hand, and contributed to discussion, "Do you give any goods, furniture, clothes, candy to the poor?" And he had tried to inform and give per-spective—"During World War II, this store gave dolls and toy cars to the 'relocated' children. But every girl got the same make of unsold doll, and every boy the same car. Kids don't like to get the same toy as the next kid. Kids walked away from the Camp Santa when they saw what they were going to get. It doesn't do any good to gift-wrap either unless there's a surprise inside. I move, the next war we send a variety of individualized toys. This isn't a voting meeting? What do you mean this isn't a voting meeting? I think every meeting in a democracy should be a democratic meeting. Robert's *Rules of Order* at least." No, of course he wasn't being facetious. He wasn't asking for pie in the sky; he knew this wasn't the place for legislating that there be no more "Relocation" Camps and no more war, but they could pass resolutions. He most certainly had stuck to the subject at hand. "Doesn't anyone want to second my motion?" There had been others who got carried away; they too thought that meetings are places where one makes motions and seconds them and votes on them. See? He wasn't crazy. "I move that we operate on a profit-sharing plan." "Let's run this store on co-op principles." "I move that we reserve one table in the Garden Lanai for feeding the poor." "Does selling candy to children contribute to their good?" "I move that the Sports Department stop selling guns and ammo." He'd even won a few victories—against selling books out of vending machines, and against blisterpacking books to protect them from spit-on-fingers browsing. Yeah, it scared him to speak up, but what actor doesn't have stagefright? An actor dead of smugness, that's who. Well, he didn't pass Management Training. A supervisor wrote him up as "disruptive at meetings," and gave him some new hours. There wasn't a scene or anything. Nobody said that part-time was a demotion. He liked shorter hours. Make stockboy soon. (The Monkey King had not minded cleaning stables until somebody told him that his title, Shit Shoveler to Avoid Horse Plague, was bottom in rank.)

Three chicks and three men with straw hats, red-and-white blazers, and candy-cane canes, men in blue pants, girls in nets, hoofed out. They led a cheer, "YOU CAN TELL—IT'S MATTEL—IT'S SWELL." "All together, boys and girls," they said. "Hit it." Taped music started up. They banged tambourines and shook sleighbells. They sang that Christmas song that rhymes "boy and" and "toyland." The Chinese-Americans in front, and Louise in front too, were having a good old time, singing along, shrugging shoulders to the beat.

The lights went out. Whistling. Clapping. "The new Mattel line!" A curtain opened—a movie screen. Green hills and blue sky, and the noise of engines. And around a turn in the road—a long shot of the road—thunders a motorcycle gang. Like *The Wild One*, like Marlon Brando riding into Hollister. The gang comes into view—right up to the camera—they are little boys in Nazi leather jackets and boots. Words splay across the sky—VA-ROOM! VA-ROOM! It was just an ad for plastic tricycles with outsize wheels that made a lot of noise. The cameras settled at a normal angle, and we see the suburban street we normally live on. Not the road into Hollister. The gang leader, the cutest little Nazi, says into the camera, "Va-room by Mattel. You can *tell* it's Mattel. It's *swell*." VA-ROOM! VA-ROOM! The end. Applause. Lights. The emcee announced how many times per day this commercial was going to run on network t.v. between now and the last shopping day before Christmas. Blitz the Saturday-morning shows for kiddos. "Demographics." "The entire country." "Going national on all three networks." "Across America." "Major." More applause. Go to U.C.L.A. film school and make industrial films.

The fishnet girls came back through a side door—costume changes accomplished during the screening—ta da! Barbie and Barbie's best girlfriend, Skipper, and Barbie's best Black girlfriend, Christie, did a skit about waiting for Ken to show up for a date, then he *does* show up. Ken and Barbie, informal, danced to Barbie's theme music. Ice-skating Skipper. Nurse Christie. Barbie-Q with her potholder and other accessories. Ken and Barbie après ski. The audience whistled and stomped for Malibu Barbie, Malibu Christie, Malibu Skipper, Malibu Ken in bathing suits and sunglasses. And the grand finale—Barbie Bride. And Bridegroom Ken and Bridesmaid Skipper. Everybody sang out together like community sing: "You can tell it's Mattel. It's swell." Oh, god, I don't belong on this planet. Then it was over, and time to leave the Jack Tar.

Louise found him. Their taxi, which she had remembered to ask the first driver to send, was waiting. You could tell why she was a successful Management Trainee and he was not. On the ride back, she talked about how cute one of the Kens was—"What a doll." Ha ha.—and how generous Mattel was to sponsor the do. "What an excellent presentation," she kept saying. Excellent. You have to be dumb to be happy on this Earth.

"You know what I think would be the best thing that could happen to me?" she asked. "There would be a grand ballroom under the stars. I would be wearing a long white formal that has a loop at the hem to loop around my wrist. I'd have a wrist corsage of a single black orchid with white ribbons. My partner would be in white tie, and the floor would be of black and white diamond tiles. We would dance forever." Wittman pictured lines of perspective extending to infinity, and Cyd Charisse dancing in the dress with the long long chiffon scarf that blew to the sky. That was it? Shouldn't the dream for her life have more to it than that? But he didn't say anything. Better than dreaming about world conquest.

"It's going to be a really nice weekend," she said. "The U.S.S. *Coral Sea* is coming into port. I know some guys on it." She'd said that already. This was where he came in. Very short loop. He vowed (again) never to repeat himself.

Back in the Toy Department, finally having mentally figured things out, he took a pencil and a bicycle up the ladder, and, using the bicycle as template, marked the pegboard where the hooks ought to go, brought the bicycle down, placed the hooks, then hung up the bicycle.

Beneath him, a mother was explaining to her kids, "I can buy a toy for one of you if I feel like it. Sometimes I find just the right thing for one of you. I don't have to buy three things for all three of you whenever I want to buy something for one of you. Just because Mommy doesn't buy you something doesn't mean she doesn't love you." She tried that again. "Mommy loves you even if she doesn't buy you a toy. I can buy one of you a toy, and on another day, I can buy another one of you a toy. I love you the same."

Another mother was leaving a child. Wittman put on his don't-fuck-with-me face, rushed down the ladder, and nabbed her. "What's your name?" he asked, notepad and pen at the ready. She said a name, but while he was writing it, it occurred to him that she'd made it up. A man said, "How about waiting on me? I have to catch a plane," in a voice that made Wittman stay with his citizen's arrest. "May I see your i.d., please?" While she went through her purse, he turned to the kid. "What's your name?" Oh, no, something was sinking in his Mexican-American eyes, and he can't jump in to save it. "Never mind," said Wittman. "It's all right. It's okay. Everything's okay. Here. Take this. A present from me to you." Pushing a red truck into the kid's arms. Taking it back, bagging it (to protect the kid from Security), giving it to him. "It's yours. Take it home. Bye-bye." "Okay," said the kid. "Okay. Okay." Don't grow up worried about how much things cost, kid. Please. The kid had nicks in his home haircut where his scalp showed.

The plane-catching man wanted a look at no other bicycle but the one attached to the wall. "It's a good thing you're taking that down," Louise called. "You've got the wrong bikes. You're supposed to put up the Va-rooms." Now how are those bulges going to sit on the flat wall?

"Look. Look," a kid was saying. "Mommy, look." The mommy turned her head too late and didn't see that, in the mirrorwall, the top of the kid's head came exactly to the height of a shelf of boats. As he walked, a flotilla of boat hats fleeted atop his head. Wittman was at an angle to have seen it.

"You're pretty damn fast with the scissors, aren't you? She's pretty damn fast with the scissors." A terrible, violent shouting. A gigantic man was shouting at Louise, then shouted his case to the masses. "How shall I be going back to Canada without my credit card? Look what you've done. Look at what she's done. I'll have your job for this, young woman. I'll have her job for this. Damn fast with the scissors. I bought a building on Castro Street today, and you're telling me I can't buy a goddamn toy? Who's your supervisor, Miss Fast-with-the-Scissors? Call him down here. I'm having your job for this. You're going to answer for this, you are."

The other shoppers were listening hard, giving the man flailing room, but acting intent on their own shopping, examining goods, their backs to the scene but prick-eared. "I have your number," Louise was saying. "They gave me your number." At last, a manager came, and the Canadian and Louise followed him away.

And the yammering began again. "How about helping me out here, you?" "Where's the restroom?" "Mommy will be right back." "Don't you have those plain domino masks? Where can I get a plain domino mask?" Come to think of it, domino masks are no more. The Lone Ranger, no longer able to disguise his Chinese eyes, rides nevermore. "Where are the refrigerators?" "I want to make an exchange."

Wittman went over to the display table and wound up a doggy. Once he had had a girlfriend whose dog named Dusty ran away. Whenever she heard on the radio, "Was it dusty on the train? P.S. I love you," she thought of Dusty on the train, paws up on the window and tail wagging goodbye. The toy dog sat down, wagged its tail, stood, barked, walked, sat again, wagged, stood, barked, walked. Wittman pressed the egg-laying hen; the eggs rolled out. Tough shit if a kid swallowed one.

Out of a box, he took an organ-grinder's monkey with cymbals attached to its hands. It had a red fez on its head. He took off its little vest, and inserted batteries in its back. It hopped about, clapping the cymbals and smiling. Its tail stuck out of a hole in its green-and-white-striped pants. "Look here, kiddos," said Wittman, and unboxed a Barbie Bride. He put her on her back with her arms and veil and legs and white dress raised, and the monkey on top of her. Her legs held it hopping in place and clapping her with its cymbals. Her eyes opened and shut as the monkey bumped away at her. "Mommy, look at the monkey fight Barbie." "Oh, how perverted." Wittman walked. The tongue of his necktie stuck out from the bicycle. A green razzberry to you, World.

Ah, Bartleby.
Ah, Humanity.

Our monkey man will live—he parties, he plays—though unemployed. To see how he does it, go on to the next chapter.

TWISTERS AND SHOUTERS

 IN THE TENDERLOIN, depressed and unemployed, the jobless Wittman Ah Sing felt a kind of bad freedom. Agoraphobic on Market Street, ha ha. There was nowhere he had to be, and nobody waiting to hear what happened to him today. Fired. Aware of Emptiness now. Ha ha. A storm will blow from the ocean or down from the mountains, and knock the set of the City down. If you dart quick enough behind the stores, you'll see that they are stage flats propped up. On the other side of them is ocean forever, and the great Valley between the Coast Range and the Sierras. Is that snow on Mt. Shasta?

And what for had they set up Market Street? To light up the dark jut of land into the dark sea. To bisect the City diagonally with a swath of lights. We are visible. See us? We're here. Here we are.

What else this street is for is to give suggestions as to what to do with oneself. What to do. What to buy. How to make a living. What to eat. Unappetizing. The street was full of schemes: FIRE SALE. LOANS. OLD GOLD. GUNS NEW AND USED. BOUGHT AND SOLD. GOING OUT OF BUSINESS. OUR PAIN YOUR GAIN. Food. Fast-food joints. Buy raw, sell cooked. If he got a-hold of food, he'd just eat it, not sell it. But we're supposed to sell that food in order to buy, cook, and eat omnivorously. If you're the more imaginative type, go to the mud flats, collect driftwood, build yourself a cart or a stand, sell umbrellas on rainy and foggy days, sell flowers, sell fast portable hot dogs, tacos, caramel corn, ice-cream sandwiches, hamburgers. Daedalate the line-up from cow to mouth, and fill up your life. If a human being did not have to eat every day, three times a day, ninety percent of life would be solved.

Clothes are no problem. He'd found his Wembley tie on a branch of a potted plant in front of the Durant Hotel, and an Eastern school tie hanging on a bush on Nob Hill. Coats are left on fences and wristwatches inside of shoes at the beach.

Musicians have a hard time of it. Sax players and guitarists and a bass player have left their instruments in pawnshops; they're away perhaps forever, trying to make money, and to eat. A lot of hocked jewelry sits in the windows overnight; the real diamonds, they keep in the twirling-lock safe. These cellos and jewels belonged to people who for a while appreciated more than food. The nature of human beings is also that they buy t.v.s, coffee tables, nightstands, sofas, daddy armchairs for dressing the set of their life dramas.

Market Street is not an avenue or a boulevard or a champs that sweeps through arches of triumph. Tangles of cables on the ground and in the air, open manholes, construction for years. Buses and cars trying to get around one another, not falling into trenches, and not catching tires in or sliding on tracks, lanes taken up by double and triple parking. Pedestrians stranded on traffic islands. How am I to be a boulevardier on Market Street? I am not a boulevardier; I am a bum-how, I am a fleaman.

Now what? Where does a fleaman go for the rest of the evening, the rest of his adult life? The sets haven't started at the Black Hawk, but no more spending extravagant money on music. Music should be overflowing everywhere. It's time to find out how much free music there is. And no hanging out at the Albatross anymore, taken over by scary Spades. To feel the green earth underfoot, he could walk on the green Marina, look at the moon over the sea, and perhaps a second moon in the sea. Keep track of moonphases; are you going through changes in sync with werewolves? But something about that nightlight on the grass that looked sick, like the Green Eye Hospital. *I saw: Hospitals.* No walk in the Palace of the Legion of Honor either, not to be by himself in that huge dark; better to have a companion, and impress her at high noon, Wittman Ah Sing as Hercules chained to the columns and pulling them down, while shouting Shakespeare. If he went to Playland at the Beach, he would get freaked out by Sal, The Laughing Lady setting off the laughing gulls. Haaw. Haaaw. Haaaaw. He had yet to walk across the Golden Gate at night, but did not just then feel like being suspended in the open cold above the Bay; the breath of the cars would not be warm enough. Continue, then, along Market.

No boulevardiers here. Who's here? Who are my familiars? Here I am among my familiars, yeah, like we're Kerouac's people, tripping along the street.

> *Soldiers, sailors,*
> *the panhandlers and drifters,*
> *[no] zoot suiters, the hoodlums,*
> *the young men who washed dishes in cafeterias*
> > *from coast to coast,*
> *the hitchhikers, the hustlers, the drunks,*
> *the battered lonely young Negroes,*
> *the twinkling little Chinese,*
> *the dark Puerto Ricans [and braceros and pachucos]*
> *and the varieties of dungareed Young Americans*
> > *in leather jackets*
> > *who were seamen and mechanics and garagemen*
> > > *everywhere . . .*
> *The same girls who walked in rhythmic pairs,*
> *the occasional whore in purple pumps and red raincoat*
> > *whose passage down these sidewalks was always*
> > > *so sensational,*
> *the sudden garish sight of some incredible homosexual*
> > *flouncing by with an effeminate shriek of*
> > > *general greeting to everyone, anyone:*
> > > *"I'm just so knocked out and you all know it,*
> > > *you* mad *things!"*
> *—and vanishing in a flaunt of hips . . .*

Well, no such red-and-purple whore or resplendent homosexual. Might as well expect a taxi door to open and out step a geisha in autumn kimono, her face painted white with tippy red lips and smudge-moth eyebrows, white tabi feet winking her out of sight on an assignation in the floating demimonde.

Shit. The "twinkling little Chinese" must be none other than himself. "Twinkling"?! "Little"?! Shit. Bumkicked again. If King Kerouac, King of the Beats, were walking here tonight, he'd see Wittman and think, "Twinkling little Chinese." Refute "little." Gainsay "twinkling." A man does not twinkle. A man with balls is not little. As a matter of fact, Kerouac didn't get "Chinese" right either. Big football player white all-American jock Kerouac. Jock Kerouac. I call into question your naming of me. I trust your sight no more. You tell people by their jobs. And by their race. And the wrong race at that. If Ah Sing were to run into Kerouac—grab him by the lapels of his lumberjack shirt. Pull him up on his toes. Listen here, you twinkling little Canuck. What do you know, Kerouac? What do you know? You don't know shit. I'm the American here. I'm the American walking here. Fuck Kerouac and his American road anyway. Et tu, Kerouac. Aiya, even you. Just for that, I showed you, I grew to six feet. May still be growing.

Like headlines, the movie marquees seemed to give titles to what was going down—MONDO CANE, THE TRIAL, LORD OF THE FLIES, DR. NO, MANCHURIAN CANDIDATE, HOW THE WEST WAS WON. Now, if there is one thing that makes life bearable, it's the movies. Let them show a movie once a week, and Wittman can take anything, live anywhere—jail, a totalitarian socialist country, the Army. Not educational films but big-bucks full-production-values American glitz movies. WEST SIDE STORY. The biggest reddest block caps told him to go see *West Side Story*, which had returned from the sixth International Film Festival at Cannes. The girl in the ornate ticket booth said that he was on time, so he bought a ticket and went into the Fox. Inhaling the smell of the popcorn and the carpet, he felt happy. In the middle seat a screen-and-a-half's width away from the front, he continued happy. In the breast pocket of his Brooks Brothers suit, on a page margin, Malte Laurids Brigge: *This which towered before me, with its shadows ordered in the semblance of a face, with the darkness gathered in the mouth of its centre, bounded, up there, by the symmetrically curling hairdos of the cornice; this was the strong, all-covering antique mask, behind which the world condensed into a face. Here, in this great incurved amphitheatre of seats, there reigned a life of expectancy, void, absorbent: all happening was yonder: gods and destiny; and thence (when one looks, up high) came lightly, over the wall's rim: the eternal entry of the heavens.* Then a thunder-clapping pleasure—the movie started with simultaneous blasts of Technicolor and horns.

"When you're a Jet, you're a Jet all the way from your first cigarette to your last dying day." Oh, yes, that's me, that's me, a-crouching and a-leaping, fight-dancing through the city, fingers snapping, tricky feet attacking and backing up and attacking, the gang altogether turning and pouncing— monkey kung fu. "You got brothers around . . . You're never disconnected . . . You're well protected."

Oh, yes, all the dances in all the wide and lonely gyms of our adolescence should have been like this. Us guys against one wall and you girls across the basketball court and along the opposite wall ought to have come bursting out at one another in two co-operating teams. The girls, led by Rita Moreno, high-kicking and lifting their skirts and many petticoats. "I like to be in America. Everything free in America."

And Tony meets Natalie Wood, and asks her to dance, and falls in love at first sight with her. Me too. "I just met a girl named Maria." And I'm in love with her too. Though her brother and her boyfriend belong to the Sharks, I love her like a religion.

In this world without balconies, climb a fire escape to court the city girl. And no sooner kiss her but have to part. "There's a place for us." Our monkey finds himself crying. Stop it. Look, identify with Chino, the reject. "Stick to your own kind." What kind of people are Tony and Maria anyway, both with black wavy hair, and looking more like each other than anybody else on or off the screen? They are on the same mafioso side, Natalie Wood as dark as a star can be. "Make of our hands one hand, make of our hearts one heart, make of our lives one life, day after day, one life." (Wittman had been to a wedding, he was best man, where his college friends had sung that song as part of the ceremony. The bride was Protestant and the groom was agnostic.)

The Jets are an Italian gang? But what about jet black? Like the Fillmore, the Western Addition. Black. Only they don't hire and cast Blacks, so Russ Tamblyn, as Riff the gangleader with kinky hair, indicates Blackness, right? (Like Leslie Caron with her wide mouth as Mardou Fox in *The Subterraneans* is supposed to be Black. George Peppard as Jack Kerouac, also as Holly Golightly's boyfriend in *Breakfast at Tiffany's*. Mickey Rooney with an eye job and glasses as Holly's jap landlord, speaking snuffling bucktoof patois.) The leader of the Sharks is Bernardo, Maria's brother, played by George Chakiris. Greek Danish Puerto Ricans of the East Coast. This is Back East, where they worry about Puerto Rican gangs, who are Black and white and blond. Don't the rest of the audience get Sharks and Jets mixed up in the fight-dancing? They should have hired dark actors for one side or the other. But not a face up there was darker than Pancake #11. Come on. Since when? A white-boy gang? Two white-boy gangs. White boys don't need a gang because they own the country. They go about the country individually and confidently, and not on the lookout for whom to ally with. "You got brothers around; you're a family man . . . We're gonna beat every last buggin gang on the whole buggin street." They mean they can beat kung fu tongs, who invented fight-dancing, and they can beat the dancing Black boxers, who fight solo.

Wittman got up and moved to a seat two rows forward, on the aisle, near the exit, but entered the movie no deeper, looking up at the squished faces. Can't get sucked in anymore. He went up to the balcony, smoked, nobody telling him to put out his smoke, and watched Tony talk to Doc, this lovable old *Jewish* candy-store guy—get it?—this movie is not prejudiced. Some of the Italians are good guys, Tony is reformed, and some are bad guys; the bad guys, see, are bad for reasons other than innateness. Wittman got up again and climbed to the back of the balcony. He would walk out except that he was too cheap to leave in the middle of movies. There weren't very many people in the audience, and they were spread out singly with rows of empty seats around each one, alone at the movies on Friday night with no place else to go. "The world is just an address. . . ." So, white guys, lonely also, borrow movie stars' faces, movie stars having inhabitable faces, and pretend to be out with Natalie, and to have a gang.

Chino does not disappear de-balled from the picture. He hunts Tony down and shoots him dead. Maria/Natalie kneels beside his body, and sings with tears in her eyes. "One hand, one heart, only death will part us now." Gangboys look on through the cyclone fence. She throws away the gun, which hits the cement but doesn't go off. "Te adoro, Anton," she says foreignly. Some Sharks, some Jets, biersmen, in rue, bear the dead away. The end.

Where are you, Bugs Bunny? We need you, Mr. Wabbit in Wed.

Wittman came out of the theater to the natural world that moves at a medium rate with no jump cuts to the interesting parts. Headache. Bad for the head to dream at the wrong time of day. The day gone. Should have cut out—the only human being in the world to walk out on *West Side Story*— too late. He'd stayed, and let the goddamn movies ruin his life.

Well, here was First Street, and the Terminal. The end of the City. The end of the week. Maws—gaps and gapes—continuing to open. But Wittman did too have a place to go, he'd been invited to a party, which he'd meant to turn down. He entered the Terminal, which is surrounded by a concrete whirlpool for the buses to turn around on spirals of ramps. Not earth dirt but like cement dirt covered everything, rush-hour feet scuffing up lime, noses and mouths inhaling lime rubbings. A last flower stand by the main entrance—chrysanthemums. And a bake shop with birthday cakes. A couple of people were eating creampuffs as they hurried along. People eat here, with the smell of urinal cakes issuing from johns. They buy hot dogs at one end of the Terminal and finish eating on their way through. They buy gifts at the last moment. Wittman bought two packs of Pall Malls in preparation for the rest of the weekend. No loiterers doing anything freaky. Keep it moving. Everybody's got a place to go tonight. Wittman bought a ticket for the Oakland-Berkeley border, and rode up the escalator to the lanes of buses. The people on traffic islands waited along safety railings. Birds beak-dived from the steel rafters to land precisely at a crumb between grill bars. The pigeons and sparrows were greyish and the cheeks of men were also grey. Pigeon dust. Pigeons fan our breathing air with pigeon dander.

Wittman was one of the first passengers to board, and chose the aisle seat behind the driver. He threw his coat on the window seat to discourage company, stuck his long legs out diagonally, and put on his metaphor glasses and looked out the window.

Up into the bus clambered this very plain girl, who lifted her leg in such an ungainly manner that anybody could see up her skirt to thighs, but who'd be interested in looking? She was carrying string bags of books and greasy butcher-paper bundles and pastry boxes. He wished she weren't Chinese, the kind who works hard and doesn't fix herself up. She, of course, stood beside him until he moved his coat and let her bump her bags across him and sit herself down to ride. This girl and her roast duck will ride beside him all the way across the San Francisco–Oakland Bay Bridge. She must have figured he was saving this seat for her, fellow ethnick.

The bus went up the turnaround ramp and over a feeder ramp, this girl working away at opening her window—got it open when they passed the Hills Brothers factory, where the long tall Hindu in the white turban and yellow gown stood quaffing his coffee. The smell of the roasting coffee made promises of comfort. Then they were on the bridge, not the bridge for suicides, and journeying through the dark. The eastbound traffic takes the bottom deck, which may as well be a tunnel. You can see lights between the railings and the top deck, and thereby identify the shores, the hills, islands, highways, the other bridge.

"Going to Oakland?" asked the girl. She said "Oak Lun."

"Haw," he grunted, a tough old China Man. If he were Japanese, he could have said, "Ee, chotto." Like "Thataway for a spell." Not impolite. None of your business, ma'am.

"I'm in the City Fridays to work," she said. "Tuesdays and Thursdays, I'm taking a night course at Cal Extension, over by the metal overpass on Laguna Street. There's the bar and the traffic light on the corner? Nobody goes into or comes out of that bar. I stand there at that corner all by myself, obeying the traffic light. There aren't any cars. It's sort of lonely going to college. What for you go City?" He didn't answer. Does she notice that he isn't the forthcoming outgoing type? "On business, huh?" Suggesting an answer for him.

"Yeah. Business."

"I signed up for psychology," she said, as if he'd conversably asked. "But I looked up love in tables of contents and indexes, and do you know love isn't in psychology books? So I signed up for philosophy, but I'm getting disappointed. I thought we were going to learn about good and evil, human nature, how to be good. You know. What God is like. You know. How to live. But we're learning about P plus Q arrows R or S. What's that, haw? I work all day, and commute for two hours, and what do I get? P plus Q arrows R."

She ought to be interesting, going right to what's important. The trouble with most people is that they don't think about the meaning of life. And here's this girl trying for heart truth. She may even have important new information. So how come she's boring? She's annoying him. Because she's presumptuous. Nosiness must be a Chinese racial trait. She was supposing, in the first place, that he was Chinese, and therefore, he has to hear her out. Care how she's getting along. She's reporting to him as to how one of our kind is faring. And she has a subtext: I am intelligent. I am educated. Why don't you ask me out? He took a side-eye look at her flat profile. She would look worse with her glasses off. Her mouse-brown hair was pulled tight against her head and up into a flat knot on top, hairpins showing, crisscrossing. (Do Jews look down on men who use bobby pins to hold their yarmulkes on?) A person has to have a perfect profile to wear her hair like that. She was wearing a short brownish jacket and her bony wrists stuck out of the sleeves. A thin springtime skirt. She's poor. Loafers with striped socks. Flat shoes, flat chest, flat hair, flat face, flat color. A smell like hot restaurant air that blows into alleys must be coming off her. Char sui? Fire duck? Traveling with food, unto this generation. Yeah, the lot of us riding the Greyhound out of Fresno and Watsonville and Gardena and Lompoc to college —even Stanford—guys *named* Stanford—with mama food and grandma food in the overhead rack and under the seat. Pretending the smell was coming off somebody else's luggage. And here was this girl, a night-school girl, a Continuing Ed girl, crossing the Bay, bringing a fire duck weekend treat from Big City Chinatown to her aging parents.

"Do you know my cousin Annette Ah Tye?" she asked. "She's from Oak Lun."

"No," he said.

"How about Susan Lew? Oh, come on. Susie Lew. Robert Lew. Do you know Fanny them? Fanny, Bobby, Chance Ong, Uncle Louis. I'm related to Fanny them."

"No, I don't know them," said Wittman, who would not be badgered into saying, "Oh, yeah, Susan them. I'm related by marriage to her cousin from Walnut Creek."

"I'm thinking of dropping philosophy," she said. "Or do you think the prof is working up to the best part?"

"I don't know what you say," said Wittman. *Know* like *no*, like *brain*. "I major in engineer."

"Where do you study engineering?"

"Ha-ah." He made a noise like a samurai doing a me-ay, or an old Chinese guy who smokes too much.

"You ought to develop yourself," she said. "Not only mentally but physically, spiritually, and socially." What nerve. Chinese have a lot of nerve. Going to extension classes was her college adventure. Let's us who wear intellectual's glasses talk smart to each other. "You may be developing yourself mentally," she said. "But you know what's wrong with Chinese boys? All you do is study, but there's more to life than that. You need to be well rounded. Go out for sports. Go out on dates. Those are just two suggestions. You have to think up other activities on your own. You can't go by rote and succeed, as in engineering school. You want a deep life, don't you? That's what's wrong with Chinese boys. Shallow lives."

What Wittman ought to say at this point was, "Just because none of us asks you out doesn't mean we don't go out with girls." Instead, to be kind, he said, "I not Chinese. I Japanese boy. I hate being taken for a chinaman. Now which of my features is it that you find peculiarly Chinese? Go on. I'm interested."

"Don't say chinaman," she said.

Oh, god. O Central Casting, who do you have for me now? And what is this role that is mine? Confederates who have an interest in race: the Ku Klux Klan, Lester Maddox, fraternity guys, Governor Faubus, Governor Wallace, Nazis—stupid people on his level. The dumb part of himself that eats Fritos and goes to movies was avidly interested in race, a topic unworthy of a great mind. Low-karma shit. Babytalk. Stuck at A,B,C. Can't get to Q. Crybaby. Race—a stupid soul-narrowing topic, like women's rights, like sociology, easy for low-I.Q. people to feel like they're thinking. Stunted and runted at a low level of inquiry, stuck at worm. All right, then, his grade-point average was low (because of doing too many life things), he's the only Chinese-American of his generation not in grad school, he'll shovel shit.

"It's the nose, isn't it, that's a chinaman nose?" he asked this flat-nosed girl. "Or my big Shinajin eyes? Oh, I know. I know. Legs. You noticed my Chinese legs." He started to pull up a pants leg. "I'm lean in the calf. Most Japanese are meaty in the calf by nature, made for wading in rice paddies. Or it's just girls who have daikon legs? How about you? You got daikon legs?"

She was holding her skirt down, moving her legs aside, not much room among her packages. Giggling. Too bad she was not offended. Modern youth in flirtation. "You Japanese know how to have a social life much better than Chinese," she said. "At least you Japanese boys take your girls out. You have a social life."

Oh, come on. Don't say "your girls." Don't say "social life." Don't say "boys." Or "prof." Those Continuing Ed teachers are on a non-tenure, non-promotional track. Below lecturers. Don't say "Chinese." Don't say "Japanese."

"You know why Chinese boys don't go out?" she asked, confiding some more. Why? What's the punchline? He ought to kill her with his bare hands, but waited to hear just why Chinese boys stay home studying and masturbating. You could hear her telling on us to some infatuated sinophile. Here it comes, the real skinny. "Because no matter how dumb-soo, every last short boy unable to get a date in high school or at college can go to Hong Kong and bring back a beautiful woman. Chinese boys don't bother to learn how to socialize. It's not fair. Can you imagine a girl going to China looking for a husband? What would they say about her? Have you ever heard of a Japanese girl sending for a picture groom?"

"No," he said.

"And if Chinese boys don't learn to date, and there are millions of wives waiting to be picked out, then what becomes of girls like me, haw?"

Oh, no, never to be married but to a girl like this one. Montgomery Clift married to Shelley Winters in A *Place in the Sun*. Never Elizabeth Taylor.

"You shouldn't go to China to pick up a guy anyway," he said. "Don't truck with foreigners. They'll marry you for your American money, and a green card. They'll say and do anything for a green card and money. Don't be fooled. They'll dump you once they get over here."

Another plan for her or for anybody might be to go to a country where your type is their ideal of physical beauty. For example, he himself would go over big in Scandinavia. But where would her type look good? Probably the U.S.A. is already her best bet. There's always white guys from Minnesota and Michigan looking for geisha girls.

"No, they won't," she said. "They'd be grateful. They're grateful and faithful forever. I'm not going to China. People can't just go to China. I was talking hypothetically." Oh, sure, she's so attractive.

"Last weekend, I went to a church dance," she said, letting him know she's with it. "I went with my girlfriends. We go to dances without a date for to meet new boys. All the people who attended the dance were Chinese. How is that? I mean, it's not even an all-Chinese church. The same thing happens at college dances. Posters on campuses say 'Spring Formal,' but everyone knows it's a Chinese-only dance. How do they know? Okay, Chinese know. They know. But how does everybody else know not to come? Is it like that with you Japanese?"

"I don't go to dances." Don't say "they."

"You ought to socialize. I guess the church gave the dance so we could meet one another. It's a church maneuver, see?, to give us something beneficial. We'd come to their buildings for English lessons, dances, pot luck, and pretty soon, we're staying for the services. Anyway, there was a chaperone at this dance who was a white acquaintance of mine from high school. We're the same age, but he was acting like an adult supervisor of children. We used to talk with each other at school, but at this dance, of course, he wouldn't ask me to dance."

"What for you want to dance with him? Oh. Oh, I get it. I know you. I know who you are. You're Pocahontas. That's who you are. Aren't you? Pocahontas. I should have recognized you from your long crane neck."

"No, my name is Judy. Judy Louis." She continued telling him more stuff about her life. On and on. Hadn't recognized her for a talker until too late. Strange moving lights, maybe airplanes, maybe satellites, were traveling through the air. The high stationary lights were warnings, the tops of hills. It seemed a long ride; this voice kept going on beside his ear. He looked at the girl again, and she looked blue-black in the dark. He blinked, and saw sitting beside him a blue boar. Yes, glints of light on bluish dagger tusks. Little shining eyes. Not an illusion because the details were very sharp. Straight black bristly eyelashes. A trick of the dark? But it was lasting.

Eyes and ivory tusks gleaming black and silver. Like black ocean with star plankton and black sky with stars. And the mouth moving, opening and closing in speech, and a blue-red tongue showing between silver teeth, and two ivory sword tusks. He leaned back in his seat, tried forward, and she remained a blue boar. (You might make a joke about it, you know. "Boar" and "bore.") He couldn't see where her face left off from her hair and the dark. He made no ado about this hallucination, acted as if she were a normal girl. Concentrated hard to hear what she was saying. "You're putting me on, aren't you?" she was saying.

"What you mean?"

"You're not really Japanese. You're Chinese. Japanese have good manners." Her piggy eyes squinted at him. He wanted to touch her, but she would think he was making a pass. But, surely, he could try touching a tusk because the tusks can't actually be there. "And you look Chinese. Big bones. Long face. Sort of messy."

"Listen here. I'm not going to ask you out, so quit hinting around, okay?"

"What?! Me go out with you? I not hinting around. I wouldn't go out with you if you ask me. You not my type. Haw."

"What type is that? Missionaries? Missionaries your type? You know where you ought to go for your type? I know the place for you. In New York, there's a nightclub for haoles and orientals to pick each other up. It's like a gay bar, that is, not your average straight thing. Sick. Girls such as yourself go there looking for an all-American boy to assimilate with, and vice versa. You can play Madame Butterfly or the Dragon Lady and find yourself a vet who's remembering Seoul or Pearl Harbor or Pusan or Occupied Japan. All kinds of Somerset Maugham combinations you hardly want to know about. Pseudo psycho lesbo sappho weirdo hetero homo combos."

"You the one sick. Look who's sick. Don't call me sick. You sick." The blue boar had eyebrows, and they were screwed together in perplexity. "*If* you are a Japanese, you shouldn't go out with a Chinese girl anyway, and I wouldn't go out with you. Japanese males work too hard. Chinese males dream too much, and fly up in the air. The Chinese female is down-to-earth, and makes her man work. When a Japanese man marries a Chinese woman, which does not happen often, it's tragic. They would never relax and have fun. A Japanese man needs a girl who will help him loosen up, and a Chinese man needs a girl who will help him settle down. Chinese man, Chinese woman stay together. I'm going to do a study of that if I go into psych."

"Don't say 'tragic.' You want the address of that place where keto haku-jin meet shinajin and nihonjin? Look, I'm just helping you out with your social life."

His talking to her, and her speaking, did not dispel her blueness or her boarness. The lips moved, the tusks flashed. He wanted her to talk some more so he could look closely at her. What was causing this effect? The other people on the bus had not turned into animals.

"Help *yourself* out with your *own* social life. Why *don't* you ask me out on a date? Haw?" The boar lips parted smiling. "Because you are scared." "Sked," she pronounced it. "You been thinking about it this whole trip, but you sked." Don't say "date."

"No, I'm not." You're homely. He can't say that. She functions like she's as good-looking as the next person, and he's not going to be the one to disabuse her.

This guise, though, is not plain. A magnificent creature. The voice that was coming out of it was the plain girl's. She must be sitting next to him engulfed in a mirage.

He touched her on a tusk, and it was there, all right. It did not fade into a strip of metal that was the window frame. The narrow eyes looked at him in surprise. "Hey, cut it out," she said, pushing his hand away from her mouth with a gentle cloven hoof. She giggled, and he backed away as far over by the aisle as he could back. What he had touched was harder than flesh. Bony. Solid. Therefore, real, huh? She giggled again. It is pretty funny to have somebody touching you on the teeth. Warm teeth.

"What was that for? Why did you do that?" she said. "Why you touch my teeth? That isn't the way to ask for a date."

"I'm not asking you for a date. I do not want to date you."

"Well, I understand. You don't like aggressive girls. Most guys can't take aggressive girls. I'm very aggressive." She'll never admit to homeliness. "Aggressive girls are especially bad for Japanese boys."

"Lay off my race," he said. "Cool it." Which was what he should have said in the first place. She went quiet. Sat there. But did not change back. The bus went on for a long time in the dark. And whenever he glanced her way, there beside him was the blue-black boar. Gleaming.

"Hey," he said, tapping her on the shoulder. Boar skin feels like corduroy. She cocked a flap of silky ear toward him. "See these people on the bus? They all look human, don't they? They look like humans but they're not."

"They are too," she said.

"Let me warn you." He looked behind him, and behind her. "Some of them only appear to be human." What he was saying even sent shivers up his own back. "There are non-humans in disguise as men and women amongst us."

"Do you see them everywhere, or only on this bus?"

"On this bus, maybe a few other places. I'm surprised you haven't noticed. Well, some of them have gotten the disguise down very well. But there's usually a slip-up that gives them away. Do you want me to tell you some signs to watch out for?"

The boar's great blue-black head nodded.

"You've seen 'The Twilight Zone' on t.v., haven't you? Have you noticed that Rod Serling doesn't have an upper lip?" He demonstrated, pressing his upper lip against his teeth. "That's a characteristic sign of the werewolf." The glittery eyes of the boar opened wider, surprised. "Their hands are different from ours. They wear gloves. Walt Disney draws them accurately. And Walter Lantz does too. Goofy wears gloves, but not Pluto. Goofy is a dog, and Pluto is a dog, but Pluto is a real dog. Mickey and Minnie, Donald and the nephews, Unca Scrooge—and Yosemite Sam—never take their gloves off. Minnie and Daisy wash dishes with their gloves on. You see women in church with those same little white gloves, huh? They are often going to church. There are more of these werewomen in San Francisco than in other cities."

"What do they want? What are they doing here?"

"You tell me. I think they're here because they belong here. That's just the way the world is. There's all kinds. There are cataclysms and luck that they probably manipulate. But there's different kinds of them too, you know; they don't get along with one another. It's not like they're all together in a conspiracy against our kind."

"Aiya-a-ah, nay gum sai nay, a-a-ah," said the creature—the Pig Woman—beside him. "Mo gum sai nay, la ma-a-ah." Such a kind voice, such a loving-kind voice, so soothing, so sorry for him, telling him to let go of the old superstitious ways.

At last, the bus shot out of the tunnel-like bridge. Under the bright lights, she turned back into a tan-and-grey drab of a girl again. Wittman got himself to his feet, rode standing up, and the bus reached the intersection of College and Alcatraz. Here's where I get off.

"Goodbye," she said. "Let's talk again. It will make our commute more interesting." She was not admitting to having weirdly become Pig Woman.

He said, "Huh." Samurai.

What the fuck had that been about? Nevermind. It's gone. Forget it. It doesn't mean a thing. No miracle. No miracles forevermore, because they may be drug flashes. I've lost my miracles. It don't mean shit.

Oh no, the plain girl had gathered up her smelly stuff, and gotten off behind him, and was following him up the street. "Are you going to the party too?" she asked. "Are we going to the same party?"

"No," he said. I'm not walking in with Miss Refreshment Committee bringing salt fish and rice, and pork with hom haw. "No party," he said, and walked off in the opposite direction of the way he was meaning to go. No more to do with you, girl. He walked quickly ahead and away down Alcatraz. The group of lights in the Bay must be the old federal pen. The Rock. As usual, Orion the Warrior ruled the city sky, and you had to know the Pleiades to find their nest. He turned left, then left again, and up the hill to the party.

The street was jampacked with cars and music, no room in the air for one more decibel. The trees held loudspeakers in their arms; their bass hearts were thudding. Wittman made his way among the bodies, some already fallen on the lawn. Above huddles of four or six, there hung oval clouds of smoke, like thought balloons. He walked the porch that wrapped all the way around the house, an Oakland Victorian, looking into doors and windows for an interesting opening, or somebody he might want to party with. From a backdoor, he went into the kitchen, where he poured himself some Mountain Red, and struck a party match. The flag flared up—stars burst, stripes curled—"bombs bursting in air"—a leftover from the Fourth of July party, which had followed the Bloom's Day party. He had, in his life, gone to four Bloom's Day parties, every end of spring semester since freshman year, missing this last one because of party dread. Dread of parties for over a year now. (The way you could tell you were at a Bloom's Day party was by a bunch of red roses in a vase, and by the date.) There was always a plot to one of these parties; the fun was in figuring out what the point was, and who got it and who didn't. Creative paranoia. Lance, who gave the parties, liked testing perception. He taught his friends, invited or not: The most important thing in the world is parties. In the bowl of walnuts was a nutcracker in the shape of a pair of woman's legs in garters and spike heels. The nut went in the crotch, and you clamped the legs shut, and cracked the nut. Nobody was using it. You'd be a fool to get a kick out of it, and a fool to be offended.

The dining room was a sane enough place—a sane zone, quieter with normal lighting—the eye of the noise. There were people he recognized from other parties; they never appeared anyplace else in his life except at parties. Party friends.

Suddenly, Lance Kamiyama, the host, and his bride, Sunny, Sunny the bride, swooped about him, one set of newlywed arms about each other, hers in luna-moth wings, dashiki cloth, and their outward arms holding their guest. Each of them kissed him on a cheek. Choreography. "You remember Wittman from our wedding," said Lance. "We're glad to see you once more," she said. A queenly We. The married We. "Once more" like "a year and a day," that is, a ritual amount of time has passed. The wedding had been the party between Bloom's Day and July 4. She had worn a sea-green wedding gown; her long Guinevere hair fell in tresses. Wittman had not met her before the wedding, but felt jealous nevertheless that during his lifetime she had chosen another, Lance. It was the first post-grad wedding, the one with music from *West Side Story*. No shame. At the reception, Wittman's last party, Sunny told him (while they were dancing, the best man and the bride) that Lance had said to her, "There's nothing in the world as beautiful as a blonde." He had something on Lance there; Sunny had been unfaithful already telling a thing like that on her husband.

"Howzit?"

"Howzit."

Checking Lance out for signs of marriage, it seemed he hadn't been married long enough to have been altered. Yet. There's something priest-like about married guys. No matter whether they're faithful or unfaithful or what. Having lived en famille once would seem to be enough for anybody.

"Isn't this one the Chinese Beatnik?" Sunny said. Discussing him. Aha, so they do talk you over. And she's given away some more of their private talk. Lance unhugged him, gesturing with that arm. "Don't my two hundred closest friends look prosperous?" he said. "We've done very well, haven't we?" Well, yes, he'd gotten them off the floor, off mattresses and gym mats, and on to furniture; the food was on tables, not on a door plank. Everybody was up on a higher level, sitting and standing. Sofas rather than automobile seats and park benches. End tables. "Lance told me, but I forgot. You're one of his business friends, right?" If the music were somewhat louder, he would not have to answer her. "Or are you primarily a social friend?" She didn't forget, she's putting him on. Do you and Lance really think like that? Does everybody? Are you mocking my natural paranoia? Isn't "business friend" an oxymoron, and "social friend" redundant? "We're old friends," he said. "We're childhood friends." A lifelong friend. The one who had turned him on to L.S.D. from the Sandoz Labs (twice), and homemade chiles rellenos, and William Carlos Williams' prose. "I was best man, remember?"

Another thing he disliked about couples—here he was ladling on the heavy charm, and looked up to see they were looking at each other, right across him. The first time a couple had done that to him, he'd been a kid in the dentist's chair. The dentist and his assistant had looked up from his open mouth, caught each other's eye, and smiled like that, the spit sucker slurping loudly and juicily away. His spit. Why was he always the one with his mouth open and his teeth hanging out in the presence of romance? He had missed the step down from the dental chair and rammed his groin into the spit fountain.

"You're looking appropriate," said Lance. "You do look the Young Millionaire." A Young Millionaire making fun of his job suit by cutting up his tie, it's allowed. After graduation, Lance started calling the parties Young Millionaires' meetings. He said "Mi-yun-neh" with Japanese-Chinese tonations. He could say it with an Oxford accent too; he'd done some study abroad at the London School of Economics.

"I've been canned," said Wittman. "Am I disqualified from the Young Millionaires? I'm going to try for Unemployment; it won't pay anywhere near a million."

"A deadbeat. But you're in luck. Here tonight you have two—maybe three—hundred business heads. Contacts. Contacts, Wittman. Recognize a brain trust when you see one. Take advantage. Hustle." He said "hunnert." He said "bidness." He didn't really talk that way; he was making fun of people who talk that way.

"Lance, why did you decide to go into the Civil Service?" I thought we were going to be brother artists.

"I like problem-solving. Actually, quite a few of our Young Millionaires are geniuses of problem-solving. Circulate. Mix." He burst out laughing at how there are hosts who'll say, "Go mix." He's probably a sociopath.

"I hate playing business games."

Sunny spoke up: "What's the matter? You aren't good at them?"

Lance laughed, delighted with her. Wittman had to laugh too. Oh, god, she's hard. No mercy. And these are his friends, toughening him up for the real world, doing him a service. She isn't so stupid; he had thought she was dumb. Why, she's sharp like her husband. Have you noticed lately that it's getting more difficult to tell smart people from dumb people? "I am too good at business games. Let me tell you what I did to get fired. You know that broken wind-up monkey in the gutter that James Dean covers with his red jacket in *Rebel Without a Cause?* We sell them. I wound one up, and put it on top of a Barbie doll. They fucked away in front of the customers and their kiddos. I should have made a bigger show—a flock of monkeys and a train of Barbies, in her housewife outfit, in her night-out formal, in her après ski, in her Malibu swimsuit, and the monkeys swooping down and up and away like the evil flock in *The Wizard of Oz.* I split before they called the cops on me. Seriously, folks, I'm like fired. I didn't even like the job, but I feel bad."

Lance said in an understanding voice, "You were just trying to make your job interesting. You can't sleep nights after all day faking a liking for your shitty job. And nothing but shit jobs ahead for the rest of your life."

"Yeah. Yeah. You stay awake over that too?"

"Who, me? Of course not." Shit. Red-assed again. The butt of the party—"Did you hear Wittman can't sleep nights over money? He's been fired, poor guy."

Then Lance showed a sincere, probably "sincere," concern. "Hey, you'll get another job soon. Everybody feels bad after getting sacked. Don't take it so hard, man. You worry too much."

"No, I don't. I didn't like that store anyway. I've got better things to do with my life." His own words always came out corny when he talked to Lance. The ironic versus the square. He wished to be the former, but couldn't turn it around. The hell with it. "I'm going to start living the life of an artist now. That was a cheap store where cheap people buy cheap presents for their cheap friends and cheap relatives." Toughen up.

"Yeah, everybody gets fired from there. Didn't you know that? By our age, the Young Millionaire has been fired at least twice. You don't want to settle down too soon. You haven't screwed up your job record at all. Most personnel managers will wonder why you were so tame you haven't been fired more often. In a lifetime, Wittman, you can make a total life change three times. All it takes to switch careers and socio-economic class—from sales clerk, as in your case, to lawyer or shrink or engineer and mechanic— is three years of re-training. I'm giving you an average. Fewer years for a nurse's aide, more for brain surgeon." It was Lance who had explained that smart people don't drive cars as well as dumb people because smart people's minds have too many alternatives.

"What G.S. are you now, Lance?" Wittman asked.

"Gee Ess Nine." Lance drew it out like suspensefully announcing the first prize. Wittman didn't know much about what exactly he did in which

Alameda federal building, but, reputedly, it was amazing for a person of their age to be a Nine. "Lucky for you, Wittman. The economic outlook is not bad," pulling a bobbin of ticker tape out of his vest pocket. Aha. Plot: Lance was wearing a three-piece suit because the theme of the party had to do with business. You were to judge ad hominem: Which suits at this party are deliberate costumes, and which came straight from work, their wearers wishing they had had time to have changed into party clothes? Those in costume and those not in costume are dressed similarly in Business District outfits, mere bowtie differences. Awareness is all, on the part of the clothes-wearer, and on the part of the beholder. A costume either disguises or reveals. One or the other. No way out of the bag.

Lance scrolled the tape between his hands. "Utilities up a quarter-point," he said. "Burroughs down 1⅜. Friday's Dow up 2.53 points in light trading on the Big Board. The Dow for the week up six good points. Run with los toros, amigo." Now, Wittman was susceptible to trance under the influence of numbers, and the evil name of Burroughs, Old Bull Lee, had been said in incantation. He heard: "The Tao is up," "Friday's Tao up 2.53 points," which is good; we were good today, not a hell of a lot better than yesterday, but holding steady and not backsliding, yes, some spiritual improvement. We are a people who measure our goodness each day. And we trade light; this is our way of shooting beams at one another. A scientific people with a measurable Tao. Wittman felt pleased with himself, that he hadn't lost his Chinese ears. He had kept a religious Chinese way of hearing while living within the military-industrial-educational complex. Wow. Lance was as good as dope—oh, god, the cosmic nature of puns. To show that he had gotten the joke, and could run with it and maybe cap it, Wittman said, "Osaka Stock Exchange, yeah. Sell G.M. Buy Kawasaki. Sell my sole for sashimi futures."

"Besides getting yourself fired, what's been happening to you?" Personally. Now his friend was making him feel ashamed for discussing work at a party. Where's his party spirit? One has to help create the atmosphere of celebration. Be more entertaining. And also candid like a camera.

"Well, I saw this guy chewing out his dog. I was taking a walk in the park yesterday. There was this queenie-looking guy dressed to kill walking his dog, this Doberman pinscher. He yanked on the chain, and said, 'You cuntless bitch.' I've never heard 'cuntless bitch' before. The dog was moving fast, like trying to get away; its ears were back. It was being publicly humiliated."

Lance was enchanted. Sunny smiled. Does she mind "bitch" and "cunt"? Not everybody would get behind this story. He and Lance liked to collect stories that most people can't appreciate.

"What movies have you seen?" Wittman asked. "Have you seen *A Nous la Liberté*?"

"Yeah. Twice. What a song. Did you see *Last Year at Marienbad*?"

"But if you sit for ten minutes at *Last Year at Marienbad* you're already repeating yourself. The point is: no point. I can't stand the imitative fallacy. I saw *West Side Story* today."

"Isn't it beautiful?"

"I like *Lolita* better, though only black and white. I like *8½* better."

"I love that part where Marcello Mastroianni whips his women around the room and the feathers are flying."

"Me too. Me too. That may be the greatest scene in cinema. But he isn't chasing them, is he? He's keeping them at bay."

"I hate that part. I hate that movie. The wife scrubbing the floor, and the aged showgirl weeping goodbye up the stairs to the attic. I hate that."

"But it's a fantasy."

"So men have a wife fantasy where she scrubs the floor on her knees and cooks for the harem."

"It's supposed to be funny. That's the funniest movie I ever saw."

"I hope you're not a man with a wife fantasy—the wife and the mistress holding hands and dancing around him."

"Fellini is a man's film-maker."

"But at the end, when everybody is running in an outdoor circus ring, didn't you like that? Didn't it make you feel good?"

"That part was okay. Everybody dressed in white, the opposite of the death dance—black silhouettes—in *The Seventh Seal*."

"Sunny, you like *Jules and Jim*, huh?"

"Of course, I like *Jules and Jim*. Everyone likes *Jules et Jim*. That's everyone's favorite movie."

"No, it's not. Everyone's favorite movie is *The Treasure of the Sierra Madre*."

"My favorite movie is *Ugetsu*."

"*Children of Paradise*."

"Yes, *Children of Paradise*."

"You like *Jules and Jim* because Jeanne Moreau has two men. We like *8½* because Mastroianni has two women."

"There weren't two women. There were more like twenty."

"That's what's so funny."

"No, it's not. It's not funny."

So, they had themselves a thorough visit right there in the middle of the bigger party, that's how good friends they are. If you have some very good lifelong friends you haven't seen or called for a long time, you have to catch up on what movies you've seen.

But there had been a time when Wittman and Lance had been the entertainment—tapdancing feet beating on skid row cement—Mr. Chin and Mr. Chan, howdy do, grin bones, grin bones, marionette arms dangling from tatter-stick shoulders, shuffle shoes, shuffle shoes. "Howdy do, Mr. Chin?" "J'eat rice, Mr. Chan?" "Yeah. Yeah. Rice and salt fish." "Crabs and black bean for me." "Wedding food, Mr. Chin." "Ah, Mr. Chan, we dance at the marriage of death and fun." Wittman quit the act; all Chinese jokes, no Japanese jokes.

The newlyweds waved to somebody, urgently, and they were off. A long-time-no-see friend has at last made the scene. Mix. Circulate. So, talking to him didn't count as circulation? Ditched. Don't anybody notice who's friendless at the party. He fought his shoulders' hunching up and his feet's shuffling, and his eyes' hunting from downbending, wine-sipping head for who was noticing that he was unpopular. If he could stand by himself alone, him and his cigarette, he would have perfected cool. In another corner, an overexcited party-goer had shut his eyes and was holding his hands in salaam position, his lips ohming and mumbling, trying to calm the space in and around him. How rude. Go home, why don't you? When you meditate, meditate; when you party, party.

Well, here's a "pool of acquaintanceship" of two to three hundred. According to friendship experts, the average American has seven "friendship units," couples counting as one unit, that is, from seven to fourteen friends. How many does he have? Below average.

Over by the fire, people suddenly burst out laughing, apparently at something the chattering fire did. "Oh, no!" "Oh, yeah!" Silence. Then many of them spoke at once, trying to get the rest to listen. "We could get arrested for watching that." "There are people who want to arrest other people for watching that." Giggles. Quick lookings around by the paranoid to check out who meant what by "that." "They want to arrest people for feeling good." Gleeful laughter. Scornful laughter. The glee winning out. Then they were all smiling calmly, gazing into the now silken flames. They were swimming in hallucinogen, ripped but appearing as ordinary as pie. So this is how the psychedelic state looks from the outside, that is, through the vantage eyes of a head straight from ear to ear at the moment. The stoned heads didn't look especially strange, a little high and red-eyed maybe, but they were smoking too, and topping mescaline and/or lysergic acid with god knows what else—combinations, asmador and Stelazine, carbogen and laughing gas, Romilar C.F. and belladonna from Vicks inhalators, whippets and whipped cream and aerosol. If peyote, the messy throw-up stage was over. They were not outwardly extraordinary; they were not actually flying around the room or going through the changes from amoeba on up. They were looking Neanderthally at the fire because we were cavemen for a long time. Then it will be a campfire on the lone prairie because we were cowboys for a generation (and more, counting the movies). And then—atomic flashes. The ages of man, though, did not visibly ripple up and down their faces. Their hair was not standing up on end as antennae for the aurora borealis. Now, all of them were calm, breathing in unison; they must be on that trip where the margins between human beings, and between human beings and other creatures, disappear, so that if one hurts, we all hurt, so that to stop war, all we have to do is drop lysergic acid into the water supply, but we don't even need to do that—because all human beings of all time are in connection—the margins didn't disappear—there aren't any margins—psychedelics only make you know about things, and do not cause a thing to be—it is—it already is—no need to reconnoiter the reservoir at Lake Chabot over beyond Canyon and the one you can see from MacArthur Boulevard, climb the dam walls and elude guards and drop L.S.D. in the water supply after all. The pleasure of acid was in knowing ideas as real as one's body and the physical universe. A girl with long hair brushed her face; the webs were bothering her. A couple of people suddenly sat up and looked around, alert. Somebody knelt like church, arms and face raised like stained-glass cathedral. Wittman did not dash over to ask what anybody saw. They were not a lively bunch. He and his compadres may not have actually flown, but when they turned into fenris wolves and dire wolves in a pack on the roam through the wilds, they had actually run barefoot through Berkeley, running to the Steppenwolf one night, having also dropped rauwolfia serpentina—"What's the trip?" "Fear and panic, man."—The fun of pure fear.—and on another night, landing at the laundromat, as you do, that laundromat on Telegraph Avenue, coming down with green paint on their faces. And recalling talking to a Black man, who was saluting a tiny American cocktail flag on top of a pyre. And they had talked, evolving language from growls to explanations of life in the universe. It must be that people who read go on more macrocosmic and microcosmic trips—Biblical god trips, *The Tibetan Book of the Dead, Ulysses, Finnegans Wake* trips. Non-readers, what do they get? (They get the munchies.)

Wittman went over below the tall black windows, where a group were talking politics. "At the rate the Masai are killing elephants," somebody was saying, "elephants will soon be extinct. Forever. From off the face of the Planet Earth." "Fuck the Masai," said this scientist girl, whom he had met before. "If I had a choice which—Masai or elephant—to conserve, I'd choose the elephants. There are too many people and not enough elephants. Elephants are peace-loving creatures, and faithful to their families and to their tribes their whole lives long. That's more than you can say for people. You must've noticed, there's a lot of anti-elephant propaganda. The movies are brainwashing us against non-human species. We have pictures in our heads of stampeding herds of elephants—rogue elephants on the rampage—man-eating elephants—trampling villages. Well, the fact is: Elephants can't run. They walk. Remember in *Dumbo the Flying Elephant* when Timothy Mouse scares the circus elephants, and they tear down the tent? Walt Disney couldn't do a *Living Desert*–type movie with elephants acting like that; he had to use animation." Oh, yes, she's the one doing her doctoral dissertation on Walt Disney with an emphasis on *The Living Desert*. "I say, Fuck the Masai. The brain energy of human beings goes into thinking up ways to kill whatever there is that moves. Fuck the Masai. Sure, I mean it. I'm on the side of life. When I shop at the Co-op, I choose the tomatoes with the bug bites and worm holes. I do." "Yeah, yeah, I'm hip. Fruit and vegetables want to be eaten," said this guy with a rep as a heroin addict. "Oranges drop out of trees and say, 'Eat me. Eat me.' " Strange how heroin addicts are always eating health food. Somebody else, who had majored in Africa, said that the Masai were hardly the elephantine consumers the Disney scholar was making them out to be. They don't cut up their cattle into hamburger and sirloins but only bleed and milk them. "The same way that Indian medicine women harvest parts of plants, some leaves from each plant, a branch, a section of a tuber system, rather than pull up the whole plant by the root." "How come Masai men are really good-looking," said a girl who traveled a lot, "and Masai women aren't?" "They seem that way to you because you're extremely hetero and not attracted to any kind of woman." "No, no, I'm speaking objectively." "What do you mean by 'good-looking'?" "Masai are like fraternal twins. Take a boy twin and a girl twin who look so alike they'd be identical if they were both boys or both girls. The boy always looks good for a boy, but the girl looks like a boy." "Yeah, like the Kennedys all look alike, but the men look good, and the women are homely." "If you watch elephants closely, you'd see that they are individual in looks and personalities." "Maybe you have a warped standard of beauty. Who amongst us in this room looks like a Masai woman? Come on, pick one out, and we can decide for ourselves whether she looks good or not." The scientist girl and the traveler girl looked at this one and at that one, turned around to look, and said that nobody there looked as ugly as a Masai woman. "Keep looking." Putting them on the spot. "You're being fooled by make-up and fashions. The range of human looks can't be that far apart. Of all the people here, who looks the closest to a Masai woman?" They waited, nobody letting the white chicks off the hook. There was a tall Black girl in the group, getting taller, and nobody was about to say it was her, and nobody was going to point out any other Black woman either. Wittman wasn't shining; time to maneuver a getaway. A newcomer was looking over shoulders, and Wittman stepped back, made room for him, and walked off, his place taken. He was getting good at shed-and-dump.

And he ran right into the most boring guest at the party, this left-wing fanatic who can't tell the difference between a party and a meeting. Each time they'd ever met, he carried on about injustice in a country you never heard of, and invited you to a "demo" in front of a hotel or a post office, which is federal property. The "demo" would be sponsored by "The Ad Hoc Committee to Save Whatever," founded by its only member, this left-wing fanatic. If you got a word in edgewise, he put it in his Marxist bag, and let you have it for not being radical enough. He had urged students to take R.O.T.C. to learn practical skills, such as shooting guns, that can be useful in making revolution. "You mean you want me to *kill?*" Wittman had asked, to agitate him; "I'll join R.O.T.C. if you join the Tibetan Brigade." Remember the Tibetan Brigade drilling on the soccer field near Bowles Hall? What happened to them? Did they ever get to Tibet? A man of principle has to hear a leftist out. It's very brave of him to picket Nob Hill all by himself, vexing delegates of governments and corporations who stay at the Mark Hopkins, the Fairmont, the Stanford Court. Tonight, the leftist was dragging around an old and tired lady. "This is Doña Maria Francesca de Ortega y Lopez"—a longer name than that—"from Sud America." Wittman, an irrelevant nobody, was not introduced by name. She didn't look at him anyway. One moment she was silent, and the next, she was spieling from deep inside, barely audible. He hoped that she was not saying what he was hearing, ". . . political torture . . . every man in the village . . . ," and names, Dons and Doñas. She rolled up a sleeve; there was a dark indentation in the bruised fat of her arm. "Bullet wound?" he asked. She shook her head, "Si"; she does that yes-no under interrogation. Please don't be saying that soldiers killed kids—niños y niñas—in front of parents. "Rapid," she said. "Rapid." As in "rapo," "rapere"? Wittman ought to come to her rescue. She is summoning him to responsibilities which would give him a life with important meanings. But he's ignorant, inengagé, not serious. "Could you tell her for me, please, that I don't want to help right now?" he said. Shame on him, so much more playing to do. The leftist rolled his eyes—a me-ay of exasperation—didn't translate such a Norte Americano embarrassment. He took the lady by the unwounded arm over to another listener, who might have a better conscience. She said, "Gracias."

Wittman hurried to pass a set of modular sofa-chairs, arranged invitingly by the married women, who were sitting safely together. They were newlyweds, young matrons, who last year were dates, but now they were wives. The adventurous girls had left for New York. The husbands were getting loaded with the boys, or dancing with the Pan Am stews. He'd gotten stuck with the wives before—stopped to say howdy-do and couldn't get away. Not a one of them was like Anna Karenina or Constance Bonacieux or Lady Connie Chatterley. Nobody bursting with sexy dissatisfaction. They were unappealing and blobby—well, two were pregnant. It was true about "letting herself go." They might as well have blackened their teeth. He had asked, "What have you been up to?" After they say they're housewives, there is nothing for him to say next. He had nodded and nodded, as if interested in "my stove," "my dinette set," "my floors," "my husband," "our pregnancy." A husband would come by and ask his wife to dance, but afterwards he brought her straight back here and left her. Surely, wives hate being stuck with wives. But how to party without being unfaithful? Why hasn't his lively generation come up with what to do with wives at parties? "Hi, Lisa," he said. "Hi, Shirley." That turning of wives' faces to him, troping him as he hurried by to join the men and single girls, wasn't because of his attractiveness; they didn't have anything else to do. They'd been sitting here like this since the last party. Watch to see when Lance starts parking Sunny.

His host and hostess were in the middle of a group that seemed to be having the best time, but he couldn't very well go over there when he'd already been conferred his turn.

"Excuse me," said a little woman beside him. She was unusual in that she seemed older and straighter than anybody. "Have you seen Sam? I've been looking all over for him."

"Sam who? I don't know anybody named Sam."

"I better go look for him. I'll be right back." And she took off. Another hit-and-run.

"I can't find him." Whaddaya know. She had said, "I'll be right back," and she was back.

"You're smart to keep track of him. Sam's a plainclothes narc."

Her eyebrows flew up, and she laughed, delighted. "Sam? You've got to be kidding. Not Sam. Oh. I'm not *with* Sam. I have been going out with him, though. I don't think it's going to work out. He's a health-food freak."

"Is he a heroin addict?"

"Oh, no, of course not. He's a health nut."

"Every heroin addict I know is on health foods. They're always trying to feel better. Another sign of the addict is strange-smelling piss. It must be the asparagus they eat."

"The only food I've seen Sam eat is lettuce with beige stuff. He took me sailing on the Bay, and we landed on Angel Island for a picnic. When he opened up the cooler, there were napkins, and his tacklebox with fifty-six kinds of vitamin pills, and this salad, which he drizzled beige stuff on top of. He talks about grinding up raw almonds in his blender. I guess that's what that beige stuff is. There were deer and raccoons; they went over to other people's picnics. He and I have no future."

"Want another drink?" asked Wittman. "Here I am letting you stand there with an empty glass. Let me freshen it up." He was getting good at party brush-offs. You ask if you can get them a drink, and dig out. Testing them, do they want to talk to you further? If so, they'll say, "No, thanks," in which case you say, "I think I'll get myself one," and cut out before you get bored or boring.

"Yeah, sure."

"I'll be right back," he said, and headed toward the refreshments. There. He'd never used those manners before. Something must be happening to him. She hadn't even been uninteresting, and he had ducked her. He could go back there and talk to her some more if he wanted. They're not supposed to feel hurt. Nothing personal. Circulating. Calculating.

He went straight out to the porch, and up some stairs to a balcony—no other party escapee here—smoked, considered hanging it up, half-ass gibbous moon in the sky—and re-entered to a corridor of closed doors. The Steppenwolf at the entrance to the Magic Theater. Lu Sooon surrounded by the eight slabs of rock doors at Fishbelly Holm. "For Mad Men Only. The Price of Admission—Your Mind." He opened any old door and went in. Movies. Also pot-luck doping going on. And they were showing a short co-produced by his own self with a stop-and-go hand-held camera. He crawled under the lightbeam and sat on the floor beneath the projector. The technique he'd helped invent was to try for a cartoon effect using face cards—you shoot a few frames, stop, move the cards, shoot again. And there they are, very bright, the Queen of Hearts, the Knave of Diamonds, the King of Spades running about on the wood table. The Knave is driving a toy pick-up truck, in the bed of which the King is suddenly hauled away. The Queen is backing off into the distance. And—deus ex machina—a black Hand (in a glove) clacking a pair of scissors beheads the Knave, picks up the King, chases the Queen, and carries them into the air. They'd filmed extreme close-ups of all three beheadings, and during the editing, decided which royal head would have the en scene star focus death. A new king and a new queen parade with the heads on pikes by torchlight. The grande finale—a cauldron of swirling water and red paint, and toy dinosaurs falling in by the Handful, and the pieces of the King, Queen, and Knave turning, and, what the hell, the rest of the pack, everything dizzying in the vortex of time. The End.

People were clapping, and they had laughed. "Not bad." "Not bad." The movie was different from when he'd run it; it was the music. There had been dirge music—the royal family moved majestically. But now there was Loony Tunes music, and the playing cards were rushing nuttily about, though the speed was actually no faster. The same story can be comedy or tragedy, depending on the music. Bad noises roaring overhead and in the streets, the world gets crazier.

Then up on the screen popped a slide of the sun setting beyond the mud flats of the Bay, the sun to the right, a branch of driftwood in the foreground on the left. Somebody said, "Sunset"; otherwise, would you know (if you weren't from around here) whether the sun at a horizon were in the east or the west, a sunrise or a sunset? In real life, there's no doubt. "Sh-sh. Look." Lance at the projector. He ejected the slide, and flipped it over, now the sun on the left and the black stick on the right. It gave off a different emotion—a shift inside the mind and chest. I felt safe, and now I am desolate. Because the first was the image as it occurred in nature? And in this reversal the stick sticks out more lonely on the salt marsh. Lance flipped the picture again, and the sun was again important and warm. Because we saw it this way first? The audience, patient on dope, and never tiring of taking out a somewhat aphasic brain and playing with it, were wowed.

At airport parties, Lance would stand at the revolving postcard rack, and arrange cards in some kind of sequence. "Do you think somebody will come along and read what I've done?" And the next time at the airport, he checked out whether he'd been answered. "Did anybody answer?" "Nope." "You mean those cards are in the same order that you left them in?" "Oh, no, people have been shuffling through them to buy." Just so, Wittman looked for some kind of a meaning to the order of the slides.

Then there was talk about f-stops, camera numbers, apertures, etc., and he went into the next room.

Where the tube was on. He sat himself down and was intercepted by a joint, which he passed on, eschewing the taking of a hit. Contact high already all over the house. The picture wasn't coming in, but the viewers were entranced, chuckling, commenting. "Wow." "Oh, wow." "Do you see what I see?" "Beautiful, yeah." Wittman had not tried the snow show straight before. What you do is turn the knob to a channel that's not broadcasting, and you stare at the snow. Try it. Pretty soon, because the mind and eye cannot take chaos, they will pull the dots into pictures of things—in color even on a black-and-white set—confetti jumping and dancing to music. Snow is not white. Regular t.v. programs are for zombies who allow N.B.C., A.B.C., and C.B.S. to take over the sacred organizing of their brain impulses into segments, sitcoms, the news, commercials. Look, where it comes again! It works both stoned and straight. There, across the bottom of the screen, rolls a line of new cars like off an assembly line in an auto plant. But each car a different make and color. And there are drivers behind the wheels. Nobody tailgating or passing anybody else. They're on an eight-lane freeway. Some people drive with their elbows out the window, and they make hand signals in another language. Girls are poking their heads out of the sunroofs, drying their hair. Can you control what you see by thinking? Wittman sped up his mind, and, sure enough, the cars speed up. A Volkswagen flips over, spins on its back, and slides along among the onrushing race. You can sort of control the pictures, but they are not strict mirrors of your thoughts. They'll do things you don't know what they'll do next. Look. A row of cars has come to a corner. Where are they going, zipping around the corner? People too, running round this edge. Wittman tried hard to see the other side, but was distracted by the girls with long hair, who fly out of the sunroofs, and become a row of feathery angels at the top of the screen. Oh, more space up there. He had been concentrating on a few rows of dots down at the bottom. There are more stars in the universe. Every jumping dot can be one of the billions of people on this planet, each one of whom you will not have time to meet, and everybody up to something. And, furthermore, there are animals. Elephants. Wild elephants.

And elephants with fringe and leis and sounding bells and other adorn-
ments. A fire truck. A float with a queen and princesses. You cannot make
something stop running to study its details. Majorettes. A marching band
passing a garage band. An Indian band riding a flatbed truck. The sitar
music was coming from the phonograph. It felt like Ravi Shankar was playing one's spine bones—the note off the top vertebra shoots into outer space
forever. Bicycles and tandems with silver spokes spinning, Gandhi wheels.
Clowns gyrating on unicycles. It's a parade. No tanks, please. No drill teams
presenting arms. No nationalistic flags. Every single thing different and not
repeating. Cars speeding up, black-and-whites behind. Car chase. Here
comes the Highway Patrol. A row of pink piggies with patent-leather hoofs
roll all the way across the screen. Yibiddy. Yibiddy. Some of them are wearing police hats. One of them is hodding bricks. Then the piggies are driving
black-and-whites with stars on their doors. Ouch. The horizontal bar rolled
up through the screen. Straight Wittman felt it smack him in the brain.
That same hit as when riding the glass elevator at the Fairmont or the Space
Needle in Seattle—while you're looking at the view, a crossbeam comes up,
and whomps you in your sightline. "Ow," said the other people too.
"Ouch. Oh, my head." The stars shoot off from the police cars and the
Highway Patrol cars and the pig hats. Ah, a line of shooting stars, each with
a golden tail. Cycle wheels of many sizes are spinning silver mandalas in the
heavenly skies. The stars are making formations and constellations—flag
stars, wing stars, sheriff's stars. Stars and stripes, and flags of other nations,
stars on wings and epaulets, kung fu stars. There goes a badge with a bullet
ding in it where it saved a lawman's life. The sitar plinks, reverberating on
and on and on, forever spacious. Wittman pinned his mind power on one
star, made it move to the center of the screen. It grows magnificently. Is this
satori? Am I going to reach it this time? And it doesn't go away? The star
blows up—smithereens of stars. Explosions massage the brain. Here we ob-
servers sit, detached as Buddhas, as the universe blows up. What was that?
Just before the bang, did you see Captain America with a star on his forehead and one on his shield, and Doctor Zhivago/Omar Sharif attach jets to
Planet Earth and blast it crazy off its axis? Wittman picked up (with his
mind) one of these iota stars, and pushed it to the middle of the galaxy,
where it pulsates intensely, and bursts again, a dizzy of birds—tweet tweet
—wun wun day—and stars orbiting around a cat's head with X'd eyes. The
pink pigs in top hats and patent-leather hoofs roll by. Yibbidy. Yibbidy.
That's all, folks.

"Wow." "Oh, wow." "Wotta trip that was." People got up; some went out; some changed seats. Did all of us get to the same place at the same time? Did we really see the same things? "Did you see the pigs roll away?" "Yeah. Yeah." "Pigs? What pigs?" Somebody has got to be scientific about all this; lock everybody up independently in separate lead-lined rooms to draw what he or she sees, and then compare.

"Look. There's more." Mushroom clouds. It was the last scene in *Dr. Strangelove*—the graceful puffing of H-bombs. Poof. Poof. Poof. "We'll meet again. Don't know where, don't know when, but I know we'll meet again some sunny da-a-ay." Electricity was shimmering between the thunderheads and the ground. A row of human brains on stems. The End. The End. The End. The End means the end of the world.

The monkey brains had tuned themselves in to an open channel to a possible future. If this many bombs were to fall, light would flash through time, backwards and forwards and sideways. Images would fly with the speed of light-years onto this screen and onto receptive minds. Future bombs are dropping into the present, an outermost arrondissement of the Bomb.

A second row of mushroom clouds bloomed, and the two rows of them boiled and smoked. Their viewers tried to shape them into other things, but the winds were dead. The Bomb, the brain, and magic mushrooms—fused. How to unlock them? Give us some peace. Some peas rolled across the screen. Helplessly, the heads watched: A parade of freaks gimped and hobblefooted across the screen—nuke mutants. See that baby attached to its mother's back? She's been running with it, carrying it piggyback along the Civil Defense route mapped out in the phone book, and it got stuck to her permanently. Werecoyotes—Los Angelenos are going to bond with the coyotes that come down from the hills and cross Ventura Boulevard into the suburbs of Studio City. Those minotaurs used to be dairy farmers and cows, or rodeo riders and toros. We're going to have a mutating generation. Nature will sport at an accelerated rate. The reason we make bombs is we want to play with Nature, so we throw bombs at her to make her do evolution faster. Nature panics. She throws handfuls of eyes at babies, and some sports will catch three or four, and some none. See that baby with sealed eyes? Before it was born, radioactivity zapped through its mother and lit up her insides. Blind calves have already been born in Nevada. Furry eyes protect them from too much light. Bees and flies will especially suffer when the light hits their many eyes and lenses. Nothing left but insects buzzing crazily. Those may be our own electrified ashes we're looking at. We won't be able to bear the touch of one another's fingertips on our faces. We'll walk blindly through the streets of unrecognizable cities. We'll be able to hear, though. Those who can see must keep talking and reading to the others, and playing music and ball games for them on the radio. After the bombs, there will be beautiful music, like the pod-picking scene in *Invasion of the Body Snatchers*. We won't have orchestras and bands; the music will be on tape. Fingers will melt together. Spadehands. Spadefeet walked across the screen. Languages will have a lot of vowels like "Aaaaaaah!"

"Remember in the days before the Comic Code Authority," said Wittman, "there was an E.C. comic book about this mad scientist who invented a potion that he gave to his big girlfriend, and she split in two. I don't mean like sides of beef. She became identical twins with red lips and long blue-black hair. Each woman was half the size she used to be, shorter but in proportion, still a normal enough height for a woman. Matter can neither be created nor destroyed. And clothes don't tear when anybody changes identities, according to comic books. Both of her had on a tight red dress and black high-heel shoes, just as before. The mad scientist takes one of her aside, and kills her. No tort case because there's still the other one alive. But that one wants to get even with him for killing her, see? She steals into the laboratory and downs some more of the drug. She's two again. Her plan is to kill him, and only one of her would have to pay for the crime. The two women gang up on the mad scientist, and he's fighting them off, when, because she o.d.ed on the chemicals, and because the two little women need reinforcements, they divide into four. No sooner does he kill one or knock one down than more form. Eight. Sixteen. Thirty-two. Geometric fucking progression. But, don't forget, every time the women multiply, they become smaller, each one half her former size. Pretty soon, there are hundreds and thousands—sixteen hundred—thirty-two hundred—of these little women in red dresses swarming at him from all over the room. They're attacking from the shelves and tables and curtains and floor. He's tromping on them and swatting them, but they come at him again and again with these little bitty screams, 'Eeeeek. Eeeeek.' " Thousands upon thousands of tiny teeming black-heeled women—a natural for the snow show—engrossed the heads, stoned beyond speech.

Wittman, one of those who talks himself through fear, talked on: "The artists drawing the E.C.s were skin freaks. They loved to draw viscous flesh dripping. Remember the one about the guy who asks a witch to destroy his evil half? 'I want to be good,' he says. She warns him, 'Are you sure that's what you want?' He can't see how you can go wrong getting rid of your evil self. The last panel took up a full page: He staggers into a mortician's office with his right side healthy, and his left side decaying and dropping worms. His word balloon says, 'Do something. I can't stand the smell.' And re-member the funnybook with this girl who had blue doughnuts erupting al-most out of her skin? Something at the amusement park had gotten her. I don't remember the story to that one. Only this picture of her in a bathing suit, lying in the sawdust, while in the background, the Ferris wheel and the merry-go-round and the hammer turn and turn." Blue rings—ringworms —the Worm Ouroboros—rolled across the screen.

"You're better than the storybook lady at the library," said Lance's voice. Some viewers laughed. We're regressing, all right. Those who'd learned to read with—because of—comic books pieced together this com-mon past—"Do you remember—?" "I remember—": There were these parents who punish their kid by locking him in the closet. The kid screams repeatedly that there's a thing in there, but they shove him in. Pretty soon he makes friends with it. They hear the kid talking to somebody. "Were you talking to yourself in there?" they ask. No, the kid says, he has a friend named Herman, and they better not be bad to him anymore, or Herman will get them. Just for that, his parents throw him in the closet again. The kid's saying, "No! No! Herman's going to hurt you." And, in the second-to-last panel—oh, yeah, the dad's a butcher, and they live above the butch-ery—there's this meat grinder with its long handle up in the air, and ground human meat is pouring out of the blades, all over the table and down the legs to the floor. And the Keeper of the Crypt, the narrator-witch who gives the moral of the story, cackles, "Hee hee hee, kiddies, the next time you eat hamburger, don't look too carefully. You might find a gold tooth. Hee hee hee."

Those comic books were brainwashing us for atomic warfare that causes skin cancer and hamburger guts. They were getting us inured so we could entertain the possibility of more nuclear fallout. Chain reactions aren't that bad; that lady in the red dress doesn't go extinct. They tried to make us despair of ridding ourselves of evil. We ought to keep heightening our squeamishness and horror.

Snow jumped and stormed on the screen. Minds were exhausted of images. Most people stood up and left. Those remaining selected a regular channel and talked back to the commercials. Wittman left too.

On his move to the main room, pouring himself another wine, past his limit already—he was one of those Chinese who turn red on a few sips— looked drunker than he felt—Wittman gave his fellow guests the once-over. Strange, there are people you've never met to talk to but they keep showing up on your rounds. See that girl in maroon? She had had to go to the Student Health Center to have a lost Tampax retrieved. That was the revenge tale against her for being a coffee girl, bringing the professors coffee, black or with cream and sugar, and sitting in the front seat and crossing her legs back and forth. You get things on people with whom you go to the same school for four years. And that one over there came back from winter break with a Jackie nose, which probably changed her looks, he didn't know, he didn't know her that well. Her friends said, "Nose job." Over there was a mathematician he had met in Chem 1A lab. Remember the smell of the wooden shed? The first experiment was about sulfur, which you cooked, then went out to the screened porch and washed it down the drains. Year round, the place smelled of sulfur and eucalyptus trees. Charley Shaw had never turned him down when Wittman asked to borrow his notes to dry lab. Where are the Pan Am stewardesses? Lance often promised career girls; he tried to make new girls prettier and possible to talk to by rumoring that they were executive secretaries from Price Waterhouse, or receptionists from the P.G.&E.—"What do you think of the rate increase?"—or Clerk Typist II's from the Bank of California. Girls won't play along with being Playboy bunnies of the San Francisco club. "What?! Me? A bunny? I go to Merritt College." All they had to do was play along being Pan Am stewardesses, and even the weather conversation would get interesting. "How's the weather in Paris this autumn?" Wittman was awaiting that woman who could make up for herself a life of world travel, Oakland only a layover. Wait, the next stew to blow in over the Pole, he had ready for her ears his life-of-crime plan: Does her airline have a job opening for baggage handler? After luggage has cleared agricultural inspection and gone down the chute, he, as baggage handler, could put contraband into the suitcases, and at the other end of the flight, before customs, another baggage handler takes the stuff off. Would she care to work in cahoots with him? What is it he wants to smuggle? A few years ago, *Ulysses*, *Lady Chatterley's Lover*, *Tropic of Cancer*, *Howl*. She didn't happen to know, did she, the titles that the customs officers are currently on the lookout for? You prepare scripts with lines for yourself and lines for her, but you have to try them on somebody brand new you never saw before, and he semi-knew everybody here. And girls won't co-operate. Actually, girls don't care to play stewardess-and-passenger, nurse-and-patient, narc-and-head. "What languages do you speak? Don't you have to be fluent in three languages to fly America's flagship carrier?" And she says, "Who, me? You must be thinking of somebody else. I'm waitressing tables part-time, Jack London

Square." You give them one more chance, "You look Pan Am, but you fly P.S.A., right? They're saying you're pit-stopping between the L.A. airport and Seattle. Is it true that air crews pirate movies, take the film cans off the planes from Hollywood, copy them, and send them on on the next flight?"

That information had come from Charley, with the degrees in math, who was moonlighting as a higher mathematician and an actor, brilliant enough to have time left over to go to parties and movies. His full American and stage name was Charles Bogard Shaw, C. B. Shaw okay on the marquee. Wittman was just thinking of him and here he was. "Seen any good movies lately?" he asked.

"No, man," said Wittman. "The movies have been bumming me out. I'm losing it. I can't take *West Side Story*. It's a bad movie, right? I mean, am I crazy, or is it like dog shit? I was losing it at *The Longest Day* too. I'm boycotting *Cleopatra*. Why don't you boycott *Cleopatra* too?"

The way a Buddhist life works is that when you need to learn something bad enough, the right teacher comes along. Charley was so good at seeing movies, he liked anything; he could "see the film behind the film." "I know the movie that will cure you," he told Wittman. "Have you heard of *The Saragossa Manuscript*? Each time I saw it, I broke through another layer of hoodwink. I am a changed person. It's been two years, and I continue changing. I'll try my best to tell you the movie. At the entrance into *The Saragossa Manuscript*, a French soldier is lost from his regiment. Explosions, cannon fire, music that sounds like *Don Giovanni*. He's running, falls, and slides down a hillside. He takes refuge in a Spanish Moorish villa; it may have once been used as an inn or a chapel but its people have fled, and dust lies everywhere. A leatherbound book, a tome, is sitting on a stand. Though this is a black-and-white movie, ask anybody who's seen it, and they'll tell you that the binding is red leather. The soldier blows off the dust, and, in the middle of war, begins to read. It is not the Bible. The camera goes inside the book: Once upon a time, there was a young soldier lost from his regiment. Cannon fire blasts the air, and cannonballs fall near him. The soldier is horrified—he is reading about himself. He runs from the villa, falls downhill, and loses consciousness. He awakes at the foot of a gibbet, and he is face-to-face with the upside-down faces of two hanged men, hung by the feet. Their heads swing on either side of his head. He escapes to a castle, where he meets a princess with long blonde hair. She gives him dinner at a table lit by candelabras of jeweled tapers and set with divining instruments. Across from her is her brother, a magician of the Cabala in a pointed hat and a dream robe that fills half the screen with crescent moons, stars, and alchemical symbols. The cabalist tells the soldier the mathematics of life and death and time. 'We are as blind men walking the streets of un-known cities.' The cabalist's beautiful sister tells a fairy tale about a dark princess—the camera goes inside her story: The dark princess, her sleeve rolled back on her beautiful arm lifting a heavy, branching candlestick, is leading a young soldier into a cave under a castle. She's somebody's sister, maybe his sister, and he falls in love with her."

Hold it. That about blind men walking the streets of unknown cities. The familiar City has been weirding out lately—flashes from a movie yet to be seen.

"The mathematics of life and death and time," said Charley, "make sense numerologically, the way that the I Ching and the periodic table do."

"What else happens in the movie?" asked Wittman, remembering when we were kids and poor. The one kid who got to go to the show— Wittman had often been that kid; so had Charley—told both double fea-tures and all of the serials to a crowd of listening friends.

"I haven't told the best part," said Charley. "The young soldier lost from his regiment follows the light from a candelabra of many branches, carried by a dark princess, one of two princesses, twins. She takes him through catacombs, where he meets houris and fellaheens. The soldier makes love to one of the dark twins, then he meets her identical twin, and becomes very confused visually and morally. What is love? What is faithful-ness when in love with a twin? One of these sisters comes to his room, which is inside the Moorish cave, and tells him that she will elope with a man with a beautiful beard. Such a man places a ladder up to her window. The ladder falls. The soldier rolls down the hill to the foot of a gallows. There is a pile of cannonballs and skulls. He screams and runs away, and takes refuge in the inn, where he reads, 'Once in a distant war . . .' Mozart-like music. Cannons boom. The soldier hurries to read to the end of this book about his life. But the movie doesn't end neat there or at the gallows. A lot happens—wars, Napoleonic, Carlist—between one gallows and the next, and you are not returning to the same place or the same time.

"I went to the movie the second time to count how many times the sol-dier finds himself on the hanging hill, and to note more exactly what pro-pels him there. The ladder falls, the man with the beautiful beard does not become part of the life of the woman in the window. That ladder is a line where planes intersect. Cannons. Perhaps the young soldier dies. Perhaps he sleeps and awakes from dreams. Perhaps he is reprieved, and is cut down, not hung by the neck until he dies—one can't die hung by the foot. No two gallows scenes are alike—the scaffold is farther away or closer, higher, lower, approached from the top of the hill, the bottom, the side. There is one hanged man or many, perhaps depending on tight shot or wide-angle. Have you seen tarot cards? One of the cards is the Hanged Man, and he hangs upside down by one foot. He looks like an upside-down 4. I think the hanged men are tricksters. During other action, they come down off their gibbets and change their costumes and rearrange their poses."

At this point, a girl of the group by the fireplace came over and inter-rupted, asking Charley very seriously, "Excuse me, but some of us have dropped L.S.D. Will you be our guide? We should have gotten a guide ahead of time. You wouldn't mind, would you?" Those were the days when heads prepared their trips carefully, and chose a watchman who promises to remain straight. Just in case. At sea, a shore. They must have picked Char-ley because they overheard his articulateness in the midst of revels. If called upon, the guide tells the tour group his wisdom, such as the reality he's see-ing back in the straight world. He sometimes takes their temperatures and blood pressures, and writes down anything memorable that is said. Such as discoveries. Mostly what you give them is your composure. No mind-fucking. "You can help too, if you feel like it." Wittman was invited too.

"I have yet to tell the best part. Good thing," said Charley, "that I saw *The Saragossa Manuscript* for the third time. The flick surprised me with logic. I love logic. I wouldn't have gone four times if I weren't getting intel-ligence. I was mapping the flow chart of the lifeplots. I counted how far in-side a story inside a story inside a story we go. And suddenly I saw that everything made sense. Because that ladder falls, the levanter with the beautiful beard does not elope with the woman in the window. Between scenes and cuts and juxtapositions are strict cause-and-effect links. Nothing is missing. The main link chain, though, is spoken. You have to listen for it. There's a man who says to the soldier that the soldier in the book is the man's grandfather. At the end, it's that grandfather as a young soldier who runs into the chapel/inn with the book under his arm, then runs out the door and up the hill. The first soldier is fighting in a nineteenth-century war. The grandfather is in a mid-eighteenth-century war. And *he* has a father, a man in a periwig, early eighteenth-century. We are connected to one another in time and by blood. Each of us is so related, we're practically

the same person living infinite versions of the great human adventure. Now I see more of my father and my grandfather.

"Here's the best part: A man with a patch over one eye climbs up through a trapdoor. As he lifts his eyepatch, and emerges into the room, he crosses over into new and larger realms. I am like him. I came out of the Cinema, and as I walked home, passing the doorways on Shattuck Avenue, and looking up at the windows of the apartments above the stores, I understood that inside each door and window someone was leading an entire amazing life. A curtain moved, a lamp switched on—a glimpse of a life that's not mine. A woman walked from one room to another; if I ran up the stairs, I'd meet her and be in another life. After that movie, Shattuck Avenue is a street of an unknown city. I'm going to spend the rest of my life discovering the streets of unknown cities. I can follow anybody into a strange other world. He or she will lead the way to another part of the story we're all inside of."

The purpose of the population explosion is to make all the multitudinous ways of being human. We are like the water of the I Ching, fluxing and flowing, seeking and filling each crack of each stream, each ocean. Charley was beautifully keeping his charges from wigging out. He got them to be inhabiting the same movie. Here we are, miraculously on Earth at the same moment, walking in and out of one another's lifestories, no problems of double exposure, no difficulties crossing the frame. Life is ultimately fun and doesn't repeat and doesn't end.

"I wanted to go see *The Saragossa Manuscript* again, and appreciate it some more, but its run was over. I've been on the lookout for it ever since. It hasn't come back to the Cinema, and it's not in the film catalogs. Do me a favor, if any of you find it, call me collect no matter from where or at what time of night. I want to play my memory against its trickiness and its thickness."

Wittman felt showered with luck that poured from the air. He'd been given a gift; someone at a party has sought him out and told him *The Saragossa Manuscript*. He can't die. He can't die without seeing this movie. Life has more enjoyment to come. Yes, life is tricky and thick.

For years afterwards, Wittman kept asking after *The Saragossa Manuscript*. He helped start a film society that held Czech and Polish festivals, but did not find it. Nor did he meet anyone else who had seen it. It will be as if he'd hallucinated that movie, a dream he'd had when he was a younger and more stoned monkey. And Charley, who saw it four times in three nights, will not see the movie again. It will become his dream too. Some of

those who heard the movie told at the fireside will think they'd seen it. All of them will remember a promise of something good among cannonballs and skulls.

Merciful guide. Heads that had sailed away were gently alighting. They had swum in and as star life, then ocean life. Then they had trogged onto land, and sensed dinosaurs, which were not bald grey as in museums; they had feathers of fiery colors. The hot wind that arose was a flock of dragons flying through the house. We had worshipped winged dragons—Mo'o the terrible lizard god, phoenixes, the Garuda, Horus. It does happen when journeying through a time of caveman wars that stoned heads will break out into fights, but everybody here was descended from tribes of benign vegetarians who had lived in gardening climates. Back in the straight world, in fact, we are citizens of a country that is militarizing us. We have to take barbiturates to keep from getting riled up. Now the wings of light were folding closed, and the heads were at word-understanding. Charley had guided them so well that the visionaries will come away talking story about this movie that they'd gone to. He set them to work applying their word-delight to finding a name to call a thing that the last time you saw it, it was in a hallucination or a story or on another planet or in a thought or dream but makes a crossover into the real world. "If we can name it, then we can more easily map the worlds," he said. "Remember the antique necklace in *Vertigo*? It was around the neck of Carlotta Valdez in the painting. Then Kim Novak as the unearthly Madeline has it; she dies—and it shows up on Judy, just somebody taking a walk on Geary Street on her lunchbreak from Magnin's. What would you call that necklace?"

Oh, what a guide that Charley is, leading these wide-open feminine minds right past the Bates Motel with its shower and the desiccated mother in the rocking chair spinning aboutface. Unafraid, they were getting off on more examples of things that cross over.

"Yeah, you mean that thing that you see after you think the nightmare is ended. An extra chill goes up you because it proves that it had *happened*. A flower or a ring or a coin that's so small, it fell through a crack in the Twilight Zone."

"You think you're home safe, but sitting on the mantelpiece or falling out of your pocket is a souvenir from the nightmare."

"Yeah, what do you call that?"

"That's what you would call the torn slippers of the twelve dancing princesses who disappeared every night."

"And Cinderella's glass slipper."

"And the rose in Sheridan Le Fanu's *Blood and Roses*, the sign of the vampiress, Carmilla, played by Annette Vadim. On the airplane out of the Black Forest, the rose on Elsa Martinelli's traveling suit withers—she's the next vampiress."

What happens if *you* were to cross over? *You* were a Saragossa or a Slipper or an Ishi, last of his tribe.

A head opened his mouth wide at Wittman, as if he were his reliable Chinese-American dentist, and asked, "Hey, objectively, do my teeth look longer to you?"

Wittman got out of the way of any biting. He nodded, smiling, not to bum the man out. "Yeah, I guess your teeth may be somewhat longer, but I'm not certain because I didn't examine them earlier for comparison." It's morally wrong to throw a hand grenade into a mind helpless on L.S.D.

"You want to look in my mirrors?" said a helpful girl. "Right now you hardly have any pores. I mean your pores are very fine. You must be going through your baby stage. You want a look?" She stood up and circled in her India Imports mirror-cloth dress, and the acid heads peered at themselves in the many many mirrors. Whatever they saw did not freak them out—not fly's eyes, or pieces of ego, or bout of the uglies, or predator's teeth. The color of their coalescent aura was salmon-coral.

"There is no physical organ for guilt," said the cathedral head. "I am so glad. I have no physical organ for guilt. But I have a question. I want to know—I do feel clearly that I have a soul. There is such a thing as a soul. I feel it. I started to send it out of my body, but got scared and pulled it back. I may have thrown my soul out of kilter. How do you reconcile unity and identity?"

"Oh, you dear brave man," said a perfectly beautiful girl, who laughed a wonderful laugh. Wittman wished that he too were spiritually far enough along to ask such an advanced question. How *do* you reconcile unity and identity? "You and the universe," said the girl, glad for each. "The universe and you."

Me and the universe. The universe and me.

At last, this party was getting somewhere, fluxing and flowing okay—when Wittman got bushwhacked. A chick who had been studying his face said, "Hey, I can see both his eyes. I'm looking at him from the side, and I can see either eye." What she say? I look like a flounder fish? Unless the right retort comes to him fast, this is going to hurt for years. Everybody was checking out his profile. Admiringly, right? "Thanks a lot," he said. Some retort. "Turn that way," said the rude girl. "See? Both eyes."

He turned full face to her. "I don't have much of a bridge," he said. What was he doing, justifying his nose. Here's her chance to say she meant a compliment. His eyes opened and shut from self-consciousness.

She said, "Can you see out of there? How can you see out of there?" She was squinting her own Caucasoid eyes to peer into his, allegedly, slitty eyes. And, god help him—instead of saying, "What is this Nazi shit?"—he explained the advantages of our kind of eyes. "They're evolved for use in desert and in snow. We don't need sunglasses." Which isn't true. We wear shades, we cool. "Finns have this kind of eyes too. Finnish people from Finland, whose language is related to Japanese." Oh, shut up, Wittman. The girl moved to his other side. "Come look," she said.

Beside him came Yoshi Ogasawara, a Nisei girl of Okinawan ancestry, whom he'd never asked out because his sexual hang-up was that he was afraid of smart pretty women. She had carried a double major of pre-med and ballet, and was now at the U.C. Med Center. Yoshi grabbed Wittman by the wrist, and announced to the world: "He's got an epicanthic fold, the same as I do. See?" He fell in hate with her. What's she taking him for? An anthro specimen. Homo epicanthus. Pushing her face forward to show her eyes, weighted down with false eyelashes, she was entertaining the party with our eyes. She batted two black brushes that were glued on with strips of electrician's tape, black eyeliner tailing out to here, blue-green mascara lids, and the lower lids rimmed with silver paste. Her eyelids were the puffy type, and the tight tape pressed into them at mid-puff; skin sort of lapped over the top edge of the tape, and made a crease per lid. She turned from side to side, giving everybody a look-see. With an index finger, she was pointing out her epicanthus, which is at the inner corner of the eye, when this (white) guy reached over and caught her finger, held it, and said, "You have beautiful eyes." It was Wittman ought to have done that. Why wasn't he the one to have leapt up, and taken her in his arms, and spoken up, "You are beautiful"? Because he can't stand her; her eyelids are like a pair of skinks.

"No. Oh, no, they're not," she giggled. "I'm going to have them operated on for double lids. I have single lids. These are single lids."

"What?" "You're what?" What? You people want two eyelids for each eye? Like an owl or a cat, one coming down, one across? Like an iguana? A shark? You don't mean you've only got one eye that's lidded. One of your eyes doesn't have a lid? They were white people, and didn't know what she was talking about. They do not have those phrases, "double lid" and "single lid," Yoshi. Those are our words. No, not ours, they are Japanese-American idioms, and just because they're English words, you think white people can

understand them. A.J.A. words. Chinese are not that subtle to have a thing about a fold in the eyelid. But, yes, eyelashes are important—they are a primary sex characteristic. Minnie and Daisy would look exactly like Mickey and Donald if not for eyelashes.

She did not know when to stop. "The upper lid—see?—is prolonged. See? The top lid dips over the inner corner of their eyes." Their. "I can ski all day long without getting snow blindness."

Oh, for the right existential Zen act that would re-define everything. Change the world. No more Mr. Nice Guy. Why were these people listening to this stupid girl, as if she were leading them in sane discussion? She was opening her eyes wide, parting her fake eyelashes top row from bottom row.

"But we came from the Tropic of Cancer," he said. What a weak thing —a fact—to say. And his vow to always identify us as born here—broken. "Eskimos wear goggles," he said. "They have to cup their eyes with these goggles made out of wood that look like egg-carton cups with a slit across them." What's he talking about Eskimo goggles? He'd made a move when he should be upsetting the chessboard.

"What is this Nazi anthropology?" he said.

She didn't get it.

"You're getting surgery on your eyelids?" asked a pitying white girl, the one who pointed out his flounder-fish eyes to the multitudes. "Are you having trouble seeing?"

The soon-to-be Doctor Ogasawara laughed. "No, I'm not having trouble seeing. I'm going to have my single lids cut, and a line sewn in. The plastic surgeon—Dr. Flowers of Honolulu, the best eye man—will remove some of the fatty tissue, and the lid will fold better. Double up."

Somebody asked why, and as she tried to answer—they were not understanding—disconcertedness overran her. How did she come to be using *this* as party conversation? "Because they—they don't like eyes like ours. We don't find my kind of eyes attractive. We like eyes that . . ." She was prating. "We like eyes like his." She pointed her finger at Wittman's face. "He's got double lids. I've got single lids." She brazened on. "You've got good eyelids, Wittman. He's got a fold. It's a common operation. It's one of the more simple cosmetic surgical procedures." She was looking to Wittman. Help. "*You* know," she said, appealing to him, Be my ally. "Oh, *you* know. *You* know what I mean."

"No," he said. "No, I don't." And walked. He left her there, kinky and alone. Sick *seppuku* chick slicing and sewing. Left her there with her shameful, unique deformity. He turned about, held his knuckles up to his eyes, and flapped his fingers at her. Like Daisy Duck eyelashes. Waved bye-bye with Daisy Duck eyelashes.

He followed flashing light and music to the room that in olden days was the front parlor—a strobe-light dance, like he first saw at "America Needs Indians." A lightshow dance at home. People breaking apart stroboscopically. Pieces hyperbright. My substantial body likewise—disappears and re-appears. A marionette who flies apart, scares kids, and suddenly reconnects. My parts dance whether I dance or not. Might as well dance. You move your crazy way; the light moves its crazy way. That hand or foot could be yours, it could be mine. Hands fanning. White sneakers stepping. White socks winking. Fanning feet. A white sleeve. The other sleeve. Angel wings feathering. White duck legs jumping. A white bra through a dark blouse. The fast, cold light will zap through to our white bones. And reveal which beautiful girl to be the White Bone Demoness. Them bones them bones gonna walk around. Step into the dark—floor's there, no abyss. White oxfords doing the splits. Come and go. Go and come. Open and shut your eyes, change the periodicity. Can't tell your blink from its blink. White gloves slapclap and fingerwave. Wittman moved any which way, invisible in his dark suit, crossing his hands before his eyes, like an umpire. Safe. Safe. Dance any silly dance you want to. The light does the rhythm. And rocknroll too loud for talk. Free of partners. I'm dancing with her and her and nobody and everybody. Loose. Is that beautiful Nanci I see? Yes, her face laughing; a curtain of hair swings over it—nope, the back of her head. Twist over in her direction. Here's Sunny the bride coming at him in fragments, her hair a splendor of gold. " 'Titania,' " said Wittman, " 'dance in our round and see our moonlight revels.' " "Huh?" Hand to her ear. "Leave Oberon, and come with me!" Shout what you want. Dance how you want. Okay to make ass. "You've been married to that guy long enough. Run away with me." She shrugged to the music, and flitted away, designs on her butterfly sleeves—two swarms of fireflies. He reached for her hand, missed, having aimed for the hand at the wrong end of the fan-out. But there's beautiful Nanci again. "Hey!" he said. "Did I scare you the other day?! I'm sorry! That I scared you! Are you pissed at me?! I wanted—I want to show you what I'm like. You did too like my poems. Hey, I know your future. I can tell your future. You'll end up with me." His feet were stumbling; headwork and mouthwork throw the dancing off. She leaned to try to hear him, smiled him a stroboscopic smile, and flew away in a rush of afterimages. She almost stayed long enough to have been his dance partner. People seemed to chase one another—chase movie—all going in the same direction, then switch and run counterwise. Were they whacking one another with rolled-up newspapers? And who's that? A very tall, very black Black man and a very tall, very blonde woman, both wearing street-fighting leathers, stood arrogantly in the center, the same couple, the same pose, at the Democratic Party fundraiser chez Mitford-Treuhaft. Daring you to call them out. Wittman moved toward them, but they were gone, went into a room where they could be lit and appreciated better. There's his old friend and enemy, Lance, looking down on me, no job, poor poems, square trips. Heads flickered by, and on the faces of the flickering heads were flickering expressions. Don't take them personally—am I keeping my discomfiture hidden? Stay very cool. Don't get caught with exertion or envy or smugness or any ugliness on your face. Nor let the light cut to a smile held tight too long, turning fake. A set of teeth were smiling on the floor, clackety-clack Hallowe'en choppers. Who choo laffin' at, boy? The cat disappeared, his smile remained. Trick or treat. Is that a mask or is it your face? Ha ha. Whose hand is that? Doing what to whom? "Suspicious, Mr. Chan?" "I smell foul play, Birmingham Brown." Whose foxy eyes narrowing at me? Wait a second. Just because eyeballs slide back and forth does not mean that conspiracy is afoot. Once paranoia starts, it keeps on coming. Okay, let me have it. Get it over with. A glower of thick eyebrows—do not react back—does not have to be a hate-stare. Keep my own face empty of suspicion and calculation. A mouth screwing up does not have to signify disapproval. A lot of people have piggy eyes and piggy noses and curly lips and flashy eyeteeth who mean no harm. Mugs are at large. No scene to comprehend expressions, and make use of them. We are blushing chameleons, ripping through the gears of camouflage trying to match the whizzing environment. Hang on. Hang on. Lobsang Rampa, who may not be a fake, says we will see monster faces, such as the ox face, on our way to death. Let them go by, he says. As Macbeth should have let pass the heads of kings without doing anything about them. Sunny winks at me. Interestedly? Lance glows greenly. Sunny hiding. Ah, sequences. Oh, no, a shmeer on my face. Don't look, everybody. Re-arrangements. Control my slidy features. Put the old face in neutral. Hold it. Is there a neutral, or does it come out bored or tired or tightass? Cocksure, ha ha. And there's the girl from the bus. Certainly didn't turn into Queen Kristine. The light jerked her away.

Flashes and music were beating together now. Wittman was getting used to things, yeah, his feet in step, the old bod bopping okay, and his monkey mind going along. His heart was beating with the bass. Go with it.

If you fight it, you will shoot off on a long slow bad trip all by yourself, un-tethered like *Destination Moon*. He went monkeying around the room, fancy feet making intricate moves, multiplexed by the light. Pardon that foot. That's okay. That's okay. Somebody else's unruly white bucks. Might as well be mine. We are as face cards being shuffled, and my fanning arms are merging into the images of the fanning arms of others. And the world is in sync. In sync at last. God Almighty, in sync at last. Feet go with drums. Heart booms to bass. My pulse, its pulse. Its pulse, my pulse. Ears, eyes, feet, heart, myself and all these people, my partners all. In sync. All synchronized. A ballet dancer and an m.s. spastic—no different—O demo-cratic light. Innards at one with the rest of the world. And why not when we're doing the twist, and Chubby Checker does the twist, "Let's twist again, like we did last summer," and the light is a strobe, and a strobila is a twisty pine cone. All right. All right. And—. And—. And—. And then—. Bang bang. Bang bang. But—. But—. But—. Banga. Banga. Lost. Found. Lost. Found. Gotcha. Gotcher teeth. Gotcher face. Boom. Boom. Bomb. The Bomb. Bomb flash. Bomb flash. In what pose will the last big flash catch me? What if. This were. Bomb practice? We're training to dig flashes. And my fellow man and woman aglow. Like fast frequent pulsa-tions of radioactivity. Why is the beat so even? If the bright intervals equal the dark intervals, like the black-and-white gingham on a Balinese butt, then are Good and Evil at an exact standoff? Paranoid again. Like we were last summer. What if Chubby Checker does not mean us well? What if Chubby Checker is up to no good? This is not Chubby Checker. Why is this tape going on for so long? Whose music is this? What. If. Music. Can. Kill. Evil drummer finds your heartbeat, and drums it. You dance along, drumbeat and heartbeat and feet together, like harmony; but what if all of a sudden—a last bang—the drummer stops, and stops your heart? But this set—ominous undertoning bass—goes on and on. This follow-along body is speeding. A race to the death. The End? The End. Is near. Ha ha. Fooled you. Longest coda in the world. To tear the heart from its mooring arteries. Hearts will flop like frogs all over the floor.

The music, however, ended before anything like that happened. The strobe lights wrought craziness. Survivors talked over what happened. Witt-man headed for normal light.

But suddenly a whistling started up, higher and higher, then a super-sonic jet war fighter plane crashed through the sound barrier right there in-side the house—the fucking house taking off. People ducked to the floor, backed against the walls, dived under tables. Hung on to the shag rug.

Sound waves pushed on them, and held them flattened. What the fuck was that? Oh, my god, they've gone and done it. This is it. Blown up the planet. Nothing left but noise. The Bomb. Has set off the Earthquake. California at last breaking loose from North America. The Rad Lab—on the fault. Blown. And resonating booming further sound. People laughed and giggled, holding their faces. Some of them might have been screaming—you could scream all you want, nobody could hear you—opening their mouths like the Munch painting. And the skull and the planet split into bowls of mush brains.

What it was were the sounds of World War II playing full blast out of the loudspeakers, of which there were twelve, hooked up to the roof and the corner eaves, engines for propelling the house away. Sound effects you can check out of the public library. Mixed with the sounds of a takeoff as you lie in the grass among the seagulls and the egrets and the jackrabbits next to the runway at the San Francisco International Airport—and this jumbo jet pulls up off the ground almost right over you, hair and feathers blowing, and just about pulls the soul right out of your body. The wind. The size. The steel. The speed. The noise. Acid flash. Acid flash. That mixed with the roars of Fleishhacker Zoo at feeding time. When you thought back on the tape, you could distinguish mortar shells from rifle shots, fighter planes diving, hand grenades, machine-gun fire, and the A-bomb at Nagasaki and the A-bomb at Hiroshima, and—finale—those bombs over-dubbed in multiplex bombilation. The boom of the Bomb, then subsequent booms, the resounding, rolling aftershocks—roaring, roaring, roaring. We are all hibakushas. The guests were thinking, "All right. Enough already. I got the joke"—and it went on and on and on.

Suddenly it was over. In the silence, people kept explaining things to one another. The amps on the roof make a giant resonator of the house. You can get sound effects from studio connections in Hollywood, the A-bombs from the Oakland Public Library. Direct from the actual bombs to your ears. "That was the Bomb." "Is that all the loud it is? It must have been louder than that."

Nobody heard police sirens. Red and blue lights swiveled onto walls and ceiling. Like the invasion of the Martians in *War of the Worlds*. Guests hiding at the windows listened to Lance sweet-talking the cops. Other guests were leaving, thank you, thank you, goodbye, taking zombie steps past the paddywagons. A two-paddywagon party. One of the policemen was asking him to go inside and bring out people who were breaking the law. Cops without warrants are like vampires; they can't cross the threshold unless you invite them. Lance asked, "Such as which laws, Officer? I didn't notice any unusual misbehavior, sir, but I'll co-operate, and look around." Then he was inside looking out the window at the police asking another person to go find *him*—"about yay tall, business suit." People were going in, coming out, like the townspeople in *Invasion of the Body Snatchers*, unloading the truck of pods, as Kevin McCarthy and his girlfriend spy from behind the blinds. Lance went out there from another direction, and said, "We withdraw all charges. Sorry, we shouldn't have called you. As you can see, no problem, no trouble-makers." And so, toward morning, it became a quiet party.

A girl, who was sitting at the top of the stairs, her sandaled toes playing peek-a-boo, was saying by heart for a crowd ranged on the steps below her every verse of "The Shooting of Dan McGrew."

> *"There's men that somehow just grip your eyes,*
> *and hold them hard like a spell;*
> *And such was he, and he looked to me like a*
> *man who had lived in hell. . . ."*

She looked right into Wittman's eyes—chose him out—and he hung over the railing, listening to the whole thing, taking a liking to her cornball ways. She stood and stuck her elbow out, the jagtime ragtime kid taking five beside his upright 88. A stranger staggers into the Malamute saloon, and buys drinks for the house. She lifted her chin, as if showing off an Adam's apple. She's knocking back a shot of hootch—"the green stuff in his glass." She brushed the swing of fringe on a buckskin sleeve, sat down, and made talon hands—the stranger clutches the keys and plays that piano.

> *"Were you ever out in the Great Alone, when the*
> *moon was awful clear,*
> *And the icy mountains hemmed you in with a*
> *silence most could hear;*
> *With only the howl of a timber wolf, and you*
> *camped there in the cold,*
> *A half-dead thing in a stark, dead world, clean*
> *mad for the muck called gold;*
> *While high overhead, green, yellow, and red,*
> *the North Lights swept in bars?—*
> *Then you've a haunch what the music meant*
> *. . . hunger and night and the stars."*

Goddamn. She knows me, and she wants me bad. The way she's looking at me, and none other, she understands, and she likes me, a heartbreaker and a rover. That's me all over. She's holding her hands over her heart, and beholding me like I'm the one breaking it.

> *"There's a race of men that don't fit in,*
> *A race that can't sit still.*
> *So they break the hearts of kith and kin,*
> *And they roam the world at will."*

That's me. She knows me and my timber wolf Steppenwolf ways, and sympathizes. She's melting my loneliness. Four years of Chaucer and Shakespeare, Milton, and Dickens, Whitman, Joyce, Pound and Eliot, and you shoot me right through the heart with Robert W. Service.

Okay, so Bloomsbury did not recite Robert Service. Neither did Gertrude Stein's Paris salon. Neither did the Beats. But Wittman Ah Sing's friends—the most artistic people he knew how to find anywhere—his generation—did. Wittman had been there at Berkeley when Charles Olson read—and drew, spreading wide his arms, a map of the universe on the chalkboard—circles and great cosmic rings. And Lew Welch dangling his legs off the corner edge of the platform and nodding in rhythm, yeah, yeah, "Ring of bone. Where ring is the sound a bell makes." And Brother Antoninus out of St. Albert's for the night, some other monk ringing the angelus bells. A Black lady from the audience questioned "lily white," and Olson answered her with a lotus vision, and Ginsberg, the social realist, had had to explain to him about politics. That's how far Olson went into his created world. And Wittman Ah Sing had been there in the room too, though nobody knew it. It was okay that nobody knew; he was just a nobody kid. He had seen for himself what an older generation of poets was like. They had not tried to include Young Millionaires and Pan Am stewardesses.

> *"They range the field and they rove the flood,*
> *And they climb the mountain's crest;*
> *Theirs is the curse of the gypsy's blood,*
> *And they don't know how to rest.*
>
> *If they just went straight they might go far;*
> *They are strong and brave and true;*

But they're always tired of the things that are,
And they want the strange and new. . . ."

Shrewd-eyed—Maria Ouspenskaya, "My son, Bela, has the curse of the werewolf."—the girl at the top of the stairs caught and opened the hand of a lucky one of her admirers, and wrote in it the lines of his life and fate. It's hard to tell, mock-corny or real corny. A rebel, reciting fervently what we're supposed to not like. Come now, "The Men Who Don't Fit In" does feel better than "The Waste Land." The brainwashing of a too hip education is wearing off. She sounds so valiant, and one feels so sad. "Ha, ha!" she shouted. If Wittman were not shy, he'd say along with her in duet:

"Ha, ha! He is one of the Legion Lost;
    He was never meant to win;
He's a rolling stone, and it's bred in the bone;
    He's the man who won't fit in."

Her audience clapped, whistled. Wittman too. She's our brave queen. We're such geniuses, we know how to like anything. The hall light shone on her, an overhead light that cast shadow bags and hag noses on all but her; on her, a halo, a rainbow. Look at her, lifting her hair with both hands. Hair's so heavy—let me just lift the gold chain-link weight of it off my neck. Oh, my burdensome hair. She sat up, the hair rippling as she leaned toward us.

Wittman held out his hand, bidding her descend the stairs to him, but she shook her head and hair, and sat amid her court. He climbed over the railing and up the stairs to the glimmering girl. She turned away, her hair a golden curtain. He was reaching down to draw it aside when she threw back her head—her hair fell back—and they were looking each other in the eyes —he tall above her, and she feminine on the floor below him. Gazing into her hazelwood eyes, he sat beside her. He pushed aside her hair, broke that hazelwand gaze, cupped her ear, and whispered into it, whispering much, until the others, left out, left the two of them alone. Eat your heart out, Nanci Lee.

O possibilities of what to say. Going over this later, Wittman, old with wandering, thought what if he'd done another one of the shticks that was flickering in the brightening air, would they have loved one another better? Everything counts; no time off ever, not on weekends, certainly not at parties. Go ahead, speak poetry to her. Seriously. Let her laugh. He would be grave. When in doubt, sez Dostoevsky or Tolstoy or Thomas Mann, always do the most difficult thing. Say to her your favorite by-heart poem, "The Song of Wandering Aengus." All the way through with no jokes. What's the use of having poems in your head if you can't have scenes in your life to say them in? And nobody to say them to? Who knows when the chance will come again. Here's a girl who has said poems, and has made a way possible for someone such as oneself to say poetry back to her. Play with her a love scene in verse. And at the same time educate her to a better poet (Yeats) than Robert Service. She won't take Aengus' vow for Wittman's vow. The silver-trout girl doesn't stay. So go ahead, Wittman, bring her the silver apples of the moon, and the golden apples of the sun, and kiss her lips, and take her hands.

But when he breathed and talked into her erogenous ear, he reserved "The Song of Wandering Aengus" for later, or for another. He praised her looks. "Thy rose lips and full blue eyes," he said. "Alfred, Lord Tennyson," he said, giving credit. He moved away from her ear; he held her hands, and beheld her mouth. He could make a wisecrack about the rosy swollen mouth on thy face like the elsewhere mouth that will leave a trail-spoor of silver snail slime. He could teach her some new words, get her to say, "En-woman me, Wittman."

He asked her her name. Taña De Weese. He will be able to find her again with an ad in the personals of *The Berkeley Barb*—"Taña, meet me on the barricades."

She asked him his name, and he gave her his first name and last name. If you give your last name, she can find you again. He let go her hands, stood, and galloped down the stairs. Leave before you fuck things up.

Oh, it's a good party now. There's a beautiful girl in hot pursuit of him. Yeah, let her come after him.

One more task to do, and the party will be complete: Clear up some friendship karma. Every get-together can be an occasion to have it out with a friend. The best parties end in a free-for-all.

And there in an alcove were Lance and Sunny, reigning side by side on the window seat. Our emperor and empress. Wittman sat down on the side next to Sunny.

"Make any good contacts?" asked Lance. "Are you having a good time?" asked his consort.

"How many people have asked *you*, 'Are you having a good time?' " asked Wittman.

"One or two."

"When people are going around polling one another, 'Are you having a good time?,' they're not getting *into* the party." He looked across her to say to her husband, "I think that it is fucked to make contacts rather than to make friends. I don't like contacts. What do you say to one? 'Of what use are you to me?' 'What are you offering?' 'To what or to whom is your end connected?' A party is a party. Or do you throw these parties for the sake of business deals? You go around assessing our connections? Why cultivate me? What good am I to you and your associates?" Wittman meant that he didn't want to do business whatsoever. There has got to be a way to live and never do business.

Lance only laughed. "Wittman. Wittman. You have to be subtle. You haven't been bruiting it among others that you've been fired, have you? Sunny and I have been keeping your secret. You do know that you can't get a job without you already have a job. You're not moving fast enough up your own organization, you go after a promotion horizontally. You never admit, 'I don't have a job.' You don't have to talk business at all, especially not at my party." Bidness a-tall. "You relax, have a good time, make friends, and at a future date, when they hear of an opening, they think of you. Make friendships longterm, Wittman. The frat brothers, or in your case, the co-op guys will pay off."

"I didn't go through Cal to make contacts."

"Of course you didn't. You would've gone to a private school for that. Stanford or Back East."

"Lance, you're using a tone on me, aren't you? Will you quit toning on me, and answer me something? There's a matter I've wanted to ask you about for years."

"Held it in all that time, huh?"

"When do you think you first met me? From what time do you date our acquaintanceship?"

"From school."

"Which school?"

"Cal."

"No. Before that. You don't remember meeting me in grammar school? I remember you. You were taidomo no taisho—leader of the kids. No. No. Try wait. General. General of the kids. You got to be taidomo no taisho in the camp. You led your army out of the camps and into the schoolyard, and beat the shit out of me. You don't remember ganging up on a tall skinny transfer who didn't fight back, and beating the shit out of him? That was me."

Shaking his head, Lance looked at Wittman, studied his face, but he looked at everyone with that intensity. In Japanese movies, noble knights, urban businessmen, peasant clowns, women—intense. In real life, Japanese-Americans don't relax. Sansei born and raised in P.O.W. "relocation" camp. He's looking at me with ex-con's eyes.

"You don't remember a Chinese kid that was in class for a while, and suddenly disappeared? My parents moved around a lot. I didn't get the knack of forming gangs. You don't remember socking a lone Chinese? There was just one Chinese boy. That was me. I got in trouble for fighting, and you didn't. You had witnesses. I think I'm running across members of your gang. Some of them were at Berkeley, grown. There are some here. None of you recognize me, huh?"

"I'm taidomo no taisho still yet. I have been and will always be the adult among children. I don't remember you. Are you accusing me of beating you up?"

Now what? Forgotten. Why is it that Wittman remembers others, such as check-out clerks, bank tellers, the coins-and-slugs collector at the laundromat, bus drivers, teachers, fellow students (many gone from parties because of graduation), but they don't remember him? Don't back down. "Yeah. And fighting dirty, and you continue to pick on me. I want to know, are we having a continuous fight that you started at Lafayette Grammar School? And, do you want to finish it now?"

"So I was a kid and didn't know better. Who wasn't? I don't fight dirty."

"You had a gang, and I was by myself."

"If you think I did that, I apologize. You want to fight, we'll fight. Do you want to fight right now, or do you want to go out in the alley?" Is there an alley, or is he being ironic about alley fights? I am not good at irony anymore. Sunny looked like she was being entertained, like they were dueling over her.

"I am less interested in hitting you than in your admitting what you have been up to all these years. You don't remember a kid who could juggle any three things? Erasers? Apples? Knives? Chomping the passing apples? That was me."

"Wittman, have you been smoking too much? You're really paranoid, man."

"The best way to help out a paranoiac is to tell him the truth about whether somebody's after him. You jack memories around, Lance, they turn on you psychologically. What you did, taidomo no taisho, you roasted goats, such as myself. You're good at defining an enemy while the rest of us have our thumbs up our asses, which is the position of most people on most topics. Whoever comes along and tells them what's going on, what the topics are, that there are topics, that a war is on, that's the one who gets to be leader. I've got your strategy, huh? You harness the polymorphous paranoia that floats around all the time, and you rule. I'm not just bringing up something that happened during kidtime, but what you do to us now. I know your m.o., man. Every school I went to, a Sansei Nihonjin, dressed in the right clothes, driving the right car, speaking with no accent, like you're dubbed, became the top bull and took over the junior prom and the senior ball and the assemblies and the student-body elections. At Cal, I recognized you right off, studying in the oriental section of the library at the table with the A.J.A. football player and the two A.J.A. girls on the pompon squad and the two Oski Dolls who were Chinese-Americans. Are you sure you didn't recognize me, the one integrating the other end of the main reading room? I noticed the way you dealt with her kind." A thumb at Sunny. "You take their shit like they're not dishing out any. You act like you're having the best time no matter what kind of racist go-away signals they're flashing at you. And you keep it up and keep it up until they, having a shorter attention span, think that you belong all along. I spot your technique, see? You A.J.A.s are really good at belonging, you belong to the Lions, the Masons, the V.F.W., the A.M.A., the American Dental Association. That's why they locked you up, man. They don't like you taking over the dances and getting elected Most Popular. (While we Chinese-Americans are sweating Most Likely to Succeed, and don't spend money on clothes, or on anything.) At camp you learned to tapdance and to play baseball, and you came out and organized everything, parties, labor unions, young millionaires."

"So? So you're envious?"

"So don't be such a conformist. Don't be such a smug asshole."

"Smug?" said Lance. "Asshole?" said Sunny.

"You better watch being so smug. That's how you're coming across, you know that? I bet you think you're coming across menacing. Well, you've turned smug. No, no. You've always been smug. You had that same smug face as a kid."

"Maybe he's got something to be smug about," said the wife.

"What are you smug about? Everything, huh? Once taidomo no taisho, general of the kids, and now the one who throws the parties, attended by all kinds. Working for the government. Asking what else your country can do

for you. Your G.S. number. Your business friends. Your Victorian house and your sofas. And your wife. And your life."

And each and every one of them a samurai. Knights of the chrysanthemum crest, or the hollyhock, or the wave and sun. They didn't come wretched to this country looking for something to eat. They'd been banished by the emperor or Amaterasu herself after taking the losing but honorable side in a lordly duel. A.J.A.s have sword names: Derek, Dirk, Blade, Gerald, Rod, Lance. Damocles, ha ha. Bart, probably a gun name. There's five or six Dereks in a school, another five or six Erics, and the rest are Darrell or Randall. "Eric" probably means "epee" or "snee" in Anglo-Saxon or Viking. Snee Sakamoto, ha ha.

"Let's go outside," said Lance. "I want to beat the shit out of you again."

They stood up, and walked, talking. "I want you to understand why you're going to get it," said Wittman. "This isn't just because of your childhood shittiness. I've let you get away with too much lately. Like when you organized the whole party to humiliate that oenologist guy from Davis. Your husband," he explained to Sunny, "emptied a good bottle of wine and put Red Mountain into the bottle with the expensive label and the price sticker still on it. We watched while the poor shmuck poured this rotgut into a stem glass, and stuck his nose into the glass, and swished the wine around in his mouth. We listened to him pronounce wine words about the nose of the full-bodied bouquet. And then, you showed him the Gallo Red Mountain jug, and everybody hooted him, gave it to him good. The worse thing was he tried to laugh and act as if *he* had been trying to put *them* on. That was a sick thing to do, Lance, and I should have stood up for that guy at the time. I should have said that the French love Gallo. Or I should have warned him. But I let you fuck him over. You prepped us to ask him, 'Has that wine got legs?' It was so premeditated."

Lance held his stomach with laughter at the memory of that scene. "*He* was smug, that wine major with a specialty in cabernets. He said the wine had 'cello tones.' Ha ha. 'Cello tones.' "

"Another time I should have done something was when you were living in that boarding house on Euclid with the rest of the A.J.A.s. Sunny, did your husband tell you that he and his buddies nailed Russell Saito inside his room? It was a team project; they surrounded his room, and hammered two-by-fours and plywood across the windows and door. You could hear him in there for three days banging with books and shoes, and crying, and begging about how he was missing his midterms. And asking about

taking a crap. He said, 'Who's out there? Is there anybody out there?' You reduced him, Lance. You shouldn't have done that. I should have let him out. Sunny, have you gotten your A.J.A. Zen? 'If the nail sticks up, hammer it down.' "

"Look, Russell Saito appreciates what I did for him. He could've moved out of Euclid, he didn't. He became known. He's going to be the first Japanese-American governor of California one day, you watch. Wittman, I didn't know you noticed all this stuff. You've got an eye for human nature. Very good."

Have you ever met a Japanese who wasn't a madman underneath? And each one far out in a different direction, the girls too. They don't get ordinary the more you know them.

"Go on," said Lance, sitting down on the rug. "Go on." Wittman and Sunny sat down with him. Get on with the unfinished bidness.

"There's a rumor about you, that you keep a list of friends in order of best to worst. Is that true?"

"Is that what they say about me? That I have a friends list?" He was delighted, and eager to hear more about his image.

"It's pretty childish, Lance, to keep track of who's your best friend and who's your second-best friend. The only people you ever hear anymore who talk about their best friend are department-store girls." He wouldn't mind knowing what number he himself was on the list but they couldn't torture such a question out of him.

Actually, he thought of Lance as his best friend, though lately he hardly saw him except at parties. When they hit the streets as a team, he could ass off, call "Pomegranates" at the girls from in front and behind. One of his kid vows, and it had been a drug vow too, was: Always tell people before you or they die that you like them. He didn't see how he was ever going to tell Lance about his oft-times being the only good friend. Remember how, unless you were totally out of it, everybody had a partner? The problem with being Lance's sidekick was that Lance got to be Don Quixote and Wittman was Sancho Panza, or, rather, Pancho to Lance's leadership role as the Cisco Kid. Wittman didn't like being Sancho or Pancho or Boswell or Tonto. Another vow was that from now on all friendships be friendships among equals. Lance had bragged about his two hundred closest friends. Who, now that I'm grown, is my best friend? Yeah, it's better not to have best friends anymore—the time has come for community.

"You have to be able to take red-ass in this world, Wittman." Speaking as a friend, for my good.

"I don't like the times you came to parties dressed as an S.S. youth. What was the point of that?"

"I was playing Tokyo-Berlin Axis. Everybody told me I looked exactly like Hitler, and that they had never noticed the resemblance before, how could they have missed it." He laughed at people who are easily fooled.

"But they shouldn't have liked it. What were your motives? Satirizing Nazis, or wanting to be a Nazi? Were you trying to offend people? Giving us a chance to get straight with Hitler? Were you trying to flush out Nazi-lovers, or what? I was offended." Shit. Admitted to having had my dumb feelings hurt.

"I look good in a Nazi uniform. Girls are very turned on by Nazi uniforms." ("We are not," said Sunny. "No, we aren't.")

"And you hate them for it. You bring stuff out in people, and then you scoff at them. Are you like sociopathic?"

"I may be, Wittman. I've considered that. We geniuses who are more intelligent than ninety-nine point nine percent of the population of the U.S., and hence the world, have to adjust to a lonely life among stupidos. We have to live among them, and help them out. They're our responsibility. They're a real pain to me." Wittman was overawed by anyone who achieved more pain than he did, given average American conditions.

"Look. To be perfectly honest with you," said Lance, "I don't remember anything that happened to me before junior high school. My memories start at about seventh grade." He *is* a sociopath, the kind that doesn't admit to dreaming in his sleep. "If it was me that beat you up, I don't remember."

He really doesn't remember. My friend is in that much pain that he has to forget almost half his life. "The camps, huh? It must have been the camps did that to you." You know that an A.J.A. has taken you on as a trusty friend if he'll give you a word or two about "camp" and "the years we were away." They've stomped the bad years deep down, like they never happened. Wittman, who didn't forget anything, was struck with pity and envy.

"My memories of kidtime events," said Lance, "come from people who insist that they eyewitnessed me. A neighbor lady—she lived in the next horse stall at Tanforan—said I took a shit at the base of a flagpole. I did that regularly even though an M.P. with a rifle warned me not to. She said, 'You were a free boy.' See? I have a history of protest that goes back to toilet-training time, taking a public dump under the American flag. I can sort of remember looking up at stars and stripes and out at a desert with barbwire all around. Hey, I can tell you exactly when my memory started

up again. I'm going to tell the both of you now, my wife, and my best friend, about when the cameras of my life began to roll." You had to admire the guy's daring; he was not afraid to declare, "You are my best friend." And disarm you.

"The moon will be full soon," he said, and, yes, over his shoulder the gibbous moon was mooning them through the window. Hoo haw. "There was blood on the full moon. But I have a new plan to wipe its face clean. I know what to do now. It's come to me what to do. Let me show you."

Lance Kamiyama led them out of his cobwebby house; they followed him around the veranda to the back porch, down the stairs, and across the grass to the end of the yard, where two willow trees grew together above a trickle of a stream. "This stream is part of the system that fills the lake at Mills College. We have crayfish—edible crayfish. I'll cook some for you one of these days. Here I will build a shrine—this is the site—for the fox spirit beside a running stream. Do you know that church they're re-modeling in Oakland J-town? The torii—do you know what that is? like a gate or door by itself, not particularly *to* anything—two uprights, like goal-posts—you've seen it, where they hang the thunder god's rope with white paper clouds and sometimes lanterns—the torii has been stolen, or lost in construction rubble. The fox is on the run again. How it came to be in Oak-land: Samurai on their way to becoming American ronin saw a red fox sail with them as a passenger aboard the *Arizona*. He was not in a cage or a bag. He walked up the gangplank on his hind legs, which showed beneath his forest-green robe. There were flaps in the hood for his ears, and his snout stuck out of the cowl. For most of the journey, he stood at the prow with his snout pointing east, that is, toward the West. One paw rested on top of the other on his new cane. The ship sailed under the Golden Gate, which is the same color he is, international orange.

"In the U.S., he cut the first notch into his cane—Issei. It was not an old cane with seals and stamps from climbing Mount Fuji and from his other pilgrimages. No more Japanese stuff. We start numbering here. From One. Our parents are Two. Nisei. I'm Sansei. There are already a few Yon-sei. American generations. What for we're keeping track? At Gosei, will something ultimate happen? Four to get ready, and five to go.

"In 1941, they had a fox hunt. Executive Order 9066 came down. Barb-wire hatchmarked the shadows of foxes running through tule fog. A Bud-dhist church that got an okay from the government as not pro-Japan hid him. For disguise, they shaved his head and hung a chain of beads around his neck.

"The fox is without a home; I'm without a home. My mama-san took me up to my room and shut the door—I thought she was going to tell me about sex. She told me that I had been raised by whites. She showed me photographs. She wasn't lying. She had newspaper clippings about a mass family murder. Done with a plantation machete. Come over here. Look at the house through these long willow leaves. I escaped alive. I saw the moon shine red through hanging leaves. There was blood on the full moon."

What is he telling me? Is this a confession of murder? Or has he spilled a plan for future doing? His family is dead for real or in his heart? Had he, as a scared child, run out into the willows to get away from the machete killer? Or did he mean, with a machete in his hand, he crept up to the house? To cut down his white foster mother, or his mama-san. The killer son. A murderer's confession would sound like this, evading or trying to transcend the worst, that is the actual macheteing. Wittman wanted to say, "What? Will you speak up please?" But if you ask for clarification, you'll interrupt the murderer into silence. You can't say, "What?! You did what?! Murder?!" Yes, a confession to murder would be part of a civilized conversation. Wow, a chronic mass murderer of not just one but maybe two families, a white family and an A.J.A. family. An Eagle Scout business-suited type like Lance, that's the type that kills his whole family, and the neighbors say, "He was such a quiet boy." They think that being quiet and being good are the same thing. Sunny's face was avid with sympathy. She was participating in cosmopolitan life-and-death events.

"Why?" said Wittman. But to be able to answer why, a criminal has to have done the highest philosophical thinking. Usually you have to be satisfied with a money or sex motive. "What would anyone have against your parents?" Lance must be exaggerating. Wittman had met his mother, a Japanese-American church lady in a pillbox hat, gloves, and a camel-hair coat.

"That A.J.A. family mortified me. I drew swastikas on fences all over the neighborhood. I didn't mean Nazis. I had a box of colored chalk, and it was fun to get those angles right. The mama-san and papa-san made me walk back through town with rags and clean off the fences, and apologize. Gomenasai. They followed me, and if anybody came out to see what we were doing, they bowed. Gomenasai. Gomenasai. They took a picture of me bowing.

"To make memories, I need documentation. At every house, there was a *Life* magazine open at the same picture: a jap soldier with his chest and stomach cut open, the slashes in the shape of a cross, according to the caption. His guts had been pulled out, intestines and heart placed at the center of the cross. It wasn't that horrible, really, unless you read the caption. He looked asleep with a smoking white fluff on his stomach; it was sort of pretty like a flower."

Wittman planned to survive the weekend, then go to the library and look up newspapers for—when?—1953?—a mass murder by machete. And the weather report would have what phase the moon was in.

"They've got a death wish out for me," said Lance. "The mama-san and papa-san held an autumn service to my memory. You weren't invited? You didn't mourn me? From school, they invited the registrar, who didn't show, and our housemother, who did. You don't remember a fall semester when I didn't come back from summer vacation? You didn't miss me? I didn't meet you yet, Sunny, and we might never have met. There's a stone doll of me in the churchyard among the other rock babies with red bandanna bibs. Tonight, I'm going to tell you where I was instead of dead. I was traveling to learn if ex-Japanese in other countries call themselves Issei, Nisei, Sansei, or if those are American words. I was sitting in the sun on one of the thousands of Molucca-Sulu islands, and looking out at the next island. For the fun of it, I was about to try swimming to it when a copra boat came along, and I hitched a ride. We passed that island, which seemed bare and uninteresting anyway, and landed on another one. I understood the boatman to say he would come back for me on his route. But he never came back.

"Days went by. No boat. I walked around and around. I could not see the tourist island I'd been on, nor any other land. I introduced myself to people, who said, 'Yes, there's a boat; it came once a long time ago, and it will come again.' I asked where was the boat I came on? They got excited —that was the boat. Why hadn't I held it for them? They sat on the ground to get over their disappointment. 'How long do we have to wait?' I asked, but their idea of time is not precision movement. I sat with them facing the sea, like *Mondo Cane* cargo cult. Three Frenchmen came along the beach. I asked them and they asked me about a boat. They'd been on that island years too long, they said, and the time has come for action. We cut bamboo and tied it together, and built two rafts. The islanders pointed their clove and cubeba cigarettes north, whence migrations of human beings and animals drifted. We paddled for a long time, and stopped on an island, but no people on it. Two of the Frenchmen went back. With the third Frenchman, an old man, I found many inhabited islands, but each with a smaller and poorer population. I left my aging old partner on an island with only one family. 'A ma puissance,' he said.

"I rowed and floated alone and nowhere until I met a boat filled with people. 'Room for one more,' they said. I left my raft, and went with them to Marore, which is the border-crossing island in the Sangihe Talaud Archipelago. But no airport, no harbor with ocean liners. A crew of Pilipinos from Mindanao, stranded for three years, told me that some years ago, a man who looked like me, a young German, came here on his way north in search of faith healers. He bought a canoe, but never rowed out of sight. The wind and sea kept returning him to the island, and at last wrecked him on the reef.

"One evening I was sitting on a pier, and eating fish jerky. A piece dropped in the water. A man with white hair dived for it, and ate it. He stayed beside me to watch the sunset. 'You live like us,' he said. 'No hotel.' I watched many sunsets with him. Mr. Sondak was his name. On Holy Saturday he said, 'Our food is your food. Our water is your water. Our hunger is your hunger. Our stories are your stories.' I must have been in very bad shape. That was the most beautiful thing I'd ever heard. I wept on the sand. He was welcoming me to remain forever on that island as my home. And give up thinking about how to get to the international airport at Jakarta or Manila."

Oh, that was beautiful. Wittman saw an island where people speak in verse, where a poet sings you a welcome to his tribe and gives you a place in its myth and legend. He asked Lance to say the mele again, and pictured its lines:

> *Our water is your water.*
> *Our food is your food.*
> *Our hunger is your hunger.*
> *Our stories are your stories.*

"But one day," Lance continued, "I walked further inland than I had walked before on any of the islands, probably through the neck of an isthmus—and entered a city again. Civilization, ho-o-o!" The cry of the wagonmaster on the Firesign Theater album. "The next thing I knew, I was riding in a taxi—Teksi, the letters on the door and roof said—racing for the airport. A Garuda plane flew overhead, and I panicked that it was my plane, and I'd missed it. But I caught Pan Am to Tokyo, where I changed planes. I waited at the boarding gate for seven hours, and took the plane to Honolulu, where I didn't leave the terminal during the stopover until takeoff for San Francisco. I've had it with islands. We shouldn't go to Asia even for vacations. We get turned around. I got made into a Kibei. A Returnee to America. Never leave, Wittman. The next time I'm curious about foreign lands, I'm traveling to Vegas or Reno. I came back in time for late registration, though most of the classes I wanted filled up already. And too late to stop my memorial service. It is absolutely necessary that I build the fox a home —in Oakland, here between these willow trees by this stream. It will be large enough for the two of us, Sunny, to use as a gazebo or a gatehouse. It will be so elegant and expensive that the fox will stay put. The stream will run; the fox will not run. The fox has come home. Here." He touched the ground with both hands. Very stoned heads will touch the earth—they dash out of the building and lie down on the street—and be well, okay. "I'm going to throw a fox-viewing party in a tent that covers the lawn. A flap rolls up. On a night when a moon is in the stream and a moon is in the sky, we're going to see the fox follow this stream, and step here under the willows. The fox will enter his house between doorposts of my design."

Wittman turned green and red with envy and admiration; a person of his generation that knows better than to make war its adventure was having himself an interesting life. Experiences befall this friend even when he means to be on vacation as a tourist. Japanese brought a fox; Chinese brought pigs and goats. And Executive Order 9066 has given to Issei, Nisei, Sansei their American history. And places: Tanforan, Manzanar, Tule Lake, Arkansas, Sand Island. And righteous politics, the Sansei's turn to say No and No to loyalty oaths and to the draft. We ought to give A.J.A.s a deep gomenasai apology without them having to ask. If only he hadn't been but a toddler at the time, Wittman would have gotten on the train that took people who looked like himself away. There had been a Chinese-Mexican kid who had done that to be with his friends.

How to kill Lance and eat his heart, and plagiarize his stories? As a friend of the hero, you're a sub-plot of his legend. When you want to be the star. And wear a beret. And go on vision quest, for which a Young Millionaire can afford plane rides to the other side of the world. The minimum-wage earner—the unemployed—goes for a walk in the park, where Wittman Ah Sing has had vision enough. Everything that comes in—that's it. Foolish ape wants more vision.

"You still want to fight?" Lance asked.

"Don't think you've talked yourself out of it. I want to kill you and eat your heart, and plagiarize your stories. Businessman."

Lance got the insult. Ranked and cut low. He put up his fists. Wittman hadn't been in all that many fights, but people putting up their dukes looked like they learned from boxing movies. He was too embarrassed to prance.

"Don't fight," said Sunny. "Please don't fight. I'm leaving right now if you fight. Do you want me to leave, Lance? Or do you want me to help? If I help, it's two against one. We don't want to outnumber him two against one, do we?"

The willows hung their branches down like weeping cherry trees in their green seasons. And into the moon-bright scene on this gibbous night walked Taña, the pretty girl in hot pursuit, who parted the willow-tail curtains, and said, "Oh, I didn't know there was anybody out here. Is the ground marshy over by you?"

Well, they had to stop for introductions in case everybody hadn't met everybody. "So you two have met," said Lance. So their attachment shows. Ignored, the married couple faded away.

"You knew I was out here," said Wittman, "and you came pursuing me."

Paying no nevermind to swampiness, she stepped right on over to him, and sat down on a log, which would moss-stain her skirt. She had bound up her hair with somebody's necktie, and another tie belted her waist—a piratess of hearts. "To find a certain type of interesting person at a party," she said, "go outside, and there he'll be, all by himself, smoking a cigarette, next to the garbage cans."

Girls who hide from the party are usually crying, and they are unsocialized wallflowers. Let that about the garbage cans go.

Too bad Lance hadn't built his shrine yet; it would be nice to go with her inside a hideaway the size of a Chinese bed. He took a-hold of her hand, and pulling her behind him, led her on a twining walk. Here and there on the grass lay sleepy bodies, girls in skirts, moth wings and daisy petals. They were the fairies of a midautumn's night; they were a slain family. Taña caught up beside him; they walked together holding hands, his every finger between her every finger. He stopped, pushed her hand behind her, her other hand caught between his chest and her breasts. A hug dance. "Let go," she said, and he, laughing and shaking his head no, kissed her. "So that I can put my arms around you," she said pleadingly. Oh, he had to let her do that for a while. Then he pulled her arm down, and, holding swinging hands some more, walked her to the porch. He embraced her by the waist, and lifted her up onto the balustrade. "Sidesaddle, ma'am?" he said. He lit up a cigarette. She took it from him and smoked it too. They were taking turns on his last cigarette.

She looked like Dale Evans as the girl singer with the Sons of the Pioneers. Dale used to wear an off-the-shoulder Mexican blouse, and looked like Marilyn Monroe but not so unstrung. Roy hadn't buttoned her up yet. Roy Rogers always wore his plaid shirt buttoned to the top, and tucked his jeans inside his boots.

Wittman leaned against a post, pushed his pretend hat back, put his boot on the footrail. "I do admire a lady who rides sidesaddle, Taña. Taña De Weese. What kind of a name is that?"

"I don't know, I'm sure, Wittman. Wittman Ah Sing. What's your other name? I should think Wittman is just your American name."

Yes, that's all it is.

"My middle name is Chloë," she said.

"My other name is Joang Fu."

"What does it mean? Joang Fu." She said it with that American uplilt that makes Chinese sound good, hearable, not lost inside somewhere.

"I don't ask you what Taña Chloë means. Why do you assume that my name means dick?"

" 'Of course it must,' " she said. " 'My name means the shape I am—and a good handsome shape it is, too. With a name like yours, you might be any shape, almost.' "

Our fool for literature is utterly impressed by her allusiveness.

He poeticated her in return. " 'By a name I know not how to tell thee who I am.' "

"Joang Fu is a secret name, isn't it? Have you given me your secret name and power over you, Joang Fu?"

"No, that's a white-man superstition. Do you throw the Ching? My name is number sixty-one, which they translate Inner Truth. You can look it up." I am True Center. Core Truth. Truth is a bird carrying a boy in her talons. She can look it up for herself. He hoped nobody Chinese was eavesdropping. Can't stand hippy dippies who trade on orientalia.

Taña leaned her head against her post and sighed. "Happy?" she asked moonily. She cracked him up. He'd found him a girl with that certain alienation.

"Happy," he said, playing along. People who aren't too smart, the ones who live by song lyrics, and who don't know their current events, those people can be happy. Yeah, he felt high, and he knew the difference between being happy and being high, neither of which is as good as joy.

"Do you like parties?" she asked. Oh, she is so understanding. She must sense that he takes celebrations seriously. He's profoundly dionysian and has standards. Too sensitive to be inside yukking it up. She hadn't asked, "Do you like this party?" She said, "Do you like parties?" Is she ready to listen to my shyness party by party? He can tell her how he hated playing Young Affordables. She hasn't heard them talk about him, has she? "He's nowhere near his first million." "He believes in voluntary poverty." "No, he's just plain cheap." But he mustn't come off as afraid of parties. He went to them. To be a no-show, you have to get it scandaled about that you don't go to parties for interesting lone-wolf reasons, and definitely not because you weren't invited. Show up, be tested. And you be cool; defensiveness is the worst of personality emanations. "He's so defensive." He has to let her know how dionysian he can be. Yes, he can be very dionysian, such as the time he rode the motorcycle through the French doors.

He said, "Now, me, what I feel about parties . . . to tell you the truth, I do and I don't like . . . I mean, it depends on what kind of party . . . the kind that . . . like paranoid . . . well, not really paranoid. . . ." It was coming out inarticulate, but that's okay. Hang down your head like sad and blue James Dean, dead already. Like your brains are too heavy. Feelings so deep that there are no words honest enough to express them. The words the world has are not good enough. His head hung ponderous, his hands a-pockets. The girl on the balustrade leaned over to peer up at his face. She reached out, and pushed aside the dark forelock. Girls' hearts break to pull James Dean's head up by the forelock. Yes, he was bowed before her. O gravitational pull of physical bodies. Felled by her. She slid off the railing, and stood before him. His head lowered helplessly toward her upturning face, and nudged at her lips to part, come on, come on, give, until she began the kissing. She was short enough to have to reach for it, and he was tall enough to have been only nodding, just thinking, nodding off, listening to some music of his own.

Taña talked and kissed at the same time, "Do you like partying now? How do you like the party now? Do you like partying with me? You do like to party, huh?" He would enjoy hearing what this girl's instinctively said sex words were. Breathing with catches in her throat, she went on to say, "I like this party. I like partying with you. You know what I wish, though? I wish that all night long you had been thinking about me, that you had been looking for me years ago before we met, and you've found me at last. You maneuvered to be invited here. Tonight you followed me from room to room, didn't you? You flirted with gorgeous girls, but they weren't me. I walked by and I made you look away from them. I made you dissatisfied. Whenever I looked up, there you would be staring at me. You were contemplating me. You went into the library, thinking I was there, and you looked behind the curtains. The toes you had seen under there might have been mine. You notice everything about me. You went out through the balcony doors, and saw me crossing the lawn in the moonlight. And you climbed down the fire escape, and caught me here. On the vine-covered veranda. As I was about to leave, you caught me in your arms. Now, tell me that happened. Tell me that was what you did. You chased me, and caught me in your arms. And hold me in your arms."

"Yeah," he said. "Yeah, looked for you. Saw you there. Caught you. Yeah, I did that. I do that. Hug you. That too." He's her nuzzling colt, her baby houyhnhnm, nuzzling for its mama.

"And hold me in your strong arms, and kiss me. And kiss me again." Oh, at last. He'd found his woman who will talk while making love. Will she blurt out everything of women he needs to know, please?

4

THE WINNERS OF THE PARTY

THE WINNERS OF the party were: Lance Kamiyama. His bride, Sunny. Wittman Ah Sing. Taña De Weese. Nanci Lee, who might have been by herself, but was sitting in the breakfast nook with Charley Bogard Shaw. And the plain girl from the bus, Judy Louis. To win, you outlast everybody else, and stay up all night. You were civilized, had not rushed off urgently with anyone. You got to talk those other people over.

Night was leaving through the tall windows. The winners of the party, those who did not find room on the banquette, sat on bar stools around the butcher block. Wittman was on one side of it, and Taña across from him. The little door for bowls and plates and for the entrances and exits of the creatures that danced on the sideboard was now shut. Lance was cooking a magic omelette ("oom-lette" he called it because it was special). He shook the grass out of a colander; the stems and seeds, he saved for tea. The heat and the scrambled eggs enriched the grassy smell, somewhat like a blend of Italian parsley and alfalfa. Doesn't the smell of the herb cooking make your limbs shaky? Your guts untangle? The windowpanes steamed up from bottom to top, the kitchen warming like somebody's mother was home, onions sautéing in butter, wooden mushrooms re-mushrooming and fluting in water. Sunny was grinding coffee beans; she fit the filter in a cone that came down by tackle from the ceiling. "The night is over," said Lance, their chieftain. "We have gotten safely through the night. We're alive." He was giving a blessing that there is a time limit to difficulties. Let any battles that were being fought among them, any bad feelings, cease. Troubles and fears are not to be carried over into daylight. Dispel paranoia. The hardiest, the geniuses, the abiders of the tribe have journeyed far and come home. "The weekend is half over," said Lance, handing out the oom-lettes on un-matched California ware. They ate quietly. "Nobody talk while the flavor lasts."

Now, to have been everywhere at once just about, to hear the parts of the party you missed: the couple-fights; who left with whom; the man-to-man fights; the identification of strangers who stood out. Like did anybody see this gigantic, slow man in the black beard? He walked around and looked at faces. He carried a handsaw, and tapped the ban-the-bomb symbol on the door. Had anybody met him before? Whose friend was he? Who was that guy? "Nobody invited him," said Lance. "He walked in from off the street. I asked him his name, and he said, 'I am Friend of All the World.'" "That's wonderful," said Sunny. "Friend of All the World. That's *why* he could walk in off the street." They had been favored. An animal had emerged out of the camouflage, and chosen them to see it.

"I stopped Eugene from throwing a motorcycle through the window," said Charley. "Somebody put chemicals in his drink—or he *thought* some-body did—and he tried to hang himself in the shower, but the curtain rod kept bending. He decided it must have been Chuckie who was trying to poison him, which it might have been; I wouldn't put it past Chuckie, but not to poison him, only to surprise him. Accident. Eugene, with the strength of a madman, tore a board off the garage and chased Chuckie around the house. Chuckie ran inside, and got trapped in the bathroom, and escaped by squeezing out between the louvers. Eugene broke in the door, then got the idea to hang himself. Everybody—girls—who came in to use the john, tried to stop him, but he kept on tying belt, necktie, towels to-gether and around his neck. Each time he lowered himself, the curtain rod bent lower too, and the knot slid down it. All the while, people were coming and going, taking a piss, taking a crap. They talked him out of it." Imagine that, living for reasons thought up by others while crapping. What reasons were they?

"Did you notice," said Sunny, "Candace got so drunk, she lost her English accent. One of her intimates asked her how come she was speaking American like anybody else. She screamed—and fainted. And when she came to, she was speaking like an English bird queen again. Do you re-member her from when she went on her fortnight junket to London? She came back with clothes from Carnaby Street, and calling us Luv and

Ducks. And birds and toffs. And she does that English babytalk—lolly and brolly and nappy and lorry and nanny and jolly and tommy and telly and ta-ta." Yes, Sunny, there are those of us right here who can no longer speak in pre-educated accents even among old friends and relatives unless stoned out of our minds.

And Nanci the beautiful, whose knees and long legs stuck out of the breakfast nook to trip one up, reported on a kissing contest. Everybody, male and female, kissed everybody else, no skipping over of anyone. She had won the title of Most Romantic Kisser. Wittman was feeling that he had missed out on the party. Where had he been during the motorcycle tossing and suiciding and fainting and mass kissing? And what had he to contribute to this after-party party? He finished his oom-lette—even square Judy ate hers—and took seconds. He didn't want to get stoned; he was hungry. Nobody has cooked for him for a long time. Grass that's eaten, in-gesta, comes on gradually; you can take a-hold of yourself, you would think. And, surely, he was now such a naturally high person that he would not get too ripped, immune now, surely. The sun was brimming pale new light over the top of the hills, and through an open window a pretty breeze blew. Why, then, was he coming down? Who's bringing him down?

"Somebody's bringing me down," he said. "So low. I'm crashing. You're feeling pain too, but you think it feels good. The food tastes good, so your brain, which is right upstairs from your mouth, thinks, 'This is good.' This is not good. Lance. He's the one making us turn the knife on our own stomach. I don't mean only now. It's longterm. We have to fight for our lives. I quit the Young Millionaires. There's nothing to buy out there. I know, I worked retail in one of the biggest department stores in the City. I didn't want to use my employee discount or my opportunities for employee theft to get anything. Nothing is worth a million dollars. You've got to let people out of the Young Millionaires, Lance."

"I feel sorry for you," said Lance. "I feel sorry for you because you can't find something you care for enough to make the money to buy it. I give parties. It costs money to give parties, Wittman. You don't return social obligations; you don't entertain. You don't know how much money I spend on my friends. Thanksgiving with turkey for me and Sunny and three or four orphans will cost fifty dollars at least. And I like serving two wines. And I have to re-stock the bar. Wittman, do I have to point out to you my lar-gesse with the grass and several kinds of mushrooms? I'm stuffing my tur-key with grass this year. I spent a couple of hundred dollars on you tonight, and you're one of the orphans I plan to invite for Thanksgiving."

"Give my share to the bums on Howard Street. I'm fasting on Thanksgiving. You ought to give the fifty dollars to a famine somewhere. Like on that island where the old man dived for your droppings. You should have stayed lost longer, Lance. You didn't go far out enough. You spent the whole trip trying to get back. Like there's no place like Oakland? I go further out than you. I'm a genius. I'm warning all of you. He softens us up on dope, then he does his imprinting. But I'll be genius enough to save your lives."

"You're having one of those trips where you think everything comes clear," said Lance.

"You're going through the delusion of clarity," agreed Charley, the mathematician and expert on metaphysical movies.

Wittman set down his cup, reached into his back pocket, and pulled out a sheaf of manuscript, the next part of his play, that had been in there all night all along. Taking the stance of Gwan Goong the Reader, who read in armor during battle, who read to enemies, who read loud when no one listened, Wittman Ah Sing read. He held his papers as Gwan Goong held his soft-covered book rolled in his sword hand. His left hand stroked his beard. His intelligent head was turned in a reading me-ay, black eyebrows winging in thought. Whether or not a listener sat with him knee-to-knee, Wittman sat bent-knee kung fu position. The man of action aggressively reads and talks.

"Remember how bedazzled you felt at black-and-white movies when it rained all up and down the screen? Light and camera through the windowpanes made the lines of rain dripping from the eaves twinkle and sparkle—setting off bodily thrills. And the star in her mermaid cocktail dress shimmered over to the window, and crumpled up a letter. The paper crackled through the sound system. Remember the pure firing milli-shocks of light, and that sound?" Yes, his friends and enemies are nodding yes. They know what he means so far. "Spangling, she crossed the screen, and the camera dollied in a close-up pan around the Christmas tree dangling with foil icicles—tiers of winking metallic rain. Coruscations. Shivering and delighting your vertebrae up and down. And the story-line didn't matter nor who she was in the shimmying dress—when that coruscation sparked and popped on the silver screen, you had corresponding feelings.

"The curtain for my play will be made out of tinsel; lights with blue gels will shaft through the very dark house and play on those moving rain-fringe curtains, which represent a waterfall. I want to suggest mermaids and flashing salmon, fluke tails flipping in the sun, sequins of water, Lorelei sequins, rainbows and trout refracting and multiplying. We'll hang one of those junior-prom rotating mirror balls. Vegas nightclub floor-show glitz production values, but we'll shoot for transcendence. You know what I wish? I wish while they're damming the Feather River, they'd build a stage. All they have to do is shape some of that concrete into risers and platforms. And I could control the waterfall to rise and fall or part and shut—stage curtains. Acoustically, use the tourist information speakers like sound boxes at drive-in theaters. And the actors—you—project hard. Yeah, open the show in Oroville. Or Santa Cruz, at the Brookdale Lodge, where the river goes through the redwood-forest lobby. The guests sit and fish. We need a rain machine. Now, it may be enough in this day and far-gone age to stage a water-and-lights happening, but here's the content: Monkeys live at the falls. All the actors who play monkeys will have to be tumblers. Tumble all over the apron, triple-somersault into the proscenium arch, pyramid barefoot onto one another's shoulders. The Wallenda pyramid breaks; they pitch against the water, which bounces them out. With almost-flying skills, the raggedy-ass and barefoot monkeys are asking of nature and one another, what is on the other side of the water curtain? 'Something to eat.' 'Why doesn't one of you go through it somehow and bring back a report?' 'Whoever does that will be king.' And off a catwalk comes flying on a rope-vine a glorious monkey. Red mask-paint rings his handsome human eyes, and points to his nose. He wears a heart on his face and has a heart on his ass. He swings out over the heads of monkeys and audience, and into the water-curtain, his tail wrapped ingeniously around the rope-vine—he can fly upside down—'Geronimo!'—and plunges through to the other side. He does not return for quite a while. The rest of the monkeys do an apron scene: 'He's not coming back.' 'Is he dead?' 'He's gone and drowned himself.' 'Was he suicidal?' 'What's the motive? Did he leave a note?' 'I think he's just testing his invulnerability.' 'He's been gone too long. He's not immortal.' 'I don't want to die.' 'Me neither. I don't want to die either.' But what's the test for immortality? There isn't a safe test to prove once and for all that some medicine, peach, or fountain water blots out one's name in the Book of Death. You keep on questing because of doubts. You can live to be over a hundred years old, and you're only long-lived. You drink from a fountain of youth, and you don't die that day, and whattayaknow, not the day after that either. Life goes along, and pretty soon you start getting suspicious for proof. So you're thirty years old, and not dead. Forty, and still not dead. Am I living forever yet? You go into battle, you live through a war. You win some hand-to-hand combats. Are you a skilled fighter, or immortal? What if you were going to survive till eighty anyway in your natural lifespan? You can be ninety, a hundred, and still not know if you're lasting forever. There are people who live to be a hundred and ten, even a hundred and twenty. I'm going to keep escaping from the old-age home, on quest until I'm a hundred and thirty.

"Plunging out of the waterfall comes Sun Wu Kong, the King of the Monkeys, hanging on to his rope with toes and tail, juggling pears and grapes and peaches and bananas, throwing them to the others, everybody juggle-eating. Monkey dives in and through the falls—the curtain opens, and we see what's behind there. 'Come on. Come on. Come on,' says the handsome King of Monkeys, leading his people into one of those sets that should make the audience gasp and stop everything to applaud the set designer. The secret and protected country has a sky that is a vaulting dome—stage it inside a blue mosque like the inside of the stone egg that Monkey hatched from, by which he is sometimes known as the Stone Monkey. He will get mountains whopped on him twice—Stoned Monkey. In the ongoing vistas, mists and streams curl around green mountains and far grey mountains. The monkeys link tails—chains of monkeys bridge the trees and canyons. They spin around and around on their knuckles. Flowers and fruit everywhere, spring and autumn coeval, each tree blooming and leafing and hanging with all you can eat. You've all driven the length of the Central Valley, haven't you, through the miles of peach ranches and plum ranches? We stage this in a barn in Fresno County, the audience will have to drive their pick-ups through a ranch of blooms—pear trees, tragic cherry trees, thorny inedible quince, and thorny citrus. Ravens (with the V-tails) and crows (with the straight-across tails) sit on tiptop branches, holding things down to earth. Welcome home to the land behind the falls. The older people will stick their tongues out of squared mouths in astonishment. And the younger people will remember that Zorro kept his black horse and his weapons and mask behind a waterfall. A black stallion in a spangly Mexican saddle gallops across the stage, and the monkeys have a rodeo."

Taña raised an arm, twirled and snapped it, roping Wittman with her invisible lasso. "Ee-haw!" Cheered by that cowgirl yell, he went on:

"Three or four hundred years go by. The monkeys spend their time eating and showing off. Their cavortions become organized acrobatics. Their moves culminate in kicking feet and boxing fists and blade-like chops of the hands. They throw fists and feet and steel stars. The shirakens—stars of steel—zip like comets—meteor showers—at targets. Bullseye targets become cop-training targets, which look like men, that is, like themselves.

Their circus parades straighten out, their hair straightens out, everybody in uniforms with scarves around their necks. Pheasant feathers wave above the heads of officers. They drill to the brass and drums of marching bands playing anthems, which the Monkey King leads with his magic rod, now the size of a conductor's wand. Straight-rule chessboard divisions, troops, squadrons, ranks and files of eighty-four thousand monkeys, horizontals and verticals like a reinforced-concrete cubiform hundred-story building viewed from the sidewalk below—you feel hallucinated at the strictness of the perspective and the monumental unwavering immensity. What I want to know about: Why the totalitarian armies that even I, a pacifist person, helplessly see on laughing gas and carbogen?

"The King of Monkeys drills and reviews troops; he leads martial-arts regimens, but something is wrong. He sprawls depressed in his throne. He has enough to eat, and the baby monkeys chase his whipping tail. But he is not entertained. It's not the militarization that's getting him down. His people are transformed into soldiers, and the landscape always has a soldier on patrol in it, but he's used to transformations, being the master of seventy-two of them himself; a slow change by a species is nothing. 'Whyfor?' he asks. 'Whyfor?' He is Aware of Emptiness. Aware of Emptiness is his middle name. His far-hearing ears have heard of a wonderful party being planned to which he has not been invited. He hardly knows the people giving the party, neither hosts nor guests; it has nothing to do with him. But he's got to be there. It's a party that they give only once every three thousand years, it's that special. A triple-millennial party. He feels so left out. Life would not be worth living if he didn't get to that party. The party of a lifetime. Whyfor did they overlook him? He was most handsome. Was it his personality? His lower-class manners? His clothes not good enough for them? He's as good as anybody. He gnashed his teeth over the feting and celebrating going on without him. Nobody should leave anybody out of anything. He'll crash that party. He'll invade it with his army. He'll make a scene. He'll eat everything on the buffet. He'll overturn tables. He'll piss in the wine. He'll show them, leaving him out."

Sunny was clearing her counters and uprighting her chairs. Dig this action, Sunny:

"A messenger comes riding but not with an invitation. Scouts patrolling the farthest ridges have spotted a king-size havoc monster coming this way. 'Help! Help!' shout the monkeys. 'War! War!' Now the drums go wild. Now there's urgency and emergency. He will blood his magic lance. 'I'll go by myself,' he says. 'It's best to meet the enemy one on one on his own turf.

I'll stop him from coming here to ruin our country. He won't get you. While I'm gone, you guard our home. You stay here just in case.' His plan is to fight this monster in the neighborhood of the party. He'll drop in sweating heroically. A monster led me a chase this way. Has anyone seen a havoc monster? You having a party? Chase that monster crashing through their party.

"The King of Monkeys, using his magic pole, polevaults away into the sky. He's off to war and party. His patriotic people beat the taiko big drums, a beat that he can hear and take heart from.

"More sound effects—bomb-like fireworks—signal for back-up. Fighting men and fighting women enter on horseback, riding from over the mountains. They sail up the streams and rivers. A band of a hundred and eight superheroes punt swift boats out of the sloughs. An offstage voice will call out the names of heroes and heroines that were once not long ago—less than twenty years ago—star roles in American theater. They have left us. We will call them back. Where are you? Come back. Gwan Goong and his brothers—Liu Pei and Chang Fei. Yue Fei, and his lifelong friends—Hong, Cheung, and Wong. And the great warrior women—Red Jade, Flower Wood Orchid, the fighting aunties from the Sung Dynasty, the ladies and goodwives of the Water Margin, Night Ogress and Pure Green Snake alias the Tigress. And Mrs. Gwan Goong, that is, Gwan Po. And the Red Peony alias Oryu alias Lady Yakusa. No, no, no. Wait. We keep the men's Chinese names, we keep the women's names untranslated too, no more Pearl Buck Peony Plum Blossom haolefied missionary names. No more accessible girls and unspeakable men. The women: Hoong Ngoak, Fa Moke Lan, Ku San the Intelligent, Mrs. Shen the Earth Star. Let the gringo Anglos do some hard hearing for a change. I don't forget actresses. I remember them better than you women do. At this roll call of paladins and mariners, the monkeys kit-chak kit-chak like Molucca-Sulu relatives. Everybody has come from eras and places to unite together on the same stage. War has bust through time.

"The heroes rein in their champing steeds and lie on their oars. On a shadow-puppet screen, they and we watch Monkey King fight the havoc monster, whose black shape looms into the sky and shoots through the crowds of armies and audience. (We can, vice versa, have Monkey en scène, and his drumming nation as shadows.) Ah Monkey dodges the snapping claw that swings out of the wings. The havoc monster is enormous; our special-effects people can build only one claw, which pokes into a side door of the theater and gropes across the stage. Ah Monkey whacks the claw with his sword-size rod, which grows—whoomp—into a battering ram. The king-size monster of havoc keeps clawing, knocking everything on the set around. The magic monkey plucks a few of his own hairs, bites them up, and blows them out, shouting, 'Beeen!' And they change presto into a myriad of little monkeys, each one wielding a monkey stick. They worry the monster, and it goes through changes—a malevolent baby, a white bone demoness, a king of swords, who mentally commands a rain of swords, a king of the lute, whose music drives the monkeys crazy, like The Fiddler against the Batman and the Flash. The other monkeys leave the cave and fight too. Wars involve everyone; every war is a world war. Ah Monkey too goes through his changes—a cormorant, a falcon, a koi fish, a temple with a flagpole tail. The war goes on for a long time. 'Kingdoms rise and fall.' "

Judy Louis was smiling her boar-like smile at this line from the classics. Wittman was encouraged to begin another movement of his play:

"Meanwhile—if this were a movie, we could use a split screen. Walt Disney ought to make the animated epic cartoon. Elsewhere—soldiers are going about the marketplace plastering recruiting posters on poles and walls. A man out of uniform had better not walk upright and show his face. The young Liu Pei, who is braiding a sandal, gets up from his squat-sit among the straw, to see what the army has to say. He reads that his country needs him badly, and he sighs, 'Aiya-a-a.'

" 'Hey, you!' says a neighbor, the butcher and vintner, wiping his hands on an apron stained with reds. 'Yeah, you, the romantic young fellow, yearning for glory while hiding from the draft.'

" 'I'm not a coward,' says Liu Pei, letting rip another sigh. 'I'd fight in wars if I didn't have to take orders. I want my own army. I have a cause of my own. I don't waste my abilities on jerkwater duels.' He hardly has to turn around to look at the heckler behind him; his eyes are far apart in his bullet-like leopard-like head.

"The butcher-winemaker sizes him up, and says, 'I myself have some abilities, and wherewithal. I've been looking for bold allies. Suppose you and I talk further.' The two of them leave their businesses unattended, and go to a tavern to drink and plan. The tavern is two tables under an awning. The crowd passes around them.

" 'We Changs have been in this county for many generations,' says Chang Fei, for it is he. 'We grow peaches and grapes, distill wine, raise pigs. I can outfit knights. I can outfit an army.'

"Among the average-size people comes a huge and mighty man pushing a handcart. The times are bad, that a man thus built be an unemployed tramp of the road. The old Chinese audience will be moved with pity because they recognize our grandfather, Grandfather Gwan Yee, also called Gwan Cheong Wun, sounds like Long Cloud, that excellent man, Gwan Goong, horseless, and no squire to carry his luggage. He sets down the cart, and ducks his head to enter the shade that the two world-changers are at work under. He's no ordinary bum-how. He sings, 'I place my bow against the wall, but I do not take off my moon-curved broadsword.' 'Be quick, innkeeper,' he shouts. 'Bring me wine. I'm in haste to get to the city and join the army.'

"Well, the effect would be the same if you shouted out your martial intentions at Enrico's or Vesuvio's or La Val's. A stalwart is making the scene; he casts his glamour over the sidewalk of tourists and regulars.

" 'Hey, stranger,' calls Chang Fei. 'Sit with us. This shoe-and-mat weaver wants to buy us drinks. I've never seen you in these parts before. Where do you come from? And where are you going pushing your belongings?'

"The interesting stranger quaffs the wine, and Chang Fei refills his cup. 'I've been a fugitive wandering the roads and the rivers for five years now,' he says. 'I can't go home to my family village.'

" 'Did you kill someone?' asks Liu Pei. 'Are you a wanted man?'

"Granddad puts his quick-draw hand on his sword hilt. His eyes flare like a pair of red birds flying up.

" 'You don't look like a pig thief to me, nor an adulterer either,' says Chang Fei. 'I'm sure if you killed a man, you had good reason.'

"Granddad drinks more wine, which sloshes on his thick and beautiful beard. Later kings and ladies will try bribing him with silk beardbags, which were once a fashion. These two brotherly men are trying to get his story.

" 'I see you keep red and healthy on wine,' says Liu Pei. 'Were you drinking the day you killed a man? If you had it to do over again, what would you do?' "

Wittman played Gwan Goong speaking out of his coffee cup, fierce eyebrows shooting rays, head down and mumbling, like Marlon Brando about to tell difficult bad memories. Brando can say anything, the ladies will listen. " 'I come from a place where the idea of governing was to make everybody obey the biggest man, and give him things, and do him favors. This executive officer taxed us for seasonal deliveries of firewood, harvest, game, three-horn joong, moon cakes, maidens. That story about mice belling the cat came from my hometown. "You do it." "No, you do it." I was the next-biggest man. It was up to me to bring the cat to justice. He was carrying off a maiden when I dragged him from his horse and ran him through. I killed him with this cold and beautiful sword, whose name is Black Dragon. And then I left town. I've been on the run ever since.'

"Chang Fei invites these two men, each of them free of the grubmoney life, to his ranch and home. They learn that one's cause is the others' cause. In the peach orchard, they invent a ritual of friendship. That friendship ritual was one thousand six hundred and twenty-nine years old when the Forty-Niners, our great-great-grandfathers, brought it to the Gold Rush. Every matinee or evening for a hundred years, somewhere in America, some acting company was performing *The Oath in the Peach Orchard*, then it disappeared, I don't know why. The theater has died. The words of that oath used to be printed on programs, and it was inscribed on walls for the World War II audience, when we were kids—that recently—to chant along with the actors, community singing. I want to bring back— not red-hot communist Chinese—but deep-roots American theater. We need it."

Anybody American who really imagines Asia feels the loneliness of the U.S.A. and suffers from the distances human beings are apart. Not because lonesome Wittman was such a persuader but because they had need to do something communal against isolation, the group of laststayers, which included two professional actors, organized themselves into a play. Players took the parts of the three brotherly friends, and improvised a ritual that made the playwright's sketch up-to-date and relevant, and showed him what happens next. Wittman thought whaddayaknow, I've written one of those plays that leave room for actors to do improv, a process as ancient as Chinese opera and as far-out as the theater of spontaneity that was happening in streets and parks. Everyone is a poet-actor adlibbing and winging it.

Lance Kamiyama will be Liu Pei; Charles Bogard Shaw will be Chang Fei; Wittman will be Gwan Goong. Nanci Lee and the other women will be audience for the time being.

"Gong boy!" said Charley Shaw, lifting his cup of coffee. "Yum sing! Mahn sing!" Which are the toasts at banquets and gambling. "Raise your wine cup! Drink to victory! Ten thousand victories!"

"Kanpei!" said Lance, taking off his apron. "Banzai!" Which were the banquet toasts, in Japanese, drunk to him and Sunny at their wedding.

"Here we are, three unrelated people," said Wittman/Gwan Goong. He stood at the butcher block, his podium. "Nobody from my family village, not even that girl that I rescued"—a thumb at Nanci—"rode with me into exile. Before I do battle again, I'd like to hear you vow that we stand by one another no matter what."

"You aren't getting me ready to kill people, are you?" asked Lance/Liu Pei, laying down his spatula. "I'm going to feel very bad if I have to kill anybody. I want to be a dove." He walked up the kitchen ladder, and sat on its top rung. Oh, come on, Lance, co-operate. These men were military heroes. And the first rule of improv is: Don't say No. "I'm warning you, I'd rather be killed than kill."

Wittman was as tall as Lance on the stepladder, and spoke in his face. "There's a war on. It comes this way, we have to take part. You can't stand aside and let your people be slaughtered. You have to be realistic."

Lance stood up on the ladder. "I'm speaking as a veteran of life and war. You should have stayed longer at that job of yours. It was your responsibility to keep track of the kids you sold war toys to. You could've guided them playing with soldiers. One day, those kids, after Ragnaroking their toy armies, will straighten out the dogpile of G.I. Joes and Sailor Bobs, and make them shake hands and become friends. As taidomo of my last gang, I led the maneuverings and the shaking of hands at the Alameda County Fair Grounds gang war of 1956. Nobody got killed or hurt much. I'm experimenting on leading people out of back-to-back, hand-to-hand situations." He tried on a pot-helmet, took it off. "You give me an army, I have additional creative ideas to try out."

"What kind of creative ideas?" asked Charley, an actor generous with the spotlight. "I was at that county fair—blue-ribbon pigs, blue-ribbon wine —I didn't see any gang trouble."

Lance walked back and forth between Charley, who sat in a straightback chair as if upon a throne, and Wittman, who leaned against the butcher block, his horse, Red Rabbit. "I carried out a war without an incurrence of cops, neither Security nor the Oakland P.D. nor the National Guard. I was working out further-along methods for taking over the world without anybody noticing. Like I am blood with the French. I gave at a Parisian mobile bloodbank. They gave me a ham sandwich and vin rouge, and saluted me, 'The people of France are grateful.' I move that we offer ourselves to the enemy as hostages-for-peace. You especially, Chang, are a valuable citizen. They'll agree to take you, especially if we throw in your land too. They can come over and live on it, feed the pigs, water the orchards. Who's ahead in this war? We are, sitting around, drinking wine, living. We can afford to experiment as to whether more lives are lost fighting or in 'unilateral surrender.' It's our duty as the latest evolvement of man to find out. I'm curious. When they get here, let's have our populace be doing something flabbergasting like spinning Gandhiesque wheels, like Frisbee, like Slinky. Invent a Frisbee-Slinky combination. Some satyagraha so interesting that they'll lay down their weapons and do it too, have us teach it to them. They'll kill a few of us from momentum, but they'll calm down by and by. What can they do to us, a wonderful country like us, we put ourselves into their arms." He was out among the audience, who could hiss or crook him or take him into their arms.

"Hai!" said Charley/Chang Fei. "Hai!" which could mean "Cunt!" or "Crab!" or "Yeah!" or "Look!" or "Hello there!" or it was just a noise. "I know you," he said, in character—tough China Man of our childhood. "I know you. You are sly. There is nothing you won't say. You say whatever, peace, whatever, and while they're thinking about it, while we're thinking about it, you do your idiocratic Dada." A Chinatown coot has spoken, sitting on his bench at Portsmouth Square, telling you who you are, and what you do.

"Nothing flabbergasts like explosives," said Wittman as Gwan Goong, sitting atop his horse. "Guns. Bombs."

"No guns. No bombs. I'm using my deepest brains to ban bombs, and to help you plan the barbecue in the orchard. You are throwing a barbecue, aren't you? You've got enough meat and wine to feed everybody." Lance/Liu poured hot coffee all around. "Invite the enemy. Always invite your enemies to parties. What to do with belligerents, we'll hold a tournament on your ranchland. And find out: Do contact sports exhaust the war energy, or is there escalation and dominoes? At pre-game activities and half-time, and everywhere they go, we'll be playing the enemy's ethnic music and speaking their language. We'll take on their ways, and slow them down, unable to distinguish themselves from us." Lance/Liu is not letting go of his tack. "For uniforms: skins versus shirts. Naked, integrated boy-girl teams. Defense—nudity as camouflage, bare skin and hair blending into nature. Nudity also works as offense; I've scared off Seventh-Day Adventists and Mormons by answering the door naked. They'll hide-and-seek us; they'll capture our flag; they won't be able to resist us. Let's invite everybody to marry everybody. For the finale, we'll have a multitudinous wedding. Our foreign policy will be: We want to marry you. Propose to every nation. Leaflet them with picture brides. We'll go anywhere and marry anybody! How do unrelated people get together? They get married." His wife smiled at this homage to marriage. Lance has already used marriage to solve a war problem. When he married Sunny, he got out of the draft. He is a Kennedy husband.

"Listen here, Running Nose," said Wittman/Gwan Goong, for that is the way Liu Pei's name sounds in American dialect. "I can tell you how many will die before they calm down. Thirty million. That's the record the human race is shooting for. Look in the *Guinness Book of World Records*. The record for Greatest Mass Killing is twenty-six million three hundred thousand, which is how many were sacrificed for the communizing of China. That broke the Russians' World War II record for the Most Killed in a War Against Invaders, twenty-five million. The number keeps going up as history goes along. There's something in us that loves to break records." These numbers had been lumbering like dead planets in Wittman's head, ruining life.

"We're inviting soldiers and civilians to a place where they quit ending up at the hillpiles of skulls," explained Chang Fei. "The right disarming, tough Zen non-violence?! What is it?" His chop-socky hand sliced the prana-filled air. He swiveled his head, eyes wide, and came to a hard stop, his foot stomped—bang!—and he held the one brother, then the other with his glare—me-ay. Charley has seen a lot of Hong Kong movies. "My dove brother. My hawk brother. These peach trees are at their fullest and reddest bloom. We vow friendship. Repeat after me. 'We three—Liu Pei, Gwan Goong, and Chang Fei—though not born to the same families, swear to be brothers. Though born under different signs, we shall seek the same death day.' " He knows. He knows. Charley is Chinese, and knows. He is a hearer of legends. And he's translating what may be the secret oath the tongs take into daylight English for all to understand. China Man ways are not gone from this world as long as an actor like Charles Bogard Shaw lives. Oh, yes, free the actors, and they will bring such gifts.

" 'In war, we will fight side by side.' " Wittman Goong gave the next part.

But Lance chimed in, and made this up: "Wherever we find a sit-in, we'll sit. A salt march along the coast? We'll march. A spinning wheel, we'll spin."

" 'Heaven and Earth, read our hearts,' " Chang Fei continued. " 'If we turn aside from righteousness or forget kindliness, may Heaven and man take out vengeance on us.' "

"Bless our chosen family," said Lance, sprinkling each man's and each woman's hair with salt from the saltshaker. "You are my chosen family."

The audience, their ladies, liked that part the best, and repeated after him, "My chosen family."

Wittman just about broke character. "Wait a minute. Hold it. Listen." He knelt on the butcher block to talk better. Lance got him with salt in the back of the neck and down his collar. He jumped off the butcher block. "You're right, we throw a barbecue. We're out on a ranch, we do a rodeo tournament and a cookout." Wittman zinged the cleaver from off the knife magnet. "Slaughter a black ox and a white horse, make them into steaks and hamburgers in full shocking en-scène view of the audience. Audience participation—they eat and they're sworn in in this blood ceremony that will change everybody into a Chinese. Yes, we invite foes too to a theater of blood that cuts through t.v. souls. Serve dog. We ought to taste puppy dog and intestinally remember our heritage, our cuisine." Nanci and Sunny put their hands over their mouths and squeezed their knees out of the way and said, "Oooo." They were the little girls you gave worms and bugs to. Taña laughed. Judy frowned. "Three hundred people came to the peach orchard to witness that first vow. The young men volunteered for the brothers' army. Later, here in the Far Out West, miners came in from the fields and paid a speck of gold for admission to *The Three Kingdoms*. And lowly brakemen came from railroad yards, and laundry guys, and migrant farm hands, and cooks from out of the basement kitchens of restaurants. They came to be part of a war oath. And to watch the rancher and the tatami-shoemaker and the fugitive be transformed into knights who fought in silks and armor and tiger shoes." Wittman prowled up to the butcher block on tiger feet, and chopped it with his sword, Black Dragon. "Our generation, who have nothing left, will remember the first movies we ever saw—the camera shoots up at the heads of Chang Fei and his black horse against the sky. The dragon-scalloped flag on his eighteen-foot spear whips in the wind —'Chang' the word on the pennon, 'Chang,' one of the first Chinese words you learned to read. 'Chang Fei,' said our parents and grandparents. And us kids stopped running up and down the aisles. 'It's Chang Fei.' We galloped along the bottom of the screen, part of the army that rides with the three brothers." Making like slow kung fu tai chi moves, Wittman pushed hands and feet circularly. The second rule of improv: A new ritual is embarrassing, it's okay. "Beneath the peach blossoms—close-up on veins and pollen—and the beginning green of leaves out of dark branches, Liu Pei rolls back his runningwater sleeves. He draws his sharp blade. And cuts the neck arteries of the black ox and the white horse. The unknowing animals step back from the red streams, then pass out. Red Rabbit, Gwan's horse, is tethered to a peach tree, and the tree rains blossoms on him. Interspersed among the trees are yellow pennons, the mulberry on a yellow field, Liu Pei's insignia and colors; the Southern Pacific flies a yellow standard to this very day. The chefs and sous-chefs of Chinatown will be cooking all through the show, and we'll serve meat rare from the fire. Our faces will turn red on wine like Gwan Goong's and Chang Fei's. We'll have dancing. Carouse all night for a week. A fat lady will dance to cave-thundering drums. Bonfires shoot overlapping shadows of her abundant body—her uplifted arms make many arms—against hillsides, where monkeys lean out like gargoyles to look at her. We could stage this at the Faculty Club at Cal —inside one of those mead-hall proscenium fireplaces. Light a fire in one fireplace, and she dances in the other. I got inside the Faculty Club as a desk clerk. I don't know why they gave me the job. Everybody else was a Greek, not frat boys, Greeks from Greece. I wrote their love letters to our American girls, and in exchange they gave me waiter's rights to turkey carcass, duck heads, champagne sleepers. You should see the goings-on—professors in drag dancing on tables. I checked-in Herman Kahn. Back to the enormous lady: Her tootsie rolls of fat bounce and jounce and rub together, breast rebounding on breast, wonderful crevices in her neck and waist and limbs and ankles, where gold coins flip and flap. Gold weights tug at the softest fattest pierced earlobes. She must turn herself on all the time. She twirls on the underbeddings of her toes. Her back is a continent of skin. She's more nude than all of us put together. All by herself, she can be Lady Yakusa's army, kimonos down to their hips and a tattooed dragon continuous across the row of their naked backs; rampant gardant, zigzagging their swords before them like the scythes of time, they scan the battlefield. The fattest lady on earth is laughing, and her laughter jiggles everything. The heroes shout and clap out rhythms for her."

"I don't know any woman who would want to play her," said Taña.

"Neither do I," said Sunny. "Fellini's done her already, huh, Lance?"

"I'm certainly not playing her," said Nanci.

"If there's anything I hate," said Judy Louis, "it's bachelor parties with girls jumping out of cakes, and stags horning around the table."

"But she's not a cake girl," said Wittman. "She's scary. What is it about her that scares you? Her size?"

"She is too a pop-up out of the cupcake," said Judy, "and I'm not scared. Everybody else wears armor, and she's naked."

"But she's bigger than they are. She'll raise the question of how come our other beauties are bony witches." He was describing the effect of mascara and eyeshadow and contoured cheeks and noses on the very women around him. Indeed, witch women were riding again, on boy's bikes, which are better made and more like broomsticks than girl's bicycles. Hair streaming behind them, they screeched at windows, "Come out. Come out." They were retrieving old names and the past by ouija board. They'd been burned at the stake in a prior life, and were tough. You play right or else, Wittman, we're going to get you, Monkey King. Not heeding a goddess when he was face-to-face with one, with four, he went headlong, "I won't leave out my large lady. There's a tradition of fatness that we have lost. All that's left are the hippo ballerinas in *Fantasia*. This fat beauty heated up kung fu opera twenty years ago, and I want to see her dance again. I want to bring her back. If none of you guys want to play her, I'm going to have to go on a star search."

"A Hong Kong actress would do it," said Nanci, whose hair color was witch black. She looked down her pale thin nose.

"Felliniesque," said Sunny. "Too Felliniesque."

"Soldiers in fatigued outfits bore me to death," said Judy. "I don't go to movies without female leads. No glamour dresses. No romantic interest. No love music. Men dramas, no good. I see on the t.v. news, suit men meeting and discussing, I know already, up to no good business."

"I hate movies about guys who don't shave digging out of some stalag," agreed Taña. "Or military guys who never change costumes inside the same submarine or foxhole for two and a half hours. I can't sit through trial movies either, twelve guys in a jury box."

"You don't understand," said Wittman. "The fat dancer has unbound feet and unbound tits and unbound hair. She busts through stereotypes. That we're puritanical. That Han people don't dance. That a fatty can't hold center stage. Okay. Here's a part you will live and die for. The drumming for the fat dance is pounded out by a noblewoman named Hoong Ngoak a.k.a. Red Jade. She led a navy to the rescue at the height of the war that you have guessed is coming up. She outfitted the crow's nest with a big-ass taiko wardrum, and she rode that swaying crow's nest through days and nights of sea battle. She kept alit a lantern over her head, and against the black sea and sky, she was a flying, drumming, lit inspiration. The white fur of her headdress circled her face. Her long black hair and the tails of ermines blew with the speed of the flagship. She is a loud-drumming will-o'-the-wisp faery, and she flies on a pair of wings, flags tucked into her sash, the flag of Han and the flag of her family, Leong. Leong Hoong Ngoak, her total name. In the midst of battle, in a star of light—the spot will pick her out in a top balcony or on the catwalk or on a flyup—she's a miraculous living figurehead. She's a target for explosives flown up to the crow's nest by missile birds, which explode and make flare the metal discs in her head-dress and in her pink silk maybe bulletproof jacket. From the fleeing ships, she appears to be a supernatural being coming after them. She whips up the drumbeat, and the wind and the waves rise. The sun comes up. We see her fleet—flats of ships, each flat larger than the one in back of it, like a fan of face cards, many ships, each one diminishing in size clear out to the horizon line on the backdrop. The ships have faces—eyes on either side of the bow, which is the nose, and there are moustaches too, and mouths—swimmers treading ocean water while talking and arguing. Lady Jade whams her club-like drumsticks, tasseled with horsehair, down and down upon the taiko for loud war. Her fleet traps the enemy in a bay—we can stage this on Lake Merritt or Lake Temescal, or in the Bay—and her sailors swashbuckle the enemy ships while she drums out victory. They burn the flags of the Gum/Gold armada, who are bearmen and wolfmen."

Unfortunately for peace on Earth, the listening ladies were appeased, and Lance had run out of plowshare ideas. Nanci and Taña and Sunny and Judy thought that if they were allowed to play war women, they were liber-ated. The time of peace women, who will not roll bandages or serve coffee and doughnuts or rivet airplanes or man battleships or shoot guns at strangers, does not begin tonight.

The unfamiliar light of Saturday morning—daybreak. A wind from the Valley blew the dawn in clouds up and over the Altamont and down into Oakland.

Sky poured pink through the windows. Everyone floated in pink air—spun sugar, spun glass, angel's hair, champagne. The friends moved toward the windows to see where this rose was coming from, and saw everything, the water of the Bay, the glass of houses and buildings, the sky, the dew on the grass, rose-blessed. Is the sun like this every morning if we but wake early enough to catch it? Is it a time of year—a season of rose air? The crew in the lightbooth has flipped on the pink gels, and tinted all the stage and the men's and women's faces. It seemed as if you could float out the win-dow on the strange atmosphere. There are Chinese people who would ex-plain that Gwan Goong was paying us a visit; the color was emanating from a building in downtown Oakland, where you could have seen Gwan Goong's good red face, or its reflection, upon ten stories of brick wall. You could have asked for any wish, and Gwan Goong would have granted it. You could have been a millionaire. As it turned out, nobody in this gathering of friends was ever again afraid when flying in an airplane. And later one or another of them in danger felt that there was someone protective beside or just ahead of him or her, making a way. They didn't discuss the rose air, didn't compare one's sensing of it with what anyone else was seeing, if anything, until years later when two happened to meet, and somebody said, "Do you remember that morning seeing the air—the air before your eyes and on your hands—pink and rose?" And then they wondered that they had not exclaimed over it at the time. (Could it have been a waft of nuclear testing gone astray from the South Pacific?)

A feeling went through Wittman that nothing wrong could ever happen again—or *had* ever happened. It's very good sitting here, among friends, coffee cup warm in hands, cigarette. Together we fall silent as the sun shows its full face. The new day. Good show, gods. Why don't I, from now on, get up for every dawn? My life would be different. I would no longer be fucked up. I set out on more life's adventure with these companions, the people with whom I have seen dawn. My chosen family. We're about to change the world for the better.

Sunny walked about her house with a brown paper bag picking up paper plates and beer bottles and plastic wineglasses, dumping ashtrays, wiping food up off the floor. "Come on, people, either keep it in your mouth or on your plate," she said. She was a full-time housewife, which she had to be in order to keep the trompes-l'oeil functioning. She was returning what she had put away that needed protection from the party. Half of a round glass table went against one side of the wall, and the other diameter on the other side, the found bottles on top filled to elegant waterlines. Where there had been dancing, she lowered a board hung on chains back down to its height as a table, découpaged with the pages of Beardsley's Savoy book. Salomé's big lips kissing John the Baptist's head, blood looping in designs like her long sleeves. On top of that, pillboxes and a vase of fake lilies, and green bananas ripening to go with the rug. She had painted the gold and black rays of Art Deco shooting out of doorframes. Lance handed out hot towels for faces and hands. O comfort.

"We've only started," said Wittman, out the door and across the porch and down the stairs and through the yard. "This play is immense. Epic. Our story won't fit a one-act on a unit set of crates and burlap bags. I'm going to bring back to theater the long and continuous play that goes on for a week without repeating itself. Because life is long and continuous. The way theater was in the old days. I mean the old days in *this* country. The audience comes back every night for the continuation. They live with us. The thing will not fit between dinner at the Tivoli and the after-theater snack at Martha Jean, Inc. or the New Shanghai Café." His friends agreed that he should work some more on the play; they would act in it, and they would be on the lookout for more actors and a venue. Then Wittman was again out on the streets, but this time with Tañia.

Dew sparked on the lawns and parked cars. A church bell rang a few iambs. Brother Antoninus, are you waking up at St. Albert's? A black-and-white cop car and a black-and-white cab cruised past each other. We're in a good part of Oakland, which used to be restricted. "No person of African or of Japanese, Chinese, or any Mongolian descent will ever be allowed to purchase, own, or even rent a lot in Rockridge or live in any house that may be built there except in the capacity of domestic servants of the occupant thereof." Lance was living there in an integrated marriage, and Wittman was walking there. Oakland Tech ought to be teaching this localest history.

Passing St. Albert's, Tañia and Wittman learned that they had something in common. On dates, each with another, they had followed the sound of men's voices chanting, carrying far without electric amplification. Hiding in the bushes outside the gate, they had seen monks in procession around the grass. Breath issued from cowl hoods. Which one of those figures was Brother Antoninus himself? Hands from angel sleeves held and shielded candles. How is it that rows of lit candles stir you so? It's automatic. The candles at the Big Game rally at the Greek Theater the night before the Cal-Stanford game get to you too, religiously. Birthday children become arsonists because if little candles on a cake can make me feel this religious, what if I set fire to a building, why don't I blow up a country? Knowing some Latin from high school, Wittman had felt on the verge of understanding the songs. "Compline," said Tañia, "the last prayer at night." The compline had been so wonderful, Wittman admitted that he'd wanted to join up but for his vow against missionary religions. This time of the morning all was still, no people on the grounds, and no lights in the buildings.

Tañia had taken off her sandals with the tire treads for a long, barefoot walk around the dog shit of Oakland. She held her shoes in one hand and Wittman's fingers by the other. He sang to her, "Tiptoe through the tulips, through the tulips with me." A bearded man, holding his head with care, climbed some front steps, and before going inside, turned and gave them a wave. Fellow tripper come through the night, come home. Not every last one of us who trips out of a Friday night makes it back home. Across the street, a couple with arms around each other hurried along, then stood to talk, then hurried on. A raven had darted a feather into her hair. He carried a black cape folded over his arm. Yes, all over town, batwings were closing. May the minds that shot off to other planets and dimensions settle gently adown to the ground of our Earth.

A single sheet of newspaper flared up into the air and flew, gliding and opening, and sailed over their heads. *Like a blank piece of paper, I drifted along past the houses, up the boulevard again.* Wittman ran after it, pulling Taña along. Please be the girl that I'm in love with.

Her sandals under her armpits, she held on to his hand with both of hers and dragged him to a stop, and up some side stairs of the California School of Arts and Crafts. She led him to a courtyard, and where she leaned back on a wall soft with moss. He leaned above her, like his elbow against her high-school locker. "Hey, wanta make out?"

She didn't laugh, but looked gravely into his eyes for quite a while. "Yeah. Let's make out."

"Let's swap spit," he said, but giggled his Chinese giggle. He had lost his previous cool. He firmed up his face. Took her face between his hands, blonde hair between his fingers. Gave her a hard kiss. Pulled back to look at her, to see how she liked it.

She looked big eyes back at him. Held his gaze. He loved the way her eyebrows frowned; she was troubled. He was getting to her. He took another kiss, longer. This time when he looked, her eyes were closed.

"Hey, Taña," he said. "Taña. Wake up. Talk to me."

She put her mouth up to his ear, and said, "You want it hot, I'll make it hot for you."

He held her chin, led her mouth away from his ear, back to his own mouth. Lips barely rubbing, he slid past her mouth and attacked her ear. "Hey, tell me. Are you blonde all over? Huh? Are you? Are you blonde everywhere? Blonde body hair? Where else are you blonde?"

"My armpits. My armpit hair comes in blonde. Why? Are you queer for blonde pubic hair?"

Shit. A queer for blondes. If she had brown hair, would he have said, "Are you brown everywhere? Do you have brown pubic hair?" "Blonde chick. White girl," he said, calling her names. "Are you a loose white girl? Where do you live, loose white girl? I want to take you home. And I want you to invite me in."

She ought to have slapped his hands away, and dumped him for acting racist. If you have principles, you do not like him anymore when you find out somebody's a racist or a Green Beret or a Republican or a narc. You ought to be able to sense such a defect, and the obstinacy of it, and run.

"Did you go to 'America Needs Indians'?" Taña asked. Yes, the first multi-media event in the world. There had been movies and slides, color, and black and white, projected against these four walls, the sky with moon and clouds overhead, and music and wise Indian voices chanting like Gregorian, like Sanskrit Buddhist. The crowds turned around and around to see everything, and their juxtapositions. A herd of buffalo charged from one side, and mustangs from the other. Indians riding across Monument Valley, and, simultaneously, close-ups of their faces. The art students had painted one another's faces with Day-Glo. People kept saying, "The tribes are gathering again," which sounded new and old. An airplane or a flying saucer—come for us—would look down and see a square flashing in marvelous light show. Now the walls were dark and no vibes. "Because it wasn't here," said Taña. "It was at the Art Institute." Wittman took her word for it, having been too ripped, and also, Chinese having no sense of direction. (That's why the Long March took so long.) Wittman and Taña might have met each other at "America Needs Indians." "What hours were you there?" "What were you wearing?" "Who were you with?" "Who were you?" "I sort of remember somebody who might have been you. Did you wear braids with a headband?" More and more in common. She can be my continuity- and direction-finder.

They walked out of the school, and he followed her through a gate, bedighted with rose vines in thorn, then along a footpath with ivy trailing upon it. Her part of the house was in back.

She had wonderful, wonderful digs—flights of mobiles, windchimes, models (bottles and dry sunflowers) for still-lifes on tables and shelves, even the dishes on the drainboard arranged in a composition, cans of brushes, the smells of linseed oil and paint and patchouli, prisms turning in the east windows, madras India Import bedspreads for curtains and bed, spectrums of yellows and oranges, coat-hanger wire webbed with lavender and purple tissue paper over light bulbs, intricate old rugs (whose mazes you could lose yourself in when stoned, a kid again lining up armies of marbles). He could live here. He was itching to rummage, and to view life through her kaleidoscopes and prisms and magnifying glasses and scientific microscope. He went right over to her industrial-strength easel under the skylight; in its clamps was a sketch of a forest with pairs of points, the eyes of animals. There were smiles in the leaves. "You're a painter," he said. "I wish I were a painter, and always had something to show for it." He spun a land-brown globe—Arabia Deserta, La Terra Inconoscivta, the Great American Desert, Red Cloud's Country, the Unattached Territories, the Badlands, Bar-

baria, the Abode of Emptiness, the Sea of Darkness, sea serpents and mermaids abounding. "Strange beasts be here." Nada ou Nouvel, whence the four winds blew. And she had a map of the universe—Hyperspace Barrier, areas of Giants, Supergiants, Dwarfs, Protogalaxies. She's another one who knows how to live on her own, where she belongs in time and space.

She went into the kitchen and boiled water, set up her drip system, ground her beans. Wittman wandered about.

Toulouse-Lautrec's *Divan Japonais* took up one wall; Taña had decorated to match that print—the furniture matte black like the man's top hat and the woman's dress, feathered hat, fan and long gloves; the madras picked up the orange hair and the yellow beard and cane. He slid open a box of kitchen matches—a bat, upright, cute face and wings akimbo, not alive. Vampiress? Taña also collected birds' nests with blue and speckled eggshells, and downy nestling feathers, and a piniony quill. A set of false teeth had a reefer crutched in its grin. Tuning forks and magnets. A cabinet of good paper. A shelf of sketch books. Nudes. A roll of new canvas. Buckets of stretcher bars. He sat at the round table with the crystal ball and apples. There were also a set of brass gramweights as in a lab, a brown velvety cloth bunched around things, collages on boxes. Flows and layers of candle wax relief-mapped the courses of many evenings staying up with friends talking and sculpting. On a postcard of Seal Rock, she had drawn a few lines and dots, and you could see that seals are born out of rocks, and rocks come from seals.

Taña brought over two cups of coffee, sat across from him, smoked. "Wittman," she said, "Darling. I've been thinking: The next time I get it on with a man, I set ground rules."

"Yes? What is it, sweetheart?" She called me a man and a darling, and she wants to get it on. I've never called anyone Sweetheart before, never called anyone anything. "Go on."

"I may not be in love with you. Say, you're the one I'm in love with, I won't let you go. But, say, I meet him tomorrow, I'll leave you. I'm being fair. You don't love me either. We're starting even. There was this guy named Edmund I was in love with when I was seventeen. I know what love feels like. I'm not in love with you. Maybe I cannot love again. But, say, I find him again, or another one like him, I'm going to have to get up and leave you. I don't have an obsession over you, though I do want to make love with you. You don't define my life. I just want you to know how I am before you decide to make it with me. Making love is my idea as well as yours. This isn't just your idea, okay? You're not going to say later that this was all my idea, or your idea. We can each of us cut out whenever we feel like it. If somebody that either of us can love comes along, why, we're going to go, okay? As of yesterday we got along perfectly well without each other. And we're not going to feel destroyed because I'm not in love with you and you're not in love with me. So, tomorrow, if one of us wants to be by himself, nobody's going to phone him up. But we could possibly go on forever not falling in love with somebody on the outside. We may get used to having each other around, and end up growing old together. Do you know Chekhov's concept of dear friends? That's what we can be to each other, dear friend."

Damn. She beat him to it. Outplayed again. He was the tough-eyed one who had been planning to let the next girl know point by point what she would be in for entangling with him. But he'd hesitated, what if she then wouldn't want to be in for it? No girl but the one in his head sat still for a read-out of rules. He'd balked, and she'd taken his lines. Now what?

Taña had been warming and softening wax in her hands and was molding it. Don't go away, Taña. Does she know she looks winsome? Truth and Consequences. He was the loser. Consequences for him. "I think I could love you," he said. "I think I do love you."

So they got it on, and they were graceful, just so much foreplay, just so much fervor and abandon and sweat, positions normal. Classic moves. Silently went at it. She didn't say much, and he didn't say much. Mouths against parts of the body, he did not make her blurt out, "I love you." Well, it was a fuck where they were hardly acquainted, after all, and one didn't want to turn off the other by seeming overly weirded out. Don't grunt and groan repulsively. Be courtly. Be mannerly. And honest. Although who's to know without having randomly made it with a large cross-section of the population—not the sampling of the one type that attracts you and is attracted by you—what's abnormally passionate. The business-like way that most people walk around publicly conducting themselves, you would think nobody does anything sexual.

Well, he was not like most people. "Hey," he said. "Play with me. Taña. Tell me, tell me, what is it you like about my body?" He was up on his elbow beside her. She lay on her back with her white arms behind her head, her hair splaying, legs splaying too. All in the light of day.

"I like your smooth bony chest," she said, bringing her slow arms down and holding the flats of her hands against his chest. She put her cheek there too and listened to his heart. "And you're thin. I can almost touch your bones, only skin between my fingers and your bones. And I like the way you

look down at me haughty like that, looking over your cheekbones. I like
your hair, thick and black. And your eyes have an expression, I don't know
what to call it. Your turn. You tell me what you like about me."

"You have pink nipples," he said. Pink nipples have got to be more sensitive than brown nipples like his own.

"And my face? What about my face?" she asked. "Tell me about my
face."

"You're lovely. Your face is lovely." (Remember in *Far from the Mad-
ding Crowd* where, of her three suitors, Bathsheba Everdean chooses Sergeant Troy, "the one to tell her that she is beautiful." Troy could also "take
down Chinese in shorthand.") "Beautiful." He stroked her arm. The hairs
stood up and moved back down. More so than the hair on her head, this
light hair on the arms was to him Caucasian. "This arm hair is how I can tell
you're a white girl," he said, aboveboard. "Your turn, beautiful Taña. Tell
me what physical feature of mine makes me Chinese to you, and how it
turns you on."

"Your eyes," she said. "Mainly your eyes."

"And my skin?"

"And your skin." Which makes me Chinese all over. "You're the same
color as me, but a different tone."

Good. She did not tell him that she liked "yellow" skin or "slanty" eyes.
She did not say he was "mysterious." If she turns out to be a freak for orientalia, kick her out of bed. She's not getting any mysterious East from me.

"Is my nose too big?" she asked.

"Everybody thinks their nose is too big," he said, wisely. "Everybody
thinks their own face has the most pores too. You have long eyelashes. Bat
them against me." She gave him butterfly kisses on his bony chest. She ca-
ressed the golden ecru of his flesh, and again he got on her, in her. Went in
unto her. And again she enjoyed herself wordlessly. She'll continue speaking after he recedes. Unstoppered. In *Hiroshima Mon Amour*, the Japanese
man listens and listens to the Frenchwoman talk. In *Snow Country*, the man
does the talking.

"What about my toes?" Wittman asked. "You notice my toes? I noticed
your toes. Your toes were pushing against your Tijuana sandals, which
strapped them tightly together. That was one of the first things I noticed
about you."

"You have a thing for feet, do you?"

"No, not me. Do you?"

"Yes. As a matter of fact, I do. I can't stand the feeling of my toes sticking together, especially the two little ones at the end. Skin to skin. It's always going on, but sometimes I think about it. Feeling them stick together drives me crazy. Especially when I have my shoes on and I'm somewhere where I can't reach down to pull them apart. You have that? They're doing it right now—look. Do you know what I mean? You know what I mean, don't you?"

"I can see if I start to think about it, I could work up an obsession. Toe skins. Yeah, I see what you mean. Lolita had that problem. Remember Humbert Humbert stuffing cotton between her toes? She's sitting on the bed, and she holds up her feet. All her toes are separated with cotton wads."

"Wait a minute." She was laughing. "Lolita didn't have this toe sensitivity. Humbert Humbert was painting her toenails. He was saying, 'Hold still.' "

"Hey, don't spoil Lolita for me. She and I are just like this." He crossed his fingers—made kings.

"I have it worse in my left toes."

"So you never heard the one about the difference between Chinese toes and Japanese toes?"

"No, what's that?"

"What do you think? Take a look at my toes, and tell me if you see anything unusual."

Whenever you find a white person you can trust, get some inside answers to questions. Spy out specific racisms.

"Is this a test to see how many men's toes I've been looking at?" asked Taña.

"I promise not to get jealous of you looking at other men's toes."

"You have nice toes. Nice long, far-apart toes."

"I can spread them at will, and pick things up with them. I got monkey feet from going barefoot as a kid. Would you say my toes are too far apart?"

"When you open them up like that, they're unusually far apart. I guess you don't have my problem feeling them smack against one another. Tell me the one about Chinese toes and Japanese toes."

"I shouldn't give you a hang-up. There ought to be a rule not to give one another new hang-ups."

"There ought to be a rule when somebody starts to tell something, he has to finish it, no fair bringing up half a secret."

"You didn't grab a peek at my toes to see whether I'm a chinaman or a jap?"

"You can tell by the toes?"

"That's what I'm asking you. Comic books and *Life* magazine said that the way to tell a good Chinese from a bad jap is that the former has more space between the toes."

"Then I must be a Japanese, and you a Chinese."

He parted her sweet, suckable Japanese toes, and bent down and kissed one. Then he sucked each little piggy, and licked the tight spaces between them. He heard her sigh, "My toes are having orgasms." Holding that sensitive foot against his chest and heart, he loved up the other one. "Wittman," she called, and he looked up to see her face, which did not make him feel embarrassed. "You gave me an orgasm between all my toes," she said. "Ten toes, eight orgasms. I didn't know toes could do that."

"I didn't either," he said; "I think we've invented a new sex act." He had not thought of toe love before suddenly doing it. Her feet were so beautiful and so human. He hoped that someday he would get to know her well enough to ask her to make love to and with his toes. Find out whether men can have orgasms down there too.

She put on her X-L t-shirt to go to sleep. Every girl he ever made it with (two) wore t-shirts to bed. They only wear negligees in movies. They want you to make love to their real self and not their peignoir.

Taña thought about complimenting Wittman on how nice and soft his penis was. But he was such a worrier over masculinity, he'd take it wrong. Men don't understand that a penis is the loveliest softness to touch, more tender than a baby's earlobe, softer than a woman's breast. And after fucking is the best time to touch and touch, but you can't do that for too long, or they feel bad they're not getting hard. Wittman was not one you could praise for his softness. Taña saved up her acclaim.

As they lay facing each other, forehead to forehead, and stared, owl eyes, she described what she saw: In another country, a path wound uphill through high waves of yellow grasses. Trumpet flowers on cactus vines blared on either side. On top of the hill there stood a house; it had never been completed, or someone was dismantling it for firewood. No windows and no doors in the frames. Wittman looked clear through to blue sky outlined by boards with driftwood grain and rusty nails. He wasn't asleep and dreaming. On the contrary, he felt especially awake, and was seeing—was walking in—this other place. "I'm awake," he said. "Taña. Taña? Do you see what I see?"

"Yes." He heard her voice beside him. "There's a girl on the other side of the house."

"She's dressed in a costume of a country that I can't identify."

"Yes. Black and red with silver, and her hair is long and coiled."

They blinked at one another. What is this?

Inside the house, every room opened to every other room and to the outdoors. The girl's heel fleeted away past a doorway. A fair breeze blew on their skins and through their hair. The sun radiated through the rooms, radiated inside their heads. Wittman looked at her beside him. "You sent me that flash. It came from you to me." She nodded yes. Just before the flash in his brainpan, he had seen it like a comet with tail whiz the short distance from her to him. His brain felt warm in one spot. "Whoa," he said. "We ought to be documenting this. One of us, the sender—you—should write down what you're about to send, and I write down what I receive. In sealed envelopes. And we get a third-party witness to open them. We ought to be scientific about this."

But E.S.P. has a quality of conviction—I am awake, more awake than ever—no doubt about it; proof feels beside the point, too slow. And it's more fun to fly around a foreign place than to be in a lab counting hearts, clubs, diamonds, and spades. What was causing this? Staying up all night? And not having dreamed? Oom-lette? A coincidence of true minds? Was this going to last forever between the two of them? Wittman added a tree to the hillside. Taña made clouds change shapes fast; strange winds were sculpting the clouds. The beyond mountains changed in a sequence: Pyramids. Glaciers. Volcanoes. Easter Island heads. Stone grandfathers of Cheju Island. Totem poles with ears. Windmills turning. Does this mean that he and she have seen the insides of each other's heads, and he needn't be scared of her? If she's the only human being he's ever encountered, perhaps ever going to encounter, with whom he can read minds, is she the one meant for him? He should never have taken drugs. Can't tell the gods' chimeras from freaks of my own.

"Let's find out if there's a roadsign that will tell us where we are," said Taña. They hiked down the palomino flank of the hill to the main road. A sign gave a traffic rule in international symbols. There was no name of a town or any advertising. There was no mood music.

"Can you do this with anybody or just me?" asked Wittman.

"Just you," said Taña.

They talked and saw more things and ate and made more love and fell asleep together. When they awoke, it was Sunday.

"Do you want to go for a drive?" she asked. "Can I drive you home?"

"Do you want to drive to the City?" he asked. No plans for the day. No job tomorrow. "I live in the City. I found a tunnel I could show you. They were going to build a subway once." He hadn't meant to tell anyone about his secret tunnel, but blabbed, showing off that he knew deep San Francisco. Oh, well, a bomb shelter should be shared.

She drove a Porsche Speedster, "1959. 1600 D," she said. It was an ovoid, softly rounded like a tan nest egg. The wrap bumper was painted white, a curve of Easter egg icing. The upholstery was chocolatey leather, and you sat low to the street. "Wanta drive?" Taña offered him the keys, and got into the suicide seat. The engine started up noisily, high in the throat, an angry muffler. James Dean had been killed in a Porsche, a silver Spyder. It was a risk car, no protection—top down, no roll bar, next thing to a motorcycle.

Showing Taña that he could talk and drive at the same time, Wittman said that she reminded him of his grandmother who dressed theater companies. When the opera costumes arrived from Hong Kong, she handed out the gorgeous raiment saying to the actors, "Treat it like shit." That's class. That's the way Taña treats this car, letting him drive.

"The windows go up and down in a Convertible D," she said. "There are only thirteen hundred of these in California."

"When we pass one of those twelve hundred and ninety-nine, do I have to give him the Porsche owner's wave? Do we flash the high sign at Karmann Ghias and M.G.s and T.R.3s? Or Porsches only? Hey, where's my car cap?" He had to talk somewhat loud above the wind and the motor. Also she put him off having to tell him the windows go up and down.

"You wave to anybody you like." Said with the confidence of a white person. "I didn't buy this car myself. I don't make that much. My parents gave it to me. The deal was: either go to Stanford without a car or go to Cal, only sixty-seven dollars a semester, and with the savings buy a fine car, and live at home and commute." So white parents also care that their kids go to a school that's cheap and close to home. "I got the car, but went to Arts and Crafts."

Wittman decided to take the long way to the City, south on the Nimitz through Oakland (past the STOP CASTING POROSITY sign), and across the long, long San Mateo Bridge. Its railings ran low alongside the low car. Better not have car trouble. The sign says No Stopping and No Turning Around. No suicides allowed. There was hardly any traffic today, and the car seemed to be shooting out on a plank. A pelican floated up from under the bridge. Wings holding still, it glided over the open car. They got a detailed look at its beak with a pouch, its legs and feet perfectly tucked into its body, like airplane wheels fitting into the wheel well. Two more pelicans came up on an updraft. Pterodactyls. And the car an exoskeletal scarab. A new age of reptiles. One of the birds landed on the bridge rail, wings folding as legs came down, all in balance, not a wobble or a teeter. "Don't look at them," said Taña. "Keep your eyes on the road. I'll do the looking."

Wittman was having a problem with his natural eye-blinks. He kept seeing three tall pepper mills with round heads, not well delineated.

"They're the windmills," Taña explained. "They're fading. Don't look at them while you're driving. They look like Egyptian cats, don't they, with long front legs and long side whiskers. Those are the vanes." She was holding her hands over her eyes, her hair blowing out behind her. Sometimes the wind tossed it into his face as if it were his own blonde hair. "Now they look like pepper mills," she reported. "Now they're keyholes. They're fading." How are you bound to the lady you dream with? And see things with?

Coming off the bridge they crossed the Bayshore and El Camino Real, and headed north on Skyline. The big bonsais were bent toward the sea, when today's wind, thick with fog, was blowing inland. San Francisco—wet as if seen through tears.

"Look," said Taña. "It's a windmill." It was the abandoned lighthouse. "What if we've been seeing the future? Do you want to stop?" No. He does not want her to contain him in her crystal ball. He wanted to be driving the Porsche by himself, his Porsche, and he did not want to take her to his secret tunnel or to his pok-mun. Where she'll be needing to go to the bathroom, and he hands her his roll of toilet paper, and she hurries down the hall among the commentators in their armpitty tank-tops.

Yes, let's stop and visit the lighthouse, then, as a theatrical family on a drive would do. Explore storefronts, mansions, barns, terraces, vineyards, caves, and imagine the theater they would house. Prisons, forts, water-pumping stations, beer factories, gas stations, lecture halls at teaching hospitals. This lighthouse could be it. The door stood open, but there was no air flow for creatures that need to breathe. A dead pigeon lay on the floor. Taña climbed the steel stairs, and Wittman followed her. The buzzardy air seemed hotter each step up. The windows were opaque with salt and dirt. On a ledge was another dead bird. "Let's get out of here," said Wittman. "We're inside somebody else's brain." The foghorns were groaning, the far-off suffering of ogres and sea dragons. "We're not going to be able to turn this lighthouse into a theater, Taña. Unless our show had vertical action, and an audience of six lay face upward. Or we could seat the audience up here and on the stairs, and they look down at a play about the abysmal."

Taña finally couldn't breathe the air from one million B.C. anymore, and they got out of there.

Zip into the City quick past El Barrio Chino, and up Telegraph Hill to Coit Tower. Wittman parked next to Christopher Columbus, who stands with a foot on a rock and his nose toward the Golden Gate and the Pacific beyond. Sailboats and whitecaps were hoving sharp out there. Masts tick-tocking, the docked boats rocked like Daruma dolls. "Welcome to my estate, Taña," said Wittman as he opened the car door for her. "Wait until you see the view from my top floor—all three bridges visible on this windswept morning." They went up the stairs that were the stairway of Rita Hayworth's mansion in *Pal Joey*, the camera avoiding Columbus in her front yard.

The elevator doors were in the middle of a mural about workers turning wheels of cable. A tower of W.P.A. artwork, a continuous epic of labor, musculatured men heroically operating turbines, women in white hats and aprons assembling milk. No place for us hummingbirds. The doors parted. Taña was not beside him. His mind was off of her for a moment, and she was gone. A wanderfooting woman. He looked for her outside.

A sweater had been left on a window ledge. He ought to try it on, a gift to him from the affluent society. A voluntarily poor person has a duty to take such a gift. Just then, a Chinese grandmother came running on gliding strides, to not pound the chi out of her system. She passed the sweater, went on circling the tower. He took the stairs up—Jimmy Stewart looking for lost Kim Novak in all the old familiar San Francisco places.

There she is, silhouetted in an arch, and she's talking to someone. Mrs. Coit ought to have put in a brass pole for her volunteer firemen; he'd slide down the hole and away. He strolled the circularama. Yes, all three bridges in sight today. And the dragon's tail zigzagging up and over Lombard Street. Alcatraz—our troupe will take over the Rock for theater-in-the-round, the audience as yardbirds, a guardwalk for the hanamichi thrust. The cellblocks were already a scaffold set like *Bye Bye Birdie*. And Angel Island too, waiting for us to come back and make a theater out of the Wooden House, where our seraphic ancestors did time. Desolation China Man angels.

Surely, one or two got off those islands and spread the theories about there being no escape against the ocean currents and sharks.

Wittman said a mantra for this place by the poet that his father tried to name him after.

Facing west from California's shores,
Inquiring, tireless, seeking what is yet unfound,
I, a child, very old, over waves, towards the house
*   of maternity, the land of migrations, look afar,*
Look off the shores of my Western sea, the circle
*   almost circled. . . .*

"Wittman. Wittman," Taña called him. He went on over, his jealousy up. She had borrowed and was wearing a lumberman's jacket off of a bearded man. Guys with beards, though, were trusting one another, for a few months more anyway, to be pure white doves, who practice right politics, that is, leftist politics. You can tell by the beard, he's a reader of books, a listener to folk, jazz, and classical, a brother of the open road to pick up and be picked up hitchhiking. Taña did getdown introductions, "Greg. Wittman." Last names unnecessary but for the government taxing you and drafting you.

"Gabe. I've changed my name to Gabe."

"He's hiding out from the draft," said Taña. "You too, huh, Wittman?"

"Yeah," said Wittman. "Me too." We won't turn each other in. So I too have a face trusted at first sight by the underground.

"I was hiding out in Mexico," said Greg/Gabe. "But I came back to see if it's possible to live a private life inside this country. Mexico freaks me too far out. Sugar skulls, bread skulls. Kids eat marzipan in the shape of death. Skulls biting on skulls. No trouble with the federales on either side of the border." Yes, the autumn skeletons are appearing in "Gordo."

"I didn't re-register after graduation," said Wittman. "And I didn't give the feds my change-of-address. If I'd known it was coming to this, I would've shown up at a church every weekend until a minister got to know me to write me a recommendation for C.O."

"There's another way to go for the religious exemption. You haven't gotten your Universal Life Church card?"

"No. How do I do that?"

"You have to be ordained by an ordained minister. I'm an ordained minister. The idea of the Universal Life Church is that the First Amendment gives each one of us total freedom to make up religion. Mine has as its main and First Commandment: 'Thou shalt not kill.' No exceptions. My god is literal about that. I'm ethically prepared if I come up against the Army philosopher. Do you want me to ordain you? I can ordain you."

"Yeah, go ahead. I'd like that. Ordain me."

"I ordain thee a minister of the Universal Life Church. There. You write a letter to Reverend Kirby Hensley, 1776 Poland Street in Modesto, and he'll send you a certificate and a card. You take that documentation to the Board of Health, and ask for a license to marry people, so you're recognized by the State of California. If you hold public rituals in your living room, you can be tax-exempt. So you're legit by the I.R.S. too. It's all legal, First Amendment. Every pacifist deed you do, keep your documentation for your C.O. defense. Educated people who read and write well have a chance at it. The Army Ph.D.s and chaplains, who've graduated from seminaries, break down the high-school dropouts. You can get help on the argumentation from the American Friends Service Committee or Catholic Action."

"I have my ideas straight. Thanks."

"You should think out whether you really want to be an official Conscientious Objector. C.O.s do service, and don't get to choose what kind. They're the avant-garde, who go out ahead of the infantry to dismantle mines. The exemption for married guys is going to stop any day. Why don't I marry the two of you? Cover all the bases. I have a perfect record; nobody I've ever married has gotten a divorce."

"Sure," said Taña. "I'd be glad to save you from the draft, Wittman."

"Sure," said Wittman, who had a principle about spontaneity. Zen. Don't mull. There's divinity in flipping a coin rather than weighing debits and assets. Taña, anyway, is probably his truest love already. Always do the more flamboyant thing. Don't be a bookkeeper. He took Taña's hand and said, "Will you marry me?"

"Yes," she said.

The Reverend Gabe had the wedding ceremony memorized, the one from the Episcopal *Book of Common Prayer* that we all know from the movies: ". . . wilt thou, Wittman ah—?"

"Ah Sing."

"Wilt thou, Wittman Ah Sing, have this woman to thy wedded wife . . . love her, comfort her, honor and keep her in sickness and in health, for richer, for poorer, forsaking all others, keep thee only unto her, so long as ye both shall live?"

"Yes, I will."

Taña also said, "Yes, I will," for her part. "My first marriage. Your first marriage too, isn't it, Wittman? You haven't been married before? No alimony? No child support?"

"No. My first marriage too." No little Chinese wife back home.

"You can also say, 'I plight thee my troth,' said the preacher."

"I plight thee my troth."

"I plight thee my troth."

Thou. How do I love thee? What if I were always to address you as "thou"? Then how could I do thee wrong? Then I will always love thee. He will gather actors and ask them to improv "thou." If his ardency flags, why, he need only call her "thee." "Thee," said Wittman again, looking at her.

"Those whom God hath joined together, let no man put asunder."

O lovely peaceful words. What if I were to think in that language? I would not have the nervous, crimpy life that I do.

A movie kiss against the sea and sky. The End.

"I'll send you the papers," said Gabe.

A Sunday of vows. The way to make a life: Say Yes more often than No. Participate. Shoulder one of the vows that are always flying about like hovering angels. *Every angel is terrible. Still, though, alas! I invoke you, almost deadly birds of the soul, knowing what you are.* Swear, and follow through. No need to invent new vows; we haven't done the old ones, and they aren't done with us. Vows remain after those who gave them are gone. Think them in kanji and in English, so no matter if a part of your brain aphasicly goes out, some word remains. A posse of angels have rounded up some strays. To keep the old promises that are not broken, though the people break. To be a brother, a friend, a husband to some stranger passing through.

5

RUBY LONG LEGS'
AND ZEPPELIN'S SONG
OF THE OPEN ROAD

 MR. AND MRS. WITTMAN AH SING monumentally
descended the sculpturesque steps outside Coit Tower.
Across their path ran the Chinese grandmother, wearing
her sweater. She met another grandmother at the parapet,
her white hair in a chignon bun, her hands on her hips,
turning her torso this way and that way, breathing. The
running grandmother talked loud to her about the price of fruit. She lifted
her arms toward the eucalyptus trees. As the inter-racial couple walked past,
she said, "Goot mah-ning." "Good morning," said Taña. So, this is the
hour they come up here to do their old-lady kung fu. Taña had better not
make a remark. Nobody had better make a remark. A girl jumped up on the
parapet; she's ballet-dancing on it. Two boys ran alongside, trying to catch
her by the hand or by her skirt, but she pirouetted away, yes, on point. At
the turn in the wall, she pivoted, and ran, leaping at her pursuers.

Taña went toward her car. She walks with her arms folded across her
breasts. She'd returned the jacket to her friend. Oh, please don't shrink up
like that, Taña. All of young and old womankind dancing but not my Taña.
It must be the effect of marriage. "Did you see the ballerina? You ought to
be more like that," he suggested. He was instructing her: Stay alive for me.
Never tire. Stay up all night, and play all day. Don't be cold in the wind.
Else, how can I keep up loving you? She didn't answer; she will get even
with him later.

To perk her up, Wittman surprised Taña with a honeymoon—a trip to

Sutro's. For the rest of their lives, they could say, "That marriage, I spent my honeymoon at Sutro's." Their third anniversary, Sutro's went up in a fire. Near the entrance, a true-to-life sculpture of a Japanese man stood almost naked, holding a hand mirror and looking itself in the eyes. Self-portrait. According to the plaque, the artist had used his own human hair for the hair on his statue. It had hair on its head; it had eyebrows, stub-brush eyelashes above doll glass eyes, nostril hairs, armpit hair. There was probably pubic hair under its loin cloth. There was a lot of yellowy-pinky skin. The honeymoon couple should have left then and there. It's not true that freakiness takes you far out and breaks through into miracle.

"I hope that he used only hair from his head," said Wittman, "clipped it and curled it for other parts of the body. How would you like to move into a studio, and find collections of eyebrow hair, fingernail clippings, eyelashes, beard shavings, pubic hair?"

"Call the cops," said Taña.

"Doesn't it make you want to cremate it?"

"He probably thinks that his statue is in some fine art museum in New York, America," she said. The commiseration of one artist for another. "It's exact, and it ought to be beautiful."

"But isn't."

"But isn't. Strange what he thought to be perfectly himself."

Oh, god, is she profound and aesthetic. And she did not say that the thing looked like Wittman (which it did not), or had anything to do with him. We umberish-amberish people are not nitpicking hair-savers, creepy fingernail-collectors, or money-hoarding coprophiliacs. No way.

Near the real-hair Japanese man was a mechanical monkey dressed in Louis XVI courtier clothes, laces and plumes, bowing to guests, sweeping his hand back and forth. "I hope that's fake fur," said Taña. Its motor heart hummed and beat.

"If you scratch its hair, part it like looking for fleas, you'll either see the pores and follicles of a real monkey or the warp and weave of cheesecloth."

"Yew. Let's not."

"It's probably real, hunted and shot by Lucius Beebe or Sutro." Taña had never been here before. He was showing her new things, keeping the marriage lively, and the momentum of life rolling apace. A bond forms between those who have seen an odd phenomenon or laugh at a joke. He could never get it on with a straight chick.

In the musée méchanique, he led the way directly to his favorite mechanical, which was the amusement park that convicts had made out of toothpicks. He slipped a quarter into the slot, and started the Ferris wheel turning; the basket chairs trembled and lifted and, at the top of the ride, cunningly dropped. How many life sentences to build the latticework of the rollercoaster trestle? No people on the rides, but the music box plinked and tinked "Let Me Call You Sweetheart."

"This is a meditation about time and doing time," said Taña. "A meld of boredom and amusement. People who commit crimes are children, and when you lock them up, they stay children. This park is their idea of freedom. When they get out on parole, the first place they'll go is the boardwalk at Santa Cruz. Amusement parks are full of criminals."

Wittman hugged her shoulders. Here's the girl he met at the party. Out in the dull world, he loved hearing Berkeley insights. And not having to make them all by himself. "Do you remember Robert Walker stalking Alfred Hitchcock's daughter Patricia's look-alike, and the merry-go-round and the Ferris wheel turning and turning?"

"*Strangers on a Train*," said Taña.

After the fire, some people will remember the amusement park, and other people will remember a mining-camp scene with men panning and carrying and dumping, and a tram going in and out of a tunnel. It would have been a replica of the Sutro Metallurgical Works.

Taña put her arm around his waist, and they walked over to another exhibit. He ought not to feel afraid. Would there be less anxiety if she were taller and stronger than he? And women were the protectors of men. There's nothing to be afraid of. Wait until he's under fire in a battlefield. Panic then.

But there is something sickening about miniatures. Scale a thing down small, work on it for a long time, some life gets compressed into it. Only a tiny bit of life is needed to make a netsuke breathe, and be scary because alive, motored for always by the exhalations of its creator, and the chi and sweat from his hands. Frankensteinish animation. But I have always been afraid. It's not the freak show, and it's not her and marriage to her. I am always afraid.

His coin brought the Electric Cassandra to life. She nodded, turned back and forth. Her jaw dropped and a voice said: "Seeker, ware—the future." Her large hands shoved a card out of an opening in the glass: "After heartbreak, you find true love." "Yours," said Taña, putting the card in Wittman's hand.

"Oh, no, it's yours. You touched it first, your fortune. Mine's the next one. I'll take the next one."

The next one was: "Follow your destiny to be rich or famous." "I choose famous," he said.

"I choose rich," she said. "I don't think I could handle famous."

"Realistically, in my life, Taña, I keep getting dealt a choice between time and money. An American peasant has to choose between time and money. I choose time."

At the diorama of the Cosmos, the moon rolled around the Earth, the planets around the sun in blue space luxurious with silver and gold stars. The Cosmos is a music-box that twinkles and spins. A comet with rainbow tail arced slowly past. Then a brindle cow jumped over the moon, and a little dog laughed to see such sport, and the dish ran away with the spoon.

There were no other people about. They could jimmy the glass case, and try to fit inside Tom Thumb's and Mrs. Thumb's carriage. Finger-dance in the tiny kid gloves and the shoes with spats. "You fan yourself with the wee fan," said Taña, "and the gloves will fit."

In the photo booth on the mezzanine above the skating rink, they took wedding pictures, a strip of four for a dollar. The first picture, "for the folks," they pantomimed feeding each other cake. The second, "our real selves," she wore a nice smile, and he looked pissed off. The last two were for each other's wallets, one of her by herself, and one of him by himself. Taña looked like a blonde movie star; Wittman looked like a wanted bandito. El Immigrante, his wetback passport picture i.d.

How is their marriage to work out when, as they could see from "our real selves," they were not on the same trip at the same time? "It's hard to take two-shots," said Wittman. "Actors have to be well directed to appear as if they belong in the same picture."

"You're photogenic, Wittman," she said. Good thing. How can those who are not photogenic walk about showing their faces? Or is she putting him on? Telling him what he needs to hear?

They hung over the balcony and watched the skaters going around. If we run downstairs and rent skates, could we be Orlando and the Russian princess zipping on the frozen Thames above the apple woman in the deep ice? Wittman, the fool for books, ought to swear off reading for a while, and find his own life.

For their wedding picnic—can't go home, home have I none—they drove to the Palace of Fine Arts. Near the No Admittance sign, he showed her a hole in the cyclone fence, and helped her through it. The green grass grew all around. In a nest of it, they ate cheese and French bread, nectarines, snappy raw stringbeans, and drank a California champagne from the bottle. This Taña could be anyone, a perfectly good enough person to be married to. She had patches of freckles on her arms and on one knee. There was blue paint and green paint—her palette—under her nails. He had been wide awake when he married her, his daylight love. Forget the dreamgirl of the dark night.

"I'm going to own this palace," he said. "We're home. These are my ducks." They threw them crumbs. They walked about, poking at the chicken wire and the insides of the hollow papier-mâché colonnades. The pink crust of the structure was breaking off in chunks. Lazy caryatids and atlantes, without a roof to hold up, draped their thick arms over the tops of the columns. The human couple walked all the way around and inside. From every angle, the giants turned their backs; backs are easier to sculpt than fronts.

"My palace was built to be viewed from up there," said Wittman, and led the way climbing the slope to the street. From the bench, they saw across the greensward a pink city on a moat lagoon. It looked like the hideout of the hundred and eight outlaws, a mountain encircled by borders of water. The caryatids and atlantes were looking down into pens at—a dog fight? A cock fight? A people fight. "Nobody wants a land, I got uses for it. I'm going to take over this ghost palace, where the atmosphere is suggestive with deeds on the verge of taking place."

"I will help you rule," said Taña.

O Central Casting, she's the consort of my life.

"The wedding present from me to you," he said, presenting her with this World's Fair site that belongs to all. He's giving her every chance to speak up if to her it was but a bogus abbadabba marriage. She doesn't like him, why, she can leave him here among the grasses and ruins. "This place and a starring role in my play that continues like life are yours. The army that we raised at breakfast will parade down Broadway and the length of Market Street. There will be a train of elephants, and in each of their howdahs, four soldiers, pointing rifles in four directions. Their uniforms are G.I. camouflage khakis. The eyes peering out from between their helmets and the tar on their cheekbones are Indochinese eyes. This part, I'm not making up. Have you read in the papers? The side we're backing in Viet Nam goes to war on elephants. A patrol of four or six elephants pick through the jungle to search-and-destroy communists. Elephants have very sensitive trunks and toes. The disadvantage is that an expanse of elephant makes a too easy target. Because of the guilt of having dropped A-bombs, we are returning to a more natural warfare. Elephants and dolphins."

Wittman was getting his inspiration from a book known as The Book of Evil; its title is something like *The Water Verge*. In preparation for warfare in marshes and rivers and rice paddies, the Pentagon was using this book too. There is a curse that anyone who tells or stages or discusses its legends would be struck mute, and his children and grandchildren also be mute. Wittman and the U.S. military may fall silent at any moment now. The ideas for strategic hamlets and agrovilles came from that book, and from Lucretius' *De Rerum Natura*, which warns that animals often backfire in battle. War animals were part of the *impedimenta* that Hannibal took over the Alps. Generals, who were wizards of the wind, blew the animals—wild boars, tigers, lions, bulls—around, and they turned on their owners. Our engineers are keeping the elephants and dolphins under control with radio implants.

There used to be three peace books too. They were found in a cave by a wind wizard, and now they're lost. This wizard had blue-green eyes and looked both young and old. He gave the books to a student who had failed his exams. This student learned control of the weather. Which could mean he had the charisma to change the atmosphere when he walked into a room. His young-old teacher said, "You can rescue mankind. You will suffer," and handed him *The Way of Peace*. That book's title is all we know of it anymore; its contents are but suspect memorizations, argumentations, and rumors.

Ho Chi Minh's favorite reading was *The Romance of the Three Kingdoms*, and it's a text at West Point too. Uncle Ho and Uncle Sam were both getting their strategy and philosophy from Grandfather Gwan, god of war.

Wittman continued telling his story as follows:

"Yonder palace is defended against the elephant army by knights on black stallions, Trigger palominos, and stout Mongolian ponies with trick riders that charge out of the intercolumniations into battle on the greensward. Archers on horseback and archers on the roof pull bows that shoot ten simultaneous arrows. On the water, a boat with blue sheets sails slowly by and collects the arrows in the cross-fire. Knights are fighting up and down those stairs that lead along the walls and into walls. Two beautiful ladies stand on those platforms amid the two clusters of columns, and sing about no one missing them. 'Two leaves from off a tree, two grains dropped from a silo.' They're the two most beautiful women in the land, and Cho Cho, as we call him in American, the brothers' archenemy, has built towers to keep them as his very own. On that tree hangs the red silk robe that he is giving as a tourney prize. Five arrows hit the bullseye, shot from horseback, shot riding backwards, shot hanging upside down from stirrups, shot from a single bow. The knights fight over it; then he gives all of them a red silk robe each. Kettle drums and cymbals and strings of ten thousand firecrackers echo like mad in the rotunda and across the water. Hookmen try to scale those turrets and the ice wall. Infantry run to it with pocketfuls of dirt, which they pile into a slope. Actors stride the tops of those ramparts. The platforms are for the soliloquies of heroes and for dialogues across chasms.

"The failed student with a peace manual and the power of the winds fights against the three brothers. His army in yellow scarves charge from over there, and the brothers charge, pounding the earth, from that side. They clang in the middle. The knights cross halberds, fleur-de-lis steel on X-ing lances. Trumpets blare, drums and gunpowder bang. Elephants trumpet. Liu Pei fights with a bullwhip; you can hear it cracking amid the firecrackers. Chang Fei flies like his name, his eighteen-foot spear before him, and pierces an elephant through the heart. Grandfather Gwan rides Red Rabbit, and cuts men in half with one swoop of his sword. You, Taña, gallop bareback on a white horse across the esplanade.

"At nightfall, the campfires (some are decoys) light up swaths of turf with a no-man's-land of darkness in between. The outnumbered brothers ambush the enemy on three sides of that triangular palace. They set fire to the turf grass. The flames throw shadows of battle up among those watching giants. The sunrise or the fire enflames the world. Each side has its wind wizard howling the weather up. The special-effects guy goes wild. Rocks and elephants roll. The brothers confer. Their wizard advises to pour pig's blood, goat's blood, and dog's blood down on the heads of their enemies, who were maybe Muslims. From the tiers of the palace cascades a storm of blood rain. Fireballs roll like burning tumbleweeds. Knights and horses and elephants explode.

"A silence descends for an interval. A black cloud settles on the field. Soldiers and animals land. The wind stops. Thunder stops. The bands stop playing. We've used up the fireworks. Rocks settle. Out of the smoke rides Liu Pei chasing Chang Chio, the student of the magic books, shooting arrows at each other from horseback. Chang Chio drops his bow, clasps his arm; he's been hit. He turns his horse about; they fight hand to hand. Liu Pei wins, but the men in yellow break through the flames. And from around the back of the palace comes another army, red guidons high; it's Cho Cho. His army drives the brothers to the Yangtze. Cho Cho does a victory dance in red silks up there on the rooftop."

Along the street behind Wittman and Taña, a moving van passed back and forth. Those who have lived near a river and a highway know that one sounds much like the other.

"The city is on fire. The people run to the river. The brothers blow up the dam, and escape in a boat. Chang Fei has to hack away at the hands of allies who could pull the boat down. They sail through devastation. Liu Pei weeps, 'Why was I ever born to be the cause of all this misery to the people?'

"Your part is coming up, Taña, and it gets larger, I promise. I have to talk fast. I may go mute at any moment. And the curse goes down three generations."

"We're going to have very quiet kids and grandkids who talk with their hands?" said Taña.

"We'll love our little muties. I better warn you; there's another curse. I'm going to tell you a wedding story from the tradition of the Heroic Couple on the Battlefield that will turn you into a Chinese. Ready?"

"Ready," said Taña.

"Years go by; battles are lost and won; kingdoms rise and fall. Lady Sun, a beautiful princess with red hair and blue eyes, has beaten all of her father's and brother's knights using their choice of weapon. She wants to try combat in a real war. News reaches her that Liu Pei's two wives have been killed. She could marry the famous old warrior, and be his partner, martial and marital. She sends him a proposal, which Liu Pei receives while mourning his wives. He has been singing an aria about growing old alone, having spent his life at war. To answer her, he sets off with a fleet of ten fast ships across the Yangtze to the southern kingdom of Wu, where Americans come from. Herding sheep and bearing wine jars, Liu Pei and half his army and navy go to the royal palace. The other half, dressed in their best civvies, shop all through the town for wedding presents.

"Liu Pei meets the gold-haired family: The old king, killer of a white tiger. Sun Ch'üan, the prince who is plotting against this would-be brother-in-law. The queen, one of the two women Cho Cho wants to keep in towers. She scolds her family, 'You're using my girl as a decoy duck.' Underneath his scholar's robe, Liu Pei wears light mail."

"Charley's not Liu Pei," said Taña. "You are."

"Yes, and you're my Lady Sun. On our wedding day, we walk between lines of red torches to the bride's apartment—which is a private armory. You've furnished your rooms with spears and swords, banners and flags, and your ladies-in-waiting are an amazon army. 'Is this the ambush then?' I ask.

"The women laugh at me, 'What's wrong? Haven't you seen weapons before?'

"I ask them to take the deadlier ones with them when they leave.

"I part the curtains of the wedding bed. A Chinese bed is like a proscenium stage, and like a very private room. The three walls and the ceiling are carved out of wood, forests of animals and people with mother-of-pearl eyes; in the grain of the inlaid marble are misty mountains and waterfalls. There are doors and drawers, and shelves for books and vases. You could peek out through gingerbread and spindles. The beautiful redhead who's in there says, 'So you don't like my weapons. Afraid of a few swords after half a lifetime of slaughter?'

" 'Take off your swords,' I say. 'Remove your armor. Disarm thyself.' You do, and I love you, and you love me.

"The gold-haired family luxuriate me. They build me a castle, where I regularly dine off gold and silver. I read in a library. Musicians always play. My men practice archery and race their horses. They don't see their leader much. A year goes by.

"Lady Sun gets her husband to swordfence with her every day, acquiring his abilities. Then we have tea in our tower, whence we look down at the beautiful land and the river. We sing duets. A wind whips up waves, rocking and pitching a tiny boat. 'You southern people are sailors, and we northern men ride horses well,' observes Liu Pei.

"At that, you jump from the balcony onto your white steed, galloping headlong downhill. You wheel around, calling, 'So the southerners can't ride, eh?'

"I lift my robe, jump on my horse, and full-gallop down the hill too. We ride side by side into the capital, where the people acclaim us.

" 'Beloved, is it true that northerners call their spouses "comrade"?' you ask.

" 'I'll call you "beloved," my beloved southerner.' Oi yun. Beloved.

" 'And are southern women the most beautiful?'

" 'Thou, the most beautiful, and the most beloved.'

"We often talk about how northerners and southerners differ. Northerners are stubborn; southerners are quick to revolution. Southerners are natural comedians; northerners laugh just hearing them speak Cantonese, the ugliest language in the world. Peking opera is for sissy academics; Cantonese opera has soul. Northerners are old; southerners are older. Educated people speak Mandarin; real people speak Cantonese, albeit the ugliest language in the world.

"One day near spring, I hear that Cho Cho, my lifelong enemy, is lead-ing fifty legions to attack the one city that is mine. A man with the gift of tears, I weep in front of my wife.

" 'Why are you sad, my beloved husband?' you ask.

" 'I've been driven hither and yon all my life. I've ridden past my ances-tral village many times, and couldn't stop at my parents' grave. And another new year is coming.'

" 'Tell me the truth. You want to leave me.'

" 'I have to save my city. I have to go, but I don't want to leave you.'

" 'Don't be sad, my husband, my loved one. I'll find a way for us to leave together.'

"Kneeling to you, I say, 'I will always love you.'

"We attend New Year's parties all day, and toward evening, you say to your mother, 'My husband is thinking of his parents. He wants to go to the river to make offerings toward the north.'

" 'As a good wife, you ought to go with him,' says the queen.

"You ride in your palanquin, and I ride my horse at the head of our small entourage.

"Sun Ch'üan goes to bed after feasting. He wakes up after his sister and brother-in-law have had a night's head start. Throwing his jade inkstone across the room, he says, 'I want their heads.' He sends cohorts after us. 'Bring back their heads, or I'll have yours. My sister plays war. I'll teach her what war is.'

"Liu Pei and Lady Sun see a cloud of dust, soldiers coming. 'You go on,' you say. 'I'll stop them.' But troops also block the road in front.

" 'I have something private to say to you.' I dismount, and go inside your palanquin with you . We enclose ourselves from the rest of the world. 'You've got me. I'm in your hands now. You win. I know there's a plot to this marriage. If you want to kill me, go ahead. You've been kind to me, and I thank you.' I face the utter paranoia of marriage.

" 'I don't want to kill you,' says my wife. 'I don't want you killed. I'll save you.' You hold me by the hand. We walk through the troops, whom you scold all the while. 'My brother sent you, so you say. You fear him more than you fear me, do you? I'll get him for this. You're turning traitors. Or are you bandits who want money? What are your names?' You take down the names of the officers. 'You're in trouble now, spoiling this holiday jour-ney that my mother ordered. What have we ever done to you?'

"You lead your group onward, but companies of soldiers follow us. 'Go,' you tell me. 'I'll hold them off.'

"I ride away. You retreat behind your curtains. Your retinue stops in the middle of the road, waiting for the pursuers to catch up. They hear your voice, 'What are you doing here, captains?' They tell you to come home with them alive.

"Out of the carriage and into the saddle of her rearing white warhorse leaps Lady Sun, fully armored, silver from head to toe. Your hair curls out of your helmet in waves of gold, and your eyes have caught the blue of the sky and the river. You draw your sword, pare your nails with it. 'Whom do I have to fight?' you ask. Your brother's knights put down the swords that had been forged expressly to kill you."

Wittman thought that with this story he was praising his lady, and teaching her to call him Beloved. Unbeknownst to him, Taña was getting feminist ideas to apply to his backass self.

"I have been waiting at the river by myself. None of my ships meet me. There are many poems about me weeping on the banks of the Yangtze, which divided kingdoms. The river will separate me from my love, I sing. I mourn for the wonderful year with the princess and for my stay in the country that lies between the Yangtze and the Pacific.

"The soldiers overtake me; twenty ships appear. And you arrive. The well-married couple run up a gangplank together. Warships flying Sun Ch'üan's flags, running with the wind, chase us to the north shore. We hear drums; there is Grandfather Gwan meeting us with fresh horses.

"That's it, my present to you," said Wittman. "Got no money. Got no home. Got story."

Taña was giving him that impressed look from the party, which she had given to everyone though. He loved that look, she's interested, beholding him, and others. That's all it takes, a few seconds of being smiled at, a while of being listened to, and he feels loved. I can go about my life, she loves me.

"I'm your beloved lady in shiny armor?" she said.

"Yes, if you'd like."

"I've already saved you from the draft. Well. Do you want a ride home?"

"Yes." Got to go home sometime.

"Are you embarrassed to take me home? Is someone there?" She does have me on her E.S.P.

"Yeah. My mother. Do you want to meet her? You feel like driving to Sacramento?" He has access to a car, might as well take advantage to see how the Aged Parents and Grandparent are doing.

"Let's drive across the Golden Gate," she said. This weekend, then, he will have crossed three bridges. The Golden Gate, the most bridge-like of bridges, swept them from the green Presidio to the Marin hills, where the manzanita and the bridge are the same red. Fog poured out of the forests. His grandmother liked being taken for Sunday drives. He had been in the backseat when the car radio said the Japanese had bombed Pearl Harbor. "Go to the Golden Gate Bridge," she said. "I want to drive across it one last time." PoPo was very good at last wishes. Taña would enjoy meeting her. They didn't have to worry about meeting Taña's family; white people don't have families. They're free.

He drove the eggshell car around the Bay and through the milky bog-land of Suisun, whereinto it merged, sunlight on tan metal, water over peat dirt. Between the whitish water and whitish sky, endless mirrorings, egrets stood on long long legs, mirror-doubled. A lone oak tree cringed like burned. Who is it that shoots the roadsigns? Every pick-up truck has a gun rack. It is eventful enough when a marshbird dips its foot and causes rings of silver going and going.

Somewhere between Fairfield and Vacaville, theirs was the only vehicle on the road. Wittman turned the car radio—shit-kicking caballero music—off. He pulled the Porsche to the roadside and killed the engine. A turn of the ignition key switched off the world's noise. They twisted out their ciga-rettes in the ashtray. It's against the law to toss them because peat smolders. At night, you sometimes see parts of an underground fire, and smell like bread baking. A stream of white butterflies frittered by, on and on. A flock of small black birds came next; the ones at the top were high in the sky, the ones at the bottom flew through the yellowing grass, and they were the same continuous flock. At last the birds tailed away. Next, yellow moths blew about; they will alight in another season, and become the mustard flowers of January. They heard a car at a distance, and then it arrived, and passed them. It had gathered eventfulness, passed, and pulled it away at sev-enty miles an hour. The silence re-closed. A soul extends in nature, then you are aware of having one. Buildings, jackhammers, etc., chop it up, and you took drugs to feel it. The extent of the soul is from oneself to wherever living beings are.

Too low in the sky came a black warplane. Its two winglights glared in the bright day. Its flat belly had hatchdoors—for bombs to drop out. The plane was the shape of a winged bomb. That humming and roaring must have been underlying everything for some time. It had no insignia, no colors, no markings, no numbers. It hung heavy in air. It passed overhead and off to the right. Wittman started the car, and drove fast to get out of there. But the plane came back around, skulking around and around. The sky seemed not to have enough room for it. Like a shark of the ocean inside a tank. How is it that I co-exist with that dead impersonal thing which moves, and is more real than the fields and more real than this unprotectable girl? Its noise replaced thought and om. Evil is not an idea. It is that. Sharks swim in schools. This thing was unpaired, singular in the isolation of the sky. Somebody ought to report it in Berkeley. And call Travis Air Force Base; one of their experiments is loose, blindly circling where Primary State 12 intersects I-80. But people who've seen the evil plane and heard it forget to do anything about it when they get back. Its dull blackness and noise are somehow subliminal, and cause helplessness and despair. They just want to hurry and get to their people. Good thing Wittman will be with his mother right away.

Ruby Ah Sing lived in sight of the capitol. A fence went around her property, a flower garden and a house with a porch and a porch swing. The years she had lived in trailer parks and her roomette on the train, she had had a dreamhouse. She'd settled down in old Sac for her boy, to give him a home, which he drove past. Take the long way. He had liked better living on the train, reading funnybooks in his fold-down bunk, everything you own at your toes. Sometimes the window had seemed to be a long television screen scrolling sideways, and sometimes another room, and sometimes a dream. In pajamas, he lay against the window, moving through a city street. Underneath him, hobos and Mexicanos were riding next to the wheels; they fell off in their sleep. Once a circus traveled with them, or they traveled with a circus. The aerialists spoke European, but the clowns were friendly with everyone. He wore his monkey outfit for them. They warned him of the circus tradition of tossing enemies and wise asses off the train. Boys and girls in Europe were riding in cattle cars, and were trampled. That was why he had had to give an anti-jap speech from the caboose. The men around the potbelly stove gave him a yellow flag. A steward let him serve lunch. Never work as an animal trainer; if an elephant shits in the ring, you have to shove a broom up there where the sun don't shine. Going through a black tunnel, a conductor said, "They say a thousand chinamen used a thousand tons of dynamite to make this cut. I don't know the truth of that." The engine puffed out words—"Elephant. Elephant."—through the semiconscious nights. Trestles, trigonometrical puzzles worked out by ancestors, carried him across canyons. His father waited at stations, where he'd be waving hello or goodbye. The train whistled woo woo. Ruby and Zeppelin had a joke about wooing each other.

"Sutter's Fort is that way," said Wittman. "Sac High. I graduated from Sac High. That's the Greyhound Station. Crocker, who invested in the railroad, built that museum. That's the old Old Eagle Theatre. The first theater was the Chinese puppet theater on I Street. That's the Governor's Mansion. That's the hotel where congressmen go to wheel and deal." He drove around the capitol. "Los Immigrantes go in that door to become citizens. There's the peanut man. I used to buy peanuts from him to feed the squirrels." It was an easy town to learn. A Street, B Street, C Street, and so on, and the number streets gridding the other way.

"The Land Hotel," said Taña. "There's a Land Hotel, isn't there?"

"Yes. Near the Senator. It's a fleabag."

"That's where we used to stay summers when I was a little girl. During the war. I didn't know it was a fleabag."

"Well, maybe it wasn't a fleabag back then."

Suddenly Wittman was coughing hard. His lungs were not made for an open-air car.

"Are you all right?" asked Taña, patting his shoulder.

"I'm okay. I always cough when I get near home."

"That's interesting. Whenever I've ridden the bus and heard somebody coughing, and I turn around, most of the time they're Chinese."

"Yeah, they're on their way home."

"It gets me in the stomach," said Taña. "Half a bottle of Kaopectate, and I'm ready to see my mother. I'm on my way out the door, and she says right in front of my date, and our double-dates, 'Are you wearing your bra? Get upstairs, young lady, and put on a brassiere. You're too big to be going out all over town without a brassiere.' Does your mother do that? It probably was a fleabag. I remember I always wanted to stay at the other one."

"The Senator."

"Yeah. One night, really hot, we had to keep the window open. I heard someone singing down on the street. In the morning, I looked out the window, and there was a sailor asleep in a phone booth. What's the main street? Is it Main Street?"

"K Street."

"On K Street, there was a captured Japanese plane, tan with big red circles on the wings. An open cockpit, and a ladder. My father made me sit in the cockpit, and I was crying because I thought it was going to fly away with me. My mother got really mad at my father. I sat in it for about five seconds. Don't laugh," she said, laughing.

"I'm not," said Wittman, coughing.

"Later I saw home movies of myself in that Zero, me in my pinafore and white stockings and real long hair, trying to climb out of the cockpit. Alice in Wonderland bombs Pearl Harbor."

The folks are going to love her, thought Wittman. Ruby and Zeppelin are really going to love her. I love her myself. No brassiere, wow! I have to buy her a leopard-skin bathing suit so we can play Sheena, Queen of the Jungle. Me Chimp.

Ruby Ah Sing, Wittman's mother, had a maple tree, the crown-leaves gold and red now. The crowns of many kings on a hat rack. The pear tree had some pears, and green leaves, and dead black leaves on long offshoots, and flowers. Wild in the time machine.

Through the screen door—the crack clack crash of mah-jongg. Oh, no, mah-jongg day. That's why, all those Coupe de Villes to have squeezed a parking space among. The son of the house would have turned about but for the girl he was with. Always do the harder thing. He opened the door, went ahead, held it for Taña.

Ruby screamed. "Eeek!" Stood up and screamed again, pointing. And Auntie Sadie screamed, and Auntie Marleese ran to him. His mother eeked him again. "Eeek!" What's wrong? The white girl? A hobo bumbled after them inside? "What have you done to yourself?!" She put her hands to her cheeks.

"You used to be such a beautiful boy!" shouted Auntie Marleese, looking up at him.

"Too much hair," said Auntie Sadie. "Much too hairy."

"You go shave," said Mother. "Shave it off! Shave it off! Oh, hock geen nay say!" That is, "Scares you to death!" "Gik say nay!" That is, "Irks you to death!" "Galls you to death!" Clack! Clack!

"No act, Ma," he said.

"Don't say hello to your mother," she said.

"Never you mind sticks and stones, honey boy," said Auntie Bessie. "Have a heart, Ruby."

A dog jumped on him. "Down, Queenie. Behave," said Auntie Jadine, its owner. "Where you manners, Queenie?" Those who usually spoke Chinese talked to the yapperdog in English. "Down, Queenie. Come heah." They spoke English to him and to the dog. American animals.

"good dog," said Wittman. It mind-fucks dogs to be called good when they're trying to be fierce.

"Wit Man has come to see his momma," explained the aunties, one to another. "Good boy. Big boy now." Clack clack clack. A racket of clack

clack clack. "All grow up. College grad, haw, Wit Man?" Nobody asked if he were a doctor or an engineer yet. How tactful. Not asking about work at all. "Sit. Sit. Sit. Here's an empty chair by me, dearie. Come meet me." Taña got a side chair at one of the dining tables.

"Oh, I be so sorry I didn't recognize you, Wit Man," said Auntie Sadie. "You so changed."

"That's okay, Auntie Sadie."

"Come talk to your Aunt Lilah."

"Hello, Aunt Lilah. Hello, Auntie Dolly," said Wittman. "Hello, Aunt Peggy." He went to each auntie, shaking hands with some, kneeling beside this one and that one for her to take a better look at him. "He was a cute biby." "Why you not visit Auntie more often?" "Me too, honey boy. Visit you Aunt Sondra too." The ladies called themselves "ahnt," and Wittman called them "ant." "Hair, Big City style, isn't it, dear?" said Auntie Dolly of San Francisco, ruffling his hair. "Beard in high style, Ruby. Wit Man Big City guy now."

The ladies at his mother's table were comforting her. "Hairy face, fashion on a plate," said Auntie Sophie. "You the one sent him to college, Ruby." Clack. Clack.

"Where I go wrong, I ask you," said Wittman's mother. "He was clean cut. He used to be soo mun." That is, "He used to be soigné." "He doesn't get his grooming from me. Kay ho soo kay ge ba, neh. Gum soo. Soo doc jai." That is, "He takes too much after his father, neh. So like. Too alike." "Moong cha cha. Both of them, father and son, moong cha cha."

"In Hong Kong now, they say m.c.c.," said Auntie Peggy, who was up on the latest.

"M.c.c." "M.c.c." The aunties tried the new Hong Kong slang. "Moong cha cha" means "spacy," spaced out and having to grope like a blindman.

Meanwhile, at Taña's table, Aunt Dolly, who was sophisticated, was saying, "What's your name, honey? Tan-ah. What a pretty name. Russian? Do you play, Tan-ah? I'll show you how to play. This is a very famous Chinese game. Mah-jongg. Can you say 'mah-jongg'?" Auntie Dolly had been a showgirl in New York, and knew how to endear herself to foreigners. She did introductions. Good. Wittman did not want to announce Taña to the room, and he was not about to tablehop with her like a wedding couple. "That's Madame S. Y. Chin. This is Madame Gordon Fong." Et cetera. "Hello," said Taña. Well, you can't expect her to say, "How do you do, Madame." And if she said, "How do you do, Mrs.," the lady would feel demoted. Meet Madame Wadsworth Woo. How do you do, Woo? "Madame" to you. Madame. Shit. Madame Chiang Kai Shek. Madame Sun Yat Sen. Mesdames Charles Jones Soong and T. V. Soong. Madame Nhu. All the cookbook ladies are madames too. And all the restaurant guys are generals. Generalissimo. "Let me show you how to play, honey." Don't trust anybody who calls you "honey," Taña. It's a verbal tic.

"My name is Maydene Lam," said Auntie Maydene. "Call me Maydene, dear."

"How do you do, Maydene."

"I've always liked your name," said Auntie Lily Rose. "Such a pretty stage name. Maydene Lam."

"Isn't it delicious? There are four little girls named after me in the Valley." Clickity clackity.

"What beautiful hair you have, Tan-ah. She's gorgeous, Wit Man!" yelled Aunt Dolly. "You are so fair. Isn't she fair?!"

"Thank you," said Taña, who hadn't yet learned that compliments need to be denied and returned.

Every auntie had jet-black dyed hair. Why do women as they get older have to have fixed hair? Because of beauty fixed at 1945. These were the glamour girls of World War II. Taking after the Soong sisters and Anna Chennault, who married guys in uniform. Whenever the aunties' pictures appeared in the papers—Chinese or English—they were identified as "the lovely Madame Houston W. P. Fong," "the beauteous Madame Johnny Tom." They were professional beauties. To this day the old fut judges vote for the Miss Chinatown U.S.A. who most reminds them of these ladies. Quite a few of them had been Wongettes—"Ladies and gentlemen, Mr. Eddie Pond proudly welcomes to the Kubla Khan the beautiful Wongettes, Chinese Blondes in a Blue Mood." "Myself, I am a blonde at heart," said Auntie Dolly. Don't you look askance at her, Taña, with your sanpaku eyes, or else I'm getting a divorce.

"Ciao!" "Poong!" "Kong!" Action. "Eight ten thousands!" "Mah-jongg!" Clack! Crash! "Mah-jongg!"

"Wit Man, over here," said Ruby.

"Coming, Mother," said Wittman. He stood behind her to look at her winning hand.

"Talk to See Nigh here," said the mother.

"You enjoying the game, See Nigh?" he said to the lady whom he had never met before.

"Oh, how well behaved," said the See Nigh, the Lady. "So dock-yee.

And such good manners. Most boys with beards are bum-how. He doesn't have to call me See Nigh. You call me Auntie, Wit Man."

His mother spoke sotto voce, in Chinese, "Who's the girl?"

"My friend. A good friend," he said in English. One shouldn't speak a foreign language in front of people who don't understand it, especially when talking about them. Don't add to the paranoia level of the universe.

"Serious?"

"Sure."

"How serious?"

"Serious, okay?"

Gary Snyder had gone to Japan to meditate for years, and could now spend five minutes in the same room with his mother. Beat his record.

"So you walk with her," said Auntie Sophie. She was translating "go with." She meant "So you go with her."

"Mixing with girls," teased Auntie Marleese. "Old enough to mix the girls." Go after girls with an eggbeater.

"She's so rude, she's not talking to me," said Mom. "She's hurt my feelings, Wit Man."

"Introduce you gal to you mama, young man," said Auntie Sophie. Clack!

"Hey, Taña," he called over to her table. "Meet my mother, Ruby Ah Sing. Ma, meet my pahng yow, Tan-ah." "Pahng yow" means "friend"; maybe Taña would think it meant "wife."

"Hi." Taña waved. Click.

"You aren't growing up to be a heartbreakin' man, are you, honey boy?" said Aunt Lilah.

"Speak for your own self," said back-talking Wittman. She was a glamour girl still raising hell at seventy-five. She gets you alone for a moment, she'll confide her romance. "Honey, this entre news is on the Q.T., and must not go further than this very room. My beloved is a sai yun. He's fifty-five years old, and so distinguished. All his clothes are Brooks Brothers. My sai yun lover is offering to divorce his wife for me, but I don't want to be married. Monday, Wednesday, and Friday are enough." A "sai yun" is a "western man," which isn't correct; we're westerners too.

"U.C., state-run public school, does not teach them to present themselves socially," Auntie Jean was explaining. She was an authority on higher education, a son at Harvard, a daughter at Wellesley, where the Soong sister who married Sun Yat Sen went, another son at Princeton, the baby daughter at Sarah Lawrence. "As I said to Mayling Soong, I-vee Leak be A-number-one all-around. They learn how to make money, *and* they learn to go around in society. Very complete." The cruel thing to say back to her is: "What eating club does Ranceford belong to?" But you don't want to be mean to her. They will graduate, and never come back.

"At U.C., this one learned: grow hair long," Mom agreed. "Grow rat beard. And go out with bok gwai noi." As if dating las gringas wasn't his idea, he had to be taught. "You ought to see them there in Berkeley. Doi doi jek. Yut doi, yow yut doi." Pair after pair (of mixed couples). "Jek," an article used with livestock. "Doi," an article used with poultry. "You meet my Wit Man too late, See Nigh. You missed out on one good-looking boy."

"You still got one matinée idol under the hair, Ruby," said Aunt Marleese. "Cut it for your poor mother, Wit Man. I remember when you were yay high. I used to change his diapers. You were deh, Wit Man. He was so deh." Click click. She gave them an example of deh, her head to one side, a finger to her dimple, coy lady pose. The aunties smiled at him like he was going to act deh any moment for his mother at least, do babytalk, act babyish, and bring out motherly love.

"Cut it off, Wit Man," said his mother. "Cut it off. I'll pay you." Clack!

"Just—. Just—," said Wittman. "Just—." Just lay off me. Cut me some slack. Let me be. And let me live.

All this time at four tables, outspread fingers with red nails and rings of gold and jade pushed and turned the tiles in wheels of bones and plastic, clockwise and counterclockwise. The sound of fortune is clack clack clack. They built little Great Walls, and tore them down. Crash! "I'm the prevailing east wind." Aunt Lily Rose is dealing. "You in luck today, Maydene." "Not luck like you, Dolly." "Poong!" "I've got a hot one," said Mom, fanning a tile like she was putting out a match. "Dangerous. Dangerous." She's got a red dragon. "Aiya." "The wind shifts to the west." "Here comes the green dragon." "The white dragon." "A hot one." "Four circles. Kong!" "Ciao!" shouted Wittman's mother, pouncing on the tile that the See Nigh had discarded. "One, two / three bamboo!" "Mah jeuk birds all in a row." (Is "mah-jongg" a white word, then, like "chop suey," a white food?) "Your mama, one cutthroat," said Auntie Sophie. "You working hard, Wit Man?"

"I've been fired." Let 'em have it.

"Fired!" His mother screamed. "Fired! Fired!"

"It's okay, Ma. I didn't like the job anyway."

"Four years college." Mom put down her tiles. She shut her eyes, a mother defeated. She's an actress. She's acting. You can't trust actors, feel one thing and act another. She put her hand on her brow. Chewed the scenery. "What are we to do?"

The chorus gals snowed her with more comfort. "He'll get a job again, Ruby." "Nowadays they try out jobs, then settle down." "Wit Man be smart. He'll be rich one of these days."

"He read books when he was three years old. Now look at him. A bum—how."

"Don't you worry. He's one good boy." "He be nice and tall." "He always has beautiful gallo friends." "He'll turn out for the better."

He should shut them up with Rilke: *It will be difficult to persuade me that the story of the Prodigal Son is not the legend of him who did not want to be loved. When he was a child, everybody in the house loved him. He grew up knowing nothing else and came to feel at home in their softness of heart, when he was a child.*

But as a boy he sought to lay aside such habits. He could not have put it into words, but when he wandered about outside all day and did not even want to have the dogs along, it was because they too loved him; because in their glances there was observation and sympathy, expectancy and solicitude; because even in their presence one could do nothing without gladdening or giving pain. . . . But then comes the worst. They take him by the hands, they draw him toward the table, and all of them, as many as are present, stretch inquisitively into the lamplight. They have the best of it; they keep in the shadow, while on him alone falls, with the light, all the shame of having a face.

. . . No, he will go away. For example, while they are all busy setting out on his birthday table those badly conceived gifts meant, once again, to compensate for everything. Go away for ever.

O King of Monkeys, help me in this Land of Women.

"And so-o-o much talent, too-o much talent." "He got upbringing, Ruby; you gave him upbringing he cannot lose." "He got foundation." "You one good mother." "He's clean too. Most beardies are dirty." Clackety clack clack. "And such good grades. Remember his report cards?" "He was so cute. Do you still have dock-yee knees, honey boy? You have got to tapdance for your Aunt Lilah again."

Mom's best friends were cheering her up, letting her brag out her happy, proud memories. "I remember, three years old, he made five dollars reading. His father bet a bok gwai lawyer that our biby could read anything. They took the biggest book down from the shelf. He read perfect. 'He's been coached on that book,' said the lawyer, and sent his secretary out to buy a brand-new *Wall Street Journal*. Our Wit Man read the editorial. He won five dollars. We let him keep it. Does he eat regular?" she asked Taña.

"Sure. He eats." Clack!

Does a mother, even an artiste mother who led a free youth, and chose her own husband, does such a mother want her son to have a free artistic life? No. Rimbaud wanted his kids to be engineers.

"You need a job?" asked Auntie Mabel. "I got one gig for you, dear. You come to Florida with me, and do my revue."

"You still doing your revue, Auntie May-bo?"

"Yeah, I do revue. You come, eh, Wit Man. We need a fella in the act."

"In Florida, you dance? You sing?"

"No-o-o. I stand-up comedy. My gals dance and sing. I train them. Miss Chinatown 1959, 1962, and 1963—all in my act." She liked breasts and balls jokes. The punchline: "One hung low. Ha ha." Miss Mabel Foo Yee, the Kookie Fortune Cookie. You had to hand it to her, though. Women aren't funny, and she's still cooking. Cook dinnah, Auntie May-bo. She herself had won beauty contests umpteen years ago. And went on to fan-dance, almost top billing with Miss Toyette Mar, the Chinese Sophie Tucker, and Mr. Stanley Toy, the Fred Astaire of Chinatown, Miss Toby Wing as Ginger, and Prince Gum Low, and Mr. Kwan Tak Hong, the Chinese Will Rogers, who also danced flamenco. Wittman had seen Auntie May-bo topless at Andy Wong's Skyroom. The first tits he'd ever seen, scared the daylights out of him. A blare of brass and a red spotlight—Aunt Mabel had slinked about the Skyroom, snaking her arms and legs like Greta Garbo and Anna May Wong, legs tangoing out of her slit dress. The light shrank to head-size, and the spot held her face. Chopsticks in her hair. False eyelashes blinked hard, and the light went out. She ran about with incense sticks, writing red script in the dark. Red lights flashed on. The front of her dress broke away. Gong. Gong. Lights out. Gong. Lights on. Auntie Mabel stood with arms and naked tits raised at the ceiling. You looked hard for two seconds, the lights went out. Gong. Lights on—she was kneeling with wrists together, tits at ease, eyelashes downcast. Lights out, climactic band music, The End.

She was saying, "My gals, queen of the prom. Court princess, at least. I teach them. Mothers of junior-high gals say to me, 'Start her on her make-up, May-bo.' I teach them hair and dress. They do not go out in blue jeans or with no gloves." Wittman had met some of these trained gals. They looked like young Aunt Mabels. They wore their hair in beehives with a sausage curl or two that hung down over the shoulder. Today Aunt Mabel had on one of her specially ordered Hong Kong dresses. The mandarin collar was frogged tight, but there was a diamond-shaped opening that showed her lace underwear and her old cleavage. Her old thigh flirted through a side slit. There was a lot of perfume in the room, My Sin, Chanel No. 5, Arpège, most of it coming from her. To their credit, no girl of Wittman's college generation would be caught dead in Chinese drag.

"Good you get fired from demeaning employment. You get back into show biz, honey. For you, Aunt Carmen has special ten percent," said Aunt Carmen, a theatrical agent. She sometimes charged twenty percent, twice as much as the regular (white) agents. Her clients, Chinese and Japanese types, who'd gotten SAG cards from *Flower Drum Song* and SEG cards from *Duel in the Sun*, and hopeful ever since, were hard to place. The go-between (white) agent had to make his ten percent too. The actors didn't ask how come these double agents weren't getting 5%–5%. She was up from L.A. to touch base with the talent in the Bay Area and Seattle, and the home folks in the Valley. She had a corner on the West Coast talent. (Auntie Goldie Joy of Manhattan handled the East Coast. The two of them had helped book S. I. Hsiung and his all-Caucasian Chinese opera, starring Harpo Marx and Alexander Woollcott, into theaters in San Francisco and London and New York.)

"You a good type, Wit Man," said Auntie Carmen. "Your gal a good type too. You an actress, darling? Lose ten pounds, you be one actress."

"No, I'm not," said Taña. "I'm an assistant claims adjuster." Why won't she tell them she's a painter?

"We need a man in the act, Wit Man," said Auntie Mabel. "You be interested, huh." Because local boys don't wear tights, Wittman had been the boy brought in from out of town to play the prince. "You were a natural, such good ideas. Tan-ah, you should have seen him, wearing his underpants outside his regular pants, like comic-book superheroes, he said. You got personality, Wit Man." There was a song that went, "Walk personality, talk personality." "Come on. Sometime we play Reno. North Shore Lake Tahoe."

"Auntie Mabel, I like do Shakespeare."

"You snob, Wit Man. You will be hurt and jobless. We have one elegant act. High-class educated gals." Yeah, like Patty (Schoolteacher) White, the stripper in—and out of—cap and gown and eyeglasses. She was showing that you make more money working North Beach than the School District, and you get more appreciation too.

"You join Auntie May-bo's revue," said Mom, "you meet prettier gals."
Clack! Putting the girlfriend in her place.

"I know a girl who would like your boy," said the See Nigh, who didn't
speak English. "She came from Hong Kong only a month ago, and already
has a job. Her sponsor pulls influence, and her papers are legal. She's a very
good old-fashioned, traditional girl. Not in this country long enough to be
spoiled. She'll make a good wife."

"Listen to See Nigh, Wit Man," said Mother. "A Chinese girl like that
doesn't like beards. You be one Beatnik, you scare her away. You be clean-
cut All-American Ivy-Leak boy, okay?"

"I've got a daughter I hope she won't marry somebody second-rate,"
said Auntie Marleese. "Gail is so smart, professors gave her a personal invitation to attend Stanford University, and pay her to go there. You know
S.A.T.? Best S.A.T. in California. Ten thousand points. Pre-med. Her
teachers tell me that they never taught a more intelligent girl."

"You still not get Gail married yet?" said Auntie Doll. Clack! The
showgirls had been young when it was smart to be catty.

"My Betty," said Auntie Lily Rose, "made valedictorian again. *And* she
is popular. *And* she is the first Chinese girl president of her parachute club.
She never told me she jumps out of airplanes till after her one hundredth
jump. She had to tell me, she landed on her face. Still pretty but. Only
chipped her tooth. She said, 'I saved the altimeter.' Any of you know of a
good boy, help settle her down?"

Wittman ought to say, "Bring me your daughters. I'll talk to them with
my hom sup mouth and touch them with my hom sup hands. Hom sup
sup." A hom sup lo is a salty drippy pervert.

"Come on, honey boy," called Auntie Bessie. "Tapdance for us. You
the cutest most dock-yee fatcheeks. Tan-ah, did he tell you he's one great
soft shoe? Come on, Wit Man, do some soft shoe, huh?" They remember,
he had taken classes in Good Manners and Tap Dance at Charlie Low's
school. Eddie Pond of the Kubla Khan had also sponsored schools, and
given to the community his expertise in engineering, insurance, real estate,
and law. The showmen competed to be most socially responsible.

"No, thanks, Auntie Bessie."

Auntie Bessie sang, " 'I won't dance. Don't ask me. I won't dance.
Don't ask me. I won't dance, monsieur, with yo-o-ou.' Not even for your
favorite aunt, honey boy?"

"Hey, Auntie Bessie, do you still say Yow!?" She had played Laurie in the Chinese Optimist Club production of *Oklahoma*. And sang and danced in all the best Big City clubs—Eddie Pond's Kubla Khan, Charlie Low's Forbidden City, Fong Wan the Herbalist's, Andy Wong's Chinese Skyroom. Benny Goodman and Duke Ellington had swung in those clubs too. " 'Okla—, Okla—, Okla—,' " sang Wittman to start her off.

" 'And when we sa-a-ay Yow!' " Auntie Bessie was on her feet. " 'Yow! A yip I yo I yay! we're only sayin' you're doin' fine, Oklaho-ma. Oklaho-ma, okay.' " She had worn a white lace Laurie dress with a half-dozen petticoats, and wigged out her hair with black ringlets. She held her hands over her heart, and sang some more,

> *"Don't sigh and gaze at me.*
> *Your sighs are so like mine.*
> *Your eyes musn't glow like mine.*
> *People will say we're in love.*
> *Don't throw bo-kays at me.*
> *Don't please my folks too much.*
> *Don't laugh at my jokes too much."*

" 'Who laughs at *yer* jokes?' " said Wittman as Curly.

" 'People will say we're in love.' " He had fallen in love with her himself. She'd kept her stage make-up on for the cast party. He had stood beside her at the community sing around the piano, and saw her powdery wrinkles. Off stage, she sang and smoked at once. "Don't daa de dada daah? Line? Line?"

Taña sang her the line in the sweetest voice, " 'Don't dance all night with me.' "

"Oh, Tan-ah can sing," said the aunties. "Good, help out."

Taña and Bessie sang together.

> *"Till the stars fade from above.*
> *They'll see it's all right with me."*

And all the showgirls chimed in, " 'People will say we're in love.' "

"Good, Bessie!" "Ho, la!" "Bessie just as good as ever." "Good, Tan-ah!" "Wit Man, you never said she's show business."

"She's not. She's an assistant claims adjuster."

"Thank you, Tan-ah," said Auntie Bessie.

"Thank *you*, Auntie Bessie," said Taña. "You have a beautiful voice."

"Tan-ah, I tell you," said Aunt Dolly, "that voice of Bessie's bought an airplane for World War II."

"And the rest of us too," said Aunt Sophie, "we were stars. We put on so many shows, and so many people paid to watch us dance and sing, we raised enough money to buy an airplane."

"We toured nationwide," said Aunt Lily Rose. "We had the most active chapter of the Association of Vaudeville Artistes."

"Remember? Remember we were dancers in the Dance of the Nations," said Auntie Mabel. "We each did a solo to honor our brave allies. I was Miss France."

"I was Miss Great Britain," said Ruby Long Legs.

"I was Miss Belgium," said Aunt Sondra.

"I was Miss Russia," said Aunt Lilah.

"I was Miss China," said Aunt Bessie.

"I was Miss Finlandia," said Aunt Maydene.

"I was Miss U.S.A.," said Aunt Sadie, who had been with another Jadine, Jadine Wong and her Wongettes, those dancing Chinese cuties.

"Money was not all that we raised," said Aunt Lilah, winking at Wittman. She had danced with petite Noel Toy and the Toyettes.

"We had a painting party," said Aunt Carmen, "and painted our airplane—a Chinese flag and an American flag—red, white, and blue."

"We painted across our airplane in Chinese and English: California Society to Rescue China," said Auntie Marleese, swooping her hand like a rainbow. "And we did, too—rescued China and won World War II."

"Auntie Bessie's brother flew it to China and became a Flying Tiger," said Auntie Jean. "And is now a pilot for China Airlines."

"Hungry, Ma," said Wittman. "What's there to eat?"

"Go eat," said Mother. "So help yourself. Sow mahng mahng." "Mahng mahng" is the sound of being skinny. "Fai dut dut" and "fai doot doot" are the sounds of being fat. "Eat. Eat. Don't wait for us."

Wittman grabbed Taña's hand, and beat it to the kitchen.

There were cartons and covered dishes on every surface, more warming in the oven, and more cooling in the refrigerator. The cartons came from the restaurants which some aunties owned and some hostessed, queens of nightlife. When you're out on the town, your rep for setting it on fire depends on them treating you and your gal right. Also, when an actor loses his will to audition, they give him a meal on the house. The food in cartons was courtesy of the chefs, letting themselves go, back-home cooking that they don't do for the customers.

"You must be very hungry," said Taña, watching Wittman load his plate. "It was getting really interesting in there. I want to tell them about *my* airplane."

"World War II was where I came in. I've heard their war stories so many times. How Mom and the aunties used their beauty to get this country to go to war, to rescue ladies-in-distress, who looked, for example, like themselves. The next thing, they'll tell about their parades that stretched from one end of the country to the other and stopped the U.S. selling scrap iron to Japan. And Auntie Doll will do her speech about buying war bonds instead of opium. Taña, you'll never meet people who love working unless they're in show business. They used to have work that they loved. Now they're housewives who have nothing better to do than sit around all day playing mah-jongg until they die. It's tragic."

Taña was looking at him out of sanpaku eyes. He'd been aware all along that she was gwutting his family with that scrutiny from another world. Judy Garland has sanpaku eyes, too much eyewhite under the irises, and John Lennon does too. Elvis and Brando act like their eyes are sanpaku by looking out from lowered heads. Over her chow mein, Taña was feyly giving him lots of eyewhite. If she says "dragon ladies," definitely divorce.

"What's so tragic about mah-jongg?" she asked. "It keeps them home. They're not out escalating our involvement in Southeast Asia." Taña's E.S.P. almost let her foresee that Auntie May-bo, Miss Australia Down Under, would take her troupe to Viet Nam.

"You don't have to be so understanding. The highpoint of a life shouldn't be a war. At the war rallies, they performed their last, then the theater died. I have to make a theater for them without a war."

"They would love to perform again, I know it. Your mother and Lily Rose and Peggy and Aunt Bessie—they're still pretty, and want to show it off. I'm sorry; I'm not going to say 'still pretty' about old people anymore. That's like 'She's pretty—for an old lady,' 'He's hard-working—for a Negro.' Some women *get* pretty in old age. I plan to be that way."

"Did you recognize any of them? You can see them on the late show. Peggy played Anna May Wong's maid, when Anna May Wong wasn't playing the maid herself. Come here. I want you to meet a respectable member of my family. I have a granny. She hates mah-jongg. She's not invited to the front room. Why don't we bring her some food?"

They carried plates and bowls to the back of the house, where he called at a door, "PoPo, tadaima-a-a," Japanese. No little-old-lady voice answered, "Okaerinasai." She had taught him more phrases than that, but when he tried them out on Japanese speakers, they didn't seem to mean anything. She spoke language of her own, or she was holding on to a language that was once spoken somewhere, or she was more senile than she appeared. Wittman opened the door, but no little old pipe-smoking lady there. They put the dishes on her coffee table, and sat on her settee and her footstool. The room was webbed with lace that she tatted from thread. The light made shadow webs, everything woofing and wefting in circles and spirals, daisies, snowflakes, the feather eyes of white peacocks. Well, if you're going to be a string-saver, you can do better than roll it up into a ball. He opened the windows and started the room buoying and drifting.

GrandMaMa owned a phonograph but mostly Cantonese opera and "Let's Learn English" records. There were pictures of little Wittman in his disguises—sumo wrestler, Injun with fringe, the Invisible Man (which he had worn only once because everybody felt bad for "the poor burned boy"), opera monkey. "Are you supposed to be a monkey?" asked Taña. "Not 'supposed to be.' I *am*," said Wittman. "That's true," laughed Taña. Pictures of aunties shaking hands with F.D.R. and Truman. A girl—Jade Snow Wong?—christening a liberty ship at the Marin Shipyards. The thermos of hot water sat next to tea glasses, which were jelly glasses caked with what looked like dry dirt. "Want some tea?" Wittman offered. "It's supposed to look like that. You're supposed to let the tea residue keep accumulating." Against the day when you can't afford tea leaves? So when you drink water, it Zenly reminds you of tea? "Like a wooden salad bowl," he explained.

"No, thanks anyway," she said, which was all right. He didn't want a girl who would gulp it right down saying, "How interesting. How Zen. Say something Chinese."

They sat quiet. He did not turn on the t.v. to watch some Sunday sport. Taña was probably picturing his grandmother as an old bride—Miss Havisham—or a spider woman. They lit up smokes. He hadn't smoked in front of Mom, who would've said, "Quit, you. You quit."

"Your grandmother's in show business too." Taña was looking at the memory village on the dresser. It did look like a stage designer's model for a set. There were rows of houses with common walls, like railroad flats of New York, like shotgun apartments of the Southwest, except no doors from home to home. The rows were separated by alleys, which were labeled with street names. Two of the houses had thatch stick roofs that opened up; ladders led to lofts. The rungs were numbered; the adobe steps with only two-risers were also numbered, one, two. One of the houses had a brick stove; the next-door had two stoves. Toy pigs, numbered, lived inside the houses and walked in the alleys. The rich man's house had a larger courtyard and more wings than the others, plus flowered tiles, and parades or boatloads of people and animals atop the horn-curved eaves. In the plaza was a well, and beside the well (where PoPo had fetched water) was the temple (where the men whistled at her and made remarks, and she dropped and broke her water jar, and the men laughed). Away from the houses was the largest building, the music building for the storage and playing of drums and horns. There were numbers on the lanes and paths out to the fields. It was autumn; the fields were shades of gold. One of the fields was edged with thirty-three lichee trees. "Twenty of those trees belonged to my great-great-uncle," said Wittman, "and three of them belonged to my great-grand-father. He didn't plant them or ever see them. He sent the money to grow them; some autumns his family thought of him, and mailed him dried lichee. Near harvest time, the boys, my cousins far removed, stayed awake nights guarding the trees with a loaded gun." A bridge went over a stream. Above the rice fields was a pumpkin patch and a graveyard. "People from this village don't like Hallowe'en or pumpkin pie. They've eaten too much of it. Pumpkins were the only crop that hardly ever failed. Like your Irish potatoes. People's skin turned orange from eating nothing but pumpkins. Slanty-eyed jack-o'-lanterns. I used to run Crackerjack cars on the paths, and boats on the rivers. Should the I.N.S.—Immigration—raid this room, looking for illegals, they can take this model as evidence, and deport our asses. Everybody who claimed to have come from here studied this model, and described it to Immigration. It is not a model *of* anything, do you understand? It's a memory village." He slid the model onto his open hand and held it like a birthday cake. "This is it. My land. I am a genie who's escaped from the bottle city of Kandor. I have told you immigration secrets. You can blackmail me. And make me small again, and stopper me up. But if I don't have a friend to tell them to, where am I?"

"Thank you, Wittman. I won't tell."

"Thank you. I'm trusting you with my life, Taña, and my grandma's life." But he was holding out on her the documentation. In PoPo's Gold Mountain trunk was the cheat sheet, a scroll like a roll of toilet paper with questions and answers about the people and the pigs who lived in those houses. Nobody had destroyed the scroll or the memory village. Wonder why.

"This room smells like a grandma's room," said Tañn. "I have two grandmas, and their houses smell like this. Tell me when I get the old-lady smell, Wittman. Or do they get it from using a powder that's out of fashion? Orrisroot, lavender."

"Salonpas. The old lady who lives here may not be my grandmother. She showed up one day, and we took her in. I've tested her for her background: I watched for her to hurt herself, and heard what she said for 'Ouch!' She said, 'Bachigataru.' Japanese. At New Year's, she doesn't go to the post office to have her green card renewed, so either she's an illegal alien or she's a regular citizen. The night she showed up she brought news about relatives that we shouldn't have lost touch with. My parents acted like they understood her, 'Yes, the cousins.' 'Of course, the village.' 'Yes, three ferries west of the city, there live cousins and village cousins. Anybody knows that.' They didn't let on that they'd lost their Chinese. You want to know another secret? She may be my father's other wife, and they're putting one over on my mom. Not to get it on sexually, she's old, but so that my mom will take care of her." The strange old lady pulled her apron to her back, a cape, and hung a twenty-four-carat gold medallion to her front, a breastplate, and belted herself with a twenty-four-carat gold buckle shield. Waving fans of dollar bills, she danced whirlygiggly the way they danced where she came from. They couldn't very well turn her away.

He wandered in back of her shoji screens, opened her closet, walked into her bathroom. No grandma dead or alive. Her long pipe was gone; her shoes were nowhere to be found. In the medicine cabinet was his grandfather's safety razor. He wet his moustache and beard, soaped up, and shaved his face clean. "That ought to freak my mother out," he said. "How do I look?"

"You look better," said Tañn. So why is she looking at herself in the mirror instead? She ought to be touching and kissing his nude face. *In any case I felt a certain shyness . . . such as one feels before a mirror in front of which someone is standing.*

"My mom hasn't seen my face for a while. I'm going to give her a break. She's my mother, after all, and has a right to see her son's face."

"Wittman, answer me something," said Tañn. "Honestly. Promise?"

"Yes. What?"

"What does 'pahng yow' mean? You called me that to your mother."

Uh-oh, thought Wittman.

"It doesn't mean 'wife,' does it?"

"No, it means 'friend.' Let's go. I'm ready to smoothface my mother."

Holding hands with his wife and friend, he led her back to the mah-jongg games. He did not let go of her hand.

"Ma, what do you think?" he asked, poking his clean-shaven face in front of her mah-jongg tiles.

"What do I think about what?" said Ruby. "You eat enough, Wit Man? You looking skinny."

He straightened up, tucking his wife's hand under his arm. "Ma, where's PoPo?"

"Out."

"Whereabouts?"

"To the Joang Wah to see a movie."

"I'll go pick her up, give her a car ride back." Leave home, come back visit, give the old folks a ride.

"No need. She'll get a car ride."

"I'll pick her up anyway."

"She may not be there. She does errands."

"She's not in an old-age home, is she, Ma? You didn't dump her? She's not dead?" Said in front of the aunties, who were all ears.

"She's alive. Strike *you* dead for saying such a thing."

"She isn't really at the movies. Where is she?"

"Wit Man, I have taken good care of her for twenty years." Arranging her tiles. Gin.

"Ruby took in a poor stranger lady, and gave her food and a home," said Aunt Lilah.

"The money you spent on her," said Auntie Jadine, "you sacrificed your own pleasures." Her commadres were helping Mom out giving her back-up. Certain aunties who were present needed to loudly let everyone know that they were against bringing a grandma over from China to be a charwoman. *They* hadn't talked *their* old lady into signing her Hong Kong building over to them, then selling it to pay for her expenses in America.

"And I taught her a skill," said Ma. "She can run wardrobe anywhere." Grandma had earned her keep, mending costumes, ironing, sleeping in dressing rooms as dark-night security watchwoman.

"Oh, you're too kind, Ruby." "Ruby has a big heart. Big-hearted Ruby —what they call you behind your back."

"Okay, Ma," said Wittman. "Where is she?"

"Your father has her."

"He took her camping?"

"He has to take care of her too. He has to take responsibility. She's from *his* side."

He walked to the door, pulling his lady with him. "I'm going to find her."

"I took responsibility long enough," shouted Ruby. "You find her, you the one responsible. You never took too much responsibility before. What for you care about the old lady all of a sudden?"

"I want to announce something to her. We gotta go. Bye, everybody."

"Tan-ah, go so soon?" "Stay, Wit Man." "Don't go already." "You going?" "Stay eat with us." "Kiss auntie goodbye." "What you announcing?" "Where you going so fast, young man?"

"Going on our honeymoon. Bye."

Out to the porch and gate and street, chasing the bride and groom, came the voices and the clacking. "Your what?" "Eeek!" "What'd he say?" "They married." "Who?" "Congratulations, honey boy." "Happy long life, Tan-ah!"

"Married!" shouted Wittman. "Goodbye, Mrs. Ah Sing!" called Taña. "Thank you for the delicious luncheon."

Taña got in on the driver's side, her turn at the wheel. "Steve McQueen taught me how to drive," she said, and peeled away from the curb. She took her passenger's cigarette, and sucked hard on it. "Let's go to Grandma's rescue." She sped out of town. Her pointy nose cut into the wind, born for a convertible. He directed her to the American River. At the turn-off, she did a double-clutch downshift from the highway to the frontage road. Her hair was blowing back, a giant brush of a mane painting the hills its own color.

"You're the only one who noticed I shaved," he said. "See how neglectful of her family my mother is? I wouldn't put it past her to give Grandma the old heave-ho."

"You have the same custom as Eskimos?" asked Taña. "You have a 'leading out of the old citizen'? I read that in William Burroughs."

"I don't know. How many times does something have to be done for it to be a tradition? There has to be ceremony. You can't just toss a grandmother on an iceberg, and run. Eskimos probably had an aloha ceremony with torches and honors, and the old citizen sat on a lit-up birthday cake of ice. She would feel bad without her farewell."

"And her body heat warms up her piece of glacier. It breaks off, calves, and Grandma is riding away on a white calf. Like Europa. It melts, and she falls into the water and has ecstasy of the deep." She put her hands over her eyes. He took the wheel, steering from the side until she got a-hold of herself.

"Thanks," she said.

Once Wittman saw the inside of an old-age home, a board-and-care. The beautiful aunties were dancing. The t.v. set had been left on out of respect for those whose heads were turned toward it. Out of a mouth hole with no teeth, an old guy farted, "Niggers." His face and eyes hadn't looked like he meant it. He hadn't meant anything; vibes from other people who had sat in that same padded wheelchair had come emanating out of it and through his body and out of his open mouth. "Nigger" is in the American air and will use any zombie mouth. Bust Grandma out of a place like that.

"Aren't you going to tell me anything about your dad?" asked Taña. "I could use some preparation."

"His name's Zeppelin."

"Who?"

"Zeppelin."

"Like in dirigible?"

"It's a perfectly respectable Chinese-American given name. Spondaic, heroic, presidential. Say your poems to him. He'll like you. He likes unusual people. You guys are really going to get along. He's the one started me on my trips. He used to play this hand organ that he won off a Gypsy for the line in front of theaters. He cranked out music, like grinding rice or coffee or wringing the wash. He didn't need music lessons. But where to put the money box? He tried leaving a guitar case open at his feet, but people are too shy to come up during the concert. They don't like to interrupt. They can toss coins, they can't toss bills. But the music's over, they go, forget to pay. And passing a hat unaccompanied, they take money out. A helper to follow the hat has to be paid. So he made little Wittman his money monkey. He paid me in peanuts. You don't have to split the take with the monkey, which is cute in itself. People like to give it money and watch its fingers take the coins, and it bites the coins with its teeth. Nowadays he does a lot of fishing. He watches 'American Bandstand' with the sound off."

On Slough Road, they passed houseboats, fishing boats, a two-room motel For Sale, piers, rafts, truck-size inner tubes, all attached to the shore. Beyond the settled part of the river, Wittman looked for a tree with familiar clothes in its branches. There. Pop's river camp. Two bird cages with a java finch in each swung side by side. A pick-up truck, hood up like its mouth open for dental work, was connected by jumper cables to a V.W., wings

open for its backseat battery. Neither engine was running; the truck had
drained the bug battery. Fishing poles were staked at the water. Taña parked
behind the mobile home, from which came masculine rumble and laughter;
you feel like a child listening to the wolf-bear sounds of Father and men
friends. Does a girl walking into this camp think about raping sites? The
trailer bounced on its shocks and springs. "Son of a bitchee!" That was Pop;
he'd learned to swear from Harry S. Truman. "Naygemagehai!" That was
Uncle Bingie saying, "Your mother's cunt!" "Say lo! Say, la!" Uncle Saga-
cious Jack losing, and shouting about death. "Kill the commies!" Big Uncle
Constant Fong winning. (He used to yell, "Kill the japs!," slap down his
cards, scoop up his money. If it weren't for the Japanese and the red-hot
communists, these old futs would have lost their spirit.) "My pop and his
friends are gambling," Wittman explained. "Poker."

He led the way through the grass to the open door of the trailer, Taña
behind and to the side of him. Be careful not to trip over the siphoning
hoses and extension cords, which were circulating juices from buckets and
machines to other buckets and machines. A cookout grill sat level on top of
black rocks. Pot-shaped rice crusts drying in the screenbox. Father is a
string-baller and rice-crust saver. The shouting stopped. Ha! Got the drop
on the old futs. We could have been robbers, County Sheriff's men, Immigration, Fish and Game.

"Wittman. Just my son," said Pop by way of greeting.

"Hi, Ba. Hello, Uncles."

"Eh."

"Um."

"Haw."

They won; he had said Hello, and they had cleared a throat, snorted,
breathed hard. Don't want to make you feel too good. He used to think it
was because they didn't approve of him for something, such as his beard, or
his studying liberal arts. But who knows what it was. General badness.

"Go sit down by the river," said Pop. "Room by the river. Have some
crackers and juice." He reached into the cooler and handed out orange soda
and strawberry soda. He didn't know the difference between soda and juice.
The soda companies take advantage of people like that.

Sitting next to the fishing poles, Wittman said, "This is his hospitality.
A seat, refreshments. He likes you. Otherwise, he'd chase us away." Taña
was drinking the orange soda. Wittman drank the strawberry, which tasted
like tobacco.

"Blonde queen of my heart, come to me at last!" yelled Big Uncle Constant. "Haw! Haw!" "Ho! Ho! Ho!" Had he picked up another queen, or was he teasing Wittman about his girlfriend? For laughs, the old futs liked to jump out from behind doors and trees and scare the shit out of a kid. That was their idea of playing with kids. I'm too old for that now, you old futs.

The young futs leaned back in their lawn chairs, looking at the river go by, looking at each other. The smell of anise and spearmint, the smell of bay laurel, like a childhood day of licorice and chewing gum. A bee-loud glade. Pop's rowboat tried to follow the current, but was tied to a mulberry tree. A gold rocker was catching and cradling whatever came tumbling by. We are water rats under the willows, which Valley Cantonese call skunk trees because we are realistic. Wind in the skunk trees and the shiverleaf aspens. The mulberry tree was dripping with purple earrings. Autumn.

"I ought to quit my job," said Taña. "Wittman, we ought to stop going to parties, and live on a houseboat. Eat catfish and crayfish and mustard greens."

The river breeze blew her hair across his eyes; through it, he saw the spanking-gold California sun hitting the blues and greens of the river, the reeds, and her beautiful sanpaku eyes. The river passed on and on.

What could come by now is a small ship, a spy ship from China, playing music. Because whoever controls music has the world spinning on the palm of his hand. Like a dreydl, like a wish-fairy. There's a plum-wine party on board. Cho Cho, now a fifty-four-year-old water rat with narrow eyes and a long thin beard, is standing alone on the prow. He makes up a song: "I built a casita, where springs and summers I might have studied my books, autumns and winters, have a home after hunting. I might have had a tranquil life but for news of the wedding of a certain woman, and news of war. Aiya, I am sad. I wasted my life at war. The ravens fly across the moon; they circle the trees, and find no nest." A guest comes up on deck, and Cho Cho asks him, "Why are the ravens cawing and knocking in the middle of the night?" "The moon is so bright, they think it's day. Don't sing such a sad song." The V of the raven's tail does not stand for "victory" in their language. "You don't like my poetry then?" says Cho Cho. For he is a warrior poet like Mao Tse Tung and a warrior actor like Chou En Lai. "What's wrong with it?" he says. His guest, a good man who has re-built farm communities and schools, says, "On the night before battle, you shouldn't sing discouraging words." Cho Cho drops his spear to fighting level, and runs the critic through. The ship sails on, flying the Big Dipper and the North Star, a flag of the night sky to guide him day and night.

And after the ship of spies and music comes Marilyn Monroe pushing and pulling the tiller of her boat with all her body, and singing "The River of No Return." Strange people—cat women, sandmen, castle builders—denizen the islands of the Delta. And some of them are one's relations, who have to be explained.

"That thing is a gold rocker. My father made it. It works. He's found gold in it. Zep had a big moment in his life. He found a gold boulder in the roots of an upturned tree. It came up out of the water like an arm and a hand with gold in its fingers, and handed it to him, a gift from the Mi-Wuks. Zeppelin Ah Sing started the Jamestown gold rush. He found his boulder in Chinese Camp, but told the newspapers it was Jimtown so as to decoy the rush away from the mother lode. He came home carrying his bird cage in one hand, and his gold boulder—like the head in *Night Must Fall* —in the other. He was living with his pet bird, inside an abandoned mine 'for free, at no cost,' he said to the newspapers. 'Americans never be homeless,' he says. Take over the mines that the Caucasians have given up on—they've done the hard digging, ha ha on them. His birds test the air. They live in thousand-year-old cages with Ming Dynasty porcelain seed and water cups. All a Chinese guy has to do is to hang out his bird, and he feels like an emperor at leisure in his castle. They think birds sing because they're happy. My dad emigrated to Australia once—'took my birds to Australia'—but came back in six months because one of the birds died; there had been two of them, twin thrushes. Gold spoiled him for regular ambition. He lives from gold find to gold find."

An especially loud uproar of swearing came from the trailer. Triumph. Losses. Zeppelin went into the bushes to piss, which you could hear. Then he came over and hunkered down next to the pretty girl for a smoke. He looked like Mescalito on the cover of the *Oracle*.

The beauty spot on a lucky part of his face, near his mouth, meant that he will always have enough to eat; if the spot were at the center of his lip, he'd have more, but he didn't want more.

"Lose?" asked Wittman, the concerned son.

"One game."

"That's what you get for playing with Uncle Bingie." Gordon (Bingie) Young Ah Doc was pit boss at the Emeryville gambling.

"Win the next. Straighten your collar. Bums wear collar up." Wittman flattened his collar. Humor the old fart, who's going to die before me. "Don't wear striped shirts, I tell you. Make you look like one prisoner. Ex-con. Bum-how." Enough already.

"I'm not wearing a striped shirt."

His father patted the collar. "Keep your collar down."

"It's nice here, Ba. Rent free."

"No. A farmer owns this land. Every piece of land belongs to somebody. You know that? The river is owned. You hear of Eminent Domain? When we got rid of King George, we should have got rid of Eminent Domain. When I die, don't pay the death tax."

"I won't. You aren't gonna die, Ba." Wittman could return affection as good as the next guy.

"Farmers have guns. If the farmer finds me, I have to pay rent."

"That's too bad."

"I'll change my parking space. Yeah, I want to stay here for the rest of my life. I'm too old to live in mines. What you been up to? You okay? Not spending too much?"

"Yeah. Okay."

"You like tea?" His father had brought out a tea tray. Very courteous of him, giving humble respect. Taña probably thinks it's like getting coffee.

"Yes, please," she said.

The teapot had been steeping in the sun. Pop poured everyone's, removed the lid, put one of the teabags on the spoon, looped the string around spoon and bag, and pulled, squeezing dark tea into his cup. A Depression trick no doubt, cheap Chang.

Taña fished up another bag, looped, squeezed. Dark tea pissed out. "The last drop," she said. Yes, Taña, he's living fully. A really Chang guy would've made one bag do for the entire tea party. Wittman dunked his bag a couple of times, and put it sloppy wet on the tray, Diamond Jim.

"Is this Indian tea?" asked Taña.

"Do you think I look Injun?" asked Zeppelin, who was wearing his turquoise belt buckle. "Some say I look Italian." He was proud to be taken for whatever, especially by one of their own kind, Mexican, Filipino. His favorite, he'd been asked by a Basque once near Gardenerville, "You Basque?" "I'm pure Chinese," he told Taña. "A pure Chinese can look Injun, Basque, Mexican, Italian, Gypsy, Pilipino." Wittman thought of Pop whenever he heard, "Some say he's black, but I know he's bonny."

"Teabags aren't a Chinese custom," said Zeppelin. "I tell you a tea custom before communists. There once was a kind of teacup with a lid. A poor man would catch a sparrow, and bring it to a teahouse. Waiting for the waiter, he put the bird inside the empty cup. The waiter opens up the lid to pour, and the bird flies out. Then the poor man says, 'Look what you've done. That was my valuable pet bird. You let it fly away. You have to pay me for my bird.' The waiter says it was a common sparrow. The poor man says, 'It was a rare almost-extinct species that flew away so fast, it looked like a sparrow to you. You owe me free tea, at least.' That's why we have the custom to lift the lid ourselves.

"I've got a new one for you, Wittman. Next time you order a cup of tea, ask for lemon, and get the whole lemon. The other day in town, I tried it. First, I paid my bill, then I waited at the cash register. The waitress said, 'Something else?'

"I said, 'Where's my lemon?'

" 'Pardon me?' the waitress said, as if she didn't understand my English.

" 'You forget the rest of my lemon?' I said.

" 'What lemon?'

" 'I ordered tea with lemon. You gave me a slice, in fact, one very thin slice. Where's the rest of my lemon?'

" 'It's in the kitchen, I guess.' Acting dumb blonde.

" 'Are you going to get it for me?' I was polite.

"She got mad. 'I should go and get the rest of the lemon? You want the whole lemon? We don't sell whole lemons. You get a slice, and another customer gets another slice. That lemon's not there anymore. It's been sliced up, and used already.'

"I said, 'Don't bully me, young woman. Your menu says, "Tea with lemon." ' I showed the menu to her and to everybody. 'What does it say? Can you read? It does not say part of a lemon. If you mean part of a lemon, you write part of a lemon on your menu. You are selling my lemon to other customers. I don't care which lemon you give me, I just want a lemon, one slice out okay.'

" 'She said, 'One lemon has to go around for ten or twelve customers.'

" 'You feed a dozen customers at my expensive.'

"She went in back, and got the manager. I had to explain it over again. 'Does the menu say tea with slice of lemon? No. It says tea with lemon. I paid fifteen cents for my tea and lemon. All I ask is the rest of my lemon. In the market, lemons are fifteen cents for two. Here I should get one lemon for that dear price.' Everybody in the diner was listening. I teach them a lesson.

"The manager said, 'You get a slice. Everybody gets a slice.'

"I repeated many times, 'I want the whole lemon. I paid for the whole lemon. I'll leave when you give me my lemon. I have a right to it.'

"He ordered the waitress to go get it, and gave me about three-fourths of a lemon, not eleven-twelfths, a compromise but all right. Lemonade for a week. You ought to try it. That's the lemon you're using right now. You understand, it's not just the lemon but the principle of the thing."

What principle of what thing? When you live in the wilds too long, and go to town, you have to boss waitresses around? Waitresses and clerks are not for giving a bad time to.

"I saw Ma," said Wittman.

"She okay?"

"Yeah. I didn't see PoPo, though. Where is she?"

"Most likely she is not your grandmama."

"Don't matter. Where is she?"

"Ee, chotto," he said in her language.

"Tell me what you did with her."

"I drove her to Reno." He was trying to sound like a good guy who took her on a vacation.

"Where is she now?"

"Maybe Reno still."

"What do you mean maybe?"

"You know your popo, she likes her gambling. She likes her gambling too much."

"You left her there?"

"I looked all over, she didn't show up. I waited, she didn't show up. It wasn't my idea, go to Reno. Your popo said, 'Let's go on a drive and picnic.' She likes that place where you can first see the Lake from the top of the mountains. We get up there—no snow, good weather for one last picnic—and she says, 'I brought my savings. Let's go gamble.' And your ma says, 'Look out. She's tricking us to gamble.' I say, 'You women argue, I dump you at Donner Pass.' Your ma, you know your ma, says, 'How you afford to gamble, PoPo, and not pay rent? How much money did you bring?' 'All,' says PoPo. 'I bring every savings I got. I an old lady can spend all.' I had to be good to her. Her last gambling trip. I drove her down to Reno."

"And dumped her there?"

"I tell you, not dump."

"Dumped."

"I like my blackjack. Your ma likes her odd-even red-black roulette wheel. Your popo likes her machines. She said, 'Amscray.' We split up. When we get back to the truck, she's not there and she's not there. Then we figure, she showed up from nowhere one day long ago, she goes away now. She lived okay by herself before she found us. Everybody has to learn to take care of herself. PoPo is self-reliant. And she has advantages—waterproof matches, fatwood kindling, Army surplus kit. Nevada one rich state from the gambling industry. Good libraries. Good services for the old folks."

"Didn't you look for her?"

"We waited."

"I'm going to look for her, Ba."

"Up to you. What you say her name is?" Pointing a thumb at his unbeknownst daughter-in-law.

"Taña."

"Taña, nice car you have. Please, may I borrow it?"

"Where are you going? Are you going to get your mother?"

"I'm not going. I want to jump-start Bingie's little V.W. Then he can drive to the junkyard, and find me a battery for the truck."

"Okay," said Taña. She backed her car up to the V.W.'s free side. Zeppelin disconnected the jumper cables from the pick-up. He crawled into the bug's backseat to adjust the clamps and arrange the cables out the other door. Then he will open up Taña's rear lid, and clamp her anode and her cathode. If there was one thing that bored Wittman to death it was hanging around while people worked on their cars. He had a block against memorizing what was carburetor, what was motor, where the oil went, what wire to stick where for a hot-wire job, though he had spent years saying, "Uh-huh, uh-huh," while handing pliers, wrenches, screwdrivers to friends. He had hoped that those adolescent days were over. He went for a walk along the river, left the mechanics signaling at one another from behind their wheels. He heard the car almost start, die, almost start.

One Christmas day in a big city where it snowed, maybe New York or Chicago, he and his father were walking through a train station. A man in a ragged coat moved away from the pole he was leaning against. His hand came out of a pocket, and brought out a toy, a plastic horse. "Say thank you," said Ba. "Say Merry Christmas." The three of them shook hands Merry Christmas all around. Wittman held the toy horse, and watched the man walk out of the station. His father said, "He's Santa Claus. That was Santa Claus." Then they were in an elevator with an old man, who kept looking at Wittman. As all of them were getting off, the old man gave him a little green car with wheels that turned. His father said, "That's another Santa Claus. He be Santa Claus too." And out on the street, a lone man reached inside his coat, and gave him a stocking bag of candy. Many Santa Clauses. Santa Claus is a bum-how, and he does not have a sack full of toys. These men's pockets were not bulgy with more presents for other boys and girls. They hadn't had a family or a home; they had had enough money for one toy, and they'd gone out into the city to celebrate Christmas by choosing one boy to give the gift to. Because of his haircut and clothes or his Chinese face or his Chinese father, they chose him.

Teen-age time, he stopped going places with his father out of shame. He ought to give him a thrill, and make the rounds with him one of these days. Appreciate a father who doesn't dictate much, nor hit, drink, nor hang around having habits that use up all the room.

Januaries, they had gone to American banks and stores to collect calendars of the solar year; Februaries, to Chinese banks and stores to collect calendars of the moon year. On the pages of time—Gwan Goong, god of gamblers, beautiful Hong Kong girls, faery girls who float among birds and bats and flowers, kids riding on deer. The world is full of free stuff. The three-hundred-and-sixty-five-page calendar. The food in back of supermarkets. His father hoisted him into the garbage bins, where he handed out cheese in plastic, cereal in boxes that the grocer had slit whilst opening the shipping carton, day-old bread, pies in tinfoil pans. Bread gets a week old at home anyway before you get to the end of the loaf, right? At the state legislature, probably of every state, you can get all the scratch paper you want— the bills that didn't pass, and the ones that did pass and were acted on already, stapled together into legal-size notepads, print but on one side—moundfuls tossed into the basement. A day out with Pop was filled with presents. The world was a generous place.

Another outing, he and Pop had gotten themselves invited to some kind of a club. In the men's room, they filled their pockets with combs, razor blades, tiny tubes of toothpaste. It hadn't been that fancy a club, no valet. Pop hadn't lifted the silver shoehorn, but the two of them had taken off their shoes, and horned them back on. Wittman, playing rich man, had left a check for a trillion godzillion dollars.

When he went to live in Berkeley, his father showed up, and took him to the back of India Imports. They recovered enough stuff to decorate his room, a madras bedspread with a stripe that hadn't taken the dye. Pop got a poncho, and Wittman, a sweater from Brazil, a strand had unraveled. The singleton earrings he took for hanging in the window. Never buy a bed, you can always take in a mattress from off the street. Find it before it rains. His school desk was a card table, one of many he's found by the curb. Must be gamblers throw them out if they get unlucky. Eat in cafeterias where the condiments are on the outside of the cash register. You buy a serving of rice or some bread, and then you load up with relish, onions, salad dressing,

Worcestershire sauce, catsup. Never leave a restaurant without taking the packs of sugar and jam. (In that same *Oracle* wherein Mescalito looks like Zeppelin, Gary Snyder says for gleaners to come to the docks. The forklifts poke holes in sacks, and you can scoop fifteen or twenty-five pounds of rice once a week.) (Grocers padlock their bins now.)

How to break the news to a wife that she's married a Chang? Don't worry; she's going to be supported but in a way that isn't going to sacrifice his free life. She's going to have to help out. He'll teach her how to live on nothing, and she'll always be able to get along, with or without him. For her birthday and anniversary, take her out to the dining rooms that feed any old body, such as the Salvation Army and the Baptist mission. Not the St. Mary's kitchen, though, because of pride, too many Chinese nearby. Don't go to the Red Cross either; after battles they meet soldiers carrying back their dead, and charge them for coffee and doughnuts, according to Zeppelin. For Wittman's twenty-first birthday, his father took him to a skid-row bloodbank, where they gave blood for ten dollars apiece. The Red Cross and the bloodbank don't preach.

The car started. The uncles were applauding. The footsteps that came up behind him were the two mechanics'. "Here." Pop whacked him on the shoulder with a sheaf of paper.

"Zeppelin! Ah Zeppelin, ah!" The gamblers were calling for more chances at him. Pop handed him the paper, and left.

"Bye," said Taña.

"Um," said Pop without turning around.

"Um," said Wittman.

The river continued flowing down from the Sierras and on to the Pacific. Taña drove, heading toward Reno and PoPo. "Pop isn't so bad," Wittman said by way of apology. "I know a family where the son had to throw a cleaver at his father's head—this was in the kitchen, a restaurant family—and got him to start saying Hi." We wouldn't mind our fathers so much if Caucasian daddies weren't always hugging hello and kissing goodbye.

Wittman used his talent for reading in a moving car without getting carsick to read to his wife, busy at her practical tasks. *Find Treasure* was a newsletter published, written, edited, typed, duplicated, and distributed by Zeppelin Ah Sing. The main article this quarter was about the mountains of Hawai'i—they're hollow inside, where continues to live the royal family that descended from navigators who came from Tahiti and Samoa via Malaysia via Israel. Even tourists and scientists have sighted the king's warriors nightwalking through certain streets of the city and carrying torches on top of the sea. When he was stationed at Schofield, Zeppelin himself had seen menehune sidhe standing on rocks. They wore bright crowns, and turned toward him with open mouths. Another evidence of the hidden kingdom is that historically there were decoy funeral processions. Inside the mountains, there live ali'i more royal than the branch on the Peninsula. When Ko'olau the Leper alone held off the U.S. Army until he ran out of bullets, he was looking for a way inside the mountains. Zeppelin warned his readers that the Hawaiians at their most glorious were pre-metal, and their treasures were feathers, stones, hair, teeth, bones, and cloth.

As in all newspapers and magazines, the Letters to the Editor were the best reading because of their non-conformity. Pop's letters came from his six subscribers: Vincent "Helicopter" Hoople of Anchorage reported that termination dust has begun to fall. Luckily, he's finished collecting the free coal that washes down to the beach from the melting glaciers. Worldbeater Tam Soong, who had been reporting about life on the Malay Peninsula—"I can't like it"—has found work on a cattle ranch in Calgary, and recommended *Canadian Short Stories* as a field guide. Rosalie Manopian complained about missing cherry-blossom time in Japan and gardenia time in Hawai'i. She is in Guam during toad season. She has to hose out the dogs' mouths, which foam from catching toads. " 'Guam is good,' " she quoted the sign at the airport. Chance S. L. (Shao Lin) Go gives up on getting near the gold and diamonds of Johannesburg, which the conglomerates have glommed, and is investing in a diving bell. He will join Mr. Arthur C. Clarke, who has news of a gold web over Ceylon. And Gavino McWong of the Americas complimented the editor for giving him info that is changing his life for the richer; he will send more details after he registers his claim on a river of opals in Baja. There was a query from Higinio Nicolas, Palos Verdes, who needs to know anything more about the treasure ship that came from China a thousand years ago and sank near the beachfront lots which he has bought up.

Find Treasure featured an abandoned mine per issue. How much wealth it might realize. How to own it. A map and a deed upon request and twenty-five dollars. Each site personally visited by Zeppelin Ah Sing. His philosophy was that the mines had been abandoned at a time when the equipment was inadequate. Using modern techniques and positive thinking, one could dig deeper. Dredge the gold mines that had been but grazed, too much rush. Politically, change zoning codes, change society. His position on using acids to leach out gold was that he was for it.

The history lesson was that Constant Fong's grandfather fainted down the steps of the Gong Jow temple-and-courthouse in Sacramento. This happened at the very moment that John Wilkes Booth shot Lincoln, and their pains were in the same places. Grandfather Fong put two and two together when the news of the assassination reached the West.

These were the filler facts: $\frac{f(x+\Delta x) - fx}{\Delta x}$ = The Limit. Many first-generation Americans are named Gordon because when their ship landed on Angel Island, and Immigration asked for their real names, they took the one off the ship, the *Gordon*.

The last page was about equipment for the retrieval of treasure, buried or sunken, types of metal detectors, prices of used machinery, where to order, etc. Professional geologists write dates and places on chunks of geode, quartz, garnet, gold with India ink on white paint. Professional archaeologists christen their sites. They dig with the Marshalltown trowel.

Wittman used his English major's skills to sneer at and correct the dumb grammar, but suddenly stopped, folded the paper away. *Find Treasures* by Pop gave him that same homey-internationale feeling as the Catholic Worker one-cent newspaper. The beans are growing at Peter Maurin Farm. I have a father who gives me a city in a coral-reef volcano. Father and son self-made men out of dregs and slags.

The highway followed the American River east, up among the turkey vultures and the red-tail hawks. They stopped to put up the top. Wittman took the wheel and drove on toward Reno. If there is a plot to life, then his setting out in search of her will cause PoPo to appear. Do something, even if it's wrong, his motto. His understanding of Kierkegaard: To think up reasons why something would not work guarantees that it will not work. Never do feasibility studies. Get on with creation. Do the most difficult thing. Keep the means moral. His path and her path will synchronize. Taña turned on the radio, which was talking about a "tragic automobile accident." "At least somebody died," she said. "To most people, tragedy is when they don't get what they want." She snapped the radio off. She sang "Clementine." GrandMaMa will hear. It can't be so easy to lose track of one's people.

He chimed in at "You are lost and gone forever, dreadful sorry." He sped up, but smoothly. He felt the drag and pull of climbing. Don't punch the gas. Shift smooth. Ahead, a slow Pilipino man in a Frank Sinatra hat peered at the road through his steering wheel. Pass him. If Wittman were alone, he wouldn't be trying to live up to this Porsche, which didn't let family cars overtake and pass it by. A car like this costs as much as a house. But as the Angelenos say, you can live in your car; you can't drive a house.

What do you get when you cross a Black with a Chinese? What? A car thief who can't drive. Ha ha. How come twenty Mexicans show up at the wedding? How come? They've only got one car. Ha ha. How do you teach a chinaman a sense of direction? How? Paint R's on his thumbnails so he can tell Right from Reft. Ha ha. A man's instincts show up behind the wheel. Wittman naturally drove like an international student from a developing country. He concentrated on counteracting his stereotype. If he were Black, no Cadillac; if he were Mexican-American, no duck ass on his head, and no 'fifty Merc, raked and deshocked, waddling through the downtown; if he were a girl, no red Mustang; if he were socialist, no V.W. with a Co-op bumpersticker. He got out of the slow lane—carefully because of having no rhythm for merging. Lean one elbow casually out the window. Drive Okie. Lew Welch says, "Think Jew, dress Black, drive Okie." Why Jack Kerouac had to hitchhike and be chauffeured was he couldn't drive. Pass the Flammable truck with car lengths to spare. The oncoming cars could crash through the poison oleanders, head-on. He went back to hugging the mountainside. But bravely tried to pass a logging truck, the logs far longer than he'd thought. The trucker seemed to race him, and not let him back in for a long time—the last moment over the hill. His mouth dry, he wanted a cigarette but neither hand wanted to leave the steering wheel to fumble around on the dashboard for a lighter that might not even be there. He could use a look at the speedometer too, but. Having trouble breathing. The altitude or an acid flash? Don't tell Taña. Shit. The log rig is too large behind him, tailgating the chinaman. He tried to step on it but seemed to go slower. He wanted to slow down, and to stop. But what if his shaky leg miscalculate the brake, and we overshoot the guardrail, or bounce off it into the logging rig? He may be about to lose it. "Isn't that beautiful?" he said at the gorges. "That's beautiful," he said at the fires of red and gold trees. The quaking of the shiverleaf aspens was inside his feet. He cannot get into an accident; the Highway Patrol will ask for his driver's license, which had expired. "Want to pull over for a good look?" asked Taña, and broke the spell. He pulled controllably into a rest stop. The logger juggernauted over the spot where he had been, its driver blasting him with the horn, giving him the finger while looking straight ahead, ignoring the bird Wittman flipped him in return. After they appreciated the scenery, he let Taña take the wheel. "I'll do the looking out for GrandMaMa," he said. She took them up and over the summit.

The evergreen pines and redwoods stood in red tangles of poison ivy and poison oak. In a Disney flick, the trees would be picking up their itchy feet and scratching them with their branches. The railroad tracks ran above here and below there. The chaparral has grown over cuts, and the mountains seem to have never been re-graded and re-shaped.

Taña was asking a question, some kind of a driving game. "See those lakes down there?" There were several flat lakes or pools, perfectly round —too round—no waves, no ducks, no campers. "You know what those are? Those are fake lakes. The C.I.A. built them. They store missiles and nuclear warheads under that glass. They press co-ordinating buttons at the Lawrence Rad Lab and Washington and Los Alamos; a lake slides open. Out of it will rise the nose of a timed rocket. It's aimed at Russia. If we were to park here, and hide—you watch—at 3:00 a.m., the lakes will open. Workers and equipment will move in and out." It was a very eerie secretive place, all right, no other cars. "It looks peaceful, huh? They're disguising the violence." She's just being her old self. He liked her old self.

Where are you, PoPo? Did you walk into the mountains and valleys, and fall asleep behind a tree, or accept a ride with a stranger, a yacht ride on Lake Tahoe? Be resting on a shoulder of the highway of life, be scraping the road apple off your shoe, I will find you.

In Reno, he parked the car, and they walked up and down the main drag. GrandMaMa was not arm-wrestling the one-arm bandits in the open-air sidewalk casinos. She was not in hotel lobbies, or in cafeterias, nor was she trading her jade at the coin-and-metals stores. At the Washoe County Courthouse, they sat on the steps that Marilyn Monroe had walked down after her divorce in *The Misfits*.

"Want to get a divorce?" asked Taña. She got the jump on him again. "Now's your chance." She was ahead by quite a few points.

"What about you? You want a divorce?" She must have noted his driving, and been disappointed in him.

"I asked you first."

"No, I don't want a divorce." Not bad, Mr. Monkey. Like "I'm not saying I don't love you." Better you should've said, "Let's go inside and really get married."

Everywhere they walked, neon hearts winked and blinked. Stuffed doves—Bill and Coo—lifted ribbons in their beaks. Legal Weddings Legal. No Waiting. Flower Bo-Kay. Photos. Rings. Garter. Hitching Post. Witnesses. Cake Reception. Se Habla Español. Ceremony by the Reverend Love in the Chapel of Love. Taña took Wittman by the hand, and pulled him under the arch-gate of white bells and valentines that led to the Chapel of Love. They looked like the couple on top of the cake. World Famous &

Reno's Finest! Civil Marriage! Commitment! Non-denominational! In revenge for his not saying, "I love you, let's really get married," she said, "I
wouldn't be caught dead inside the Chapel of Love again. Once you get inside, they separate the men from the women. The bride and bridesmaid go
into this room, where they change into dresses. The wedding march starts,
and an amber light goes on, the signal for the bridesmaid to walk out. She
emerges at the top of these stairs that go down to the altar. Like church.
And at the top of the other wing of this double staircase, the best man walks
out his door. Like a cuckoo clock. Then, green lights go on in the dressing
rooms, and here comes the bride and the groom. In sync without a rehearsal. And the Reverend Love of the Chapel of Love marries them."

She's been married before? She's a divorcée? A bigamist? Nah. She'd
been the bridesmaid, not the bride. Her gang of friends drove across State
Line and married one another for kicks.

"I'm glad we're already married, and don't have to go through that," he
said.

They went into a coffee shop to tank up for the drive back. They filled
out the keno cards with crayons. Tables in Reno have salt, pepper, and a
carton of crayons. Numbers lit up on the boards. Although Zenly one
doesn't care about winning and losing, one feels a thrill and satisfaction at
each number that matches. It's sort of like watching the board at the U.C.
library to see if they've got your book. Flash. Your book is *in*. Lucky. Gamblers think they want money, but they're really after the hit-the-jackpot
pinball lights. Like satori.

"I can't stand to lose," Taña said. "But if I win, I'll get addicted. I have
an addictive personality."

"I don't. Do you think I would be more stable if I acquired some habits
like a rabbit?"

Should they stay and make Reno their home? There was a Berkeley plot
to take over Nevada, which is the state with the smallest population for its
land size. Establish residency in kibbutzim of tents and caves, and vote our
people into office. Two U.S. senators easy, same as New York, California,
Texas. The prostitutes and gamblers of Reno and Las Vegas and Mustang
would, of course, be leftish and help send hip representatives to Congress
and Carson City. They will legalize marijuana, and re-appoint the draft
boards, and ban bomb testing from the desert, and send our own friendly
ambassadors throughout the world. The center of world revolution was
supposed to move from Berkeley to Nevada.

No, not yet. Still more private life to lead. Find GrandMaMa. Wittman paid for gas, and drove. Fall off a horse, get right back on. Same with a car. The sun going down, the casino lights going up, the night softening the Sierras, he'll take it through. Taña looked for GrandMaMa on the right side of the freeway; Wittman looked to the left across the oncoming traffic. One more chance, PoPo.

Silverado. Silver cities. If you know your history, you can see more clearly the ghosts in the ghost towns. There had once been Chinese parades. To the surprise of their neighbors, one day every Chinese in town and from out of nowhere, including the women with bound feet, had dressed up and paraded. On a buckboard stage, the few women, representing eighty-seven faeries, played banjos and flutes, and strewed flowers, and waved branches of quince and poles of streamers and tassels. A faery seemed airborne, dancing in the circles of ribbon she twirled on a stick; ribbon dancing will be an Olympic event, wait and see. The men walked with their birds or sat on antique throne-chairs on haywagons. Farm-hand clowns did handsprings and bird calls and animal calls, and acrobatic pile-ups. Those who remembered opera sang the parts of kings. They fanned themselves and their birds and the townspeople with elaborate vanes of feathers, paper, wood. At the end of the street, the procession turned around and went through town again, and again. The main streets were very wide, not for quickdraw gunfights, but so that wagons, which had no reverse, could turn around. A buckboard carried a pyramid of buns for everyone to help themselves. A man walked among the crowds inviting them to look inside his gourd, and to drink from it. Merchants and traders—this happened on a workday—came out on the plank walkways and the balconies, and were amazed at their cook and babysitter, their laundryman, their cowhand, so changed. Why, but a few years ago, they had been pogrommed in a drive-out, and here they were parading. Yes, the citizens of the town will marvel at the comeback. They'll find these human beings so beautiful that they won't want to massacre them anymore. Already the lifetime of the town had never seen the like—when overhead sailed men in a basket lofted by a red silk balloon. It floated low. The people in the air seemed wonderstruck to see the people on the ground. Their runningwater sleeves streaming in the sky, they pointed at this one and that one. They dropped notes upon them. They called in a foreign language. Each wore a different shape of hat. They had long moustaches. The wind caught the balloon up, and they blew away to see the Indians and buffaloes. They went in the direction of one of the four words on the sides of their basket. Those words might have been the compass points, or perhaps they said, "We discover you, America." Nobody could read Chinese, they could've said anything. It had been an exploration all the way from Cathay.

In Truckee after dark, a warm light drew the car, which came to a stop under a wooden sign twined with ivy. La Vieille Maison. Usually, both Taña and Wittman fought against being waylaid by the advertised, but they were cold and hungry, and in need of bathrooms.

As he held the car door open for her, some cowboys in a pick-up truck shouted something, whistled. Fucking rednecks. The way they get you paranoid is you can't tell whether they're admiring the car and the chick, or they're giving you racist red ass. Flipping them the old finger isn't satisfying enough. They run away, and don't catch your reaction.

The amber in the windows was coming from a fireplace, which the maître d' seated them near. Given a choice, Wittman would have chosen that hearth table anyway. Who cares if it's the conspicuous, overheated table that they couldn't get rid of? Right off he ordered a carafe of the house red. The waiter brought homemade bread rolls and said that the butter was "drawn and whipped." This restaurant was famous for boarding the cast and crew of *The Gold Rush*. Charlie Chaplin might have sat right here and invented the Oceana Roll. Wittman stuck his fork and Taña's fork into two rolls, held these feet under his chin, and danced his head across the table, kicked left, eyes left, kicked right, eyes right, run run run run, and bowed. Taña applauded, and ate one of the feet. Chaplin had hired eleven thousand tramps from the Yellow Jungle of Sacramento to build the Yukon in the Sierras. Every structure in the area had had its artist-in-residence. Wittman leaned back, looking through his wine at the firelight and at his woman. Taña raised her glass, he raised his. Clink. Can you stay in love with somebody you've been with—let's see—for how many hours straight? Thirty-six continuous hours. Some kind of a record, he bet. Romeo and Juliet weren't together for that long their entire lives.

Oh, yes, to have an orderly table three times a day every day, plus second breakfast and a high tea, five sittings a day, a pressed tablecloth, cloth dinner napkins, utensils lined up, a plate for salad, a plate for bread, clean ashtrays, flowers, oneself fitting just right in front of his place setting. At the clink of maybe real crystal, holding the stem between thumb and finger, Wittman resolved ways to make life better for himself: He ought not to eat and work at the same table; clear off the papers and decant the catsup, put away the Peace Brand nori furikake fish flakes, except when that meal required a dash. Wash coffee cup between usings, use its saucer strictly as saucer, not for a sandwich plate or an ashtray. Set up each course and activity. His whole outlook would change. Be more Japanese and French. Take time to fix food; take as long to eat it. Serve it presentably. No more naked lunches. He's got to stop eating with his head in the refrigerator or bent over the pot on the stove. Peel an orange into the garbage bag, okay, but then walk a ways off, don't slurp over the bag. His parents hadn't raised him on organized meals; they didn't know better, scarfing hot dogs and soda pop while taking a walk between the matinée and the evening show. He had forgotten how to live, but it was coming back to him. End the day gracefully. See each day out, toast it, feast it, sing its farewell. At least, sit down and eat with another human being.

Across from him—Taña. He loved the way her hands moved, a long finger going down the menu. She's in no hurry to get to the next thing. An artist's pace. She pretended to untie the laces of a bread-shoe; she picked its bone-nail from between her teeth. With a silver blade, the waiter scraped the crumbs into a silver crumb-catcher, then brought the appetizer—wonderful escargots. She got down to business. The same garlicky buttery pleasure that is coursing from my mouth to my soul is gladdening your insides too. We are communicating. Her sixth and last shell empty, she traced the snail whorls with her menu finger. Hers are sculptress's hands. "Will you cook for me?" her dinner companion asked with his mouth full of the Gruyère crust of the onion soup. "I could have French onion soup every meal. You'll make it for me?" Yes, he could take this for the rest of his days.

This monkey man of hers has lessons coming to him. He should have said, "I love French onion soup. I love you. Let me cook it for you, and feed it to you. Then you cook it for me. Let's cook for each other. You taste my version, I taste yours, we know each other's taste buds."

"Every damn Sunday at this time, I get brought down," Taña said, cutting her rumsteake. They had ordered the rumsteake maître d'hôtel pour deux personnes and pommes frites and carottes râpées au citron. And a salade de saison and a fromage. They had yet to choose the mousse au chocolat with strawberries or the tartelette aux fruits avec Chantilly or le mystère. And coffee with a B&B. "I start thinking about calling in sick. What do you think? Should I call in sick? Help me decide what I have. Nobody can lie about sick leave. Whatever you say you have, you get."

Here was another chance for Wittman to let his woman know how he loves her. He should have said, "Eat your French fries. Go wild on strawberries. You don't have to worry about your job anymore. I'll do the providing."

Instead, he gave her advice on what to do about Mondays. "I've never worked on a Monday, restaurants and theaters dark Mondays. At this job I just lost, Monday was one of my days off. I'm going to go on Unemployment. Six months off."

"I'll say diarrhea. Diarrhea gets to them. They don't know what to reply to a diarrheaist. They don't want anybody with the runs around the office. It's one of my best excuses. You have my permission to use it when you get a job again. 'I can't come into the office. I got the runs. Gotta go, bye.' Hang up quick, don't give them a chance to discuss it and say no."

She doesn't understand, he doesn't want a job again. Fired, he's got more self-respect than ever.

They were smoking between courses, and did not make it to dessert. The voice of a loud man at Wittman's back said, "Every Mexican in town has one."

The party at that table laughed and laughed, repeating in appreciation, "Every Mexican in town has one."

Has one what? Go ahead.

More laughs. Wittman turned to see what they looked like. They looked like the kind who entertain one another with race jokes. The vigilante of parties has got to go into action when he hears jokes against any color. He knows, it started out as a chink joke, but they had looked about, saw one, and changed it to Mexican. Like a heroic Black man who has overheard a jiggaboo junglebunny joke, he got up, turned, walked over to that table, step by step, closer and closer. "You talking about me?" he said. "What you say? You say a joke about me? Say it to my face. Come on, let's hear it." So I can have right paranoia.

He struck the two men and two women speechless. He prompted them, "I want a laugh too. Every Mexican has one what? I want a laugh too."

"You're causing a disturbance," said the joker. "This is a private party." The men got to their feet to defend their table. "You're spoiling our dinner." "Waiter. Waiter," said the other man.

Their waiter and the maître d' and a cook or owner in a black rubber apron came running. "What's wrong? Be seated, please. No fighting in here, gentlemen. Sir, return to your table, please."

Wittman spoke loud for the dining room to hear. "You like jokes? I tell you joke. What's ten inches long and white? Nothing, ha ha. Every gringo doesn't have one. Why you not laughing? I funny, you not funny. You nauseating. You ruin my dinner. You slur all over my food with dirty not-funny joke." He pointed his finger at each nose. "Don't you tell jokes anymore. Don't let me catch you laughing against any raza again. You tell a gringo joke, wherever you are, I'm coming to get you. Understand? You sabe?" He held the edge of their table ready to overturn it.

"We weren't telling dirty jokes," said one of the ladies. Her husband will get her later.

"Ignore him," said the other woman. "He's disturbed."

"Are you going to eject him, or do I have to?" said the joke-teller.

"I'm leaving," said Wittman. "I might throw up my gorge, barf eating next to you. You're getting off easy this time. I give you a chance. Next time, out of luck." He turned to the help: "If you want to run a gourmet cuisine place, you shouldn't allow pigs."

He paid his bill and tip with virtually all the money he had left, and no wages ahead. It was worth it. He had come up with excellent rejoinders. His americanismo was intact. Everybody had sat up and taken notice. Taña didn't give anybody a disloyal look or shrug. He wished he could speak private Chinese to her, and she to him.

Outside, she asked, "What were those people saying? I didn't hear what they said."

"They were racists. They were telling a race joke. I didn't overhear it all the way through. During jokes, I have trouble hearing anyway. I get this blockage in my ears, like a wall or a roar that protects me. Line by line, I'm thinking, Is here where I break in and call them out, 'Don't tell coon jokes'? And try to educate them as to the unfunniness of the genre. Or can I laugh, it's not a coon joke? I'm a good sport, I'm ready to catch on and laugh, or catch on and bust ass. They get quiet when I walk into the party. I don't get to hear as many jokes as most people. I caught the punchline in there. It went like this: 'Every Mexican in town has one.' Do you know how the rest of it goes?"

" 'Every Mexican in town has one.' No, but I can find out for you." Will he be with her at that by-invitation party where she listens for Anglos making merry prejudice?

As they crossed the street, a voice demanded, "What time is it?"

Wittman didn't look about. Not every shout is meant for you.

"You. You have the time?"

"No," Wittman shouted into darkness. "No. I don't own a watch."

"What's the time? What time?"

"No watch. No watch." He could not see who was there.

The way they drive you crazy is you can't calibrate your paranoia. Like "Your time is up"? Like "Your time is up, chinaman"? You can't be too paranoid in these small towns with separate outskirt Chinese cemeteries full of graves with the dates of young men. A few years ago, he'd gone up to Middletown to join an anthro dig; the storekeeper said, "You ain't gonna find nothin' but the bones of the chinaman, ha ha ha." He'd said that to the white kids too, nothing personal. In these parts, anyone who wants to cash a check has to turn himself in to the sheriff.

Wittman escorted his lady safely through the main street toward the car. They window-shopped and looked for GrandMaMa. Notches to the tops of doorframes recorded snows. He got in the driver's side. He drove well, the while inventing a ratsbane parade. These towns need banging.

Ba-baan! Blow the ram's horn—announcing public executions. On prancing Red Rabbit, Grand Marshal Grandfather Gwan, god of war and theater, rides again. Halberdiers and gunslingers carrying scythes, samurai swords, grenades, railroad spikes, chef's knives, Mrs. Winchester's rifle, whatever there is around the house, make an exit from the theater on the esplanade and processionally walk to the temple in the middle of town. No permit, tough shit, we parade anyway. Four days of parading a town, leaflet-ting it, advertising ourselves. The flyers quote *The Sacramento Union*: "It would appear that John Chinaman means to remain with us for an indefi-nite period and to enjoy himself the while." You bet your booty and sweet patootie. Yes, it must have been a show-of-force parade that the *Union* reacted so meanly. King Mulu walks his beasts, white tigers, kirins, camel-opards on bridles which also guide the winds. Chuko waves his feather fan that can sic elephants on a populace. Doctor Woo will be there, flashing his fishbait lures: "Step right up for a peek between my hands. The lure is lighting up. Ten cents to look. One dollar to buy. The lure is difficult to see by daylight, but. It allures in the dark. It allures you for to dig your mine tunnel. Good for a lifetime. Dig for fifteen years, guarantee you find pros-perity. You will find you a palace of chrome. You will meet the Queen of Silverado, who looks like this lovely lady. At no extra cost, she will take from her own head to you very own head the wolf helmet. You wear the ruff of a wild wolf all around you face, you hear and remember the lucky strike chant I be singing." Eddie Toy swags and slides his lariat noose. And here comes our all-girl drum corps shuffling along in slippers. And Miss Chinatown and her court of runner-up princesses on the backs of convertibles. Roll flam-flam flam-flam. Roll flam-flam. Each girl mad to turn into a swords-woman, her secret identity. Running about everywhere and interacting with everybody—blue-faced varmints and clowns in skull-white. You won't be able to make them laugh, even tickling them keelee keelee in the armpits. And riders are coming in warpaint, each with its peculiar menace—black-winged eyes and eyebrows, curlicues around round noses, grooves beside their red mouths, red and green diamonds on foreheads and chins. None of the horses is gunshy because of the bats and words painted on their hoofs and rumps (over the Bar-B-Q brands). Stomach-echoing ear-blasting cherry bombs go off. And fountains and showers of fireworks rise and fall. Fire falls hurtle down mountainsides. And at the end, six white horses pull a stage-coach delivering in its belly ten thousand gold eagles won by a Chinese gambler.

The black shapes in the sky were ravens, those on the ground were a herd of tumbleweeds. They had broken from their roots, and were traveling on the freeway. Wittman slowed down for a couple of thickets to cross, did not get tail-ended, and drove under a bouncer, big as the car, swerving around a sitter. In his rearview mirror, he saw a gnarly snarly mass switch directions to chase a windbreaking truck. Taña said that he played dodge-the-tumbleweeds very well.

Yes, he was getting into driving. The Porsche Speedster smoothed out the plodsome world, which he controlled with the steering wheel. The Sierras rolled by like movie scenery to the background music from the radio, *Fanfare for the Common Man* by Aaron Copland. For long stretches, no other traffic messed with him.

But then he started thinking about the moving light yonder. Didn't it seem to be staying with them? What was it, and was it coming this way? In emptiness, brainwaves home in on one another. There may be thinkers tracing you. Try not to attract killers, and things from outer space. People are always meeting flying saucers in Nevada and being taken aboard to Venus. Anything could have happened to GrandMaMa.

At State Line, Taña told the ag inspector that the only fruit they had was Juicy Fruit. That's why he likes her—she is socially aggressive.

GrandMaMa probably won a jackpot, and the casino is sending her home with an escort at its own expense. The news of her winnings may have reached Sacramento by now. Her friends are waiting at the Grey-hound Station.

Oakland came up before San Francisco. Good. He would drop this girl off. He had gotten here on the bus, he could take the bus back. If you don't get back to your own pok-mun alone when the weekend is over, you start becoming the husband part of a longterm living-together couple. She was worrytalking about Monday morning turning her into an assistant claims adjuster. (Can a monkey love an assistant claims adjuster?)

"I loathe my job," Taña was saying. "You know what the most creative

part of it is? I mean, besides making up excuses. I match up a monetary figure with a loss of a body part, so much for a hand, so much for each finger,
so much for an eye, one leg, two legs, a foot, a toe, more for the big toe than
the baby toe. Loss of an extremity is usually accidental. In beatings, people
get hurt in the torso. That's the most interesting information I've gotten out
of the job. You know what the most common occurrence in the human
body is? Cysts and fibroids. At parties, I say, 'I'm an assistant claims adjuster,' I may as well say, 'I'm just a housewife.' I never meet these people
with the cysts, or the one eye and one leg. I just match up the number of
stitches with the number of dollars. I type out the checks. I write letters
denying pregnancy coverage for the unwed daughter of the family. The
most excitement we've had was when my desk partner recognized the signature on a physician-verification form to be the name of the acid killer
doctor. An autograph of a killer. I've got to change jobs, but Claudine—
that's our Office Manager—isn't going to give me a good letter of recommendation."

    She carried on like that all the way back to the curb of her house. Here
was Wittman's chance, come to her rescue. At least walk her to the door.
And come on in for a sit and a listen. Don't leave her like this. "At eight
o'clock a.m., this chime goes off. The first four notes of Lara's theme in
Doctor Zhivago. We have to be at our desks. It goes off again at ten-fifteen,
coffee break, and ten-twenty-five, end of coffee break, and at twelve noon
and twelve-forty, and at two-fifteen, second coffee break, and two-twenty-
five, end of coffee break, and five o'clock—commute hour. I live for those
two ten-minute coffee breaks and the forty-minute lunch hour. They com-
pute those sixty minutes against us. We get paid for eight hours when we're
at the office for nine hours, plus two rush-hour commutes. Plus getting
ready, dressing for work, nylons and make-up you wouldn't wear otherwise.
When we get so sick that we have to stay home, they call that a benefit. If I
lost a toe or got beaten up in the torso, I ought to be able to type myself a
check. They keep congratulating themselves for giving us a girls' lounge.
The girls crochet and knit and read *Bride* magazine in there. Men never
come in. I don't know where the idea of office romances comes from.
Males and females don't have much to do with one another. When one of
the men does talk to you, he tells you that insurance is the answer to everything—especially death, everything. The girls knit ten minutes at a time,
and after a couple of years, they have a sweater or an afghan to show for it.
Some of the older girls knit booties for their grandbabies. Most of the girls

graduated from high school; they think they have to obey bells. The men don't go by the chimes. It's not fair. The men go to lunch from eleven o'clock till two or three, and it counts as work. They eat with clients. You can smell what they had to drink. And they get paid many, many times as much as the girls, plus commissions. Claudine told us not to compare paychecks. She said pay envelopes are confidential. So whenever I'm alone with a girl in the restroom or the elevator, I tell her how much I'm making, then ask her what she's making. Most of them say it's none of my business, and that I'm breaking the rules. I did get a couple of girls mad, though; they've been there longer than me and I make ten dollars a month more than they do. We think it's because I went to college. We've got to start a union, but white-collar workers don't like unions. And do you know what's really unfair? I'd have to hold organizing meetings on my own time; bosses get to have union-busting meetings on company time. The job of executives is to fuck over employees. When I brought up unions, some girls said I was a communist. In fact, they reported me to the American Legion, who called on Claudine, who told me to watch my step. If I quit my job, I won't be able to get back in elsewhere. I'll be blacklisted by the insurance industry. Ordinarily, I'm not political, Wittman, but most people are so dumb, I can't just stand by and enjoy having brains. We have to take responsibility for the dumb people." Wittman hoped that those scared office workers, whom he pictured typing their lives away at infinite banks of desks, weren't Chinese-American girls. Most likely they were, and Claudine was too. "I can finish my work by the second coffee break. I tried reading, writing letters, making phone calls. Claudine told me to spread insurance forms on my desk. 'Look busy,' she says. I was reading a very educational book, but she made me put it away. I've got to get out of there."

Wittman can't be her rescuer. The only way he could see to rescue her was to take her place, and he had just escaped from wageslavery. But what kind of a monkey would he be not to stay and try to change her trip? Anyway, he had lost the energy to go out into the streets and catch the last bus of the drear night, stopping all along San Pablo, transferring, ending up at the Terminal again, walking to his poor room. And here were clean sheets, a made bed, and this girl getting into her lavender tie-dyed t-shirt. He had to have his feel of her. He ought to have said, but not any good at saying, didn't say, "Thank you for being brave, showing me the insurance side of you. I love you nevertheless. I love you." He loved her up quietly, stilling her chatter. Bodies have their touching ways, their own dumb language.

Look into eyes and face, watch the giving in and the changing. The reason we're made of flesh that feels pain, we're evolving to be careful creatures who handle one another with all considerateness.

Taña lit up a Balkan Sobranie, and offered Wittman a Gauloise, both brands on her headboard shelf for decoration, the packs almost full because they taste worse than shit. Taña sucked a mouthful of smoke, rounded her lips. She puffed out a smoke ring that drifted upward. "Let me practice my call-in on you, okay? 'Claudine?' Picture an S.S. Nazi concentration-camp guard on the other end of the line. 'Claudine, I can't come in today. I've got . . . I'm embarrassed to say . . . running diarrhea.' Can you tell I'm lying? I get all hesitant and inarticulate lying. 'Claudine, I'm pregnant. Puking all morning. I'm going to be late puking in the mornings from here on in. I'll get there as soon as I can. Upchucking goes away after the abortion.' They probably fire girls for abortions. They fire you for getting pregnant, married or not. We're always having baby-shower farewell parties, where Claudine says, 'We can't have you big as a cow in a business office, now, can we?' I've got it. I'll say, 'Claudine, to keep my job I got an abortion, resulting in feminine complications. How much sick leave do I have?' Good night, Wittman, my dear. I need to get some sleep, and get up early whether I go to work or not. Even when we're legitimately sick, we can't sleep in. We have to call as soon as the switchboard opens, before the clients start phoning. Claudine has hung up her coat and put her purse in her file cabinet, and hasn't noticed that I'm late or missing, her phone's got to be ringing, me on the line. They ought to let us call the night before, so we can relax."

She pulled the covers up, turned her back, shut her eyes. Wittman panicked. Taña, please don't go. Don't shut me out. He leapt out of bed to the vase behind the door, whereout he pulled two fencing foils. When naked making love with a stranger, locate the weapons. "Taña, wake up. Here, take this sword. Fence me." He found her lipstick, and painted a pink heart under his left tit. "Show me some moves. Come on, Taña. Be a good hostess."

She sat up, picked up her sword, undid the safety tip, thrust, parried, parried again, and touched him at the heart.

"No fair. You've taken lessons," he said.

"Good night, Wittman," she said, sliding down, rolling over, her sword between her side of the bed and his.

He sat on the footboard, his sword between his knees. In the shining steel handguard, his penis reflected huge. Behind it, his pinhead peeped out a long ways off. How odd, his head, the container of his mind, which contains the universe, is a complicated button topping this gigantic purple penis, which ends in a slit, like a vagina. "Hey, take a look at this."

She acted asleep. Well, he couldn't expect her to watch him play with himself. He brought the sword mirror up to his face, a Jiminy Cricket face with a bug body. Hey diddly dee, the actor's life for me. What interesting reflections of pinks and mauves and tans. She's asleep, might as well explore her place. In the kitchen was another Toulouse-Lautrec, 75 *Rue des Martyrs*. Yeah, he ought to be living in Paris, home for his type. Taña had matching canisters, alphabetized spices, glass jars with red beans, green peas, sugar, pasta. Domesticity. Don't get domesticated. In the living room, he sat himself down at her dainty secretary desk. Looking in the pigeon-hole dioramas, he found no letters either to or from her. He could write her a note saying that the buses aren't running, he had to steal her car. Two a.m. already. Should he remove the Isolde sword, and uxoriously crawl into bed? No fair; "uxorious" refers to men, and "husbandly" also refers to men. He ought to use her expensive texture-weave stationery and the pen of her desk set, and write more play. Back in the bedroom, he went inside the closet. Behind her clothes were shelves of labeled shoe boxes—huaraches, slingbacks, spectators, red shoes, white pumps, etc. "Beeeen!" said the evolutionary monkey.

The curtain opens—he flung her dresses aside—the great killer ape in chains sees the audience. Bloodshot eyes roll, sharp teeth gnash. Roar! Roar! He opened his mouth wide like in the silent movies. Laughing at me, are you? Look at my red lashing tongue, and down my gullet—a real ape, not some fool inside an ape costume. Feel my guffs of hot breath. I will slip these chains. White hunters, you will die. Let me make my hand small here, change it into a wing, a red fin. Oh, no, I'm stuck at ape. I'll grow then—to one hundred thousand feet. The chains snap. "Bring down the curtain!" shouts the stage manager. The curtain swings across. Down drops the asbestos wall. The shape of the gargantua ape swells and bulges. He tears through man's puny barriers against reality, and leaps out of the proscenium into the stampeding audience. Swinging his chains—tool-wielding ape—he lassoos the chandelier, pulls himself up, and rides it. He screams louder and higher than the ladies. Swooping Fay Wray up in his mighty arm, he and she swing across the ceiling of the San Francisco Opera House. Down rain crystal and loose excrement—cee—on to the audience. Balso Snell. O, say can you cee? The ape is loose upon America. Crash their party. Open his maw mouth, and eat their canapés and drink their champagne. The party is mine.

No one left but me. And this fellow in milady's dressing-table mirror, and in her hand mirror. With opposing mirrors, I can see my profile. I look like an ape. I have an ape nose. I do not look like a flounder.

Who's that human being unconscious down there? Dead? And here is her suitcase for going away to death camp. I alone am left alive. She is a mother dead beside the evacuation road. I am her babe clinging to her dead body still warm. Tanks are coming. And bombers in the sky. If I run after the others, I leave her dead alone forever.

He put his cheek and ear close to her face, felt her breathing. Alive, whew. He picked up her sword, and put it on the floor. He lay down at her side, and slept.

6

A SONG FOR OCCUPATIONS

 WITTMAN AH SING, for one who wanted badly to be a free man, was promising quite a few people that he would help them out. He had to create for Nanci Lee a theater. And find his PoPo. And keep Taña for richer, for poorer. "Forsaking all others." That part of the ceremony ought to include the saying of the names of the forsaken, so that we can specifically and publicly give them up. The bride's catalog of the forsaken. The groom's catalog of the forsaken. I forsake thee, Nanci Lee, et alia.

He did too have a philosophy of life: Do the right thing by whoever crosses your path. Those coincidental people are your people.

He rode into the City with Taña, who went to work after all, having wakened too late to call in, and late for work too, though it was early. The air was yet unbreathed through too many engines and lungs. The sun was a dime in the rearview mirror as she bravely drove into the fog of the Bridge toward the City, which looked like a grey thought. Drag boats were visible section by section crossing blue clearings. The City emerged, unmoved. Among its necktied men and heeled women, Wittman was yogore, a mess on a business day. Taña dropped him off near the Unemployment Office, where he would try for full benefits, six months of money to finance all that had to be done. She volunteered a plan for the rest of their lives: alternately, each spouse work half the year and collect Unemployment the other half. Bending over the roofless car, he kissed her goodbye.

He walked past two clochards sitting on the curb with a bottle of vin ordinaire. One poured a red trickle into his cupped hand, started to wipe his face with it, and flicked it in the other's face. Good morning. They bust up laughing—they still have laughs in them. The man with wine-wet face took the bottle, put his thumb over its mouth, and shook a rain of wine down on his friend. A toast—to superabundance for grasshoppers. They passed the bottle between them, drinking, swapping germs, mingling fates.

Inside a smoke shop, four bad boys, why weren't they in school, were at the magazine rack. It had to be porn that they were reading so intensely, warping their imaginations. But the tallest kid was reading aloud to the others, and it was *Astounding Stories*. The next tallest kid hung on the reader's shoulder and stared at the page as though there were illustrations. The littlest one rested his head on a shelf. The fourth kid sat on a bundle of magazines with his chin on his fists. Everybody enrapt.

At the corner across the street slouched a tough-shit girl with raccoon make-up, black motorcycle jacket, short skirt, fruit boots. Wittman prepared for rude eye contact, but at the light's change, she waited to walk slow with her old-world grandma. He slowed down too, an additional pedestrian body in the crosswalk against cars jumping the light. The girl bent down, speaking in kind Spanish to the babushka head.

How to behold strangers: longer.

The reason he was receiving all these beneficences must be because he was free from work. The city becomes an easier place. Indian summer was holding steady.

And parked at the parking meter in front of a deli—a red toy bull in a shopping cart. Of course, no pets allowed. Wittman went inside and ordered a pastrami on rye. The owner of the red bull was not there. The guy at the counter reached into the refrigerator and handed him his sandwich. "Could you heat it up please?" Wittman asked.

"You want it hot? I'll make it hot for you," said the deli man. Wittman laughed in the street. He left the sandwich in the shopping cart.

At the Unemployment Office, the jobless were lined up clear out the door. He went inside to figure out whether that long line was indeed where he had to start. Nobody told him to get his ass back out there. No information booth or posted instructions to help him out. What do the dumb people, who are most of the people in the country, do? The unemployed, his fellow man, waited before windows marked A, B, C, and D, and 9:00, 9:30, 10:00, 10:30. Rows of them waited in chairs arranged as if the down-and-out were an audience. A man in a boss suit jumped ahead to the counter. "Half a sec. Half a sec," he kept saying, a fired executive who hasn't learned that his time isn't valuable anymore. Everybody ignored him, and he left. Come on, give him the benefit of the doubt, he's no different from you and me. Tail him, and he'll lead you to a secret neighborhood of skylit lofts and underground poetry readings, and to the studio where he is making something beyond your imagination. Look at us: artists, squandering our creation time. Please give us our grants to do the work we were born for. We won't waste our lives in front of the t.v., we promise. Wittman decided on line A, a beginning and also his initial. This maneuver put him out the door. Well, he'd learned patience at registration for classes. When inside again, he followed a stripe of yellow tape on the concrete floor. Yeah, hitting his marks. All together now: "Follow the yellow brick road. Follow the yellow brick road. Follow, follow, follow, follow, follow the yellow brick road." The people did not look particularly employable or unemployable, or tired or abashed. Some women and a few men had brought their children. The movie stars were traveling incognito. No communists leafletting the crowd. Some unshaven guys starting beards. Some ladies in curlers, and some Black guys in stingy-brim hats, a few in do-rags. There were a bunch of Chinatown ladies; he didn't know them. They were talking about the advantages of migrant labor. "At the grape camp, I felt like a Girl Scout." "Just like college girls in one dormitory." "I forget my boy in Army. Indochina." A good life, harvest the tomatoes, harvest the grapes, collect Unemployment between crops. They spoke good and loud because the low fawns can't understand them. Wittman let his cigarette ashes fall, then his cigarette butt, and stood on it. No ashtrays for the poor. He wondered how much money he was going to get, whether this waiting and whatever else they'll make him go through was worth it. Good thing he was a stable person, otherwise run amok. Nobody was running amok. How patient most people are. How law-abiding. He was standing amok. So, it has come to this. Lew Welch teaches us to stop and say every now and then, "So it has come to this." So it has come to this.

The best dresser in the place was a very pretty Black lady a couple of lines over, the C line. She wore a halo hat, suit, gloves, and very high-heel shoes, on which she was rising on tiptoes above the situation. Her hair fluffed out around her Nefertiti face. She must be a high-fashion model back from Paris after the haute-couture showings. Two Black guys, who came in together, spotted her, and their faces changed—were gladdened— their postures straightened up, inspirited by her. There ought to be such a girl doing the same for our unemployed, but our career girls wouldn't be seen at the Unemployment Office, too shame.

After about an hour, all at once, the clerks flipped the cards over the wire—11:00, 11:30, 12:00, 12:30. Eventually he got near the front of window A, where he stayed behind a white stripe perpendicular to the yellow line. The unemployed person gets privacy at the window. The one behind him could not overhear the right answers. Then our pilgrim passed the test of waiting. It was his turn to step over the white stripe. "Good morning," he said cheerfully, to take the initiative, to keep up his end of the day, to shoot this government worker some sarcasm, it hardly being morning anymore.

She didn't say Good morning back, but had her hand out for him to give her something.

"I want to sign up for Unemployment," he said.

"Your form?"

"What form?"

"Application form."

"What application? I thought when I made it to the front, you were going to hand me my money." He didn't really think that, but was suggesting to her a possible vision.

"You're supposed to've filled out a form that looks like this"—she held up a sample—"before you got into line." Don't deck her out. She's an artist too, artists and wayfarers all, earning her livelihood, meeting me in her path.

He reached for the application form. "Can I borrow your pencil?"

"I have to use it. I'm using it."

He turned around, keeping his place, and said across the foot-fault line, "Anybody got a pencil I can borrow? Hey, can you lend me a pencil?" A kind soul threw him a pencil.

"You can get a form over there." She put hers out of his reach.

"Then do I come right back here? I don't have to stand in line all over again, do I?"

She looked at him like she didn't know what he was talking about. Nobody in the history of Unemployment ever asked that before.

He did not but should have rushed the counter. Kick over file cabinets. Spill I.B.M. cards. George C. Scott as the social worker in "East Side West Side" revolutionizing the bureaucracy.

He stepped over to a wall table. List your previous employment, beginning with most current. Retail clerk, Management Trainee, ZIP sorter, busboy and grease-trap rongeur, U.C. Psych Department subject. Wittman Ah Sing, this is your life.

Line A came this side of the door now. He gave the blunt pencil to the next poor man to enter, someone even more behind than he was. Pass it on.

The cards with half-hour increments flipped once more before he got to the front. The same clerk was in the window, but she did not recognize him. She asked him the same questions as were printed on the application, made a mark beside each of his answers as he re-answered them orally. Her supervisor is a checker of checkmarks. We unemployed keep many scribes employed.

"I.d.?" she said.

He said his Social Security number.

"You don't have a driver's license?"

"I don't have a car."

"You don't have your passport?"

What's this? Is she calling me a wetback? "I'm not going anywhere."

"You don't have a credit card?" A wide-open invitation to give her his speech against installment buying. "Is it government policy to encourage the jobless to go into debt?"

"All I'm asking you for is a firm i.d. card."

"I'm morally against credit cards."

"You shouldn't leave the house without identification," she said. He felt scolded.

"You're speaking for the government, right? As a representative of the state, you're ordering me to have papers on my person at all times?" The Berkeley rumor was that the computers in Washington, D.C., cross-referenced your I.R.S. file with your bank statement with your F.B.I. record with your Motor V Registration. It's your duty to confound them. Any conspiracy we can get paranoid over, the U.S. Government is already carrying out. "Here's the number assigned to me by the feds," he said, handing her his Social Security card.

"A Social Security card is not an i.d.," she said.

"Why not? I'm the only one in the world with this number, right?" Social Security and the I.R.S. had promised the Americans of Japanese Ancestry that their Social Security numbers and their tax returns would not be used to hunt them down.

"How about your draft registration card?" Oh, shit. Oh fucking shit. She'll see his expired 2-S. She'll turn his evasive ass in, and he will go to jail. He gave her the stub from a paycheck, and his A.S.U.C. Activity card, and a party invitation (in a court summons theme). And his library card. Here. This is the most important thing about me—I'm a card-carrying reader. All I really want to do is to sit and read or lie down and read or eat and read or shit and read. I'm a trained reader. I want a job where I get paid for reading books. And I don't have to make reports on what I read or to apply what I read. Ah, girl, don't sear me with trade, smear me with toil. Hand over my money and let me get on with it.

"Next time, bring an official picture i.d.," she said, and gave him a yellow card. She wrote his name and Social Security number in a tiny yellow booklet, stamped the date, and wrote an appointment time. "Your interview is for 1:00. Here's your literature."

"Thanks." Thanks for nothing. My dole and your salary come out of the same budget. "Didn't you just now interview me? What else do you want to know?"

"I'm registering you. They'll interview you over there. This isn't the interview."

"You mean I stood in line just to get to stand in another line?"

He went to the 11:30 line, calculating that when the cards flipped, that one would say 1:00. His booklet said: "Unemployment Compensation is paid for by employers." Somebody's lying. The money has been taken out of our paychecks, everybody knows that. And we're entitled to get it back. How come so many people say so if it isn't true? The State of California is putting out "literature" to snow our common knowledge. The truth must be that employers pay at a penultimate step; the workers' paychecks absorb the money in the long run indirectly.

Wittman had free time, and an old Chinese lady caught a whiff of it. "You Chinese?" she asked. When you have a moment of idleness, an old Chinese lady will always appear, and give you something to do, keep you from going lazy. He looked around, a wise guy, like she could be addressing somebody behind him.

"Yes," he said.

"Good boy." She was praising him for accomplishing the excellent geste of being a Chinese boy. "You tell them for me that I can work, and I want work, and I need work. I must have work. I went looking every day this week. I had a job at the Fruitvale Cannery putting three molly-see-no cherries"—maraschino—"in the fruit cocktail. Not two. Not four. Three." Lowering her voice for a secret—"The boss floorlady told everyone: I—the exactest Chinese lady in the cannery. Do you understand me? I want you to tell them for me. Okay?"

"Okay," he said. Though she shouldn't need translation. She spoke back and forth, a shuttling scuttling weaver of Chinese and English.

"Never never eat fruit cocktail. Do you know what a molly-see-no cherry is? An onion. They bleach it white, no more onion smell, no onion taste. Then they soak it in red dye and sugar syrup. Fruit cocktail is bad for you health. Don't eat fruit cocktail." She was making him a gift of her insider advice. It was in exchange for the upcoming translation work. "Have an orange," she said, rummaging in her plastic shopping bag.

"No. No, thank you."

She came up with an orange in her gloved hand. She was wearing long white prom gloves. "Keep it for later. Don't eat canned. Do you know how they take skins off peaches? Lye bath. My job is to gwoot out the pit with my fruit knife." She had her fruit knife in her bag too, and showed him its crescent blade, honed fine by long and abundant peach seasons. "Aiya, I have to learn how to work fast left-handed."

"Why's that?"

"Do you want to see my hand?" She handed him the orange, the fruit knife, her purse, her shopping bag. She pulled the glove off her right hand, her back to the counter windows. "I can move it a little." Her thumb and index finger were swollen purple-grey and stretched too far apart. Her hand was tautening into a claw, a fruit knife. "When we talk to them, you tell them I must work. Must. You sabe? It hurts a lot but. I will get Unyimployment, and give my hand a rest." She pronounced "Unemployment" with a "yim," as in "salt," the sweat of labor, the salt of the earth. "Don't tell them about my hand. Tell them I'm healthy, and can work."

Grimacing, she pushed her fingers closer together and tugged the glove back on. "This is as tight as I can bring my thumb and pointer together. I can't shut my hand but. Everything will be all right. Yesterday I went to the Workman's Comp office. I told them I was hurt on the job. I'll be all right. I'll get Workman's Comp and I'll get Unyimployment."

"Wait a minute," said Wittman. "Can you do that? It says here in this booklet and on this card that you have to be physically able to work."

"So?"

"Well, what if the Government says you lie?"

"Oh." He felt very sorry that he was making her falter.

"What happens if Workman's Comp sends to this office the paper that says you're too hurt to work, but here you say you are *not* too hurt to work? And the Government notices that the answers don't match? Do you see what I mean?"

"No. No, I don't. No."

On the cover of the yellow handbook, there was a box around all caps:

PENALTY FOR FALSE STATEMENT—
UNDER THE LAW IT IS A MISDEMEANOR
TO WILLFULLY MAKE A FALSE STATEMENT.
CONVICTION IS PUNISHABLE BY FINE
OR IMPRISONMENT OR BOTH.

"It says here one could go to jail for lying." He was breaking the news to this innocent: Meat comes from piggies and cowcows and little lost lambs.

"Aiya," she said. "Here. Change the answer to 'No.' " They were moving up in line. She gave him her card and a pen. He found the question about being physically able. Somebody had written the 'Yes' in ballpoint. He rubbed it with spit; tails of paper epidermis rolled off. He wrote "No."

"You don't need to stand in line and go through all this," he advised. "Go home and take care of your hand." He meant she wasn't going to qualify anyway.

"But I can work. I use my left hand. Change it back to 'Yes.' "

Her card looked suspect. "Are you sure you want me to do that?" he asked. "Your card will look messy. 'No.' 'Yes.' 'No.' "

"What do you think I should do?"

"I think too much trouble to apply for both Workman's Compensation and Unyimployment. Decide on one, save yourself the standing in line and the paperwork."

"Oh, I have the time to stand in line. And I get double chances. And win both if I'm lucky."

"If your hand hurts a lot, then the Government is not going to give you Unyimployment."

"My hand hurts a lot. Should I leave that square empty and ask the Government lady what's best to write down?"

"The Government lady is going to say write down what's true."

"The best answer is 'Yes,' I am going to work. Put 'Yes.' "

"Remember yesterday you filled out a form that said that you're not able to work, that you want them to pay you because your hand was injured at work."

"You mean that I best write down on this card the same answer today and yesterday. But." To hear her think to surrender stuck a pain into his heart. She was co-operating with the authorities, which included himself. "I like work," she said.

"All right. All right. 'Yes.' " He blackened out the 'No,' and wrote 'Yes' beside the blot. Enough Unemployment counseling; the Government can do its own dirty work. See what you have to put up with if you want to have community? Any old Chinese lady comes along, she takes your day, you have to do her beckoning. The hippy-dippies don't know what they're in for. They couldn't take Communitas.

"Let me help you fill out your card right," she said. "I've been coming to this office between seasons for twenty years, so I know. They give the same test questions every week, and we have to give the same answers. Listen now. I teach you. Learn. You ready? Remember these ten answers: 'No.' 'None.' Number Two is not 'No.' The right answer is 'None.' Don't forget, 'None.' That's the tricky part right there. I start over, okay? 'No.' 'None.' 'Yes.' 'No.' 'Yes.' 'No.' 'No.' 'No.' 'No.' Always answer like that. One more time, okay? 'No.' 'None.' 'Yes.' 'No.' 'Yes.' 'No.' 'No.' 'No.' 'No.' 'No.' "

" 'No.' 'None.' 'Yes,' " repeated Wittman. " 'No.' 'Yes.' 'No' 'No.' 'No.' 'No.' 'No.' " (That first "Yes" is the answer to Number Three, "Were you physically able to work full-time each of the seven days that week?")

"Ho, la. Smart boy. One wrong answer, they send you inside to the office. And they take the money away. Don't forget. Always answer like that. One wrong answer—no more money."

"Why is it better to say 'No' to Number Seven?" he asked. "That's the one that asks, Did anybody in this office or anywhere else tell you about a job?" He considerately told her the question in case she couldn't read or remember.

"That's called 'refer.' No matter what the refer is, you have to go try for that job. But they hardly ever refer. Twenty seasons of cannery, they referred me one time. I think they drew my name out of a bad-luck lottery. They referred me on the telephone. My mistake, I put 'No' on Seven the same as usual. So the Government lady sent me to interrogation. I said, 'Oh dear, I forgot. Now I remember, you refer. The answer is "Yes." ' There *had* been a Sai Yun voice on the phone." To call them Sai Yun instead of White Demon shows the classiness of the speaker, and also gives the Caucasian person class. "For punishment, they delayed my Unyimployment for one week."

The two of them crossed the stripe on the floor together. "How old is she?" asked the Government lady.

"Tell her sixty-five."

"Sixty-five," said Wittman.

"Tell her," said the Government lady, speaking slowly, enunciating, "that I have to inform all the senior citizens that there's a bill in Congress to deduct Unemployment Compensation from their Social Security checks. So her benefits may total no more than her Social Security. This bill may not pass, but we have to tell senior citizens about it."

"No sabe," said the old lady.

"The Government lady says," said Wittman, "that you get Social Security, you might not get Unyimployment. Maybe. They might subtract one from the other. Sabe?"

"No sabe. Tell her I don't understand English." She meant she didn't like what she was hearing.

"She doesn't get it."

The clerk repeated the whole thing. "In other words," she said, "she could be making extra paperwork for herself, and for us, and she wouldn't be getting more than her Social Security."

"I no sabe." Sometimes if you act stupid, you get your way.

"She wants to apply anyway," said Wittman.

The clerk marked the answers to Number One and Number Two with red checks. Some of the new Hong Kong people say that writing with red is unlucky, but it's unclear for whom, the writer or the written about or to. Her red pencil hesitated at the answer to Number Three, which had been worked over. "Is she physically able to work?" she asked.

Wittman said to the popo, somebody else's grandmother, now his responsibility, "Are you physically able to work?"

"I can do a great many things." She folded her gloved hands on the counter.

"Can she do her usual job at the cannery?" Good question.

"Better than most people," answered the popo.

" 'Yes' or 'No.' "

"Not outstanding as usual but. I will be okay one day soon."

The clerk said, "Please sign here for me."

Her poor hand could not close over the pen. She took it in her left hand and wrote her signature, copying her name that a relative with careful penmanship had written out. Mrs. Chew.

"Have her wait in line D for an interview."

"Tell her thank you," said Mrs. Chew.

"Thank you."

"Thank *you*."

As long as he was up here, Wittman pushed his own papers forward.

"Did you work last week?"

He recognized the first question, to which the right answer is "No."

"As a matter of fact, yes," he said. "Tuesday's the first day I won't be going in to work. But I'm eager to get a jump on my paperwork, get the machinery rolling, as it were. In case I don't find a job right away, possibly later on today, who knows, no time wasted. I have drive. I'm no O.E.O. deadbeat. I'm a go-getter. An active job seeker." The "literature" said that he had to be "an active job seeker."

The Government lady asked him the rest of the questions. He was grateful to Mrs. Chew for the answer ("No") to Number Four, which is one of those negative subjunctive questions that if you stop to think about it too much, your brain gets confused, doubling back, turning around. " 'Was there any other reason you could not have worked full-time each workday?' "

He wished that this were not a force-choice test. He would say, like an Englishman, "Would that there were. Ah, would that there were."

"You have to go to two more interviews—the intake interview for a new claimant—that's you—and a job counseling appointment at the Employment Office."

He followed the green stripe to sit next to Mrs. Chew in line D, which was the row of chairs against the wall. Aiya, there ought to be a nice waiting room for us like at the dentist's with carpets and magazines. Where are the potted plants and music? Where's a receptionist offering coffee or tea? No comforts for the unemployed. They're punishing us for losing our jobs. When they ought to be honoring us. We people who have unbusied ourselves to scout around, to review the system, to do some doubting and questioning, the ones who try if it's possible yet for the human race to live on air and sun.

The two Chinese-Americans, who looked like relatives, ate an orange. Its peelings filled the stand-up ashtray that Mrs. Chew had found and pushed between them. "Now we're going to be interrogated," she said. "This is the worst part. They give you bad news in that inside office. You should avoid going in there if you can. You are coming in with me, aren't you?" It was now 1:45, as he could tell by looking on the wrists of people who owned watches.

"Sure," he said. "Don't you worry."

"Are you married?" she asked. "Do you have kidboys?"

"No. Yes. No. No kids."

"Don't worry. I know a very kind rich girl. Fix you up, okay? She puts in the money; you do the hard work, you do the English-speaking; you can have a restaurant, children, everything. You're clever enough, I can tell. You remind me of the boys from China I met on Angel Island. You're older than most of them but. You'll get down to business and work harder. They were fifteen, sixteen, seventeen years old, not broken in. They had no patience for I.N.S. red tape. They didn't like the food, they had food fights. I didn't like the food myself. Noodles with tomato sauce. Jell-O. We didn't know how to eat Jell-O. We spread it on the white bread. Jell-O sandwiches." She laughed at the greenhorns they used to be. "There was too much we didn't know. The ground on Angel Island is covered with jade. We walked on dark green jade clink-clinking underfoot from the boat to the Wooden House. When the soldiers turned their backs, I picked up a piece. We thought, the island is made of jade; the mainland must be made of gold. Now I know, it's just mock jade. Monterey jade. For breaking rules, the boys got locked up one at a time in the closet. They built a trapdoor which was a dove-tail puzzle. It was also their shit- and pisshole. The closet was always clean no matter how long a boy was locked up. That's how Chinese got the reputation for being able to hold it in.

"We ladies had a big bathroom with flush commodes and showers. But we didn't shower; we bathed using basins. Whenever in the middle of the night, we heard someone in the showers, we knew that a woman was going to hang herself. We wouldn't try to stop her because she had her reason— she failed her interrogation or she couldn't bear the waiting any longer or nobody came for her or she was being deported. It was her own business. The suicides wore their wedding dresses; they tied the sashes around their necks, and hung themselves from the shower pipes. The commodes sat up on stands all in a row. The women, who were from the country, were very modest. For privacy, they put pillowcases over their heads. Can you picture it? A row of peasant ladies shitting and pissing with bags over their heads."

Mrs. Chew didn't need to go, did she? "Do you have to go to the bathroom?" Wittman asked. "Do you want me to go look for the ladies' seesaw?"

"No, thank you. You're very considerate. I know you would make that kind rich girl a good husband. I'm just talking-story to pass the time."

"I thought you were about to tell me a hero story. Didn't any of those guys try to escape through the trapdoor and swim to the Big City? I don't think we ought to spread crap stories about how tightass and clean we are, and how sneaky sly we are." Chinese do not have a thing about boxing them/ourselves up inside puzzle mazes; Kafka was the one, made that up. And we didn't come here to make money off of America; we burn money.

"Oh, but we have a tradition of shitting and pissing," said Mrs. Chew.

"The reason we have war on earth was because of a fart. Do you know the story of Ngok Fei? You remind me of him. Maybe you know him as Yue Fei? Yue Fei, the Patriot. What in your dialect?"

"Ngok Fei." Most Americans would say Ngok. "The man with the words cut on his back." His own old grandmother had received a postcard from a Hong Kong wax museum of a young man on his knees, and a hag with a knife behind him. The young man, fleshy and acquiescent, had made him feel sick. "The words on his back mean something like 'First—Save the Nation,' correct?"

"Oh, very good." Mrs. Chew clapped her hands. "Your name wouldn't happen to be Gwock Wai or Wai Gwock, would it?"

"Not me. If I had a name like that, I'd change it. I don't agree that my first duty is to serve a country. Mrs. Chew, I'm running away from the draft. I'm helping my country but. What I'm going to do for the U.S.A.: I'm not going to kill anybody. An American who doesn't kill—that's what I want to be. You're not trying to talk me into joining the Army, are you? You don't see a war in my future, do you?"

"I'm no hag witch."

"Tell me about the fart that started a war. Was Ngok Fei a farter?"

"No, no. He was against farting. That's why you remind me of him. A long time ago, back before Ngok Fei was born, a Buddha was chanting with students in the sky. They were so loud and so lovely that saints—. Do you know what a saint is? A sunseen? A fut? A good person who has lived and died and gone to live Up There. A bunch of those sky beings encircled this Buddha and his students." She was tripping him out as on drugs—spheres of protons and neutrons resolve into orbiting planets with rings and moons that resolve into the bald heads of monks, Buddhaheads. "And suddenly a girl student farted." Mrs. Chew did a razzberry right there in the Unemployment Office for dramatic illustrative sound effect. A religious fart. "Well, the Red-bearded Dragon laughed; and the students laughed. You know how students are, always laughing at farts. But Gold Wing did not laugh. With one peck of his scissors-like beak, he stabbed that farting girl student." These are bodhisattvas, Wittman thought, like in *The Dharma Bums*. A farting bodhisattva. With Toshiro Mifune as Red Beard. "She fell down dead." So people in Heaven can die? "And landed in our world as a baby, who grew up to marry a man with a red beard. Red-Beard Dragon reared over everyone's heads and almost caught Gold Wing in his claws and teeth. The bird-angel flew up, turned, and jabbed out Red Beard's eye. The dragon thundered, and flashed lightning all through the skies. Gold Wing flew downward, where he tried to hide as a human being. But. He has just killed somebody, don't forget. For punishment, he could not become human right off. The dragon searched everywhere, flooding burrows in the ground and washing away nests in trees. At last Gold Wing was born as a human baby. Guess which baby he became? I told you a hint already."

"Ngok Fei. I see, he's 'Fei' because he flies. When he was a boy collecting firewood, he fell lightly out of trees because he was a bird. He and his mother were in a jar floating down the river because the dragon was after him. And years later, when he was a political prisoner, his stay of execution lasted until the rainy season because you-know-who controls the rain." Wittman loved link-ups. He had just learned the pre-human events behind the boy who learned to read by stealing lessons outside the schoolhouse window and to write by scratching with a stick upon the earth.

"Mrs. Chew Ying May? Mrs. May?" Unemployment was calling. The senior citizen walked through the swinging gate while naming heroes for the young man behind her. "Gold Wing's cohorts were led by Wong, Cheung, and Hong. You've heard of those families, huh?" Yes, common in America. This is the way we would go to the gas chambers or the locomotive furnace in *Man's Fate*. They reached the interrogation desk a long way from the finish of the story, Chinese stories having no end, sons and ghosts continuing to fight in the ongoing wars.

Mrs. Chew picked up a G.I. metal war-surplus chair with her prom-gloved hands, and carried it over to the desk for her interpreter, Wittman. He and the Government man both offered to help, but she was too quick. When everyone was seated, the Government man leaned forward across his desk and said in a kind voice, "Now, Mrs. May, can I help you? What's the problem?"

His sympathy undid her. She pulled off the glove, and said, "Let me show you. To wear this glove hurts. And in the cannery I wear tight, hot rubber gloves." She has this guy mixed up with a doctor. "Let me show you. See how it's turned blue here? Like a Santa Rosa plum."

"That must hurt a lot. It's hurting you now, isn't it?"

"Oh, yes, it does. It hurts bad. Aiya. Oh." She's going to get her way by trying to make the Government feel guilty and sorry at the sight of her poor hand.

"Have you been to a doctor? Has she seen a doctor?"

"Have you seen a doctor?"

"I have a doctor," she said, handing over a prescription order she hadn't had filled. She's saving money not filling her scrip. She's proud to keep this documentation that she does have a physician.

The man picked up the phone, and dialed the doctor's number. He asked whoever answered about Mrs. Chew Ying May. "Uh-huh. Uh-huh. Shingles, huh? Shingles," he said, hanging up. "Listen, when your hand gets better, you come back here, all right? You come back here and see me. I hope it gets well soon. Thank you for coming in, Mrs. May."

"Thank you," she said. "Thank you very much." She tried to carry Wittman's chair back to where she'd gotten it.

"No, please," said the man. "That's all right. Leave it there. I'll take it back."

"Thank you. Thank you too much."

"You're welcome."

"You're welcome too." Thanking, being thanked, thanking Wittman, thanking the man, she got turned around and out the gate.

"Wittman Ah Sing?" His turn on the docket. The same Government man read through his application form and said, "Laid off, fired, quit, strike, or other?"

Definitely not out on strike, and he'd decided never to answer "other" to anything ever again. Come to think of it, he hadn't had a confrontation scene where anybody said, "You're fired." He hadn't had his chance to say, "You can't fire me. I quit." "Laid off," he said, which is just the right answer.

"Since you came in on a Monday, Tuesday, or Wednesday," said the Government man, "you get backdated to Sunday. You get credit for this week as your one-week waiting period." He was being given good news; if he'd waited to come in on Thursday or Friday, they would've started him off the following Sunday. "Wait a minute. I have a file on you." Sitting on the blotter was a Notification of Changes or Terminations Due to Personnel Action re: Wittman Ah Sing. The store must have hand-delivered it by messenger, they were in such a hurry to unemploy him. "You might be interested in this," said the Government guy, pointing to Comments: "He seems to hate merchandising, and can benefit from psychiatric counseling." Wow. Written evidence that the establishment is monitoring our minds. He was to get his head shrunk on the recommendation of a department store. It's official, he's not fit for commerce. In this society, retailers define saneness. If you hate the marketplace, and can't sell, and don't buy much, you're crazy. In black and white and carbon copies on file here and at the store and in Sacramento—"He seems to hate merchandising, and can benefit from psychiatric counseling." Wait until the S.S.S. gets a load of this. Too crazy to fight for capitalism. He giggled. The Government man did not smile in return. Wittman should contain himself, shrink his head, shrink his face, but he let out another baboonish heh heh heh. The Chinese giggle. One of twenty theatrical laffs.

Jauntily, he tossed the Notification of Changes back. "Who is it that doesn't get the boot now and again?" he said. "One can be too Steady Eddie." Shut up already. He never said "one," or "get the boot," or "now and again," or "Steady Eddie." Where does this diction come from out of his Chinese mouth that was born with American English as its own, its first language?

"Every young person gets canned a couple of times before he settles down," said the Unemployment guy. Huh? What you say? "That store has a big turnover. They fire everybody. You'll find better stores to work for." Ah, I have brothers around. He thinks I'm funny to get hung up on a job nobody else wants.

To qualify for Unemployment, Wittman had to report within three days to the Employment Office near Chinatown. (Why the Chinatown one? Because of my looks and ghettoization accordingly? Because that's my address? Or merely because every place in the City is near every place else?) After his waiting period, which he had already begun, he might be eligible for twenty-six weeks of benefits. The penalties they dealt out seemed to be week-long increments of waiting, no hardship really. Think of a string of twenty-six markers at Mike's Pool Hall; whether you slide them from this end or that end, there are twenty-six of them.

Almost enjoying the dread-laden fall of the afternoon and of the season, he reported to the Employment Office near Chinatown, where he was headed anyway. Why fuck up another day? Waste the rest of this one, which is shot already. You took the best, take the rest. I cannot go on I go on.

The Jobs Office of the Department of Human Resources was better lit than the Unemployment Office, cleaner, fewer people. Two receptionists, men, greeted him, and sent him right through to an Employment Counselor. There wasn't the deadface waiting; people were reading printouts of jobs. The white collars sat at tables under a sign that said White Collar, and the blue collars were at Blue Collar. A sign also said that only those with an E.S. i.d. card were eligible to use the printouts. Some Hamlet ought to stand up and say, "Would not this, sir, and a forest of feathers—if the rest of my fortunes turn Turk with me—with two Provincial roses on my razed shoes, get me a fellowship in a cry of players, sir?"

The Employment Counselor was a Mexican-American guy about Wittman's age; you expect right understanding from him. He was dressed extremely Ivy League, argyle sweater with V neck setting off an oxford collar and well-knotted black knit tie. Don't you look down on him. The token has to excel over everybody of every kind for that one job. He's overqualified to get this far. Sitting on the desk was one of the c.c.s of the Notification of lunacy. "Let's see," said the counselor, Mr. Sanchez, "Mr." on his nameplate as if it were his given name. "What kind of work are you looking for?"

"Playwriting," said Wittman. "I'm looking for a playwriting job. I'm a playwright."

Mr. Sanchez leaned forward, frowned. "What's the last job you had? And the one prior to that? What company you last work for as a playwright?"

"I'm not a playwright for a corporation. I'm not a corporate playwright." I'm no playwright who scripts industrial shows and hygiene films for the educational-military-industrial complex.

"Did you write plays at your last job?"

"I wrote plays during my last job, yes."

"Did you get paid for them? Paid for writing plays?"

"No." If you don't make money, it doesn't count as work.

"What did you get paid for doing?"

"Sales." But I don't want another selling job. I never want to sell anything to anybody as long as I live.

"Then that's what you should write down. The last job you had was retail, and the one before that, retail. So you write down that you are seeking a retail job."

Actually, the job before this one, he worked for one day at a vet clinic, a pet hospital which was also a dog pound. He unloaded flat cats off this truck into the incinerator. Mounds of fur, some necks with collars. Gassed dogs. Teeth, tails. Auschwitz, Bergen-Belsen. He also held pets for the vet to work on. An aged half-dead mangy dog got expensive surgery while a perfectly good dog got put away. Tranked, Rover and Fluffy and Anonymous slid sideways out of consciousness, then out of life. Memorial ashes cost ten dollars a box. There was this one stiff dog that its owner kept weeping over. "What's wrong with Poochy?" She wouldn't listen to Wittman's diagnosis but kept bugging the vet, who had to tell her, "What's wrong with him is he's dead." Wittman only lasted the one day. He didn't list that job in his vita; a spotty job record is worse than no experience at all. He had stayed until closing time. He did his duty, found out what was going on behind appearances. A liberal-arts education is good for knowing to look at anything from an inquisitive viewpoint, to have thoughts while shoveling shit.

Another job, he hadn't stayed the day, he was wired up to a dictaphone —earphones in his ears, hearing a boss's voice that kept saying "Dear" and "Sincerely" and "Truly" and "Yours," with all manner of repulsive business bullshit in between. Which his fingers typed, and his eyes read, and his foot forwarded, rewound, forwarded. Only his dick had been free.

"I see here that you've had management training experience. Take advantage of that. You should go out for management positions. Listen, about this playwriting thing, hombre, I get a lot of college graduates in here who were t.a.s for one semester. They get a taste, you know? To get paid for intellectual discussions and released time to do research, thinking, the writing of a play, whatever. They sign up for college teaching. Universities. They snoot J.C.s. When there's hardly any openings. Colleges don't hire through this office. A theatrical producer has never called. You have to be realistic. I'm hip to your side of the street, man. The one thing people like us have to learn after graduating from college is—be realistic. Let's face it, there is no connection between your major and a job. That's why they told us that we should work to learn, and not for grades."

No, you're not hip to my side of the street, man. Does this look like the hair of a realist? This is poet's hair. You can see this hair and talk to me like that? If you're so hip to my side of the street, why don't you give me some ideas on how to make long hair look short for interviews?

Or is he hinting to me a loophole? Like go ahead and sign up for college teaching. Our office will never bother you with phone calls and leads. You stay home, work on your play. This Sanchez hombre majored in a social science, and he's trying to apply it on me, counseling my ass.

"I am a realist," said Wittman. "It's the business of a playwright to bring thoughts into reality. They come out of my head and into the world, real chairs, solid tables." He knocked on the desk. "Real people. A playwright is nothing if not realistic." He offered Mr. Sanchez a cigarette, which he took. They lit up, laying their matches in the clean ashtray. Wittman said, "Confucius, the realist, said, 'Neither a soldier nor an actor be.' I have no eyes for either line of work." (If he can say "hombre," I can say "Confucius." Nobody's going to put anybody into a bag.) The truth was he didn't want a job of any kind. He was empty of desire for employment.

"You Chinese?" said Mr. Sanchez. "You went to Berkeley? I can tell by the way you talk. You went to Berkeley, didn't you? I went to Berkeley."

"Yeah," said Wittman. "It shows, huh?"

"How were your grades? Your G.P.A.?"

"Not bad. Not too good."

"Did you get a lot of Cs? You got a lot of Cs, right?"

"Some."

"I thought so. Those were Chinese Cs."

"They were what?"

"You haven't heard of the Chinese C? The professor I t.a.'ed for told me to give guys like you the Chinese C, never mind the poor grammar and broken English. You're ending up engineers anyway."

"I wasn't an engineering major. What do you mean? Do you mean they kept me down to a C no matter how well I was doing?"

"No, they were raising you to a C. They were giving you a break who couldn't learn the language. They were trying to help out, get the engineering majors through the liberal arts requirements."

Monkey powers—outrage and jokes—went detumescent at the enormity of the condescension. Too late. He should've been informed of the system, then could've gone into their offices and reasoned with them until they heard his English was gradable.

Mr. Sanchez was saying, "I read all my blue books and papers, and wrote comments. It wasn't like I just read the Chinese name and assigned a C."

"You ought to put in my file that my Cs are worth more."

"Actually, I think they're worth less. Okay, I'll notify employers that you're a really unusual Chinese, who was able to graduate in the liberal arts. You're an idealist. You want to go into a service profession."

"I know just the service I'm qualified to perform. I've invented a job for myself. Let me run it past you up the flagpole."

Wittman put out his cigarette; he had drawn one of those horse-manure numbers that they slip into a pack now and then. "I want to save the world from the bomb. I have an idea how to do it: We implant the detonator inside a human chest. The only way the President can get at the red button is to tear a man open. He has to reach inside the chest cavity with his own hands, and push the button with his personal fingerprint. That will make him think twice before bombing Cubans or Russians. Look, as a pacifist, I volunteer to be the one holding the detonator. It would be better to put it inside the chest of a little kid, but. I'll be the fail-safe detonator. Put that down. I'm signing up with you. Fail-safe detonator. That's what I'll be."

"I won't put that. You can't put that. You're volunteering to be a human sacrifice. The Army already has its pool of human sacrifices. We don't send people on jobs that will never be. And you don't have the experience or qualifications to do bomb work."

"Yes, I do. I worked in a science lab. We, these German ladies and I, harvested R.N.A.-D.N.A. It comes from worms, which have a light-sensitive end. That end—ass or face—rears up at the lights overhead, and we nip it. The ladies were hired for the exactness of their touch. I got hired for my touch too because I look like a delicate and precise Japanese. We gave the worms, which were very clean and pink, a pinch, and out squirted raw R.N.A.-D.N.A. life stuff. It shot into a test tube. We wore goggles because we sometimes shot ourselves in the eye. While the physicists were making bombs, I was storing up life. I know where it's kept. I made friends with the lab tech who had the job of taking the tubes to an underground vault. He showed me the location. Whenever any test-tube washer says to me, 'Hey, man, you want to see something trippy?'—I go with him. I've been to some far-out labs. I've seen kitty cats with electrodes sticking out of their heads. I saw a core sample, which is a piece of the center of the earth brought up from as far down into the ocean floor as they can drill. It looks like shit. I've been inside the Livermore Rad Lab out in the Altamont. They *say* they're studying earthquakes, they mean the earth quakes when they bomb it. I dated a research assistant who took me up to the cyclotron (which is built on top of the Hayward Fault—it may go at any moment). She spun subatomic particles in the cloud chamber and counted them. She let me count some. Because of the Heisenberg miracle, it's the duty of artists to volunteer to do particle counting. Don't leave creation up to the accountants. My eyes have influenced the laws of the universe. I spoke over the particles. I laid trips on them. I made faces at them. I played connect-the-dots—constellations of my own—on a strip of film. My girlfriend threw me out of the lab. Scientists are paranoid. The ones that teach won't tell you the meat of the projects they're working on. They lock their file cabinets. They lock their refrigerators, where they're making winter to hatch baby grasshoppers in 'spring.' They take their briefcases home. I took Physics for Non-Majors from Dr. Edward Teller, who mostly appeared to us on closed-circuit t.v. He didn't teach us dick about fathering the A-bomb. I got assigned to do my reports on the dance of the bumblebees and soap bubbles. Dr. Teller had me working on babyshit when he should have been teaching me the bomb. I learned more from research assistants. An r.a. in physics and an r.a. in biology independently told me that they were working on isolating a chronon —a time ion. Like time *is* a clock. The physicists are looking for it inside the atom, and the biologists are looking in the pituitary gland. Alvarez's team is looking inside pyramids, which they were getting ready to X-ray with lasers that measure cosmic rays. The models and the blueprints looked like set designs for *Aida*. But the Sudan crisis came up, and I don't know what happened next. We are not talking mad scientists here. These are sane scientists.

"Anyway, back at our Frankenstein lab, this techie friend of mine says, 'Do you want to see where they store this stuff?' I helped him carry a vat of R.N.A.-D.N.A., followed him walking on this dirt path in the woods above Strawberry Canyon. We came to a mound with a grass groundcover. The trees were in a circle. The mother tree had died, and its outmost ring had shot up a grove. On top of the mound, under a flat of sod, there's a metal manhole cover with a ring in it. My friend grabbed a-hold of the ring, and turned it in a combination, which I memorized. He lifted the cover off. There was a metal stopper that pulled up like a piston. A mist floated out hovering close to the ground—dry ice. Yeah, I myself have looked inside the vault that stores the essence of life. There's a pool, a well of raw life. We poured in the new stuff. It ran in a rainbow stream. Ribbons and streamers of pure R.N.A.-D.N.A. We stirred it with a glass wand that flashed with the running snot of pure germ. You should be glad to know, in case the bombs go off, the quiddity of pure life is hidden away to start us up again, unless a bomb lands smack dab on that vault on the mound in the circle of trees.

"That was one job that I knew it had a purpose. Boring nevertheless. Hour after hour. Me and the German ladies. Pinch. Squirt. Pinch. Squirt. Pinch. Squirt. Until my techie friend invented a machine that laid all of us off. What if we darkened the room and put the light at the end of the table? You should have seen those greedy little pinkies. Like actors, 'Get outta my light.' They stretch out, important end craning. And this juggernaut-guillotine roll-chops it off. Pop squirt pop squirt pop squirt. We saved us a lot of dainty time. I didn't put that job on my résumé because of being phased out so soon. My friend who invented the worm light and pinch-squeezer lost his job too, and is now an oenologist in Sonoma County.

"No, no, what's so unlikely? I'll tell you the unlikely part, which I left out. The Tibetan Buddhists predict that there will come a time when human beings will be only fourteen inches high. Some say eighteen inches. What year this evolution is supposed to happen is hard to translate from Tibetan time into our time. But I think it will be after the bomb, like in *The Time Machine*. We're going to be mutants like Yvette Mimieux, Weena of the Eloi, but smaller and not everybody a blonde. Because of a contribution I made, which I'll tell you about. What we were doing in our lab was working out the science of how we'll come to be fourteen inches high.

"I went one more time to the stash of R.N.A.-D.N.A. I remember the way to the mound, and went there by myself. I held the ring, and turned it so many clicks this way and so many clicks that way. What the hell, I'll give you the combination. Mr. Sanchez, you could be the survivor who uses it to save mankind. I'll bet anything that there are vaults hidden throughout the Berkeley hills, and the Marin hills, and in the Altamont all around the Lawrence Rad Lab. The combination to that vault—ready?—easy to re-member—is: clockwise to fifty-four, counterclockwise passing fifty-four three times to thirty-two, clockwise two times to ten. Nothing to it. Fifty-four right thrice—thirty-two left twice—right to ten. A countdown, get it? As crackable as a bicycle lock. There I was, all by myself at the well of life. I wet my hands in it. I let it run from hand to hand in the sunlight. I've touched and played with the clear mucous gist of life. When the bomb goes off, the radiation will cook the stuff, see? And these fourteen-inch guys will be animated. They will incubate in the pregnant earth. One of us has to let them out. Out from their bomb shelter will come hopping the prettiest little men and women avid for daylight. The next Big Bang will destroy and create, just like the last Big Bang. Well, there I was alone in the forest, and the sun smiling down on me, alive. I didn't want to die. So I added my two cents to the stuff in the vat. I mean I donated some sperm. There'll be some of me jumping out of the earth. Yvette Mimieux as Weena of the Eloi has Chinese eyes. She'll get them from me. Mr. Sanchez, after the wipe-out, we need to start the earth up with new life. Help me out, man. You have to put me down for a job in science."

"I can't send you to interviews talking like this. Scientists won't buy it. Physics for Non-Majors was just for the fun of it, and to make us well rounded. It doesn't qualify you to work for NASA. Like you aren't fit to be a beekeeper either, or a soap-bubble physicist. All right, all right, I'll put you down for a playwright job. We have never had a call for a playwright, I'm telling you. You better put something else in addition, a fallback position that you can realistically get, such as retail clerk."

"Is there a law that says I have to try for retail clerk and/or retail management?"

"No, I'm suggesting it to you. You want to be humanitarian, you could clerk in a charitable organization, or a political organization."

"Yeah, I could do that. If one of those organizations calls me up, I don't have to take the job, do I?"

"No. This isn't an agency for slaves or human sacrifices. You have to try for the job, though. You ought to go see the movie too." Mr. Sanchez pointed to an arrow that said To Movie Room. "Yes, you better go see the movie." He was writing "Playwright" on the form. Wittman was being humored. Then he wrote "Clerk."

"Okay. I'll go see your movie. Hey, thanks a lot, huh, hombre? I appreciate the counseling. You gave me some good ideas. Adios, huh?"

"Adios," said Mr. Sanchez. When Wittman looked back at him, he was shaking his head muttering, let's hope, "Fifty-four right thrice—thirty-two left twice—right to ten."

Wittman followed the arrow, and joined about a dozen of the pre-employed sitting in front of a roll-down screen. They were evenly spaced away from one another, nobody wanting to sit with a deadbeat. A civil servant finished re-winding the film, and said, "Lights out, please." Wittman, who sat nearest the door for a quick getaway, flipped the switch. Deadbeats and freeloaders in the dark.

It was a cartoon about going for a job interview—how to dress and cut your hair—your personal appearance. Good grooming for that all-important interview. Come to think of it, what everybody in that room had in common was that they were bad dressers. Bad hair. Bad clothes. Bad skin. Nobody in here but us bandanna heads and fishnet torsos and flipflop feet. And ethnics who carry lunch greasing through a brown paper bag. Wittman had been sized up and found sartorially incorrect. (Where had he lost his chewed-up tie?) "Good grooming hints," said the sound track. "Mind these etiquette tips." "Hints." "Tips." Like this was no major deal. Watch, they're going to use his other unfavorite words, "peeve," "hue." Personnel's pet peeve—necktie and socks of the wrong hue. "You mean business. Dress for it." An X crisscrossed a brunette with a low-cut blouse and tight skirt and a cigarette hanging from her lips. She had a beauty spot on her cheek. Rita Moreno. Light rays shone around a woman with a Peter Pan collar and a blonde flip; she was smiling into a hand mirror and patting her hair. Trashy Rita Moreno versus employable Sandra Dee. Who would you hire? An X through the man in a greasy d.a., t-shirt and jeans. Light rays for the man in three-piece suit and barbered hair. X the tennis shoes; gleam all over black shoes with black socks. We the underdressed had to sit there taking one insult after another against our every style and taste. Checkmark: Take a bath or shower, Trim nails and cuticles, Shake hands firmly. X out red pointy fingernails, chewed nails, claw-dirt nails. Another word he didn't like, "cuticles." Do other people really push that bit of nailskin down and cut it off? This is a Watch Bird watching a Nail Biter; this is a Watch Bird watching YOU.

"DO wear a friendly facial expression. DO ask informed questions. DO NOT ask about perquisites and salary right away." The voice read the words on the screen for you. This was not your Cinema Guild and Studio audience. Nobody snickered or made a wisecrack. Oh, shame. Gone are the audiences who laughed at suits and white sidewalls over the ears. But, you know, the average person is not bright. Somebody here may now be reformed to use mouthwash and deodorant. There's a Basic Training hands-on class on how to use your G.I. toothbrush, which some Americans cannot afford. They join the Army, and get their first toothbrush and first pair of new shoes. The Army civilizes. Kill and die with clean teeth. "CHECK the heels of your shoes. DO wear clean linen." Linen? "BRUSH your teeth. COMB your hair." And you'll be all right. "DO sit up straight. DO NOT slouch. DO NOT chew gum. BE on time." He vowed never to polish his shoes or cut his hair again. "PRESENT yourself at your best." Like female monkeys in heat present lipstick-red asses. "A positive attitude," said the voice. At-tee-tood, thought Wittman. "Well turned out. That out-of-the-bandbox look." What the fuck's a bandbox?

"COME ALONE to the interview. DO NOT take friends or relatives with you." An X through my people. Adios, mis amigos. There it is, up on the screen, and in the handbook too: "DO NOT take friends or relatives with you." An American stands alone. Alienated, tribeless, individual. To be a successful American, leave your tribe, your caravan, your gang, your partner, your village cousins, your refugee family that you're making the money for, leave them behind. Do not bring back-up. You're doing it wrong, letting your friends drop you off in a ratty car full of people who look like they live in the car. Out you come wearing the suit and the shoes, carrying the lunch your mamacita made. The girls sitting on the floor outside offices are waiting for commadres taking typing tests and mopping tests. Personnel walks those corridors and lobbies to see who brought a horde. No job for them. Wittman got lonely for that tribesman that said to the Peace Corps volunteer, "We don't need a reading class; we've already got a guy who can read." That's the tribe where he wants to belong, and the job he wants, to be the reader of the tribe. O right livelihood.

Wittman had wanted a tribe since he was a kid at the theater late one night when the cleaning man came, an immigrant from a South Sea island. It was he that had the job but his wife helped, and an elderly grandfather and four kids. They brought a t.v., which they plugged in down in the green room. They enjoyed the use of the rug as a kang, everybody and Wittman sticking their legs under the one blanket, the baby for warming laps. The daddy had people to have his breaks with, eating home-popped popcorn and drinking sodas. He wasn't at all lonely working. Jobs ought to be like that.

"DO write neatly on your application. STRESS your qualifications for the job. AVOID gum chewing, fiddling with a purse, or jingling coins in your pocket. DO NOT SMOKE unless invited to do so." Wittman lit up; it's a free country. "DO NOT apply during the lunch hour or after working hours. AVOID talking about your personal, domestic, or financial problems. RELAX. SPEAK clearly and answer questions honestly. BE business-like and brief." Don't let them smell your fear that you won't make the rent, and you're hungry, and your child is going to die the death of a ragbaby. No flop-sweat. If you're desperate for a job, and why else would you want one, it shows, and they won't give it to you. Act like you don't need money. The End, they don't even say Good luck or any blessing.

At the slapping, snapping tail end of the film, the projectionist said, "Lights. Lights, please." Wittman was so offended that he refused to be light monitor, went right out the door. Where did my monkey powers go? He should have pulled the film out of its sprockets, festooned it around the room, and torn his papers and other people's papers into confetti.

The film that we're going to make after the revolution will give practical information, such as Down with dress codes. Come as you are. The F.O.B.s ought to be told: After the tryout period, nobody wears interview clothes. Bring your greasy lunch in a briefcase, or bring money to eat out. The revolutionary monkey will give lessons on how to tell jokes that crack up employers. He'll teach an etiquette good enough to talk to anybody.

Walking back to his pad, Wittman planned his twenty-six weeks of subsidized living. Forty-four dollars per week to fund subsistence and theater. Jobless, no more pilfering of office supplies and trick-or-treat candy, but no more dry-cleaning of the suit. Stop buying newspapers. Pall Malls are long enough to cut in half for two smokes. Eat one meal a day; fast one day a week. Start shoplifting food from chains. He never did look beyond the year at the furthest. The Bomb could very well fall before Unemployment runs out. He had always taken maximum exemptions—fourteen—and gotten his money in case of bombing before the spring refunds.

Back in his demesne, he found in the mailbox the last paycheck from the store, and the dimmest carbon of the Notification of Changes enclosed. Where's the thank you for your services? Enough bread, though, until Unemployment comes through.

He sat himself right down at his desk and got a head start on the next Claim card. No. None. Yes. No. Yes. No. No. No. No. No. On the flip side were blanks for the names, addresses, and phone numbers of three places where one has inquired for work. As his first contact, he listed Lance Gentaro Kamiyama, President of the Young Millionaires. If Unemployment phoned Lance, being fast on the uptake, he would answer Yes, Wittman had indeed come in for an interview, a good prospective employee, yes. No need to call Lance up requesting and explaining. He was a true friend. On the sheet for keeping an ongoing record, he again wrote Lance's name, and an "I" next to it for "Interview." Interviews would be most troublesome as compared to contact by letter ("L") and contact by telephone ("T"). Surely, U.I.D., the Unemployment Insurance Division, doesn't check every contact, but if they do, may they randomly pick Lance. Whoever needs to cover an Unemployed ass can always write in Wittman Ah Sing as a prospective employer; he would never fail to lie to the Government for the sake of a friend eluding a job, either civilian or military. There. One down. Two to go. Wait a few weeks, put Lance's name again. ("DO make repeat contacts with employers.")

In six months, a Claim every two weeks, twelve cards times three contacts per, that's thirty-six employers. Everyone should form a hui of thirty-six friends. According to friendship scientists, it takes a pool of one million people in order to make twenty friends. But how many of those can you count on to let you use their name on a U.I.D. Claim card? The befriending is hard work in itself.

For the second entry, he wrote, "Chinchillo Fruit Co., a Tillie Lewis Co." That sounded like two employers in a space for one; how hard he's trying. Those canneries pick up busloads of los braceros y los hobos at the hiring halls and on street corners, and drive them to the fields. The U.I.D. won't waste the taxpayers' bucks for a long-distance check-up call. There's no list of those who tried but didn't get a seat on the company bus. Hanging around a hiring hall would count as an interview—"I."

For his third contact, he put the John Simon Guggenheim Foundation. That would be an "L," contact by mail. Next card, the Rockefeller Foundation, then the Ford Foundation, the Woodrow Wilson National Fellow-ships, the Rhodes. He'll cull *Grants and Fellowships* at the library—enough names and addresses for years of Unemployment.

There. Done. Ass covered for next week. Free to go about his true life. Looking for a job could've become a full-time job; and he'd covered two weeks' worth of interviews in fifteen minutes. And it's only Monday. Number Five, "Did you try to find work for yourself that week?" "Yes." And Number Six, "Was any work offered you that week?" "No." Log in first thing every other Monday, and the rest of the fortnight will be his.

Too bad no more spaces already. He was getting hot. What the hell. Fill out some more. Put the F.B.I., and on a later card, the C.I.A. The F.B.I. and the C.I.A. will deny that Wittman Ah Sing was a candidate, then he'll say to Unemployment, "Well, of course, the F.B.I. doesn't tell anybody the everyday-identity name of a G-man trainee-to-be. They can't blow my cover. They offered me a spy job, as a matter of fact, but I don't sign loyalty oaths." NASA, the Pentagon, Scotland Yard. "T," phone calls, hard to trace.

His aunties, the showgirls, would vouch that he had talked to them about work. Start with Auntie Carmen, the agent, then Auntie Mabel's revue. List the casinos in Reno; Unemployment won't question his talent as a croupier, all Chinese are gamblers.

And another thing you can do—put Chinatown businesses. Your con-tact is Woo Ping Sao or Go Wing Mao or Soo Hoo Ting Bao. If Unem-ployment were to say, "We can't find that name in the phone book," you say, "You must have looked under Sao. Sao's not his last name. Woo is his last name. We put the last name in front, see?" And if they say they did look under Woo, you say, "Oh, it must be under Ng. In my dialect, we say Ng instead of Woo. Sometimes he goes by Ng. Try looking under Quinto. They came up out of Bolivia." Or you find some actual name in the China-town phone book, and when that king of tofu hears the white Government voice on the phone, he'll say he doesn't speak English. Throw flak all around. Outsmarting the government is our heritage.

Wittman's not crazy and he's not lazy. The reason he doesn't have right livelihood is that our theater is dead. A company of one hundred great-great-grandparents came over to San Francisco during the Gold Rush, and put on epic kung fu opera and horse shows. Soon the City had six compa-nies—not those six business companies—six theater companies—the Man-darin Theater, the last to die; the Great China Theater, which runs movies now. The difference beween us and other pioneers, we did not come here for the gold streets. We came to play. And we'll play again. Yes, John China-man means to enjoy himself all the while. "If some of us don't live this way, then the work of the world would be in vain," says Lew Welch, poet guide, whose California incarnation is Leo, the Red Monk. We played for a hundred years plays that went on for five hours a night, continuing the next night, the same long play going on for a week with no repeats, like ancient languages with no breaks between words, theater for a century, then dark. Nothing left but beauty contests. Wittman may be untalented, poor, not called upon, but he will make vocation; he will make theater. *Had not one had a hundred times to promise not to die?*

From a shelf higher than his head, he took down the *I Ching*, which is a book and also a person dressed in yellow. He—the Ching—jumps reality to reality like quantum physics. Wittman found any three pennies from his pocket change, shook them, ringing the changes, and threw the Big Have. Dai Yow. Hexagram Number 14, Possession in Great Measure. Dai Yow, a name we give our gambling houses—The Big Have—and Dai Loy, the Big Come, ha ha. When you get something terrific like that, you don't believe it. He threw again, and got Dai Kuo, the Big Crossing, or, as they say, Pre-ponderance of the Great. The Ching says Go. The pre-Americans, before they crossed the ocean to here, went to a church-casino to throw with God. They bet the Big Crossing, and here we are. He threw again. The Ching said, "Youthful Folly. It is not I who seeks the young fool; the young fool seeks me. At the first oracle I inform him. If he asks two or three times, it is importunity." Let us go then, you and I, to make the world our own place.

Through the windows, the San Francisco weather gave no hint as to what time it was, afternoon grey or morning grey. *Here he rises from his meditations and goes to his window; his high room is too close to him, he would like to see stars, if that is possible.* Wittman's stars were the pinholes in his roller blinds, constellations like none in the sky. He shook his pillow out of the pillowcase, stuffed in his sheet, bathroom towels and dishtowel from off the fire escape. He took off the green shirt, stuffed it in too. He put on one of his chambray blue shirts, and his black knit tie, collar down neat, and changed to jeans and tennis shoes. He gathered the socks and under-wear from off the shelves of stacked-up crates and off the floor and out of corners. The good thing about living by yourself in an uncomfortable room is that it forces you out into the marketplace and the forum, a notebook and a couple of books under the arm.

His afterschool and afterwork homecoming neighbors went at him again in the halls and stairwell. "College graduate, believes too much what they teach over there." "Bum-how." "No job. Useless." He faced a woman down, "Have you eaten yet, Grandmother?" "I'm not *your* grandmother, boy. Jook tsing." Bamboo head. "Ho chi gwai jai." Earth paper boy. Just the community's way of letting you know we care. He ought to bring his white girl up here for a tour, give them something to talk about. *Now since I have been drifting about alone like this, I have had innumerable neighbors; neighbors above me and beneath me, neighbors on the right and on the left, sometimes all four kinds at once. I could simply write the history of my neighbors; that would be the work of a lifetime. It is true that it would be, rather, the history of the symptoms of maladies they have generated in me. . . .* The smell of other people's dinners was filling the air with hungers.

He turned up his pea-coat collar, slung his seabag over his shoulder, and walked toward his ship, which had been torpedoed during World War II. He was the ghost of one of the five fighting Sullivan brothers. Five roles for five Caucasians. The sun looked like a foggy moon. The old eyes of the man in the moon, up again during the day, were drooping tearfully. The street, the buildings, the people seemed spackled, blending them into a coherent set. The laundromat was on a corner; the traffic took right turns around the windows like sharks at the Steinhart Aquarium. There were pools of water on the street and on the floor. He bought some soap out of the vending machine, shoved everything into a small washer, stretching his money. President Truman had washed his own socks in the White House sink, so as not to make Bess his laundress. "Nobody should have to wash a man's socks for him," he'd said. Wittman was having the same consideration for Taña. But he did miss laundromats near a campus; there had been propaganda leaflets you could agree with, recent magazines and newspapers and good paperbacks left behind to share the wealth, and readers and writers at the chairs with a desk-arm. Though too often a head was watching t.v. at a front-loading washer.

He picked up a postcard from off the floor. It was porno, two or three fleshy people cheesing into the camera. The girl looked Chinese or Japanese or Korean. Arms and legs were bent funny because of balancing on high-heel shoes while fucking while looking at the birdie. There was an address and phone number, which the Steppenwolf would have gone to or called up, letting whatever wrong number trip him out into somebody else's movie. No, thanks. Wittman, a man of purpose, had in mind a place to go while his clothes were washing.

At his bus stop, a very strange person, a blonde Black lady, also waited. She stood closer and closer. She was wearing too many clothes, not knowing why she was uncomfortable. They had been boiled in dark dye, as PoPo used to do to costumes. He felt her stares touching his face. "Do you know what they did to the pretty little oriental girl?" she asked. He put his books on his shoulder, blocked her view. But didn't fool her into thinking he was invisible. "They killed the pretty little oriental girl. And do you know why they killed her?" Why did they kill her? "I'll tell you why they killed her." Dramatic pause. Five, six, seven, eight. "They killed her for her kidneys." No shit, Dick Tracy. He walked fast to another bus stop, lost her. Her voice came on the pouring fog, ". . . kidneys," chasing him for quite a while.

"Is that you? Is that you?" What is this? One for each bus stop. Who? Me? Yes, pointing at him, addressing him, shouting him out from across the traffic was a white lady in a raincoat and scarf. The shark cars were cutting her off from coming over to his side of the street. "It's you, isn't it?"

"No, it's not," Wittman answered.

"Sure, it's you."

"No. No. I don't think so." Hey, wait a second. That's not right. She's tanglewitting him.

"Georgie. You Georgie?"

He knows the answer to that one. "No, I'm not. I'm not Georgie."

"Georgie, you go home and phone your mother. You phone your mother. You hear? Go home, Georgie. Phone your mother. Why won't you call your mother, Georgie? You call your mother. Georgie, you call her right now."

Street talkers choose him. They're always recognizing him. It takes one to know one. The bus came, and he rode away, passing both his ladies. What is it about me that I am picked out by the touched?

Well, yes, he ought to give his mother a call, tell her she can stage a memorial service. PoPo is not getting herself found.

When a familiarity pervaded a certain neighborhood in the Avenues, Wittman got off and walked. He peeked like X-ray eyes through cracks between buildings and saw the ocean. Sea dragons were rolling about sounding their foghorns. He came to a Queen Anne house that he had seen before; it hadn't been a dream or a wish. That red plant they make soup out of, who knows its English name, was growing in the strip of dirt between the sidewalk and the street. Over the front door were three words that looked like the Chinese on houses that his parents and grandmother had pointed out to him in Vancouver, Seattle, Sacramento, Stockton, Denver, L.A. "Ours." A house not much different from others on the block except for the sign that was a board off a crate: Bow On Hong, which isn't even how you pronounce Benevolent Association but the best the founders could spell. Wongs and Lees have headquarters that are architect-designed office buildings; they own the block, the shopping center. The Ah Sings had had to join up with a bunch of other families, and they still weren't much. Not one of your power clans. "You need help," said his father, "you go there." Zeppelin went to the New Year's banquet and July 4 picnic as a philanthropist, a big donor, a buyer of many raffle tickets with his last twenty-dollar bill. The only beggarmen at the Eighth Month Fifteenth Day party were Black bum-hows and white bum-hows, who walked in off the street, no shame.

An old fut in B.V.D. undershirt came out to the curb with a watering bucket. Wittman turned and walked away. He needed to go around the block practicing what to say. Admit it, he was sort of afraid of the Bow On Hong. There are non-Chinese who understand that. At school, he'd met a Jewish girl who was afraid of Hadassah ladies. Same thing.

He folded the collar of his pea coat down, and came at the old fut from the other direction. He was watering the curb vegetables with warm piss. Smell it, hear it bubble, see it steam. Fresh. "Sir," said Wittman, that is to say, "Teacher." "Teacher, may I speak with you awhile?" Sloshed the old honeybucket there almost onto one's shoes. Then picked up a broom and started sweeping his way across the sidewalk and up the stairs. Swept that Wittman aside. "Teacher, may I please have a word with you?" Importuning, crabwalking.

The old coot bent over with his ass in one's face, and swept into his oil-can dustpan. He could have stood straight, using the upright handle. He was giving Wittman the ass on purpose. "I have an idea I want to discuss with you," said Wittman.

"No speak English," said the old fut, heading up the stairs, blocking the way with his equipment. Oh, come on, he can speak English. Anybody can speak English who feels like it. "Boss not here," he said, like Wittman was some health inspector, some tourist, some Caucasian salesman. But Wittman's half-ass Chinese would have insulted him, as if he were not good enough to use American on. The boss is too here. This is our president, Mr. Grand Opening Ah Sing. Do they call him Grand Opening to his face?

"Teacher, I need to talk to you about something very important," said Wittman, as he had rehearsed, stepping over things to beat Mr. Grand Opening up the stairs.

The old fut banged his broom, oilcan dustpan, honeybucket. Wittman sat down on the top step. "Let's sit and talk awhile, Teacher. Rest," he said, beckoning the old fut to have a sit, like host inviting guest. This place is my place too.

"Talk then talk, la." Like suit yourself. The old fut kept walking on up.

Wittman jumped to his feet, yanked the screen door open, "Let me help you," grabbed the wet honeybucket. "I came here with a good idea for you, Uncle." But quick, the old fut rattled through the door and locked it. His hair stuck up from its whorl in a topspin. He laughed, hoisting his droopy drawers by their suspenders. He's no president; this is our village idiot who has no other place to live and no family, our charity case in exchange for caretaking the estate.

"Hoi mun!" shouted Wittman. "Open the door!" The old guy stood there looking at him. " 'Knock knock.' 'Who's there?' 'Hoimun. Hoimun Who? Hoimun, I want to come in, ah.' Ha ha. Get it? Herman, open the door."

"Go away," said the old fut. "You go."

"No, no, I'm not ah Go. I'm Ah Sing. Are you an Ah Sing too, Uncle? I'm Ah Sing. I'm not a robber." You can trust me not to steal this honey-bucket. "I want to talk to you. I'm Ah Sing. I'm Zeppelin Wadsworth Ah Sing's boy. You know Ruby? Ruby Long of Chicago. I'm Ruby Long Legs' boy." Shit. What's GrandMaMa's name? "I have a popo. I'm Ah Sing PoPo's grandson."

He was grabbing look-sees over the old fut's shoulders. A large living room with a pair of heavy carved throne-chairs at one end—the stage area. "My Ah Sing PoPo was here at the New Year's party, do you remember her? My mother gave a lot of money to this association, Sacramento branch. My baba is a past president of the Six Companies. I just want to visit, okay? Just visit. Just just. Please, Ah Sing Uncle, may I come in and sit?"

"Come in then come in."

Wittman brought the rest of the pissing and cleaning equipment inside. He set his books on the conference-dining table, and sat down before them. They like you to have books. He gestured the old fut toward a chair, "Sit. Sit," acting as if he were a dues-paid active member, whose family were founders from way back. The old fut took the seat at the head of the table, next to a chalkboard. "So what you want?" he said.

"I want to put on a play here. For free. It won't cost you anything. It will make money for you. For us. For the Family Association, who doesn't have to pay to see it. The Association can sell tickets, and make money. Will you please donate the use of our hall for a play? We could open up these doors to make the living room and eating room one big room. Only move this long table."

"What you mean play?"

"A bock wah. A bock wah, wah." White speech. Pure speech, as in a play. "Jew hay, wah. I like to jew hay." To make air. To give to airy nothing a local habitation and a name. "I like to make a play with Gwan Goong. A Chinese play." But he doesn't mean a Chinese play. Is there a Chinese word for Chinese-American? They say "jook tsing." They say "ho chi gwai." Like "mestizo." Like "pachuco."

"Gwan Goong be here." The god of actors and writers and warriors and gamblers and travelers was on top of the mantel.

"This house be a good house to make a play," said Wittman, said all the spiel he'd prepared, and began repeating himself.

"You no can play in here."

"Listen, we must play in here. Else, what Association for, huh? Collecting dues? What you do, huh? You bury old men. You be nothing but one burial society. Better you let United Farm Workers use the bathroom and kitchen. Let them crash overnight. Be headquarters—Hello, Strike Central —for union of waiters and garment workers." Where's more language, for to amplify and ramify? In Berkeley, a Black Muslim spoke about "sanctuary that the Chinese brothers provide one unto another." He had looked right at Wittman, a member of a people with a genius for community. Black guys see too many kung fu movies. They think a Chinese-American can go anywhere in the country and have a safehouse where a stranger can be served a family dinner. Well, there had been a time, any old Chinese stopped you in the intersection and scolded you to be careful crossing streets. Scolded you to be a good boy, like they all took a hand in raising you. The ethnos is degenerating.

"We no can have Black gwai and bum-how meeting here. Don't say old men dead."

"Okay, okay, old men not dead. Nobody dead. Everybody plays. Look, I'll show you." Wittman jumped up and ran to the fireplace, to the flags and the oranges and pomelos and the dusty plastic fruit and flowers. "Here. Gwan Goong and Chang Fei be here. Kung fu. Hi ho, Red Rabbit." He picked up a feather duster, which represents horse. "Sabe? Move this." He shoved the big table. "Chairs. People." Moved chairs away from the wall, turned them toward the front. "Talk big stories."

"What you doing?" said the old fut. "What you doing?" He moved the chairs back. He pushed against the other side of the table. "What you do, jook tsing boy? You ho chi gwai. You monkey." But the old fut was asking a question. Always take questions as signs of friendliness.

"Monkey kung fu," said our monkey. "I do monkey kung fu." He grabbed a flagstaff. "Monkey gim." The gim is the double-edged sword. Wave the red-white-and-blue, wave the horse. "Monkey at war." The magic monkey twirls his rod that turns into needle, gim, staff, the Empire State Building, a soft-shoe swaggerstick. "Monkey fights Lao Tse." "Lousy," he pronounced it, trying to hit the tones. "Monkey fights lousy," which is all right; Monkey lost that fight. "Monkey fights Kwan Yin." He picked Kwan Yin up from the mantelpiece, and shook her, shook himself as if she were doing it, bonked himself on the head with her, and disappeared, yanked, behind the chalkboard. He ran out, carrying the flag sweeping the furniture and floor. He stopped at the fruit, and bit a plastic peach. "Monkey drinks the wine and eats the peaches. Monkey pisses in the cups. Priests drink monkey piss. Pfooey." Funny face toward the audience. "Monkey changes seventy-two ways. Bee-e-en! Monkey bird. Monkey fish." Bug eyes, blowfish cheeks, mouth and eyes opening and shutting, his fingers swimming like gills and fins beside his face. "Monkey as temple." Stiff and articulated like an Egyptian, his flagpole-tail erect, salute it. "Be-ee-en! Monkey as a dancing bouillon cube. Help. Help. I'm diminishing. Bee-e-en!" Jumping up and down, voice fading, cooking in the cauldron of life. He picked up the jar of sticks, and shook them onto the hearthstone, like jackstraws. He threw the three coins in his pocket against the baseboard. There were three turtle shells, and he threw them on the floor. "Did they land lucky, huh, Uncle? Good luck, huh? We okay for a play? Monkey bets God." He wrapped himself around the porcelain footstool-drum, and banged out a rhythm. "Come see the bock wah, laaaah." He fell into the throne-chair. Come on, come on, where's the applause? "Seriously, sir," he said, "let me give you a tryout free sample story. If you like it, we have more show for everybody. You don't like it, I leave. Fair?"

"Okay okay," said the old fut.

"Okay?! Once upon a time, the one hundred and eight outlaws fought against an army that took arrows through their hearts, and got stronger and stronger. There came word or a dream about a weapon that would keep that army down. Tai Chung, the messenger of the outlaws, would go get it. 'Take me with you,' said Li Kwai, the Black Whirlwind. Now, some say he's black because he was bad and his weapon was the ax. He killed anybody, little kids, girls. He didn't mean it but. He was like a storm. He knuckle-rapped this girl singer's forehead, and she died. He had wanted her to stop singing while he talked-story. You could get rich taking the adventures of the Black Whirlwind to Hollywood. He was trying to civilize himself, bringing his old mother to the community at the Water Verge. She got eaten by a tiger while he fought the wrong tiger. He made too much trouble for his own side, losing. He might as well go on errand. I say he was Black Li because his skin was black. He was Chinese and black, a black Chinese, many roles in our bock wah for all kinds of us.

"Tai Chung, the Flying Prince, says, 'You may come along if you promise not to eat meat on the way. Will you do whatever I tell you to do?'

" 'No problem,' says Black Li.

" 'Good. We'll be traveling fast. Don't lag behind.' " Wittman did two voices, me-aying his head back and forth. "They go only three or four miles before Black Li suggests that they stop for wine. Tai says that wine is about as bad as meat. They run until evening. At an inn, Black Li serves Tai vegetables, but doesn't touch them himself." Wittman brought the plastic fruit over to the big table. " 'Why aren't you eating with me?' asks Tai. 'Aren't you hungry?'

" 'I be back,' says Black Li.

"Tai tails him to a back room. He's eating platters of beef and pork." Wittman pretended to gobble up the plastic fruit. "The next morning, they get up at four a.m., and both eat vegetables for breakfast. Tai says, 'Yesterday wasn't fast enough; we have to make three hundred miles today. Pack tight.' " Wittman wrapped his tie around his head, and stuck paper—letters and dispatches—into his belt. He knelt at the old fut's feet, untied his shoes, could've tied the laces together. " 'I'm giving you leg armor that was hammered from enchanted metal.' " He blew and spoke on the shoes, which the old fut was re-lacing. " 'There. You've eaten your peas and carrots. You're going to run well. One more magic: You carry our dark banner. Feel the wind pulling at it? I'll carry everything else.' " He put the broom in the old fut's hand, and picked up the honeybucket, the basket of gifts for negotiating with friends and strangers. "Black Li sails away, his legs moving in long strides without touching the ground." Wittman grabbed the old fut's hand, and pulled him around the table. "Run *this* way, Uncle," he said, his feet going ahead of him, the rest of his body trying to catch up.

"Stop," said the old fut, "stop, you." He gave a yank, and Wittman fell down, landing on his butt. The old fut laughed. Fall down, make 'em laff.

Wittman got up, continuing in character as mercuric Tai.

" 'Move those feet. Hear the storms rushing in your ears. See the trees and houses whirl by. You're passing inns and can't stop for a drink. Your feet keep moving under you. Swim, Black Li. Fly. All I see of you is a black streak, you're going so fast. I'm two yellow streaks—my yellow turban and my cummerbund. I catch up to you when the sky is red with sunset. Brother Black Li, why aren't you stopping to eat?'

" 'Elder Brother Tai,' you say, 'save me. I'm dying from hunger and thirst, and I can't stop running. Help. Food. Please.'

"Tai holds out a bun. They miss the relay. He eats it himself.

"Black Li turns around, feet running ahead, hands reaching for the bun far far behind. Tai catches up. 'Things are very strange today,' he says, 'as I can't seem to control my legs.'

" 'I can't either,' says Black Li. 'My legs won't obey me. I feel like chopping them off.'

" 'Yes, where's your ax? We go on like this, we won't stop until New Year's Day.'

" 'Please don't play tricks on me, Elder Brother. If I cut off my legs, how can I go home?'

" 'You must have disobeyed me and eaten meat. I think that's why strange legs.'

" 'I don't lie. I ate some meat yesterday. But not much. Only six pounds. When I looked at your vegetables, I just had to have a little meat. What do I do now?'

" 'Stop!' Tai catches hold of Black Li's leg, and yanks." From behind, Wittman scooped the old fut into a chair. " 'I see you're having trouble with gravity. Let's take off one shoe, and slow you down by half. Walk this way.' " He did a banana-peel run, slip-sliding around the room.

"They rush past wine flags and grog flags, but the waving of a fingery pennon draws them both to a halt. They find themselves at a crossroads where grows a tree that five men holding hands exactly encircle. There's an inn with a woman leaning out the window. She's wearing a green see-through coat, a low-cut blouse, and a pink underblouse. The buttons are real gold. In her hair are gold combs and red flowers. She has red-rouge cheeks. 'Good meat,' she calls. 'Good wine. Come refresh yourselves.' She walks out to meet them. Her skirt is red and short. They follow her through the grape arbor outdoor café to the cedar tables and stools inside. There are no other customers. 'We have very tasty bow and dim sum.'

" 'Bring forty then,' says Black Li.

" 'Bring vegetable bow,' says Tai. 'Bean filling.'

" 'What are you afraid of?' The woman laughs. 'That we use dog meat?

These are good times; no need to eat human meat or dog meat. We serve pork and beef.'

" 'I've lived through many travels,' says Tai. 'I know about inns where they cut up fat men to fill dumplings, and toss thin men into the river. Vegetarianism makes my senses strong, and I'm smelling a strange meat.'

" 'What a way you have of flirting with me. As a vegetarian, you've come to the right place. We're famous for our peas and beans. My husband's nickname is Vegetable Gardener.'

" 'I'll test the meat,' says Black Li. 'I'll taste what these bows are made of.' He takes a mouthful.

"Tai pulls a long hair out of his bow. 'Now isn't this a human hair?'

"Their hostess giggles and scratches her head with a comb. 'It's one of mine. I'm sorry. I do have a profusion of hair, don't I?'

" 'Sister, why isn't there a man about?' asks Tai.

" 'My husband, the Vegetable Gardener, went to visit friends, and is bringing them home for dinner.'

" 'How long has he been gone?'

" 'So you are flirting with me.'

" 'Woman, this wine is weak,' says Black Li. 'If you make better wine, let's have it.'

" 'I have a thick red I've been saving for a special drinker.'

" 'Bring it. And two tubs of warm water for our feet.'

"She goes out and comes back with a dark and dull wine. She's laughing to herself.

" 'This wine is cold,' says Tai. 'Could you warm it please?'

" 'You want it hot, I'll make it hot for you. I'll redden that vegetarian body of yours with grog blossoms.'

"While she's gone, Tai whispers to Black Li that the wine has been poisoned. They should pretend to drink but pour it out the window.

" 'No waste,' says Black Li, who downs it. His eyes close, and he falls off his stool. Tai also shuts his eyes, and lays his head on his arms. He hears the woman clap her hands. 'Ha, I washed my feet in that swill you drank.' She undoes their belts and pouches, feeling for money, laughing all the while. 'I've caught two big ones. Meat bow for days.' Her henchmen come out from the kitchen. 'Carry the meat to the butcher block,' she orders. They drag Black Li off. Tai lies rigid; they can't move him. 'You lazy clowns,' she scolds the helpers. 'You eat and drink but can't work. I'll lift him myself. Why, he's going to be as tough as water buffalo.' She takes off her green see-through coat and her red silk skirt. She throws his arms over her shoulder, trying to get him into a fireman's carry. He clamps her in his legs. She screams. And just then, her husband comes home, banging through the swinging door with his gang of friends. Black Li crashes in from the kitchen, chased by the cooks with butcher knives. Tai tries to hang on to the Night Ogress, for it is she. They have a free-for-all bar-room brawl fracas and melee all over the place. Black Li swings from the rafters and kicks stomachs and jaws and asses. The Vegetable Gardener lassoes the paddleblade fan, and rides it around the room, swiping at Black Li. The mirror behind the bar shatters in a storm of reflections. A cook throws a wok. It carries him off the balcony. The bartender falls out through the swinging doors into a horse trough. Aces, kings, queens, and knaves fly." Wittman was running all over the Benevolent Association, up and down the stairs, on and off the furniture, the old fut chasing him.

"They fight to a tie and draw. Tai has his foot on Night Ogress's neck. 'Your mother farts like a dog,' she curses. 'He's accusing us of murder,' she tells her husband. 'He's saying we're cannibals.'

" 'There are body parts in the kitchen,' says Black Li. Tai lets go of the Night Ogress to have a look.

" 'Oh, no,' says she. 'What must you be thinking?' She flusters around with the featherduster, just a housewife caught behind on her housekeeping. She picks up a hand. 'You're thinking that I—that I—cook and serve and eat—? That this is food? Oh, how could you? Why, you're looking at trophies. These are the pieces of armed and dangerous men with prices on their heads. We don't have room in the house for their whole bodies. I'm not strong enough to bring back their entire remains. I just clip a part for identification—a scalp, a distinctive patch of tattooed or branded skin. This hand is the hand of Three-Finger Jack.' Well, there are two fingers missing, all right; the famous trigger finger is still there. 'And this head is the head of Joaquín Murrieta.' " Wittman took hold of the old fut's head by the chin.

"Tai and Black Li examine the head with respect. There was the handsome eagle nose, the handlebar moustache, the brown eyes, looking at them even in death. But throughout the Far Out West were many heads of Joaquín Murrieta. Stagecoaches miles apart were held up at the same time by a man who said, 'It is I, Joaquín.' Of course, those who were robbed insisted that no lesser Joaquín Murrieta than El Famoso had done it. How do we know this head is the head?

" 'I have the hand from the selfsame body,' says the Night Ogress a.k.a. Mrs. Chang a.k.a. Mrs. Sun a.k.a. the Goodwife Sheng. 'This hand of his has the correct finger dedigitated. We got El Famoso, all right. Next time you go to Sacramento, honey, take me and the head and the hand with you. I need to redeem my bounty coupons. We have fifteen thousand dollars coming.'

"Now that everyone has calmed down, Chang Ch'ing alias the Vegetable Gardener says, 'My wife and I invite you to dine on chicken and goose al fresco under the grapevines.' Though Chang fought hard, his black cap is still on his head, and his white coat is clean and neat. 'Honey, you got carried away again,' he says to his wife in everyone's hearing by way of apology.

" 'How did we get so drunk?' asks Black Li. 'We didn't drink much. The wine must have been very good. We'll have to remember the inn under the great tree at the crossroads, and drop by on our way home.'

" 'Please accept my apology,' says Tai to Mrs. Chang, 'for messing up your house.'

"She accepts, and everyone adopts one another as brothers and sister. Flying Prince Tai invites the couple to start a restaurant-guardpost at the Mountains of the White Tigers and the Two Dragons, Shantung. There the stranger, the weird and the alienated make their own country. And have one hundred and seven brothers and sisters. The one hundred and eight banditos, banished from everywhere else, build a community. Their thousands of stories, multiples of a hundred and eight, branch and weave, intersecting at the Water Verge. An inn at each of the four directions run by four couples, famous for serving their guests generously and sweetly, account for the strange things that happen at city limits."

"You give wrong impressions," said Grand Opening Ah Sing. "We not be cannibals. We not be bad."

"But, Uncle, we bad. Chinaman freaks. Illegal aliens. Outlaws. Outcasts of America. But we make our place—this one community house for benevolent living. We make theater, we make community."

"But you wreck the restaurants. The tourists will ask, 'What is this stuff inside the dim sum? What kind of meat you put inside the char sui bow?' Business goes down, no more Chinatown."

"But they ask anyway, huh? Answer once and for all."

"Answer what? Cannibal meat."

"You're getting the idea, Uncle. White meat."

"Bad advertising. What's the matter for you, boy? The tourists save money for years, working all their lives until they retire, and they come here to see us. Whyfor you want to hurt them? They want to see the Gold Mountain too."

The monkeys which had broken loose, jumping all over the old man and the young man, tickling toes, armpits and groins, keelee keelee, rubbing paw-hands, oh boy, oh boy, stopped their funny business. Wittman said, "I promise: no bad advertising. May I put on a show, okay?"

"Okay okay."

"Okay?!" Wittman grabbed the old fut's pissy hand and shook it.

"You come go outside now. Meet again."

"Don't forget you said okay; we shook on it. Thank you, Uncle. Thank you. Lucky meet again."

"Meet again," said the old fut, latching the screen door, and looking at him through it.

"When?" asked Wittman. "When do we meet again? How about tomorrow everyday nighttime I bring the troupe? And grand-opening night be Tenth Month, thirty-first day. Guai Night. Hawk Guai Night." Imitation of Ghosts Night. Scare the Ghosts Night. Hallowe'en. "Call a meeting for our play, okay? Take a vote. Okay? Okay."

"Yeah yeah yeah," said the old fut.

Wittman hopped the bus back to the laundromat. Yes, he was in luck, laundry all there. He jammed it wet back into the pillowcase, to be hung up to dry on the fire escape. Pea-coat collar up against the foggy dusk, which can break your heart—your true love has left, and you're lost, when you haven't even found her—he walked through ambiguities. Poems blow about that nobody has put into words. Old poems partly remembered sniff at your ears. Nah. Lew Welch warned that it isn't the moon that's sad, it's you. The moon is never sad, says the Red Monk.

North Beach was lit up, jumpy with neon. Chinatown was bright too, paper lanterns over light bulbs, a party neverending. On Stockton Street was the biggest Joang Wah, the Consolidated Benevolent Associations. Majestic stairs going up to the locked gates and locked doors, roof curlicuing above gilt words—it ought to be a theater. Give our little Family Association first crack at a hit play; the Consolidated Benevolent will invite it here, and get revolutionized. Bust the men in suits. They haven't done useful politics anymore since China Relief. United Farm Workers, when you march on Sacramento at Easter, you are invited to bivouac here and at all the Associations en route from Delano up the Central Valley. I, Wittman Ah Sing, welcome you. And while you're at it, liberate the twenty-one missions that Junipero Serra built a day's walk apart—perfectamente for protesters. Then take the Gong Jow temple. Please. They don't do nothing in there but worship goats. No kidding. GrandMaMa once sent a postcard of a statue of goats climbing a pinnacle. A ram stood on its hind legs; it held wheat shafts in its mouth. She said, "Goats saved Gong Jow." I come from a people who worship billygoats.

And, of course, who should Wittman see—find—crossing kittycorner on the green light though it wasn't a Scramble Walk, just when he was thinking of her—but PoPo. The traffic was jammed up, and she walked slow and old in it. Break, my heart. She has gone out without her cane, to show off her legs. Her head—a mantilla comb was stuck high in the geisha-style coils of her very black hair—baubled among the cars. The light changed; the cars picked up speed, a metal river before her and behind her. She kept on coming. A quick nick and one grandma closer to orphanhood. Wittman went out into the intersection, and took from her her purse and her pink box of pastries. He didn't rush her, walked slowly with her, let her take her time, let the fucking honkers run over the both of them. (I am Carlos Bulosan's manong pinoy come home from the city to take the reins of the carabao from the old mother's brown hands, and plow the wet rice field.) It takes youth and willpower to stop cars—look the drivers in the eyes. He brought GrandMaMa safe through the street and up onto the curb.

"How did you get to Big City, PoPo? I've been looking all over for you."

"By miracles. I was upstairs at the Gong Jow giving my thank you."

"What do you do up there, PoPo? Who do you thank? Goats? What's upstairs?"

"Pile up some fruit, stick three incense sticks in the pile. You don't have to go to temple, you can do it anywhere; the kitchen is okay. Oranges, grapefruit, not lemons but. Then hold your hands together like this, and say something."

"Say what?"

"Whatever you feel like saying. Say it all out."

That's all there is to it.

He's going to have to find out if our organizations take upon themselves the reputation as law-abiding, super-patriotic do-nothings so that they can hide illegal aliens, and be a peace sanctuary for fugitives from the next war.

Hardly resting at the street corner, she kept walking; she wasn't going to lose her momentum. "Your grandmama was an abandoned grandmama," she said. "Give me a cigarette, honey girl." Managing the purse and the box, and his laundry, he lit a smoke for her and one for himself. "Your mother and your father lost me on purpose to die in the high-up Sierras.

Left me like an extra cat or dog that's cute no more. Oh, you should see the ex-pets dumped in the wild woods. Perfectly good dogs. I fed them my food. I made a wish at those dogs to turn back into wolves. But they forget how to be animals. They thought I was going to take them home. I walked up and down the roadside, and two dogs and a skinny skinny cat and one creature I don't know what it was followed me."

"Did it have a tail? How big was it?"

"It might have had a tail tucked up. It was brown and white and about this big. O life. The hundred and eight outlaws had a saying: 'Even an ape will cry when another ape is sad.' Your parents are heartless, little Wit Man. Oh, my poor honey girl, you had to be raised by them." Well, he had been raised by her too, and he would probably be better off psychologically if she didn't call him "honey girl," mutt hong nay, which doesn't sound good translated or untranslated. "I tell you, honey girl. Your mother said, 'Do you want to go on a picnic, PoPo?' We went in your father's pick-up truck. I sat in the back. They sat up front plotting against me. We bought takeout, a fire duck with plum sauce and steam rolls."

"Do you want my jacket, PoPo?" She was wearing one of her Malay dresses, and you could see her bony tan shoulders through it. They took turns holding the purse, the pink box, the cigarettes, the heavy wet laundry; he took off the pea coat, she put it on. It hung heavy and long on her, an old urchin of the U.S. Navy.

"Your father drove high, high; he wound around in the mountains so I didn't know east or west. The wind was getting me. I pressed against the backs of those two in the cab. They were talking too much to each other. They were passing picnic spots by. Pretty soon, no benches, no barbecue stoves. We were driving into the wild woods. They acted as if they couldn't hear me banging at their heads and calling Stop.

"At the top of the mountains, they stopped, and your father lifted me down from the pick-up. He carried me. He said, 'Upsy Daisy.' Your mother handed me the blanket and said, 'Spread the blanket under that tree, PoPo.' They put the bag of duck on the ground. I cleared off stones and pine cones. I got tangled in the blanket trying to shake it out in the mountain wind, and do you know what those two kai dai did?" Wittman didn't know the translation for "kai dai," such a dirty word that the dictionary leaves it out and nobody claims to know what it means. "Those kai dai got in the truck and drove away. I thought to myself, they're hurrying down to State Line to do some gambling before we eat. But they didn't come back, and they didn't come back. I ate fire duck without them. Some picnic. A dog came out of the forest carrying a doggie dish in his mouth. I fed him their duck; it served them right. I had lunch. I had dinner. I stood beside the road —they had gotten me off the highway to a hidden road—and looked for the pick-up, and never saw it come back or go by. I gave steam rolls and soda to that dog and another dog and the cat and the creature animal. I patted them —'Good dog. Good dog'—and kept them with me. Those animals were so worn out, they didn't read my mind that I might need to eat them by and by. Oh, honey girl, I'm a perfectly good grandmama, and they dumped me. But a 'perfectly good dog' isn't as good as a 'good dog,' is it? Oh, honey girl, I began to cry. I wept loud. The sun was setting. Oh, who wouldn't cry? It's not fair. Why hadn't they warned me? They could have given me a chance. Judges and employers give people chances. Did they think they had already heard all my conversation? If they were tired of me repeating myself, they could have told me so. I would have done something about it. I repeat myself but not because I forget that I've told a story already. I know I told it before. I tell a thing over again because I like going through it again. I could keep a calendar, and not tell the same things so often. I'm going to read more, and know facts that nobody's heard yet. Maybe they don't like my habits? Your mother and I were at a banquet, where a bit of food spilled on my skirt. I licked my finger and cleaned the spot. Your mother said, 'Stop that, PoPo, that's an old-lady habit.' I stopped, and don't do that anymore. She didn't notice I changed. That was my last chance. It's hard to keep being new and different, honey girl. I was falling behind on the news. The newspapers were piling up in my room. Don't grow old. Otherwise, out you go."

"Yeah, be fun or else, no more use for you. Otherwise, old-age home. Otherwise, divorce. Otherwise, up for adoption. Dog pound. You're a perfect and good grandmother. PoPo, you come live with me. We be cronies." It's not fair, a crone is an old sheep, but a crony is a friend through time.

"Oh, but no, thank you. You one good boy, Wit Man. I found me a place to live. Let me tell you what happened."

"You were waiting by the side of the road, the sun going down."

"I was weeping by the side of the road, the sun going down. High high in the cold, far mountains, the trees are thick, and the woods are dark long before the sun goes down. Oh, those two ex-children of mine acted so caring of me. 'Why don't you get out here and take a pee, PoPo?' 'Go ahead, start eating, PoPo. Don't wait for us.' Under the tall red trees, I cried and cried and cried. There was no other sound in the air.

"It happened that an old Chinese man was driving through that forest with his windows down. He heard crying, and thought, 'Who can that be weeping in the dark woods?' He braked beside me, and stuck his head out the window. 'Lady, why do you weep?' 'Sir,' says I, 'I have been forsaken by ungrateful children.' 'Aiya,' the old man said, 'no-good children. Come with me. Come home with me. I've been seeking a wife. Will you marry me? And return to the City, and live with me?' I put the picnic blanket in the car, and got in next to him. Fortunately, Reno was nearby. We drove there, and were married. The numbers we bet on were our wedding date and our ages. We won a great deal of money. Such a lucky day. We're living together now on Washington Gai. You can tell your no-heart mother and father that their plot to kill me has failed. My love story is the talk of China-town."

A miracle, all right. Wittman hoped that when he grew old, he would become like that old man. A babe goes bouncing down the street; a wrin-kled popo lags along. Why, he'd whistle at the latter and mean it. He was beginning already. He liked the way her eyelids draped at the corners. Debbie Reynolds eyelids. She wore October opals at the top tips of her ears, perhaps a fashion of a country nobody else knows about or comes from. Perhaps her family sold her, but earmarked her to find again.

"Tell me some more about your old man," he said.

"He's important. A big shot. He owns the building we live in. He col-lects the rent from a whole building. I help him collect. His office is on the ground floor, and our apartment is the top floor. We don't work and live in the same room. Do you know what he was doing in the Sierras? He was waiting for a storm. He wanted to ride a tree, as he did when he was a lum-berjack. He hugged the trunk at the tiptop of a sequoia—the tree whipping around and around in the thunder and lightning. It staggered backward and forward, arms waving, almost losing its balance. My old man, the best tree rider, could let go of his tree and fly to the next tree. He went for one last ride, but it didn't storm, and he found me."

Wittman pictured a tree flinging the old man—slingshooting him out of a fork—and he catches another tree. And many lumberjacks riding a for-est, and flying from tree to tree. Angel shots. "PoPo, will you do me one favor, huh? Will you ask your old man for some costumes and make-up and lights? I like put on a play. He doesn't have to do work; he could just help out with money."

"What will my old man think of me? No sooner does he take a wife, but my needy greedy relatives come out of hiding. The next thing he knows, he's sponsor of a village. They want airplane tickets, and they want to be house guests, and they want clean jobs. And they want a college education for every kid all the way up to M.D. and Ph.D. And they want Wilson tennis rackets. There's a lady in our building whose cousin is living in her guest room; he sits all day long to be served like he's king of America. Relatives keep asking for more until everybody is down to living on shrimp paste on rice. Any pair of undershorts my old man buys for himself, they'll call a luxury. They don't understand that nowadays we don't live in a bare room and eat hom haw on rice so they can go to college. They ask too much. I've seen it before. I'm protecting my oi yun from relatives." GrandMaMa was the witch under the eclipse in *King Solomon's Mines*. "I've seen it before. I've seen it before."

"Yeah," said Wittman, "they think they can come over here and take advantage of us Americans, they got another think coming. We're wise to their actions. Good thing we don't have any more people to come from China. You're the last one. I'm not asking for money for keeps, PoPo. We make our nut, your oi yun can have all the profits. Everyone will call him Angel. Come on, you used to help me do plays. You like be in my play, PoPo? Play Mother Hsü. You get to tell off Cho Cho. 'Kill me or lock me up in the tower; this hand will never write a ransom note.' And you scold your son, stupid, foolhardy to ride to your rescue and get captured. You can take care of yourself; you don't need rescue. Onstage downstage-center death scene, PoPo. Climactic and dramatic seppuku harakiri. You fall on the longsword—the gim, your oi yun needs to help me buy. His name will be on the program: Angel—Mr. Oi Yun."

PoPo giggled. "His name isn't Oi Yun, Mr. Beloved. He's Mr. Lincoln Fong."

Wittman's English better than his Chinese, and PoPo's Chinese better than her English, you would think that they weren't understanding each other. But the best way to talk to someone of another language is at the top of your intelligence, not to slow down or to shout or to talk babytalk. You say more than enough, o.d. your listener, give her plenty to choose from. She will get more out of it than you can say.

PoPo said, "Who I really want to play is the princess with the eighty-seven attendant faeries, represented by two dozen beautiful actresses, leading up to my entrance. Did I tell you I played such a princess on the London stage?"

"Yeah, you have, PoPo. How about I arrange six beautiful girls representing the eighty-seven faeries?"

"How about ten or twelve?"

"How about eight? And your oi yun plays K'ung Ming, the tactician for the three brothers. We'll invent a way to give him a tree ride on stage— K'ung Ming controlling the winds. And controlling the atmosphere. Everywhere he abides, gibbons and birds fill the forest; villagers sing in taverns and fields. He outlives the three brothers, and takes over the try for emperor."

"Yes. Yes, that sounds like my beloved."

They were then in front of Wittman's pad. "Well, PoPo. I live up there now. Do you want to come in and drink tea? Do you want to sit awhile?"

"No, thank you," she said. "My oi yun has a car. We're going to meet at a dim sum parlor, and he'll drive me home. Am I sah chun or am I not? Sah chun, ma? If you need a ride anywhere, you call your popo. Look up Mr. Lincoln Fong of Washington Gai in the telephone book, Lincoln Ho in the Chinese phone book. Honey girl, you aren't lonely living up there by yourself, are you?"

"No, no, not me. Don't worry about me. I just got married myself, PoPo. Isn't it lucky, we two newlyweds meeting on the street?"

"Yes. That's very good. Lucky. You and I, a bridegroom and a bride." She smiled up at him. "A tall newlywed and a short newlywed." She made him laugh. She patted him on the arm. "Lucky." She took off his coat, and took her purse and the pink box. "You want some money? Here."

"No, thank you, PoPo. It's okay. Too much. You buy something for your oi yun." She was giving him a roll of tens.

"No, no. Wedding present. You buy persimmons for *your* oi yun. Sayonara, honey girl." His sah chun grandmama sashayed away sassy down the street. She was wearing a batik cloth tied over her skirt, and her feet were bare brown in sandals. Persimmon season. She's lived for a long time, and in many places. Lucky to have her here now. It was her that Samuel Pepys saw in *A Midsummer Night's Dream*, which featured four peacocks and six monkeys and twenty-four Chinese faeries.

There. Wittman Ah Sing had gotten married, found a venue for a theater, found his grandmother, who gave him money that he did not have to report. Good work. Phone the wife, and so to bed. A reader doesn't have to pay more money for the next chapter or admission to the show if there's going to be a show; you might as well travel on with our monkey for the next while.

A PEAR GARDEN IN THE WEST

 THE CHINESY BANK with dragons coiling its red pillars was closed for making change, so Wittman Ah Sing went to a newsstand and bought cigarettes with a part of the grandmother money. He intended to pay her back out of Unemployment money. At his phone booth, he called his people. Yes, he does have people, and they belong to him whether they like it or not.

"Ma? I'm not sick or in trouble." He always had to say that right off.

"Good. Why you call then? You find a job?"

"I found PoPo."

"Aiya."

"Not her body. Her. She's alive, and she's married."

"Aiya. That old body, married? Who married her old self?"

"I think, Ma, that there are people who know how to prefer old bodies. Good thing too, else we're going to be lonely most of our time."

"What kind of man is he? Did you meet him?"

"A good man. He gives her everything. You don't have to let her take back her furniture. She's here in the City, and lives in a building that her old man owns."

"I knew she would make for herself a happy ending. How about you? Job yet? Don't grow up lazy, Wit Man, that's the worst." He showered her voice with long-distance dimes.

"Ma? I'm producing a show. I'm a show producer. And our Joang Wah will sponsor. They like see you and the aunties do your historic War Bonds Rescue China act. Do you remember how it goes?"

His mother went quiet. He dropped in some more dimes. "Ma. Ma, are you there?"

"Remembering or forgetting the act is not the problem, Wit Man. I contributed to the world war effort that ended up with A-bombs. I'm changed now. I did those shows because I wasn't thinking. You were a baby. But now you're draft-age. I'm not sending you off to Viet Nam. I'm not helping drop the H-bomb. Don't you think about Viet Nam? What's the matter for you? You're too carefree, like your father. I want you to run for Canada. Go." His mother was so advanced, he could hardly keep up with her.

"I do think about Viet Nam, Ma. I'm against it. You put on your show after all these years, it won't be the same but. You guys are old nowadays. Not so smooth on your feet, okay. Tap shoes skid, okay. Legs kick crooked, okay. Make the audience see through propaganda." Still talking down to her, he was trying to explain Brechtian.

"You young kid, don't know nothing. The legs are the last to go."

"Ma, if you can stir up a war with your dancing, you can stop one, right? Why don't you and the aunties make up an Anti–War Bond show, and see what happens? If it doesn't work, I'll go to Canada."

"Maybe I take you to Canada. I don't want to stay here and get persecution when I refuse to roll bandages and knit socks. Wit Man, do me one favor."

"Sure, Ma."

"If you go to Viet Nam and get shot down, I don't want you to scream Mama. I can't take that, hurt soldiers yelling Mama on the battlefield, crying for their mother in the hospital. Scream Daddy, why don't they? You don't yell Mama, okay? Have consideration for me for once in your life."

"Teach Daddy to the audience at the Anti–War Bond show."

"I'll talk to the girls. Some are for Viet Nam but. I have to argue them out of it. Good night, Wit Man. Long distance costs too much." She didn't ask after Taña.

A group of tourists walked by, a lone man with his herd of widows. And crossing the street, a family of tourists, all dressed in the same fabric.

He dialed Lance's number. "Howzit? This is Wittman." Lance liked to put you through identifying yourself. Beat him to it.

"Howzit? What's up?"

"You're not giving a Hallowe'en party, are you?"

"Sure, I'll give one if you like. Feel like partying again already, huh?" Always pinning you with motives.

A woman's voice came from another place, "Hallowe'en party? I was about to send out invitations. You're invited, Wittman." It was Sunny on the extension.

"Sunny, is that you? Hi." It's a marriage where he won't be able to talk to his friend alone again. He has to address the both of them, the Kami-yamas as one. "Listen, will you do me a favor, and not give a party that night?"

"*You're* giving the party?" "A party costs at least fifty dollars."

"Well, yes. That night will be opening night for our play. I need your party guests for audience, and you up front." That is, the plural you. If he were to ask to go out with just one of them, would there be a break in the marriage? "The read-through is tomorrow night at our Benevolent house. Bring people for me to read, okay?"

"We're looking forward to it, Wittman," said Sunny. "Hold it," said Lance. "It's a kung fu challenge, Sunny. He's couched it in Japanese polite-ness, but he's handing us a kung fu challenge all right. His gwoon is about to raid our gwoon; we have to beat him to the punch." "What's a gwoon, Lance?" "It's a school of martial arts. The students of a gwoon will march or drive to another gwoon and attack during practice. That's the walk-through-town of the Seven Samurai and the Magnificent Seven. They fight aikido against chi kung, tai kwan do against zazen, monkey style against wu style against push hands against karate. For keeps. Winner takes all. The sensei roshi whose students lose has to give over his gwoon, his teaching business, his students, his reputation, the Benevolent house, and he has to admit that his form of kung fu is not the superior form. I know what you're after, Wittman—you heard him, Sunny—my mailing list and my phone tree. I accept your challenge. I and my men will be there at your Benevolent house tomorrow night." "Oh, Wittman," said Sunny, "you better be ready. His jiu jitsu is getting so superior." "Chinese against Japa-nese, Wittman, just like in a Bruce Lee movie. This time, Japanese win."

"Thanks for warning me," said Wittman. "Bring your gang and your artillery and your bombs. I'll fight you single-handedly." His own only kung fu was acting like a monkey. For defense, he would count on what he had seen Bruce Lee do on a t.v. talk show. A challenger was waving hands and feet at him, and Bruce Lee knocked him out with a good old American right cross to the chin. "Sometimes a black belt is only good for holding up pants," said Bruce Lee, who showed himself capable of a street-fighting move, an alley-fighting move.

"By the way, I gave Unemployment your name, " said Wittman.

"Are we going to let him use our good name, dear?" "We can't be-grudge a man getting on the dole, dear." "Goddamn it, darling, is our tax money paying for his Welfare?"

"Not Welfare," said Wittman. "Unemployment."

"Wittman is siphoning off funds from the war machine." "Oh, come now, Lance, the Pentagon has a separate budget from Welfare. He's drain-ing the California taxpayer, us." He should hang up, and let them talk to each other. "I'm disgusted by thieves who call sponging and shoplifting rev-olutionary activities." "You're right. Lifting a steak in one's bookbag is not a complete political act. You have to distribute it to the poor, then call in a news release to KQED." Listen to them, showing off for each other. Witt-man slowly lowered the receiver hook. He'll have to tell Taña that he won't have a marriage that makes friends feel left out.

Speaking of whom, he called her next. "What's your phone number, Wittman?" Taña asked. "Where're you calling from?"

"I'm at a payphone."

"You don't have a home phone?"

"Nope." Nor a home. "At a pay phone, I can dig the street. Do you hear it? There's a blind guy waving his broken cane at the cars. It's hanging by a string. Blind guys and magicians use the same kind of collapsible cane. He's shouting. Can you hear him? 'The next son of a bitch who runs over my cane is gonna be a dead son of a bitch.' " *I saw an old man who was blind and shouted. That I saw. Saw.*

She was silent until he finished laughing. "You put me at a disadvan-tage," she said. "You have my number; I don't have yours."

"I didn't mean to put you at a disadvantage. I see what you're thinking. 'Don't call us; we'll call you.' I don't operate like that, Taña. I just don't have a telephone, that's all, honest. Do you want me to get one? I'll get one if you like, and you'll be the only one I'll give the number to. You can call me any time of the day or night."

"The telephone isn't the problem. I do want to be married to you, but I don't want to be the wife. I think it's very important, Wittman, that we tell each other our ideas about marriage. There's a certain proposal that I want from a man. He'll love me and understand me so much, he'll say, 'Taña, let me be your wife.' I got carried away with you, Wittman, and forgot to ask which one of us would be the wife."

"You want me to be your wife?!"

"I hadn't thought the proposal would come in that tone of voice, Witt-man, but, yes, I do."

"Wait, wait. We take turns. I want a wife too sometimes, you know."

"Now you've proposed to me, but I haven't proposed to you. I don't want to be a woman who waits for proposals from men. One thing I've never done, I've never asked anyone to marry me. I want to do that some-day. I'll get down on one knee and offer my hand and a diamond ring. When are we going to see each other again, Wittman? How about tomorrow night?"

"Tomorrow night I'm gathering a troupe to read-through the play. Will you come? Please come, Taña. We'd see each other and work together every night for months, like marriage."

"Say 'I love you,' " said Taña, who was better at loving than Wittman was. She was also tougher at using the phone.

"I love you."

"I love you too. Where do I meet you tomorrow night?"

He gave her the address, and they said good night agreeably.

Nevertheless, he next called Nanci, who was home alone, as the most beautiful girls are.

"Nanci? Wittman Ah Sing. Did you have a good time at the party? I saw you dancing." Did you notice I was with the blonde? Ask why I didn't ask you to dance with me.

"Yes. No. It was okay. I don't like big parties."

"Me neither. I don't think I'll go to them anymore." I ought to ask her to go out with me on a real date. Dinner with harp and violin music at the Garden Court of the Sheraton Palace. A gardenia for fifty cents at a flower stand. Dancing around the rain forest at the Tonga Room. Ah, the hell with it, let her see his ordinary self and love him for it. "Say, I didn't scare you with my poems, did I? I'm sorry if I scared you."

"No, you don't scare me, Wittman."

"You haven't been cast in anything yet, have you?"

"No."

"I've found a theater site, and we're opening on Hallowe'en. Will you read for me? After seeing those improvs? I mean, they were only improvs but."

"I liked those scenes, Wittman, and I don't mean to criticize but." While she criticized, he watched the street. A showgirl in a sequined cheongsahm yelled after somebody driving off in a white car, "You dumb fuck" or "You dumb cluck." Then she had to walk in her impossibly high heels.

"What's so funny?" asked Nanci.

"The street is wonderful tonight. You ought to be out in it." At a street phone, you can't run out of what to talk about; it comes to you in the on-swirling lifestream. "I get what you're saying about the play, Nanci. You're saying: Do better. Will you be in it nevertheless?" . . . *I entreat you, request you and desire you . . . meet me in the palace wood, a mile without the city, we shall be dogged with company. . . . I pray you, fail me not. We will meet; and there we may rehearse most obscenely and courageously. Take pains; be perfect: adieu.*

"I'd love to be in it. Bye-bye."

"Bye-bye."

With his last dimes, he called the stockroom of his ex–department store. After quite a while, somebody who must be living there picked up the receiver. "Hello?" said Wittman. "Is this the Yale Younger Poet I'm talking to? Is it you?"

"Who is this?"

"It's me, remember?" Not by my looks, and not by my race, nor by my deformities, I will yet identify myself. "I was moving bicycles."

"Yeah. What's up?"

"I got fired. I'm on Unemployment."

"That's too bad. Or, do you mind?"

"It's all right. I don't mind. That play I was telling you about? I found a venue. You said you'd think about it. If you come out of hiding, people wouldn't know it was you. You could wear make-up or a mask. You'd have a good time. It's not like poetry."

"Heh." He sounded like an old fut.

"You'd be helping me out. Do me a big favor. I need to integrate the cast. You have lots of parts to choose from. Let me tell you about them. You have time?"

"Yeh. That's what I have. Time."

With his last dimes, Wittman gave the ex-poet a catalog of heroes whom he looked like. "Choose: Lee Yoon, the Blue-eyed Tiger (green, blue, Chinese don't distinguish), is in charge of building a commune for a population of one hundred and eight outlaws, some with families. By architecture and city planning, he arranges space—where who sleeps with whom, communal kitchen, dining commons, outdoor cafés, plazas, no jail-house—so that anarchists can live together. He fights Black Li, the most unruly commune member, to a draw.

"And/or you could play Liu Tang, the Red Hairy Barbarian. Excuse me, but we call your type barbarian. He was a big man with dark skin—you can use pancake—a broad face—broad faces are best for the stage—with a red birthmark, and black and yellow hair on his head and feet. We'll spray you with Streaks 'n Tips. He appears one morning asleep on the altar of a temple. The outlaws take him in to share their food and fate.

"And/or Tuan Ching Chu, the Gold-haired Dog, who wins from a Tartar prince a wonder horse named White Jade Lion That Shines in the Night.

"And/or Doctor Huang Pu Tuan, Uncle Purple Beard, a horse vet and a horse thief, the last outlaw to join the community. He's got blue-green eyes and blue-red beard and hair. To look like a barbarian does not mean you're ugly. These were not Caucasians; a Chinese can look like anything. A sign of a person being special—extra smart or brave or lucky or spiritual —was that he had something odd about his looks—eyebrows down to his knees, bumps or horns on his head, very skinny, very fat." Yes, in our theater, we will have regard for all kinds no matter they're disregarding us.

"You get to win the last battle in the play, okay? King Sun Ch'üan, who also had your looks, leads his navy west up the Yangtze, eight warships disguised as merchant ships with thirty thousand men hidden belowdecks. You ride your horse along the shore of that oceanic river, and capture lighthouses. You signal the ships, and you signal Cho Cho, your ally, who is head of a million men. He is sailing east, singing a poem about ravens. You meet at the enemy's walled capital. 'We're merchants, and we bear gifts,' you say. The gates open. You take the city. Gwan Goong flees. His brothers are missing, probably dead. The locals will not help him when he's losing. You post a reward of ten thousand gold pieces for his head, then you yourself capture him alive. 'How strange life is,' you muse to him. 'Gwan, my prisoner. I can't get over it. That we fought against one another, and now it has come to this. Why not be my brother instead? Come over to my side as ally and family.'

" 'My blue-eyed boy,' says Gwan Goong. 'My red-whiskered rodent, I have my allies and family. I won't be brothers with a traitor.'

" 'I could execute you as a traitor,' you say. 'I could kill you like any soldier. But I'm offering brotherhood, familyhood, a marriage for your daughter with my son. Our war chests could pay for one munificent wedding celebration.'

" 'My tiger girl will never marry your son, a mongrel dog.'

" 'You're the barbarian,' you say, 'for keeping the war going.'

"Gwan Goong's son, Gwan P'ing, interrupts, 'We don't surrender.' He draws his sword. 'We have not lost. I'll kill you, and we win.'

"Gwan Goong stands between his son and you. He has a way of standing so that the reality of his presence disperses illusions. His son lays down his sword. We have lost the war.

"Gwan Goong at the age of sixty and his son were beheaded in the winter of 220 A.D., our time."

Before hanging up, Wittman got Yale Younger to agree to his dropping the script off, such as it was, soon to be completed by improv and workshop.

Everyone came—friends, and friends' friends, and family. Not because Wittman had charisma or leadership, and certainly not because of his standing in the community. Nor were they here to feel sorry and give charity, which one human being has to give another anyway if he or she is to stay Chinese. They came because what Boleslavsky said is true: "Acting is the life of the human soul receiving its birth through art." Everyone really does want to get into the act.

They were bawling one another out for long-time-no-see. Those who weren't such talkers riffed the jungs, banjos, erhus, fiddles. Drummers were hitting the wooden whales—knock-knocking, that is, dock-docking truths out of their wide mouths. PoPo and Mr. Fong asked kung fu boys to carry up trunks—lifetimes of wardrobe, which the actors unfurled and unfolded. "Oh, remember? Remember?" Some remembered wearing these costumes, and some remembered seeing them on stage or in a movie. Out of sleeves came lengths of worn and torn ripplingwater inner sleeves like lines of magician's hankies. Too few pants, but Levis will go with anything. Time, the wardrobe mistress. PoPo shook out an operatic brocade, and here we are again—inside the cedarwood, sandalwood, camphorball, mothball atmosphere. Aunties were crowning one another with headdresses. Peacock feathers and silver eyeballs were waving around looking at one and all. Somebody was growl-speaking from the depths of a dragon head. Beautiful Nanci was tippy-toeing in fake bound-feet shoes. The Goodwife Taña and Auntie Bessie and Auntie Sophie were tappety-tapping "The Sidewalks of New York." Pop was scuffle-shuffling in raggedy shoes. (Huck's Pap too had done "play-acting at the palace.") So word-of-mouth had reached even the bo daddy river, and Zeppelin's battery was well enough to bring a truckload of uncles. Mom and Pop together in the same room. Archenemies running into one another. PoPo on the arm of her new old man walked past Pop—and slapped her ass at him, one of her Japanese gestures. She sashayed up to Ruby Long Legs, and said, "We're cutting you out of our wills. The money will go to Wit Man, and he can build a theater if he wants. Nada for you." The old fut (who is our president after all, Mr. Grand Opening Ah Sing) brought the rest of the tribal council, who voted okay. And there's the cannery lady with her prom gloves on. She and fellow workers and fellow unemployed artists were catching up on news of one another's between-gig gigs. The program notes will be interesting for the bios of caterers, furniture movers, stevedores, housesitters, lifeguards. After laboring all day, they come here to work on the impossible. Our most famous Hollywood movie star and tree trimmer, the one who's had an Oscar nomination—oh, we're all available—was telling about his chainsaw that jumped loose and missed his jugular vein by a graze. So close, we might have lost him. Judy Louis was dressed for fiesta, and setting out refreshments. She looked nothing like a boar. Oh, everyone. Yale Younger—with a Barbie from the Mattel Industrial Show! A Miss Chinatown who got too good for Auntie Mabel's revue was saying to Charles Bogard Shaw, "Yes, that was me on 'Hawaiian Eye.' I didn't tell anyone to watch for me because they made me wear a Suzie Wong dress. So shame." Most people brought as costumes and props Chinesy things they happened to have around the house, such as nightgown kimono, wedding kimono and obi, dragoned jackets that they sell to G.I.s in Korea, yarmulkes, borlas, a samurai grandfather's armor and swords that had been buried under the house and dug up to give to a sansei on his twentieth birthday. A backscratcher from a Singapore sling, a paper umbrella from an aloha mai tai, a Buddha bottle with head that unscrews—make something of it. Use it. From these chicken scraps and dog scraps, learn what a Chinese-American is made up of. Yes, the music boat has sailed into San Francisco Bay, and the boatman is reunited with his troupe. Write the play ahead of them to include everyone and everything.

Wittman pounded a drum for order. Standing in front of the chalkboard, he welcomed the players, and thanked them for embarking tonight on an enormous loud play that will awake our audience, bring it back. For a century, every night somewhere in America, we had had a show. But our theater went dark. Something happened ten years ago, I don't know what, but. We'll cook and blast again. We have so much story, if we can't tell it entirely on the first night, we continue on the second night, the third, a week if we have to. He handed out Xeroxes of the script that had lots of holes for ad lib and actors' gifts. Gwan Goong, standing on the mantelpiece, was using his powers over illusions to sway the house to theater—

Crash! Through the door came a grand entrance—Lance and a

kung fu gang. "That's him, there." Lance was siccing their champion on
Wittman. The champ kicked over the jackstraw pile of weapons, and
walked at him while rolling up his sleeves. "I hit strong kung fu. My kung fu
win." The force of his voice blew slam-bang at the listener. They don't
"do" kung fu or "play" it. They "hit" it. A tiger was flaming on his forearm, and a dragon was flaring on his other forearm, branded on, according
to the movies. At the graduation test, he had lifted a five-hundred-pound
red-hot iron cauldron by hugging it to himself. Lick-on tattoos, thought
Wittman, body paint. "You're welcome to a script, Siew Loong," he said,
showing the guy that he can read his jock jacket—the Little Dragon. Me
too, born in a year of the dragon, but I don't advertise Wittman Dragon,
nor would I call myself Little. "Your gwoon, help yourselves to scripts too.
Do they read? Do they take direction? Don't I recognize you from
parades? You do dragon dance, huh?" Yes, he was the dancer at the head of
the dragon, who lifts the head with those branded arms, and dances beneath
its beard.

Siew Loong pushed the script aside, and stuck out his pinky and said,
"See this finger? I can kill with this finger. I be careful." "He's restraining
himself," explained Lance. "You be careful too, Wittman. He's got the
touch that kills. He knows places on the body that all he has to do is touch,
and you die on a specific date years hence. He'll have an alibi of being nowhere near the death scene. Watch out, he's getting into position for the
vibrating palm. It can wreck the flow of blood and air."

"Oh, Jesus, the poor guy," said Wittman. "You shouldn't let oppression
do that to you, Siew Loong. I understand. You walk around lonely among
the tall and racially prejudiced, and you start getting crazy ideas. A foreign-
exchange student, lonely on campus, no dates, no money for round-trip
tickets during vacations, staying by yourself in the empty dorms, no maid
service, nobody to talk to. You start thinking, they better not fuck with me,
I'm just keeping myself from touch-killing them with this mighty finger."

There was a turn of the hand somehow that Wittman didn't see what hit
him, but suddenly he was coming to. What do you know, you really do see
stars. And, oh no, his mother has climbed into the ring, holding his head.
"Are you alive, biby?"

"I'm all right, Ma," he said, getting to his feet. Eyewitnesses were saying it must have been a force of directed energy. No punch had been
thrown; none landed. The champ had been gesturing, and some chi got
loose. Ruby Long Legs stuck a long leg out to trip Siew Loong, but he

stepped over it. Some of us must be born doves; Wittman had no instinct to hit back. He was glad to learn that his pacifism went deep.

Siew Loong said, "I have a script here. You help me put on one show?"

"You're bound to do it, Wittman," said Lance. Mrs. Lance was handing out copies. It was only a page long, let him have his say.

The Little Dragon stood where Wittman had been standing, his gang leaning against the walls; they do the gang swagger standing still. F.O.B.s run in a gang, no cool American independence. Their leader talked-story like so: "A kung fu monk walks into town in old California. He thinks, this be one ghost town. The long long main street is too quiet because the citizens are chickenshit that a gang of bad guys are coming to showdown. They see the monk has no gun, so they haw him for being chinaman. They pull his short pigtail, which he grew for to disguise himself." Siew Loong pulled out a whipcord—no, it's a queue—and stuck it to his head. "He is far far away from Shaolin, Hunan, where monks invented kung fu to be strong in body because Buddhism heavy to carry. You understand? How did he come west to here? Okay, backflash: The monk as a kidboy bang-bang on the back gate of the Shaolin temple, and waits and waits. A teacher opens the gate, but there is an inside gate, and another inside gate inside the inside gate. At each back gate, he sees no-good students kicked out or run away. At last, he gets inside the gwoon. Don't say 'dojo,' Japanese. Say 'gwoon.' He studies hard years. Training is allthesame hell. Arrows and spears shoot out of walls. Stones and axes fall down. Eagle stars—they look like cutting wheels that cut up pizzapie—whiz-shoot at his eyes. The skeletons are the bones of students who failed tests." Wittman imagined Billy Batson going down the hallway between the statues of virtues and vices, and reaching Shazam on his throne, who gave him the holy-moly herb and the word that changes him into Captain Marvel. "The monk graduates high. And makes kung fu revolution to kick invaders and opium out of China. One night at the international ball thrown by Empress Suzie—"

"Kiai!" The kung fu jocks came off the walls and swung into action, chop-socking and barefoot-kicking, and swinging from doorways right side up and upside down. They fought through the crowd, flexing feet, stretching spines, levitating, bilocating, radiating colors, screaming, "Kiai!" They played the good guys, and they played the enemy. Their eyes bulged round and red and saw through darkness. A fast finger plucked out an eyeball, and no evidence of it remained but a coin—a quarter—in the hand. They cracked you up; you could die laughing. A bad guy laughed to death. They attacked a fort, represented by the tall table that had had fruit on it. "Kiai!" They conquered it with their dexterous feet.

Suddenly, the Little Dragon did the most amazing thing. He sucked in his cheeks and puckered his lips into a tight 8. He knelt and concentrated himself into a ball, from which his hands were flapping—two blurs at his shoulders. He did fly up onto the table. A buzzing came from him, from his mouth or from the whir of wings. Those tiny thalidomide wings flew him up. He landed in a crouch, and looked at everyone with inhuman eyes. It was the weirdest, most foreign thing an American audience will ever see; that man changed into a bee.

The boxers escape-exited—they had the power to escape anything. They held their hands in front of their chests like paws, and walked sideways heel-and-toe out the front door, their spinal tails whipping. They came back inside to wild applause. Chop-socky flix kix and lix tickle box office. They took bows, all dozen or twenty boxer jox dressed in Hong Kong Pop Art t-shirts. On each chest was an egghead of Gwan Goong's red face with hood-eyes, like the Hawkman, or Chang Fei's face, which was a blue-and-black ovoid like the Atom's; Cho Cho looked like black Dr. Midnight. The gang had given one another those home haircuts, every one with hair that stuck up in black shocks; the chi energy they fool around with does that to hair.

Squatting on the table, Siew Loong continued talking from his outline or treatment: "Kung fu—hit fair, hit square and courageous. Get you ass near to opponent. Hit him with bare hand. Your own fingers de-eyeball him. But. The enemy—Germans, Austrians, Italians, French, Russians, British, mostly Japanese, mostly Americans—no-fair fight with tanks and gunboats. Us against the world."

He got off the table and stepped to one side, letting Lance, good at English, have the floor to do elegy. "Those on the side of the animals and the wind should have won. Tigers, crabs, white cranes, eagles, monkeys, bees —'Kiai!' the fighting cry of cats and of birds—hands and hair moving with the wind, our team blew toward the cannons, which blasted them to pieces. Bare hands, bare feet, the weapons of poor people—bare human bodies lost against machines. Why hadn't it worked? Right politics ought to make the body bulletproof. They had practiced on blocks of wood and ice, bricks and tiles, materials out of which forts and castles are made. Had the masters cheated their students by firing blanks at them? Are monkey style and white-crane style and wu good for nothing but morning calisthenics? The victorious martial arts are fighter jets and bombs. Clip a coupon and get the secret of the East: A black belt is only good for holding up pants."

"So," continued Siew Loong, "the Shaolin monk crosses the ocean to America to raise money for guns. He leads the townspeople to fight the gang of bad guys, and he has victory, okay. He travels on to the next town, New York, Hawai'i. American ladies wave hankie after him, and hold hankie to eyes and in teeth. He has many adventures, suitable for t.v. series. He goes to university, and studies science." Using the tail end of his queue as a compass, he drew a perfect circle on the chalkboard. "He gets M.D. He works restaurants, cook and dishwasher. He gives speeches for revolution. He makes parades and flagsful of money. He dances tai chi among sick people in hospital and cures an epidemic. When he moves, the air changes, and sick be well. He meets Two-Gun Cohen, faithful Jewish Canadian sidekick and bodyguard. They go back to China and win revolution this time. You see me before? You see Hong Kong movies, you see me before. I was ming sing—bright star—in Hong Kong, but I have a dream: I go Haw-lee-woot. I bought one Z card, and I trampsteamer out to Little Mexico, and jumpship in the Bay, Fisherman's Wharf. I been all over this land ball"—"ball" as in "pompon." "All over this pompon of Earth, I took this script. To Warner Brothers and A.B.C., I said, 'I be a Hong Kong ming sing. But I like be one Haw-lee-woot ming sing. Have I got a great idea for you—an eastern western—*Kung Fu*. Every week I be Shaolin monk, and have another eastern-western adventure.' But. They said No. They said Chinese man has no Star Quality. The hell with them. Good for me. I did not let Haw-lee-woot change me into the dung dung dung dung dung with the little pigtail in back." His hand slice-whacked off the queue, which a freedom-fighter grandfather had cut off, and his lady saved. "The hell with them. I act you theater; you act me theater." His fist beat-beat on his hand, then beat-beat on his heart.

Yes, hurry—do the play now or else the generation of actors that talk like that go unheard. "See the players well bestowed. Do you hear, let them be well used; for they are the abstract and brief chronicle of the time." That chi charge that had come off of him was a blast of actor's energy. With his presence—his Star Quality—we could have our first Chinese-American male sex symbol. All he's after is an act or two in a play that will go on for sixty acts lasting forever. Give it to him.

"Okay," said Wittman. "I act you theater; you act me theater. Only one thing but. You're going to stay F.O.B. as long as you hear and say 'Revolution,' and be thinking 1911, 1949. Forget Tobacco Shit War and Kung Fu

War. Seventeen seventy-six, Siew Loong, July 4—our Revolution. We allthesame Americans, you sabe? Get it?"

Shut up, Wittman. On with the show already. As promised, Lance read Liu Pei, and Charles Bogard Shaw read Chang Fei, he himself Gwan Goong as before, and Yale Younger as Sun Ch'üan. He asked Siew Loong to read Cho Cho, and Step-Grandfather Fong to read K'ung Ming. The part about the death of the Chinese kings—the old country, gone—went like this:

Gwan Goong, one of those people who has to tell his dreams at breakfast, tells his last dream: "A black boar or a black bull charged into my tent, and bit my leg. I leapt out of bed and took up my dagger, but I woke up stabbing the tent."

"It's only a dream," says a soldier. "A dragon floated through your tent last night." Another of his men tries to read his character: "It means that you're alert, and you face difficult problems head on." Others think dreams are omens: "You're going to be awarded a large medal with an animal crest on it. You'll win the tiger-head breastplate." "You're not going to be killed in battle."

Gwan rubs his leg. "It still hurts. I'm awake, and the pain is still there. I often have aches and pains now. I'm getting old. Sixty this year."

Sure enough, their every interpretation turns out true. He isn't killed in battle. Sun Ch'üan captures him, and executes him. To banish Death, Sun piles up pyramids of grapefruit, oranges, tangerines; he steams flocks of chickens and roasts herds of pigs. Surrounded by altars of food, he wraps up Gwan's head, and sends it to Cho Cho with this message: "I want to join you against his brothers. I pledge you my kingdom."

Cho Cho silently looks at Gwan's head. Then out of a piece of wood, he carves a body for the head. He dresses it in the brocades which Gwan had refused as gifts. (He had accepted one gift—the horse Red Rabbit.) Branches of hands and feet stick out from the stubby trunk. Gwan looks to be an ogrish, trollish chunk, which makes perspective crazy. Out of his big head the once-beautiful hair frizzes like lightning. Pinpointy dots stare out of goggle eyes.

Cho Cho talks to his lifelong enemy: "You've been well, I trust, General, since we parted?" Which were the very words that Gwan had said to him after besting him in combat.

And the Gwan Goong thing—like the votive statue over there—hears Cho Cho. Its eyes roll, and it opens its black mouth as if about to speak. Cho Cho faints in a fit of terror.

He moves to a clean new house, but a tree that is hundreds of years old bleeds on him—the branches hang over and drip—and a voice comes out of it: "I come to take your life." And at midnight, into his lighted bedroom walks Lady Fu, a queen he murdered long ago. "You," she says. "Y-o-o-ou. Y-o-o-ou." (Taña with her pale hair hanging did that very well.) She calls, "Children. Oh, chi-i-ildren." Two boys come trailing. The ghosts follow one another through the wall. There's a tearing sound, and that section of the house breaks off.

Night after night, voices howl. Those of us who can hear them will perform them for those who don't have the ear for them. The howls—weeping, groaning—come from wars and hungry children. Some of us can hear the actual sounds no matter how far away. Cho Cho thinks they are the voices of people he's killed. "For thirty years, I've ridden across the empire doing battle against heroes. I have only two equals left to fight. But my health is gone." He orders seventy-two decoy tombs, appoints his son emperor, and dies at the age of sixty-six.

Gwan visits Liu Pei. At the sight of the cloud-soul, Liu Pei knows that his brother is dead. Gwan's voice says, "I beg you raise an army. Avenge me." "I am getting old," says Liu Pei, "and I have spent my life at war." He sings, "I Have Grown Old Waging War."

The brothers do not reach death on the same day. Trying to fulfill another part of their vow, Liu Pei declares the three kingdoms united, and himself the emperor. Chang Fei kneels to him, and says, "You've achieved our cause, emperor now. Avenge our brother." Against the advice of their spiritual and military guru, they attack Sun Ch'üan.

Through the nights, Chang Fei drinks too much, promising that in the morning he will be leading the troops as usual. "Or else tie me to a tree, give me a flogging, and have me beheaded." He sleeps with his eyes open, but does not see two men steal into his tent. They are men he had flogged with fifty lashes apiece. They stab him to death at the age of fifty-five, and cut off his head, which they take to Sun Ch'üan.

Sun Ch'üan receives that head, and sends it to Liu Pei. The messengers try to assassinate Liu Pei as they hand it to him. But he chops off their heads, and sends those two heads back. (Hollywood, do not stick pigtails on any of these heads—they were free men, who lived before the Manchus. Set a long table with a row of heads, like the banquet scene in *Titus Andronicus*.) Liu Pei fights on alone, wearing white armor and flying white flags. His banners in the sun whiten the land for seven hundred leagues.

Sun receives his assassin-messengers' heads. With heads on his mind, he leads his army onto the battlefield. Galloping out of the smoke and dust comes Red Rabbit. On his back sits a headless horseman, who wields a blue-dragon sword. The voice of Gwan says, "Give me back my head."

That night in his throne room, Sun hears that voice come from one of his men, "My blue-eyed boy. My red-whiskered rodent, have you forgotten me?" The man walks up the steps to the throne, knocks Sun off, and himself sits on it. Gwan no longer looks like a troll or a cloud-soul. His eyebrows and the creases beside his mouth are vertical black lines; his eyes and face are blood red—War incorporated. He speaks out of the earthly body he's using: "So I crisscrossed the empire for forty years, and fell into your trap. You have me with you, then. I failed to taste your flesh in life; I shall give you no peace in death."

Sun leads his army up the Yangtze, setting fire to everything. The trees are torches from which flames jump back and forth. Curtains of flame hang and blow. Liu Pei, running from the heat, enters a grove of woods, which break into fire. Fire chases him to the river, but its banks are burning. Chang's son leads him through forests of torches up a hill. He sees everywhere below him—fire, which has left the country barren of trees to this day. And then Sun's army shoots flaming arrows up the hill. Gwan's son finds a way down it, and Liu escapes.

In hiding, badly burned, he mourns his brothers. Spots appear in front of his eyes, and he blacks out. On a still night, a draft blows against him. He sees two figures in the candlelight. "I thought I dismissed you," he says to servants. He looks again. "Then you are still alive."

Gwan Goong, who has a more normal shape now, says, "We are ghosts, not men. The time is not far off when we shall be together again."

"We will the three of us all go home," says Liu Pei.

O home-returning powers, where might home be? How to find it and dwell there?

In the morning, Liu calls for K'ung Ming. "I am dying," he says, "and my children are not wise enough to rule. You be emperor after me." The wizard of the wind knocks his forehead on the ground until blood runs. Liu tells his sons to serve the new ruler, and dies in 223 A.D.

This was not the end, only the end of a night's performance. Just because they all die, it isn't the end. Gwan's grandchildren were gathered to find out: Then what? Gwan Goong has the ability to travel anywhere, crossing back and forth the River of Stars to visit his brothers and his enemies. An ocean-going ship will cross the stage behind a scrim of time, and he will be on it. Gwan Goong on Angel Island. Gwan Goong on Ellis Island.

The night was growing late, yet people who had to go to work graveyard or in the morning were taking up lines of a play that the savage world beyond the black windows didn't know or care about. Look at their heads bowed over words. The oldest ladies have the blackest hair. Too many older women—a chorus line of beautiful ladies—without men friends. If only we could match them up with the kung fu boys. Everybody should leave with somebody—a bad boy placing his jacket on the shoulders of a Flora Dora girl, and a stage kiss becoming a real kiss.

At the inconclusive ending of this first rehearsal, Wittman tried out on the crowd—actors make the best audience—an intermezzo (that he had practiced and set in front of the mirror). He took both parts.

Ah Monkey is bragging to Tripitaka, "I crashed the party in the sky, and ate up the food. I've been cooked in the pot on the moon. I'm a chase-master, and catch arrows in my teeth. I climb skyscrapers. I bet you I can polevault over those clouds."

Wittman turned facing where he'd been standing, and said in a different voice, "I bet that you can't clear this hand." Tripitaka holds an open hand at waist level.

The monkey laughs, opening wide his big mouth and showing his big teeth. "It's a bet." His pole elongates between his hands, and shoots up into the air, his eyes following its enormous growth. "Watch. At the height of my parabolic jump, you won't be able to see me. Watch now. Watch." He rocks heel-and-toe, his tail and nose twitching. "I'm off!" He polevaults into the sky. Clouds go by. The moon and sun and stars go by. He arrives on a mass of pink-and-white ether and meteorite dust. If this were a decent theater, he would be up in the catwalk. "Ha," he breathes, waving his tail like a flag. "Look at me. Nothing to it. I can do anything. Higher than his hand, ha!" He strolls among clouds of many levels and shapes. "These must be the white columns that hold up the sky. I'm going to leave proof that I've been here." At the tall middle pillar, he pulls out one of his hairs. "Presto be-e-e-en change-o!" The hair becomes a pen wet with ink. He writes his graffito: "The Greatest Wisest Man wuz here." He saunters over to the thickest pillar, turns his back to the audience, unzips, and takes a piss. He returns his pen to his hair, and his penis to his pants, and jumps down off the cloud. "I jumped clear of your hand and your head and of Earth," he brags, "all the way to the top of the sky."

"Fool ape," says Tripitaka. "You never left my hand." He holds up his hand to the monkey's nose, and to the noses of the audience, who said, "Pee-yew." Wittman dangled his hand out there like it was somebody else's, looked at it, sniffed it, "Pee-yew! Monkey piss." Then Tripitaka sticks up his middle finger. "What's this?" He studies that middle finger, holds it to his eyes for a close look-see. "Why, there's writing on my middle finger. 'The Greatest Wisest Man wuz here.' " With thumb and finger, he picks up the monkey, and lowers him into his other hand. "You never left my hand." And to the audience, "Do you see the tiny monkey on my hand? See? See? A teenyweeny gorilla? See his little hat with the feathers? See his cute tail?" Like King Kong with Fay Wray in his hand, but vice versa. At the table where the bee had sat, he suddenly smashes his hand down. Bang! The audience jumped, some let out a scream, and laughed. "A mountain holds Ah Monkey imprisoned for five hundred years." (James Dean covers with his red windbreaker the toy monkey broken in the gutter.)

Wittman handed out a schedule of rehearsals to the actors going out the door. They would work scene by scene, then run-throughs, then open on Hallowe'en. Promise. We will meet again in the Pear Garden. They walked out wearing the shoes that will give them a way of going about in character.

But people didn't say Good night right off. They had to say, "Good but." "Good but you left out our millionaires. What about our millionaires?" "Good but bad impression of us. We not be uncivilized, we not be monkeys. We got inventors. We got scientists." Oh, stop looking over your shoulders, why don't you? And best friend Lance said, "Good but can a cannibal be capable of tragedy?" "What about an omnivore?" said Mrs. Lance. Wittman didn't argue with wise guys, said Thank you for the constructive criticism.

At least nobody quit. The kung fu gang whose practice room this was did not take away the use of the hall.

Nanci was talking to one of the agent aunties. Without looking, he could sense the whereabouts of loveliness. Her atmosphere included him. She was leaving slowly, awaiting him? If he were a different type, and she were a different type, he could help her on with her coat, while saying in her ear, "I've missed you. I love you. I want you. Come with me." He felt her tug toward the door. He stood in the path of the doe stepping into the night forest. "You aren't going out there by yourself, are you? Do you have a ride?"

"We'll give you a ride. We have a car." It was Taña, his wife, with not a guile in voice or face.

"I live on Red Rock Hill now. Near the steps. It won't be out of your way? Yes, thank you all."

Everybody pulled his or her coat collar up. The fog and their cigarette smoke entwined in the San Francisco night. Out with two beautiful women, one on either side, if only a couple arrangement had not been made already. Wittman, of course, had to talk too much. "I love it when good actors come on stage, meet, interact and go off. In oceans and seas of time and space, amidst all the creatures and species, this one and that one find one another for a while of eternity on the same schedule and life-route as oneself. Nanci, you're an actress who can deliver a Hello that makes us see the miracle of meeting, and a Goodbye that echoes all the partings and dyings." Now, Nanci could say, "It's your wonderful play that does all that for an actress."

"I like the play," Taña said.

"Me too," said Nanci, giving him the opportunity to look at her. Say some more. Say, "I also like you."

"I also like you," said Taña, and put her arm through his.

They unzipped her pretty little car. Taña got in on the driver's side. Wittman jumped into the air and landed in the space behind the seats. Taña reached over and opened the door for Nanci. Well, what did you expect? To ride through the suggestive City with her in his lap, his legs entangling with her legs? A hand at her waist curve? Scrunched amidst her and the gear shift? His back to the driver? As it was, he sat in the back with his head behind her head, and his feet sticking out the driver's side. Black hair blew in his eyes and his mouth. One arm was like casual along the top of her door. The other arm was pinned. He can't whisper into her ear, the wind blowing voices away. The Great Monkey would have given the neck in front of him a dracula bite. Dracula-bite them both. "Turn here," she pointed, and jabbed him in the face with her elbow. She was not aware, then, of the air between them, and the exact boundaries between their bodies? She was sitting sort of upright. If she would fit herself better into her bucket seat, and back up against him, they could feel their connection through it. Come to think of it, he's not feeling it much. Does this mean that it's over? That would be okay, for it to be over. Let it be over. Let me out of love. *How he thought then of the troubadours who feared nothing more than being answered.* She was yelling the directions to where she lived, the Divisadero, near Ashbury, Vulcan Street, you know where the planet streets are, Mars,

Saturn? The city lights streamed over the low car, and they dropped her off at her planet. Good night. . . . *because I never held you close, I hold you forever.*

In all scrupulosity, he can't go home with Taña. She dropped him off. He spent the rest of the night looking for the plot of our ever-branching lives. A job can't be the plot of life, and not a soapy love-marriage-divorce —and hell no, not Viet Nam. To entertain and educate the solitaries that make up a community, the play will be a combination revue-lecture. You're invited.

8

BONES AND JONES

ON HALLOWE'EN, the red marble head of Sun Yat Sen breaks off, and kremlin gremlins fly out of the aluminum body and spook the City. His red marble hands move. Kids who once hid and waited in Portsmouth Square to be scared by this miracle had grown up. This year, these adults put on costumes again, and go-out clothes and fake and safe-deposit jewels, and went to an opening night of their own making. More maskers were at large than ever. They were trick-or-treating the Benevolent Association house. Jaywalking with children by the hand, they followed a boom-booming that pounded and sounded like Come come come until they arrived at the sight of the drummers. Two men and a woman banged the taikos with all the might of their workers' arms. The tails of their sweatband-fillets jumped and flipflapped. A barker with pants rolled up over peasant legs ran barefoot up and down the sidewalk, calling friends by name and you and you while plinkplunking on his porcelain drum. Welcome. Welcome. The crowd walked through flowers—arrays of carnations and aisles of chrysanthemums sashed with red ribbons and calligraphy—and became audience.

A call—la-a-a-a!—out of the dark grew nearer with each of four soundings. The Talking Chief crosses the white rainbow. His eagle feathers flare —sun up—and he rains the audience with water from the Atlantic and the Pacific. Overhead flies Garuda, whose wings like a wheel we were wearing on our batik clothes, which Peace Corps volunteers were sending home from Southeast Asia. Ranga of the long fangs, long hair, long tits, shakes her scythe-like fingernails at a young man, and makes him arm-wrestle himself, his right hand trying to stab his bare chest, his left hand wrist-twisting his knife hand. Suddenly, he breaks from that Damballah trance and does the bent-knee hula—his thighs clapping, his hands rising from between his legs and up to the sky in enormous praise of the volcano goddess. Hanuman, the white monkey, swings in and out the windows. The black-and-white Abba-Zabba man—the one with the clown-white skull-white face and the black turtleneck—giving away Abba-Zabbas was Antonin Artaud, who had had to evoke genies of a crueler theater. Caliban is raging at not seeing his face in the mirror. Good red Gwan Goong is riding good Red Rabbit again, and has led eight genies through the streets to here. A sunseen man opens his water gourd that cools water as the sun gets hotter; the audience looks inside, and sees—everything, the Earth, everything. At any moment, one or another of these genie of the theater may interfere in a gambling scene and change the luck, or whisper answers to a test. And chant, "May he live" or "May he die." The Talking Chief will cast his yo-yo, and hunt up children, twins, soldiers.

Across the stage, which was the size of Tripitaka's hand, forward-rolled acrobatic twins, tied together—four heels over two heads that did not gravity-drop katonk. They backflipped off. And re-entered—verbal twins in green velveteen connected suits. Yale Younger and Lance Kamiyama as Chang and Eng, the Double Boys, pattering away in Carolina-Siamese. Chinkus and Pinkus.

"Sir Bones, how you feeling?"

"I feel like I'm being followed, Mr. Jones. The footsteps go where I go and stop where I stop. They don't seem to be getting any closer but. I'm paranoid."

"How do you do, Mr. Paranoid. I feel uneasy myself, you peeking at me sideways like that."

"I have an idea that would make us be more like the normal American person."

"What idea is that?"

"Let's change our name."

"What name would befit us?"

"Bunker. They like you in green velvet, and they like you being named after battles. Chang Bunker and Eng Bunker."

"I'm dubious."

"Ah, Mr. Dubious, the footsteps pursuing us come on feminine feet. You all see that belle give me the eye?"

"She's looking at me."

"Do you think she'll marry me?"

"She wants to marry me."

"You all think every beautiful gal wants to marry you."

"No, no. See that gal dancing with the Yankee officer? That's Miss Adelaide, who wants to marry me. Her sister, Miss Sally, wants to marry *you*. And finds me repulsive. And vice versa."

"Oh, such marvelous order in the universe. I'm beside myself with happiness. You'll introduce me, won't you?"

A tasteful scrim, a golden net, falls and a just-right pair of beautiful women hold out their arms and dance with him/them. Not the Virginia reel. It's sort of a square-dance waltz. You never saw such a sight in your life. Two men dancing with their wives, Mrs. Bunker and Mrs. Bunker, née Adelaide and Sally Yates. And these lovely white ladies of the wider American world don't spoil the brothers for the Chinese girls. Adet and Anor, Lin Yutang's daughters, accept a dance. As do the Eaton sisters, Edith and Winnifred, a.k.a. Sui Sin Fah (Narcissus) and Onoto Watanna of Hollywood and Broadway and Universal Studios and M-G-M. Not a loner woman among them, each and every one a sister. And more concurrence: the brothers dance with their colleagues, Millie and Christine, the Carolina Black Joined Twins.

Eng: I'd like to buy you from Mr. Barnum. You be my slave. I have thirty-one slaves. You won't be lonely.

Miss Millie: Why, no, sir. I won't be your slave. Mr. Barnum pays me an artiste's salary, the same as you. I'm a free woman.

Miss Christine: You are making her an indecent proposal, sir.

Chang: We shouldn't be seen together in society. *Re*jects shouldn't settle for *re*jects. We need to better ourselves. There's nothing as rejected as a Black woman but a yellow man.

Eng: Speak for yourself, sir. I for one am an uncommon and rare man. And Miss Christine and Miss Millie are uncommon and rare women.

Miss Narcissus, who writes for newspapers: Are you fraternal twins or identical? You certainly do look alike.

Chang: I am alike.

Miss Narcissus: Tell me about your meeting with President Lincoln.

Chang: He told me a joke. Something about an Illinois farmer with a yoke of oxen that won't pull together. He was making fun of me.

Eng: You're always taking things personally. You're too sensitive. He was speaking metaphorically and politically. The punchline goes, "To make a more perfect union."

Miss Watanna: I'm so sorry for your sad life and persecution, and your loneliness. I sympathize.

Chang-Eng: Loneliness?

Miss Watanna: I'd advise a Japanese identity. Americans adore cherry blossoms and silk fans and tea ceremony and geisha girls and samurai and Mount Fuji and Madame Butterfly and sea waves and dainty vegetables such as a tempura of one watercress leaf. (Were this a movie, an extreme close-up: the Eaton sisters have blue eyes, which belie that the brown-eye gene is dominant. Their father was an English painter, and their mother was a Chinese tightrope dancer; such a miscegenation produces American children.)

Chang-Eng: Identity? (He are baffled.)

Eng: South Carolina, the rice capital of the world, also has cherry blossoms and butterflies, and women who are artful with fans and women with flower names. We have a seacoast and tea and watercress sandwiches, and our soldiers are aristocrats.

Miss Watanna: You've lost your identity.

Miss Narcissus: You're assimilated, Mr. Eng. And you too, Winnifred.

The sisters go away, and from across the ballroom comes a beautiful girl, Miss Sophia, played by Taña. She holds out her hands and clasps the outside hands of each twin. They are in a ring-around-the-rosy circle. In an English accent, Miss Sophia says, "Will you marry me, dear? I love you, Chang-Eng."

"No, thank you, Miss Sophia," says Chang.

"I can't marry you, Miss Sophia," says Eng.

"May I see you now and then, dearest?"

"No, Miss Sophia."

"May I write to you? Write poems to you? And mail them to you?"

"Yes, I'll read your poems."

"Goodbye, Chang-Eng dear."

"Goodbye, Miss Sophia dear."

Alone, Chang says to Eng, "I love her very much."

"Me too. I was in love with her."

"She had no discrimination. She had the capability for impartial love. She will write democratic love poems. I'm sorry I can't marry her."

"So am I."

A stagehand in black spins the lottery drum that was once upon a time a

Gold Rush cradle, and a voice calls out: "The United States Army wants you, Mr. Eng Bunker."

Eng: We've been drafted into the Union Army. They need men to tear up the North Carolina and Piedmont Railroad.

Chang: What you mean "we," white man? (As Tonto says to the Lone Ranger when they are surrounded by Indians.) As Confucius said, "You are you, and I am I." I'm not going to tear up any railroads, and I'm not freeing any slaves. I don't want to go to war.

Eng: Shall I make a plea of conscience?

Chang: You all ought to make a plea of the body. You all weren't constructed to be a soldier.

Eng: I am an able-bodied man. Twice as able-bodied as most. I have to think out a deep philosophy against war.

Chang: Point out that you have an attachment to a dove of peace.

Eng: I'm on your side. And a good thing too. If you were to join the Confederate Army, I don't see that we have enough room to shoot long rifles at each other. Does a conscience have to be pure of self-interest? When I think about fighting against my own son and your own son, I get a limpness in my trigger finger, and an anchoring in of my heels.

Chang: Yes, I feel that too. That's our conscience all right, real and most concrete. Brother Eng, aren't you afraid of going to Salisbury Prison as a traitor and a coward?

Eng: Only one thing I'm scared of—myself.

Chang: Mr. Jones, you strike me as ornery. I drink to you, an ornery American man.

Eng feels the liquor too. And they do drunk shtick, slurring and weaving, and falling down, which gets a laff.

But the circus crowd wants more. "Let's have a look!" "Let's see! Let's see!" They rush the brothers and pull at the green velveteen to try to see and touch the ligament. A doctor gets between the twins, examines it, and says, "He is as human as the next American man." The brothers hit the doctor from either side. Chang chases him, dragging Eng after him.

The lights throw bars of shadow across the stage; Chang is jailed for starting a riot. He yells at the audience through the bars, "We know damned well what you came for to see—the angle we're joined at, how we can have two sisters for wives and twenty-one Chinese-Carolinian children between us. You want to see if there's room for two, three bundling boards. You want to know if we feel jointly. You want to look at the hyphen. You want to look at it bare."

"My, you all are a violent man," says Eng. "How am I to make my plea of conscience?"

"Mr. Bones, your troubles give me a pain in the ass."

The brothers are let out of jail and out of the draft on technicalities. Only one of them is a rioter and only one a draftee, so what to do with the extra man but let him go?

But they cannot evade age and death. Chang dies. He does death throes, then hangs there dead with his pigtail fanning like a fishtail sweeping the floor. The world has been contemplating the horror of being attached to a corpse—the albatross tied to the sailor; Ripley's camel roaming the desert with the dead legionnaire tied to its saddle. The remaining brother pushes at the dead one, runs without getting anywhere, and says: *Now it was there. Now it grew out of me like a tumor, like a second head, and was so big. It was there like a huge, dead beast, that had once, when it was still alive, been my hand or my arm.* Eng dies too after several days and nights of sympathy and fright.

Then here come The Flying Lings! The Living Target! The Frame of Knives! The Chinese Coin and the Enchanted Straw! Experiments in Human Elasticity by the Boneless Boy! The Bowl of Water and the Charmed Sling! The World Record Number One Balancer of Eight (8) Stools on the Nose—Going for Nine (9) Tonight Only! The Magic Balls! Bird Calls and Animals of the Farm! The Revolving Oil Jar! The Most Ambidextrous Jugglers in the World! The First Chinese Woman in America! And off fly the Lings, Four Muscular Orientals, to Mystic, Connecticut.

So, several families of brothers are dead. Kingdoms rise and fall. World war again. Vaudeville time! The screen for changing costumes behind— black silk stockings and a red feather boa flung over it—fell with a crash-bang! It's Ruby Long Legs and the Flora Doras with all their clothes on. They ran out of their huddle and got into chorus-girl formation. They rolled their shoulders, winked over their high almost-Pilipina sleeves, wiggled their peplum asses. Ruffling the air with dusting powder and French perfumes, Auntie Dolly, Auntie Sadie, Auntie Bessie, Auntie Maydene, Auntie Lilah, Auntie Marleese, and Mom, all together now—knee kick, full kick, knee kick, full kick. "Can you do the cancan? I can do the cancan"— segueing into "There's a place in France where the ladies wear no pants." They gave us their backsides, and lifted their skirts. Each auntie was wearing undies with the flag of an ally on them. It's the Pants Dance of the Nations. The audience went wild for each auntie doing her national special. Clicking castanets over her head, Auntie Dolly with a rose between her teeth stamped her feet in tight circles, and flung that rose at her old man. "La cucaracha. La cucaracha." "King Georgie had a date. He stayed out very late. God save the King. Queen Lizzie paced the floor. King George came in at four. She met him at the door. God save the King." Skirts down and hands proper, they sang as regally as queens. Aunt Maydene, Miss Finlandia, sang, "Dear land of home, our hearts to thee are holden." "Yo-ho-HEAVE-ho-o!" The aunties bent their backs and pulled, a chorus line of Mother Courages. March march march, tappy toes, tappy toes, salute, salute. "From the halls of Montezu-uma to the shores of Tripoli." Aunt Bessie sang "Mae Ling Toy and her Chinee Boy"; she danced, wagging her head back and forth between pointer fingers pointing up and down. The merry widows—they *wore* merry widows—were yet breaking hearts at forty feet; and at five feet, which was how close the front row was, their kicking spike heels could knock your head off. The oldest stars in our firmament sky were radiating. The audience whistled for encore after encore, drawing the aunties out amongst them, where they sat on laps, rubbed bald heads, gazed into eyes, vamped "I'd like to get you on a slow boat to China all to myself alone." Ruby Long Legs parted her legs, and did the splits, sliding down all the way to the floor. Then everybody on her back—legs wide open making V for Victory.

As the pink feathers settled, here come the bathing beauties down the hanamichi thrust runway. The old-guy judges say, "Beauti-foo. Beauti-foo," when "foo" means "pants," and choose Miss Chinatown U.S.A.: the tallest girl with the tightest blackest curls and reddest lips, the roundest nose, the reddest apple cheeks in the whitest face, the plumpest cheongsahm.

Little girls in loose, fluttery cheongsahms bring Jade Snow Wong a dozen long-stem American Beauty roses, and orchid corsages for her mother and sister. Jade Snow is wearing an embroidered black satin coat with slits, but all you see through them is her pleated skirt. Youngest Sister Wong is sweet in peach-blossom silk, and their mother is dignified in a pale blue gown, everybody's hair marcelled. "It was almost like a wedding," says Jade Snow. She reads her essay about absenteeism in factories, which won first prize in a contest sponsored by the War Production Board's War Production Drive. This essay was sent to President Roosevelt, and you can read it in the *Congressional Record*. The prizes are a war bond and the christening of a liberty ship on a Sunday, and sending it to war. The loudspeakers play our crash-bang music. Jade Snow hits the ship with a bottle of champagne beribboned in red, white, and blue. "I christen thee the *William A. Jones*." Welders cut away the plates that hold the ship to the pier of the

Marin County shipyards, where Jade Snow works. "Burn one!" "Burn two!" The maiden ship is free on the water and sails to war.

The Soong sisters and Anna Chennault, dressed in suits that the bride wears at her wedding reception, travel all over the country and give speeches. "Freedom," they say. "Liberty." Their accents were schooled Back East. They prove that the ladies-in-distress aren't bucktoof myopic pagans. Women not unlike Katharine Hepburn and Myrna Loy are burning the rice fields as they flee the invaders. (The invaders are the ones with the buckteeth and glasses.) These excellent dark women should have overcome dumb blondes forevermore. Women get their wish: War. Men, sexy in uniform, will fight and die for them.

All hell broke loose on the third night of this play, for which the audience kept growing. The public, including white strangers, came and made the show important. The theater went beyond cracking up family, friends and neighbors come to see one another be different from everyday. The take at the box office paid for the explosives for the climactic blowout. The audience sat on the staircase and windowsills; there was no longer an aisle.

We are in a show palace on the frontier. We have come down out of the ice fields of the Sierras and the Rockies and the Yukon, and up from Death Valley. Three authentic crescent oil lamps were pulled up and down throughout the evening that seemed endless because time is a dragon that curls and smokes. Trappers, hunters, prospectors, scouts are spending their earnings to see fellow human beings. As still as animals, they suddenly shout because they haven't talked to anyone for a long time. They need to hear people, and to tune their voices again.

When the sun is farthest from the Earth, Lantern Festival lights up the five days of deepest winter. Curves of scaffolding form a white dragon; the white lanterns are its scales. Each holding a lantern, children file singing through the ice tunnels. Dragons are playing with flames englobed in ice— the pearl that is the universe or Earth. A thousand lanterns—phoenixes in paper cages—hang from the Blue Cloud Tower, the most famous restaurant ever, with over a hundred dining rooms. At crossroads, shopkeepers and householders build mountains of buns as in Marysville. But this is not Marysville. This is Tai Ming Fu, the Great Bright City, and to this City of Big Lights on the clear silver-and-gold night of the full moon will come the hundred and eight bandits. Or so warns the poem on the gate, scrolls of poetry unfurling on walls and posts. Sung Chiang, the Timely Rain, leader of the hundred and eight, has written a guarantee-poem giving fair warning that the bandits are about to attack. But the innocent shall not be harmed;

the imprisoned shall be free. Teams of husband-and-wife knights enter the city from different routes. It's the Dwarf Tiger and the Tigress, played by Zeppelin and Ruby; the Vegetarian and the Night Ogress, played by Charles Bogard Shaw and Nanci Lee; the Dry Land Water Beast and Devil Face, played by Lance and Sunny Kamiyama; the Pursuing God of Death and the Lively Woman, played by Mr. Lincoln Fong and PoPo. They're wearing party clothes to account for glamour. They shop and eat until time to reveal themselves as the toughest fighters of all.

Dudes and schoolmarms from Back East, and picture brides from back East, and Frank Cane step out of the stagecoach. "Get back on that stage and keep riding if you know what's good for you." See that woman in a poke bonnet leading her workhorses? She's a runaway slave. She turns around; you see she has a Chinese face. That man walking here and there in a cangue—like locked in stocks that are not stuck into the ground—has committed so many crimes, ten-pound and twenty-five-pound iron weights have been added to his burden; the papers that list his penalties seal the joins and cover the wood. He's been collared. But on this holiday, kind people are making his cangue into a feasting table—roast duck and buns. Horses have brands on their butts, while men have them on their faces. You can read on cheeks and foreheads their places of exile, where they're supposed to be. The men with hanks of straw tied around their blades are swords-for-hire, walking up and down the marketplace. The clomp and stomp of boots on wooden sidewalks satisfy the ear, no shuffling and scuttling in slippers.

Friends and enemies find one another. Agon.

Into the dungeons Night Ogress Nanci carries paper flowers and paper butterflies, which hide brimstone and saltpeter, the ingredients for gunpowder. Her accomplices are the Forest Dragon and the Horned Dragon, who once knocked down a fir tree with his head. The jailers have gone out to celebrate, having put their poor relations in charge. "Where are my brothers?" asks the Ogress, taking her swords out of her belt. "I've come for my brothers. They were framed. It's time you let them out. Before I deal with you, I want to hear your idea of justice. Should you lock up the man who stole the tiger or the two innocent boys whom he stole it from?" "Let me think. I need to think," says the amateur jailer, backing away from her. He bumps into a prisoner, who bangs him over the head with his cangue. The Ogress fights the guards while the dragons free prisoners and set gunpowder. Outside, the Vegetable Gardener ties the jailhouse bars to his pommel. His horse pulls the wall down. The other Perfect Couples of the Battlefield open all the city gates, just as, amid fireworks, the Blue Cloud

Tower blows up. At the sight of that flambeau, Miss Hu the Pure, played by Judy Louis, spurs her ash-grey horse. Twirling her red silk lasso overhead, she leads the main army of four thousand men and amazons into the city. Snow falls. A fire dragon and a snow dragon have come at once.

As in real life, things were happening all over the place. The audience looked left, right, up and down, in and about the round, everywhere, the flies, the wings, all the while hearing reports from off stage. Too much goings-on, they miss some, okay, like life.

Inside a grocery store, some bad Caucasians plant dope among the mayjing and the black-bean sauce, then call the cops. A lynch mob raids the store, where the grocers both work and live. They jerk the chinamen through the streets by their long hair. Ropes hang from lampposts and fire escapes. Nooses are lowered over heads. The accusation and sentence are read: To be hung by the neck until he dies for dealing opium, which debauches white girls for the slave trade. The kung fu gang leaps to the rescue. Everybody dukes it out. The opium war in the West. John Wayne rides into town, asking, "Where's the chinaman? Gotta see the chinaman about some opium." The police break up the riot, and arrest the grocers for assaulting officers. So Chinese-Americans founded the Joang Wah for the purpose of filing legal complaints with the City of New York against lynchings, illegal arrests, opium, slavery, and grocery-store licensing. A tong is not a crime syndicate and not a burial society. It is organization of community, for which Chinese-Americans have genius.

A storyman arrives on I Street, and unpacks a troupe of puppets, the tribe and clan that he carries with him. Pretty wife doll and courtesans and warrior girls and faeries. With puppets, you can bind their feet as tiny as you like, ladies' slippers on their feet, foxgloves on their hands. The troupe has a hundred bodies and a thousand switchable heads. The gambling house is in front; the hundred-seat theater is in back. The gamblers drink and play pai gow standing up, one boot on the railing, which has U's like stirrups, worn into it. Guns are at-ready in holsters. Motivated by human nature, the poker players sock one another across the tables, and crash through the wall. Puppets whack the live actors on their heads and in their faces. The set spins about; another life is going on on the reverse side. The bar mirror falls in a sleet of crashing reflections. Gamblers and cheaters swipe at one another's eyes with jagged bottles. Puppets lose their heads. Hand-puppets lose their insides, which change into fists. The puppet master, invisible black ninja, kicks ass. Wail. Bang.

The floor caves in, and those who don't fall in jump into the hole—gold dust has been raining down through the floorboards for years.

Meanwhile, Rudyard Kipling (played by the Yale Younger Poet), the first white explorer to write an account of crossing America from west to east, sets foot in "the Chinese quarter of San Francisco, which is a ward of the city of Canton set down in the most eligible business-quarter of the place." He guides a tour group of ladies and gentlemen through our town. Look at how strange the tourists are, pale outsiders abroad in their own country. Sir Kipling gives them *American Notes*: "The Chinaman with his usual skill has possessed himself of good brick fireproof buildings and, following instinct, has packed each tenement with hundreds of souls, all living in filth and squalor not to be appreciated save by you in India." The poor tourists follow him down into a basement. "I wanted to know how deep in the earth the Pig-tail had taken root. I struck a house about four stories high full of celestial abominations, and began to burrow down. . . ." He descends a level below the cellar, and another one below that. He goes into what Frank Norris called the Third Circle of Evil. (The First Circle is the shops and restaurants; the Second Circle is the home life.) Three levels down, Kipling discovers that "a poker club had assembled and was in full swing. The Chinaman loves 'pokel,' and plays it with great skill, swearing like a cat when he loses. One of the company looked like a Eurasian, whence I argued that he was a Mexican—a supposition that later inquiries confirmed. They were a picturesque set of fiends and polite, being too absorbed in their game to look at a stranger." A fate of the cards set the Eurasian Mexican (played by Mr. Leroy Sanchez of the Office of Human Development) and a chinaman against each other. "The latter shifted his place to put the table between himself and his opponent, and stretched a lean yellow hand towards the Mexican's winnings." A pistol shot bangs out. Smoke obscures the scene. Kipling and the Eurasian-Mexican hit the floor. The smoke clears. "The Chinaman was gripping the table with both hands and staring in front of him at an empty chair. The Mexican had gone, and a little whirl of smoke was floating near the roof. Still gripping the table, the Chinaman said: 'Ah!' in the tone that a man would use when, looking up from his work suddenly, he sees a well-known friend in the doorway. Then he coughed and fell over to his own right, and I saw that he had been shot in the stomach. I became aware that, save for two men leaning over the stricken one, the room was empty. It was possible that the Chinamen would mistake me for the Mexican—everything horrible seemed possible just then—and it was more than possible that the stairways would be closed while they were hunting for the murderer. The man on the floor coughed a sickening cough. I heard it as I fled, and one of his companions turned out the lamp. . . . I found the doorway, and my legs trembling under me, reached the protection of the clear cool light, the fog, and the rain. I dared not run, and for the life of me I could not walk. I must have effected a compromise, for I remember the light of a street lamp showed the shadow of one half skipping—caracoling along the pavements in what seemed to be an ecstasy of suppressed happiness. But it was fear—deadly fear. Fear compounded of past knowledge of the Oriental—only other white man—available witness—three stories underground—and the cough of the Chinaman now some forty feet under my clattering boot-heels. Not for anything would I have informed the police, because I firmly believed that the Mexican had been dealt with somewhere down there on the third floor long ere I had reached the air; and, moreover, once clear of the place, I could not for the life of me tell where it was. My ill-considered flight brought me out somewhere a mile distant from the hotel; and the clank of the lift that bore me to a bed six stories above ground was music in my ears. Wherefore I would impress it upon you who follow after, do not knock about the Chinese quarters at night and alone. You may stumble across a picturesque piece of human nature that will unsteady your nerves for half a day."

You would think that that Chinese guy had killed somebody instead of having gotten killed himself. Rudyard Kipling exits, chased off by cherry bombs and cymbal clangs. Nobel Prize winner. No wonder the Yale Younger Poet was depressed in spite of honors.

At the Fook Tai Lottery Co., Liang Kai Hee, an actor and a gambling man, has broken the bank. Everybody stops fighting as they recount in wonder how he did it, which is a legend to this day. He bought a ticket for fifty cents, and picked six numbers, like a hexagram out of the Ching, and won ten dollars. He put those ten dollars on the same six numbers and won the jackpot—ten thousand dollars. The stagecoach with wheels spinning like coins and its belly sagging with the gold and silver weight of the fortune rolls to him. Black and white boys are chanting, "Ching chong chinaman sitting on a fence, trying to make a dollar out of fifty cents," caterwauling the vowels and honking the "n"s, slurring us. The kung fu guys chase them, and they run like the cowards they are.

Firecrackers boomed in the chimney. A mother-and-sons bomb ricocheted crazily inside a garbage can—a big mother bang detonating and creating seventy-five scatter bombs that bounced about for a long time. An

M-80 barrel bomb went off. Night mirages filled the windows, reflecting and magnifying—a city at war and carnival. All aflare and so bright that we understand: Why we go to war is to make explosions and lights, which are more beautiful than anything.

At the climactic free-for-all—everybody fights everybody everywhere at once. The hundred and eight bandits and their enemies (played by twenty-five actors) knock one another in and out all entrances and exits, sword-fighting up and down the stairs and out amongst the audience, take that and *that*, kicking the mandarin-duck kick, swinging the jeweled-ring swing, drums and cymbals backing up the punches. The intellectuals grasp their five-pronged pen holders, and make of their hands claw-fists. Everybody chased one another outside and battled on 22nd Avenue among the cars. Audience hung out of window. Ten thousand San Franciscans, armed with knives and shouting, "Death to capitalists," attack the railroad office, and set fire to Chinatown. Four thousand Sacramento's Order of Caucasians sing a scab song, "Ching chong chinaman sitting on the fence." Bullets and arrows zing from the false fronts of the sharpshooter roofs. Gunslingers and archers jump from balconies into the saddle. Rain barrels explode. Puppets pummel and cudgel and wack-wack. Tenderfoot drinkers of lemonade and sarsaparilla and milk bust out through swinging doors and over hitching posts into water troughs and rain barrels and Ali Baba wine jars. Through the smoke, a juggernaut, an iron roller with spikes, thunders across a hollow floor. The audience got to its feet in participation. The sheriff will surely come soon to stop the show with a cease-and-desist-disturbing-the-peace order. Jail us for performing without a permit, like our brave theatrical ancestors, who were violators of zoning ordinances; they put on shows, they paraded, they raised chickens within city limits. They were flimflammers of tourists, wildcat miners, cigar makers without the white label, carriers of baskets on poles, cubic air breathers, miscegenists, landsquatters and landlords without deeds, kangaroo jurists, medical and legal practitioners without degrees, unconvertible pagans and heathens, gamblers with God and one another, aliens unqualifiable to apply for citizenship, unrelated communalists and crowders into single-family dwellings, dwellers and gamblers in the backs of stores, restaurateurs and launderers who didn't pass health inspections, droppers of garbage into other people's cans, payers and takers of less than minimum wage, founders of martial-arts schools with wall certificates from the Shaolin Temple of Hunan, China, but no accreditation by the Western Association of Schools and Colleges, Unemployment-check collectors, dodgers of the draft of several countries, un-Americans, red-hot communists, unbridled capitalists, look-alikes of japs and Viet Cong, un-licensed manufacturers and exploders of fireworks. Everybody with aliases. More than one hundred and eight outlaws.

In chain reactions, thousand-firecracker strands climbed poles to the microphones and blasted out the loudspeakers. Blow it all up. Set the the-ater on fire. The playwright goes down with his play like the historians who were killed at the ends of their eras, their books burning at their feet. No asbestos-and-metal guillotine curtain here. The Globe and the Garrick had many fires, then holocaust. It's a theater tradition. Chinese hold all the Guinness records—1,670 audience members and actors killed in Canton in 1845 at the Theater, which was enclosed by a high wall. The fire at the The-ater in Kamli killed two thousand in 1893. The Fu Chow playhouse burned down in 1884 under bombardment by the French fleet. Every theater you've ever been to or heard of has had its fire. The Bowery Theatre in Vauxhall Gardens, New York—burned and rebuilt six times. Eleven hundred theater fires all over the world during the last hundred years. In London and Paris and Budapest and Silver City, Eureka, Virginia City, Leadville (three times), Marysville, Placerville, Meadville, and in San Fran-cisco alone, not counting earthquake fires—the Adelphi Theatre, the Jenny Lind Theatre, Ronison & Evrad's Theatre, the Olympic Circus, the New Jenny Lind, the Lyceum (twice), the Music Hall, Pickwick Hall, the Rus-sian Gardens, the Grand American Theatre I, the Grand American Theatre II, the Winter Garden, and the Chinese Theatre of San Francisco. Floors caught fire when winter stoves under the stage heated up the boards too hot. The candles in the luster pooled and became a bowl of sheet-flame. The gasman at the Baltimore Front Street Theater held his pole-torch up to a jet, and a gust of fire shot out through the stage, which is a wind tunnel. The hay bales for dragging the floors clean caught sparks and smoldered. For the sake of verisimilitude, the actor-soldiers at the court theater in Ol-denburg set fire to a stage fortress, midnight, 1891, and the rest of the build-ing went with it. On Bastille Day, 1873, cannons were shot off indoors, which destroyed the Grand Opéra House and the bibliothèque. The last act of *Faust*, the masked ball, caused many theaters to burn, including the holo-causts of the Leghorn and the Teatro degli Acquidotti. There was a cinema-tographe fire in Paris in 1897; and in 1908, at the Rhoades Opera House, Boyerton, Pennsylvania, a motion-picture machine exploded and killed a hundred people. And just this past spring in Saigon, three hundred children were killed at a waterfront theater. We'll do anything for lighting, die for it, kill for it.

In the tradition of theater fires, in remembrance of the burnings of Chinatowns, and of the Great Earthquake and Fire, and of the Honolulu plague fire at the New Year and the new century, and in protest of the school fact that Chinese invented gunpowder but were too dumb to use it in warfare, and in honor of artists who were arrested for incendiarism, Wittman Ah Sing—"Gotta match?" he asked. "Not since Superman died," answered a chorus of kids in the audience.—lit every last explosive. Go up in flames and down in history. Fireworks whiz-banged over and into the neighborhood. Percussion caps, powders, and instruments banged and boomed. A genie of the theater ran around with torches—Antonin Artaud torches the grass-hut theater of Bali, and the actors gesture through the flames.

The neighbors turned in four alarums. Fire engines were coming, wailing louder than Chinese opera. On cue—the S.F.F.D. was bringing the redness and the wailing. Sirens. Bells. A hook-and-ladder truck. The audience ran out into the street. More audience came. And the actors were out from backstage and the green room, breaking rules of reality-and-illusion. Their armor and swords were mirrored in fenders, bumpers, and the long sides of the fire trucks. The clear clean red metal with the silver chrome glorified all that was shining. The emergency lights reddened faces and buildings. "Fire!" "Fire!" The *Chron*'s banner tomorrow: Chinese Fire!

"Where's the fire?"

"No fire. Chinese custom."

"Do you have a fireworks permit?"

"Permit?" Only three flashpowder technicians in the State of California had a Class C license for setting off theatrical explosives. Wittman Ah Sing wasn't one of them.

"You don't plan to keep this racket up all night, do you?"

"The noisy part of our ritual is done. Would you like some tickets to the quiet part? You're invited to come in and see it." And to the crowd of neighbors, "We invite you too," papering the house. "I promise to be quiet."

The next part of Wittman's night could have had him caged and taken through the City in a paddywagon. He might have seen the streets through grillwork and between the heads of a pair of cops.

Instead, he was given a chance; Chinese are allowed more fireworks than other people. He went back inside, and continued the play. We'll let him tell you about himself by himself.

ONE-MAN SHOW

It came to you to be yourself. Your fellow-actors'
courage failed; as if they had been caged with a
pantheress, they crept along the wings and spoke
what they had to, only not to irritate you. But you
drew them forward, and you posed them and dealt
with them as if they were real. Those limp doors,
those simulated curtains, those objects that had no
reverse side, drove you to protest. You felt how
your heart intensified unceasingly toward an
immense reality and, frightened, you tried once
more to take people's gaze off you like long
gossamer threads—: but now, in their fear of the
worst, they were already breaking into applause: as
though at the last moment to ward off something
that would compel them to change their life.
—Rilke, *The Notebooks of Malte Laurids Brigge*

I. I. I.
I. I. I.
I. I. I.
—Monkey's aria, *The Journey to the West*

OF COURSE, Wittman Ah Sing didn't really burn
down the Association house and the theater. It was an illusion of fire. Good monkey. He kept control of the explosives, and of his arsonist's delight in flames. He wasn't
crazy; he was a monkey. What's crazy is the idea that revo-
lutionaries must shoot and bomb and kill, that revolution is
the same as war. We keep losing our way on the short cut—killing for freedom and liberty and community and a better economy. Wittman could
have torched the curtains and the dry flowers; he could have downpoured
the oil lamps onto the chairs and fruit crates. He'd been envying that
Japanese-American guy that got shot allegedly helping to set the Watts

fires, yelling, "Burn, baby, burn." But, no, Wittman would not have tried to burn the City. It's all too beautiful to burn.

The world was splitting up. Tolstoy had noted the surprising gaiety of war. During his time, picnickers and fighters took to the same field. We'd gotten more schizzy. The dying was on the Asian side of the planet while the playing—the love-ins and the be-ins—were on the other, American side. Whatever there is when there isn't war has to be invented. What do people do in peace? Peace has barely been thought.

Our monkey, master of change, staged a fake war, which might very well be displacing some real war. Wittman was learning that one big bang-up show has to be followed up with a second show, a third show, shows until something takes hold. He was defining a community, which will meet every night for a season. Community is not built once-and-for-all; people have to imagine, practice, and re-create it. His community surrounding him, then, we're going to reward and bless Wittman with our listening while he talks to his heart's content. Let him get it all out, and we hear what he has to say direct. Blasting and blazing are too wordless.

On the third night, the one hundred and eight bandits climbed the stairs to become stars in the sky, except for some of the Juan brothers. They escape westward, that is, to Southeast Asia. They shunt their skiffs through the tule fog and shoot out in Viet Nam. Juan II, Juan V, and Juan VII (pronounced the Hispanic way, not like Don Quick-set and Don Jew-On the way we learned at Berkeley), played by Chicanos, become the One Hundred Children who are the ancestors of the Vietnamese. Though Vietnamese will deny that. Everybody would rather be the indigenous people of a place than be its immigrants. Another Indian punchline: "Are they going back where they came from yet?" A door like two golden trays opens up for a moment in the sky, which tears like blue silk, and a hundred and five bandits go to Heaven and three start a new country. The audience clapped loud, bone-proud of our boys and our girls, just like graduation, where we take the hardest awards, math and science. The End.

Except: A Chinese-minded audience likes the moral of the story told in so many words. And the American theater was rejoicing in scoldings; Blacks were breaking through the fourth wall. Whites were going to the theater and paying good money to be yelled at by Blacks, and loving them for it. Wittman Ah Sing waited for the audience to stop applauding, whistling, calling out names—"Kamiyama!" "Shaw!" "Nanci!"—a kabuki tradition. The actors had taken solo bows after arias and scenes and acts. He held up his hands—enough, enough already—turned his chair around, lit a cigarette, smoked, straddled the chair. He wanted to address the world as the shouting Daruma, fists upthrust pulling force up from lotus butt base, his body a triangle of power, and hairy mouth wide open and roaring. Not the Daruma doll that you knock around but Daruma the Shouter.

"I want to talk to you," said Wittman. "I'm Wittman Ah Sing, the playwright." The audience clapped for the playwright. He further introduced himself by giving them the mele of his name. "I'm one of the American Ah Sings. Probably there are no Ah Sings in China. You may laugh behind my family's back, that we keep the Ah and think it means something. I know it's just a sound. A vocative that goes in front of everyone's names. Ah Smith. Ah Jones. Everyone has an ah, only our family writes ours down. In that Ah, you can hear we had an ancestor who left a country where the language has sounds that don't mean anything—la and ma and wa—like music. Alone and illiterate, he went where not one other Chinese was. Nobody to set him straight. When his new friends asked him his name, he remembered that those who wanted him had called, 'Ah Sing.' So he told the schoolmarm, 'Ah Sing, ma'am,' and she wrote down for him the two syllables of a new American name."

Wittman waved the newspapers in his hand, and whacked them against his knee. "The reviews have come out. You've seen the reviews, haven't you?" The audience, which now included the actors, gave the reviews a round of applause. "I want to talk," he said. They gave him another hand, welcoming him to go ahead, talk. "So. You were entertained. You liked the show, huh? I myself have some complaints and notes but. Let me discuss with you what the *Chron* and the *Examiner* said, and the *Oakland Tribune*, and *The Daily Cal* and the *Berkeley Gazette*, and the *Shopping News*, and the *Barb*. They've reviewed us already, thinking that opening night is no different from the second night and tonight. You like the reviews? I am sore and disappointed. Come on, you can't like these reviews. Don't be too easily made happy. Look. Look. 'East meets West.' 'Exotic.' 'Sino-American theater.' 'Snaps, crackles and pops like singing rice.' 'Sweet and sour.' Quit clapping. Stop it. What's to cheer about? You like being compared to Rice Krispies? Cut it out. Let me show you, you've been insulted. They sent their food critics. They wrote us up like they were tasting Chinese food. Rice, get it? 'Savor beauteous Nanci Lee,' it says here. That's like saying that LeRoi Jones is as good as a watermelon. 'Yum yum, authentic watermelon.' They wouldn't write a headline for *Raisin in the Sun*: 'America Meets Africa.' They want us to go back to China where we belong. They think that Americans are either white or Black. I can't wear that civil-rights button with the Black hand and the white hand shaking each other. I have a nightmare—after duking it out, someday Blacks and whites will shake hands over my head. I'm the little yellow man beneath the bridge of their hands and overlooked. Have you been at a demonstration where they sing:

> *Black and white together.*
> *Black and white together.*
> *Black and white together*
> *someda-a-a-ay.*

Deep in my heart, I do believe we have to be of further outrage to stop this chanting about us, that 'East is east and west is west.' Here's one that keeps quoting longer, like more learned. I won't read it to you. My mouth doesn't want to say any more wog-hater non-American Kipling. 'Twain shall.' Shit. Nobody says 'twain shall,' except in reference to us. We've failed with our magnificence of explosions to bust through their Kipling. I'm having to give instruction. There is no East here. West is meeting West. This was all West. All you saw was West. This is The Journey *In* the West. I am so fucking offended. Why aren't you offended? Let me help you get offended. Always be careful to take offense. These sinophiles dig us so much, they're drooling over us. That kind of favorableness we can do without. They think they know us—the wide range of us from sweet to sour—because they eat in Chinese restaurants. They're the ones who order the sweet-and-sour pork and the sweet-and-sour spare ribs and the sweet-and-sour shrimp. I've read my Aristotle and Agee, I've been to college; they have ways to criticize theater besides for sweetness and sourness. They could do laundry reviews, clean or dirty. Come on. What's so 'exotic'? We're about as exotic as shit. Nobody soo-pecial here. No sweet-and-sour shit. No exotic chop suey shit. So this variety show had too much motley; they didn't have to call it 'chop-suey vaudeville.' I am so pissed off. But. This other piece says that we are *not* exotic. 'Easily understood and not too exotic for the American audience.' Do I have to explain why 'exotic' pisses me off, and 'not exotic' pisses me off? They've got us in a bag, which we aren't punching our way out of. To be exotic or to be not-exotic is not a question about Americans or about humans. Okay, okay. Take me, for example. I'm common ordinary. Plain black sweater. Blue jeans. Tennis shoes ordinaire. Clean soo mun shaven. What's so exotic? My hair's too long, huh? Is that it? It's the hair? Does anybody have a pair of scissors? Here, help me spread these newspapers on the floor. I'm cutting my hair. If I bend over like this, I can see it, and cut it fairly straight. What's so funny? It ought to be the same around each ear? No need for symmetrical, huh? I don't want to snip off my ears. Earless Oichi. I'll lean over this way, and off comes this side. And this side too. And the top. The do-it-yourself haircut. Can be done without mirrors or friends. Whatever you get, you wear. Natural. Fast. Cheap. Just cut until you yourself can't see any more hair. Go by feel. I like the feel of sharp blades sandily closing through hairs. Sure, it's my real hair. I'm not wearing a wig, I'm honest. Wow, I didn't know I was carrying so much hair on my head."

Winging it, the monkey was indeed cutting off his actual hair. Black hair covered the newspapers. Wittman was performing an unpremeditated on-the-spot happening, unrepeatable tomorrow night. His prickly pear head cracked the audience up. The hair down his collar kept him in aggravation.

Wittman turned the chair flush toward the audience, sat up straight facing them, classic talk-story pose, and said: "We should have done a soap opera that takes place in a kitchen about your average domestic love agonies and money agonies. The leading lady is in hair curlers and an apron, and her husband, who has a home haircut like mine, stomps in, home from work. He knocks the mud off his workboots. He lets down the bib of his farmer or mechanic overalls. He drinks his beer while kneading his toes. She empties his lunchbucket, and they argue about whether a napkin does or does not count as one lunch item. A radio is on, and it's tuned to some popular station broadcasting whatever happens to be on, show tunes or a ball game or the news. No ching-chong music, no epic costumes, you understand? The highpoint will be the family eating and discussing around the table—where the dramatic confrontations of real life take place; that's why meals are the hardest scenes to block. You know what the *Tribune* will say? 'Exotic.' Or they'll say, 'Whaddya know? Not exotic. The inscrutables are explaining themselves at last. We are allowed into their mysterious oriental world.' " Pause for the thinkers to think. "Okay, let's say in this soap opera, they hear bad news about their only son—killed in war. (Don't you whites get confused; he's killed fighting for *our* side. Nobody here but us Americans.) The mom is weeping big sobs with nose-blowing, and the dad howls, 'Aiya! Aiya! Aaaaaaa! Say, la! Naygamagahai! Aaaargh! Say, la! Say, la! Aiyaaaah!' and like in the funnies, 'Aieeeee!' "

Wittman stood and vocalesed a wail of pain that a dad might cry who'd given his only kid to his country. His eyebrows screwed toward each other, and his mouth was bent into the sign for infinity. Some audience members laughed.

"And guess how too many people will react? They'll say, 'Inscrutable.' We do tears. We do ejaculations. We do laffs. And they call us inscrutable.

"I have an idea how to make them cut that inscrutable shit out. Our next task is to crack the heart of the soap opera."

"I've gotten work on the soaps," said Charley. "They're starting to hire minorities now."

"Me too," said Nanci. "I played a nurse."

"Did you play the lab tech again, Charley? Or the court stenographer? You guys are too grateful. The job of the characters they let you play gets upgraded from criminal or servant to semi-professional, and you're fooled that we're doing better. Just because you get to wear a nurse's uniform rather than a Suzie Wong dress doesn't mean you're getting anywhere nearer to the heart of that soap. You're not the ones they tune in every day to weep over. We need to be part of the daily love life of the country, to be shown and loved continuously until we're not inscrutable anymore.

"Wait a minute. Let me try that again. We're not inscrutable at all. We are not inherently unknowable. That's a trip they're laying on us. Because they are willfully innocent. Willful innocence is a perversion. It's like that other perversion where people fly to Japan or Denmark to have their ex-hymen sewn shut. People who call us inscrutable get their brains sewn shut. Then they run around saying, 'We don't know you. And it's your fault. You're inscrutable.' They willfully do not learn us, and blame that on us, that we have an essential unknowableness. I was reading in a book by a Black man who travels far from America to this snowy village in the Alps. No Black man had set foot on that part of the Earth before. The villagers are innocent of slavery and of standing in the schoolhouse door and even of having ever seen a Black person. Their innocence pisses him off. On his walks, the kids call to him, innocently, 'Neger. Neger,' which makes echoes of another word to his American ears. He doesn't make a scary face and chase those kids, and he doesn't lecture them. He is a very quiet guy, who thinks at them: 'People are trapped in history and history is trapped in them . . . and hence all Black men have toward all white men an attitude which is designed, really, either to rob the white man of the jewel of his naïveté, or else to make it cost him dear.' "

Wittman was quoting from "Stranger in the Village," which is in *Notes of a Native Son* by James Baldwin. After getting educated, a graduate has to find ways to talk to his family and regular people again. It helps, when you want to tell them about your reading, to leave out the title and author. Just start, "I was reading in a book . . ."

"We have a story about what to do to those who try to hang on to the jewel of their naïveté. Cho Cho will get them. Once after losing a battle, Cho Cho hides out in a farmhouse with a well-meaning family. So many kids of various sizes run all over the place, they seem like the hundred children. The farm folks are going about their chores and speaking ordinarily, but all is fraught; the birds are stirring and beating their wings. Cho Cho walks here and there, peeping through doors and windows. What are these people up to, treating him so well? They say they are not political; they welcome the stranger as a guest. They certainly laugh a lot. Cho Cho steps into the wine cellar; a tall boy ducks into a jar. 'Aren't you too old to be playing hide-and-go-seek?' And where did the father go? Cho Cho strolls in the fields and orchards. No father. 'Where is he?' he asks this kid and that kid. 'He went to market to buy a fat pig.' The same answer from everybody. Had they had a meeting, and rehearsed that answer? Some kind of code? They say, 'He went to market to buy a fat pig,' and look at one another and laugh. Grandma brings a butcher knife, and a sister brings a boning knife. The mother sharpens them. 'Why are you sharpening the knives?' 'We're going to slaughter the fat pig that Father is bringing home from market.' Did she say 'pig' like she meant *him?* Why's everybody giggling? A brother and a cousin are talking behind a tree. What are they laughing at? What's so funny? There were eight of them—they could gang up on him. Nothing for it but to pick them off one by one. He catches a brother alone in a lean-to, and quietly kills him, and hides the body behind the storage. Kills the mother, and hides her in the loft above the kitchen. Kills the grandma with her own knife, tucks her behind the grain jars. The rest of the family goes about their routine, not missing the others. He kills them one and all. Got a sister in the courtyard, a brother in the fields, another brother in the barn. Very neatly. No fights, no hysteria. Killed that family clean. Got them from behind, a hand over their eyes, fast. They didn't know what hit them. Nobody suffered.

"He leaves the farm, and meets the father on the road. He is trundling a fat pig bundled upside down in a basket. The rattan binds against its human-like skin. A pig's eye looks out between wickerwork bands. One has to look closely to see that it is a pig and not a naked man; sometimes there are naked men trussed up like this as a punishment for adultery, adulterer in a pigpoke. So the family had been acting secretive and excited because they had been planning a surprise party. The father says, 'The party's for you. You'll act surprised when the ladies tell you, won't you?' 'I'll do that, yes,' says Cho Cho. The father will have to go too, a quick stab in the back. The poor man is spared the suffering of finding his family slaughtered. Cho Cho takes the pig and continues his journey."

The listeners did not applaud this tale of paranoia. They were not ready to slaughter innocents. The white people were probably getting uncomfortable. The others were watching to see Wittman get struck mute.

"I think," he tried explaining, "that history being trapped in people means that history is embodied in physical characteristics, such as skin colors. And do you know what part of our bodies they find so mysteriously inscrutable? It's our little eyes. They think they can't see into these little squinny eyes. They think we're sneaky, squinnying at them through spy eyes. They can't see inside here past these slits. And that's why you girls are slicing your eyelids open, isn't it? Poor girls. I understand. And you glue on the false eyelashes to give your scant eyes some definition. I could sell all this hair for eyelashes. Make a bundle."

The girls and women who were wearing them did not lower their eyelashes in abashment. Wittman was just part of a show, which did not upset them; he's talking about other girls. Bad Wittman did not let up. "I have been requesting my actresses to take off their false eyelashes, to go on bareface and show what we look like. I promise, they will find a new beauty. But every one of them draw on eyeliner, top and bottom rims, and also up here on the bone to make like deep sockets. Then mascara, then—clamp, clamp. They kink their stubby lashes with this metal pincher that looks like a little plow. With spirit gum and tape, they glue on a couple of rows per eye of fake-hair falsies. A bulge of fat swells out over the tape—a crease, a fold—allthesame Caucasoid. That is too much weight for an eyelid to carry. There's droop. Allthesame Minnie Mouse. Allthesame Daisy Duck." Wittman held the backs of his hands over his eyes, and opened and shut his fingers, getting laffs.

Judy, the awfully beautiful pigwoman, was agreeing with him, nodding her natural head. And Taña, who did not have an eye problem, also understood. She will let that tactless husband of hers have it later in private. The ladies with the mink eyelashes ought to speak up for themselves. But through the make-up they did not feel assaults on their looks.

"Worse than make-up," said Wittman, "is the eye operation. There's an actress who dropped out of the show because she was having it done— the first Chinese-American I know to cut herself up like an A.J.A., who have a thing about knives. I won't tell you her name. Too shame. She's hiding out in a Booth home for girls during double-eye post-op. She didn't want to show her face with black stitches across her reddish swollen Vaselined eyelids X'ed across like cut along the dotted line. You girls shouldn't do that to yourselves. It's supposed to make you more attractive to men, right? Speaking as a man, I don't want to kiss eyes that have been cut and sewn; I'd be thinking Bride of Frankenstein. But I guess you're not trying to attract my type. I can tell when somebody's had her lids done. After she gets her stitches pulled and the puffiness goes down, she doesn't have a fold exactly, it's a scar line across each roundish lid. And her mien has been like lifted. Like she ate something too hot. The jalapeño look. She'll have to meet new guys who will believe she was born like that. She'll draw black lines on top of the scars, and date white guys, who don't care one way or the other single-lid double-lid."

Several pioneer showgirls were present who had secretly had that operation done long ago. They were laughing at the girl with the jalapeño expression. They did not admit that all you have to do is leave your eyes alone, and grow old; the lids will naturally develop a nice wrinkle.

"As a responsible director, as a man, I try to stop my actresses from mutilating themselves. I take them for coffee one at a time, and talk to them. You guys need to help me out, there's too many beautiful girls who think they're ugly. You're friends of a raccoon-eyed girl, tell her how beautiful she might be without make-up. She says, 'No, I look washed out. I look sick.' You say, 'You shouldn't wear stage make-up out in the street. Will you take it off for me? I want to see what you look like. Go to the ladies' room with this jar of Abolene cream, and come out with a nude face. Be brave. Go about bareface. Find your face. You have enormous eyes, not enormous-for-a-Chinese but for anyone. I want to kiss your naked eyelids, and not feel false eyelashes on my lips.' Okay, I get nowhere. Maybe I say it wrong, you laugh, they laugh. But you guys who get chicks to listen to you better than I do should give them a talking to.

"Please don't end up like a wife of some military dictator of a nowhere Southeast Asian country. Trip out on the before-and-after Madame Sukarno and Madame Thieu and Madame Ky and Madame Nhu. Their eyes have been Americanized. They wear shades, like everything is cool, man. They've been hiding stitches or maybe a botch job. They have round noses but Madame Nhu's is the roundest, hardly enough bridge to hang her glasses on. Any Mongolian type you see fucking with their eyes, you know they've got big problems. You girls ought to step right up here, and peel those false eyelashes off, and cast them down amongst this other hair."

Nobody took him up on that, but they didn't walk out either, and Wittman went on:

"Speaking of plastic surgery, did you see on t.v. this dentist named Dr. Angle, D.D.S., who invented a way to straighten buckteeth? He's fixed thousands of people—the champion bucktooth fixer in the world. He brought along audio-visual aids, shots of make-overs. The interviewer asked him what his standards are for a good bite. He said, 'That's a good question. I thought hard about that very question.' His answer did not have to do with chewing, or being able to talk better, or teeth in relation to the rest of the face. He said, 'I use my own teeth as the model. Because they're perfect. I've got perfect teeth.' And he does. Dr. Angle looks just right. Regular eyes, regular nose, regular teeth. No mole or birthmark or crookedness I can use to describe him so's you'd recognize him.

"Like Dr. Angle, I declare my looks—teeth, eyes, nose, profile—perfect. Take a good look at these eyes. Check them out in profile too. And the other profile. Dig the three-quarter view. So it's not Mount Rushmore, but it's an American face. Notice as I profile, you can see both my eyes at once. I see more than most people—no bridge that blocks the view between the eyes. I have a wide-angle windshield. Take a good look. These are the type of eyes most preferred for the movies. Eyes like mine sight along rifles and scan the plains and squint up into the high noon sun from under a Stetson. Yes, these are movie-star eyes. Picture extreme close-ups of the following cowboys: Roy Rogers. Buck Jones. John Wayne. John Payne. Randolph Scott. Hopalong Cassidy. Rex Allen. John Huston. John Carradine. Gabby Hayes. Donald O'Connor, if *Francis the Talking Mule* counts as a western. Chinese eyes. Chinese eyes. Like mine. Like yours. These eyes are cowboy eyes with which I'm looking at you, and you are looking back at me with cowboy eyes. We have the eyes that won the West."

Now, Wittman was giving out what he thought was his craziest riff, the weirdest take of his life at the movies. But the audience stayed with him. His community was madder than he was. They named more cowboys with Chinese eyes—Lee Marvin, Steve McQueen, Gary Cooper. And more—Alan Ladd and Jack Palance in *Shane*, a movie about a Chinese against a Chinese. Gregory Peck. Robert Mitchum. Richard Boone. Have you heard: James Coburn is taking Chinese lessons from Bruce Lee, his "little brother." There's this guy, Clint Eastwood, who can't get work in Hollywood because of Chinese eyes, working in Italian westerns now. Some are traitors to their Chinese heritage. Richard Widmark took a role as a U.S. Cavalry expert on Indians in *Two Rode Together*, where he says, "I've lived among the Apache. They don't feel pain." The Lone Ranger masks his Chinese eyes. So does Cato.

The poets who sit zazen get Japanese eyes: Philip Whalen and Gary Snyder.

The ladies refused to be left out. They found for themselves actresses who have Chinese fox eyes: Luise Rainer and Myrna Loy and Merle Oberon and Gene Tierney and Bette Davis and Jennifer Jones and Katharine Hepburn and Shirley MacLaine. Rita Hayworth is Chinese. The showgirls have a souvenir program of the Forbidden City's All-Chinese Review, and there she is, Rita Hayworth, in the middle of the front row.

"Marlon Brando," said Wittman, "is not Chinese, and he's not Japanese either. To turn him Japanese, they pulled back his hair and skin and clamped the sides of his head with clips. They shaved his eyebrows clean off, and drew antennae like an insect's, like an elf's. Sekiya scoot-scoots about, procuring his sisters for the all-white American armed services."

Lance Kamiyama stood up from the throne-chair where he was sitting at the back of the room. Sunny sat in the other one. He held up a banana, and made as if to throw it. "For you," he said. He tried to walk with it up to the stage area, but the floor was too crowded. He handed the banana off, "Pass it on, no pass back." It went from hand to hand up to Wittman. What signifies a banana? If I were Black, would I be getting an Oreo? If I were a red man, a radish?

" 'Is this a dagger which I see before me, the handle toward my hand?' " said Shakespearean Wittman. "No, it's a banana. My pay? Thank you. Just like olden days—two streetcar tokens, two sandwiches, one dollar, and one banana—pay movie star allthesame pay railroad man. Oh, I get it —top banana. Thank you. Ladies and gentlemen of the Academy, I thank you. Hello. Hello. Nobody home in either ear. I feel like Krapp. I mean, the Krapp of *Krapp's Last Tape* by Ah Bik Giht. He wears his banana sticking out of his waistcoat pocket. I'm going to wear mine down in my pants. Have you heard the one about these two oriental guys who saved enough money for a vacation at the seashore? They're walking on the beach and desiring all the bathing beauties. They make no eye contact with bullies who kick sand in faces. The smaller oriental says, 'I strike out with the chicks. I try and I try but. How you do it?' The bigger oriental says, 'I been studying your situation, brother. I recommend, you put one banana in your bathing suit.' 'Ah, so that be the secret. I'll go buy a banana and try it.' He does that, and too soon returns in disappointment. 'I don't understand. I buy one big ripe banana. I stick it in my swimsuit. I walk on the beach—and the chicks laugh at me. What be wrong?' The big oriental says, 'I think you're supposed to wear the banana in front.'

"Seriously, folks, this banana suggests two parts of the anatomy that are deficient in orientals. The nose and the penis. Do you think if I attached it between my eyes I'd get to be a movie star? Do you think if I attach it between my legs, I'd get the girls?

"I ought to unzip and show you—one penis. Large. Star Quality. Larger than this banana. Let me whip out the evidence that belies smallness. Nah. Nah. Nah. Just kidding, la. I'd only be able to astound the front rows; the people in back will tell everybody they didn't see much. I've got to get it up on the big screen. The stage is not the medium for the penis or for the details of this face. For the appreciation of eyelids, double-eye or single-eye, we need movie close-ups. So you can learn to love this face.

"Is there anybody out there who's heard the joke all the way through that has the line, 'The chinaman don't dig that shit either!'? That may be the punchline. All my life, I've heard pieces of jokes—maybe the same joke in fragments—that they quit telling when I walk in. They're trying to drive me pre-psychotic. I'm already getting paranoid. I'm wishing for a cloak of invisibility. I want to hear the jokes they tell at the parties that I'm not invited to. Americans celebrate business and holidays with orgies of race jokes. A white friend of mine has volunteered to hear for me what comes before 'The chinaman don't dig that shit either!' Don't dig what shit?"

"It's about this horny bushy guy who comes down out of the Arctic Circle," said Lance.

"He wants a girl for fifty cents," said Zeppelin. "But she costs too much—one dollar."

"No," said Lance. "No girls available, but for one dollar, you can have the chinaman. This manly guy doesn't want the chinaman. He says, 'I don't dig that shit.' "

"No, no, that's not the way it goes," said Zeppelin. "He can afford fifty cents but they up it on him to one dollar."

"The exact amount of money," said Charley, "is beside the point. Whatever they say the cost is, this guy thinks it's too much, especially since he wouldn't even be getting a girl. He goes away. He's very horny, so comes back for the deal on the chinaman. But now they want to charge three times as much. Let's make it simple, three dollars."

"Three dollars?!" said Zeppelin. "How come three dollars. Awhile ago, you offered one dollar. I don't dig that shit."

"One dollar for the chinaman, and two dollars for the two guys to hold him down," said Lance. "The chinaman don't dig that shit either."

"American jokes too dry," said Siew Loong.

"No wonder they call you inscrutable, you don't laugh at jokes," said Wittman.

"You guys feel so sorry for youself," said Auntie Dolly. "But you tell tit twat cunt chick hom sup low jokes."

"All you joke experts be here, why don't you men tell us, 'Is it true what they say about Chinese girls?' " said Auntie Bessie. "Is *what* true?"

"The full line," said Wittman, "is, 'Is it true what they say about Chinese girls' twats?' They think they're sideways, that they slant like eyes. As in *Chinese Japanese Koreean*." He put his fingers on the tails of his eyes, and pulled them up, "*Chinese*," pulled them down, "*Japanese*," pulled them sideways, "*Koreean*." He felt immediately sorry. He had pulled tears of anger and sorrow up into his eyes. White men let little yellow men overhear that twat joke to make them littler and yellower. And they fuck over the women too. Kick ass, Wittman. "The King of Monkeys hereby announces: I'm crashing parties wherever these jokes are told, and I'm going to do some spoilsporting. Let me educate you, Mr. and Mrs. Potato Head, on what isn't funny. Never ask me or anyone who looks like me, 'Are you *Chinese* or *Japanese*?' I know what they're after who ask that question. They want to hear me answer something obscene, something bodily. Some disgusting admission about our anatomy. About daikon legs and short waist or long waist, and that the twat goes sideways, slanting like her eyes. They want me to show them the Mongoloidian spot on my ass. They want to measure the length of my ape arms and compare them to Negers' arms.

"And don't ask: 'Where do you come from?' I deign to retort, 'Sacramento,' or 'Hanford,' or 'Bakersfield,' I'm being sarcastic, get it? And don't ask: 'How long have you been in the country?' 'How do you like our country?' "

"The answer to that," said Lance, "is 'Fine. How do *you* like it?' "

"The one that drives me craziest is 'Do you speak English?' Particularly after I've been talking for hours, don't ask, 'Do you speak English?' The voice doesn't go with the face, they don't hear it. On the phone I sound like anybody, I get the interview, but I get downtown, they see my face, they ask, 'Do you speak English?' Watch, as I leave this stage tonight after my filibuster, somebody's going to ask me, 'You speak the language?'

"In the tradition of stand-up comics—I'm a stand-up tragic—I want to pass on to you a true story that Wellington Koo told to Doctor Ng, who told it to me. Wellington Koo was at a state dinner in Washington, D.C. The leaders of the free world were meeting to figure out how to win World War II. Koo was talking to his dinner partners, the ladies on his left and right, when the diplomat across from him says, 'Likee soupee?' Wellington nods, slubs his soup, gets up, and delivers the keynote address. The leaders of the free world and their wives give him a standing ovation. He says to the diplomat, 'Likee speechee?' After a putdown like that, wouldn't you think Mr. and Mrs. Potato Head would stop saying,'You speakee English?'

"And I don't want to hear any more food shit out of anybody. I'm warning you, you ask me food shit, I'll recommend a dog-shit restaurant. Once when I was in high school, I met one of the great American Beat writers— I'm not saying which one because of protecting his reputation. He's the one who looks like two of the lohats, beard and eyebrows all over the place. He was standing next to me during a break at the *Howl* trial. I told him I wanted to be a playwright. I was a kid playwright who could've used a guru. While he was shaking my hand, he said, 'What's a good Chinese restaurant around here?' I tell you, my feelings were hurt bad. Here was a poet, he's got right politics, anti-war, anti-segregation, he writes good, riding all over America making up the words for it, but on me he turned trite. Watch out for him, he's giving out a fake North Beach. He doesn't know his Chinatown, he doesn't know his North Beach. I thought about straightening him out, and almost invited him for crab with black-bean sauce, and long bean with foo yee, and hot-and-sour soup, but I didn't want to hear him say, 'I likee soupee. You likee?'

"I know why they ask those questions. They expect us to go into our Charlie Chan Fu Manchu act. Don't you hate it when they ask, 'How about saying something in Chinese?' If you refuse, you feel stupid, and whatsamatter, you're ashamed? But if you think of something Chinese to say, and you say it, noises come out of you that are not part of this civilization. Your face contorts out of context. They say, 'What?' Like do it again. They want to watch you turn strange and foreign. When I speak my mind, I spill my guts, I want to be understood, I want to be answered. Peter Sellers, starting with the Ying Tong Goon Show and continuing throughout his bucktoof career to this day, and Mickey Rooney in *Breakfast at Tiffany's* and Warner Oland and Jerry Lewis and Lon Chaney are cutting off our balls linguistically. 'Me no likee.' 'Me find clue to identity of murderer.' 'Ming of Mongo conquers the Earth and the universe,' says Ming of Mongo. 'Confucius say,' says Confucius. 'Me name-um Li'l Beaver,' says Li'l Beaver. They depict us with an inability to say 'I.' They're taking the 'I' away from us. 'Me'—that's the fucked over, the fuckee. 'I'—that's the mean-ass motherfucker first-person pronoun of the active voice, and they don't want us to have it.

"We used to have a mighty 'I,' but we lost it. At one time whenever we said 'I,' we said 'I-warrior.' You don't know about it, you lost it. 'I-warrior' was the same whether subject or object, 'I-warrior' whether the actor or the receiver of action. When the turtles brought writing on their shells, the word for 'I' looked like this." Wittman wrote on the blackboard:

"It looks almost like 'Ngo' today, huh? 'Wo' to you Mandarins. This word, maybe pronounced 'ge,' was also the word for long weapons such as spears and lances and Ah Monkey's pole and the longsword. This longest stroke must be the weapon. And 'ge' also meant 'fight.' To say 'I' was to say 'I fight.' This isn't a Rorschach craziness on my part. I'll bet somewhere in China, a museum has collected that turtle shell in the same exhibit with the longswords. To this day, words to do with fighting and chopping off heads and for long weapons have this component:

as does the word for 'I.' We are the grandchildren of Gwan the Warrior. Don't let them take the fight out of our spirit and language. I. I. I. I. I. I. I. I. I. I-warrior win the West and the Earth and the universe.

"They have an enslavement wish for us, and they have a death wish, that we die. They use the movies to brainwash us into suicide. They started in on us with the first movies, and they're still at it. D. W. Griffith's *Broken Blossoms*, originally entitled *The Chink and the Child*: Lillian Gish as the pure White Child, Richard Barthelmess as the Chink, also called The Yellow Man. They were actually about the same age. The Child has a drunken father, so the Chink takes her into his house to protect her. One moonlit night, she seems to be asleep in a silk Chinese gown. He yearns for her. Ripped on opium, he looks at her out of stoned, taped eyes. His fingernailed hand quivers out for her, and barely touches a wisp of her gossamer hair, lacy and a-splay and golden in the moonbeams. The audience is in nasty anticipation of perversions, but before he can do some sexy oriental fetishy thing to her, his yellow hand stops. He kills himself. The Yellow Man lusts after a white girl, he has to kill himself—that's a tradition they've made up for us. We have this suicide urge and suicide code. They don't have to bloody their hands. Don't ever kill yourself. You kill yourself, you play into their hands."

Nanci was saying something to Auntie Marleese. "Poor Wittman." The two of them shook their heads. "He's so oversensitive."

"I am not oversensitive," he said. "You ought to be hurting too. You're dead to be insensitive, which is what they wish for you. You think you're looking good; you think you're doing fine, they re-run another one of those movies at you. And the morning cartoons get you wearing that pigtail again. And Hop Sing chases after the white man, and begs, 'Me be your slave. Please let me be your slave.' John Wayne has a Hop Sing, and the Cartwrights have a Hop Sing. They name him Hop Sing on purpose, the name of the powerful tong, to put us down. Here's another custom for orientals: Deranged by gratitude, an oriental has to have a master, and will tail after a white man until enslaved. In *Vertigo*, which could have been my favorite movie, James Stewart dives into the Bay and saves Kim Novak. He brings her back to his apartment that has a railing with the ideograms for joy. He lives within sight of Coit Tower. He tells Kim Novak, who's wearing his clothes and drying her hair by the fire, 'Chinese say if you rescue someone, you're responsible for them forever.' Think carefully; you've never heard a real Chinese say that; the ones in the movies and on t.v. say it over and over again. Every few days they show us a movie or a t.v. episode about us owing them, therefore thankfully doing their laundry and waiting on them, cooking and serving and washing and sewing for John Wayne and the Cartwright boys at the Ponderosa. The way Hop Sing shuffles, I want to hit him. Sock him an uppercut to straighten him up—stand up like a man.

"I want to punch Charlie Chan too in his pregnant stomach that bellies out his white linen maternity suit. And he's got a widow's hump from bowing with humbleness. He has never caught a criminal by fistfighting him. And he doesn't grab his client-in-distress and kiss her hard, pressing her boobs against his gun. He shuffles up to a clue and hunches over it, holding his own hand behind his back. He mulls in Martian over the clues. Martians from outer space and Chinese monks talk alike. Old futs talking fustian. Confucius say this. Confucius say that. Too clean and too good for sex. The Good Mensch runs all over Setzuan in a dress, then in pants, and fools everybody because Chinese look so alike, we ourselves can't tell the difference between a man and a woman. We're de-balled and other-worldly, we don't have the natural fucking urges of the average, that is, the white human being.

"Next time you watch insomnia television, you can see their dreams about us. A racist movie is always running on some channel. Just the other night, I saw another one that kills off the Chinese guy for loving a white lady. I'm not spoiling it by giving away the ending. They always end like that. Barbara Stanwyck is the bride of a missionary, and she is interested in converting this guy with tape on his eyes named General Yin, played by Nils Asther. He talks to himself, rubbing his hands together, plotting, 'I will convert a missionary.' Which is racially and religiously very fucked up. Chinese don't convert white people but vice versa. (Someday I'll tell you my theory about how everyone is already a Buddhist, only they don't know it. You're all Buddhas whether you know it or not, whether you like it or not.) General Yin's religion has to do with burning incense in braziers and torturing slavegirls. He keeps faking wise sayings about conquering the Earth. I liked him. He seemed intelligent. Whatever his cause, he's lost. He's fought his last battle, and lost his army and friends. He's alone in his palace with Barbara Stanwyck and one last slavegirl, Anna May Wong, whom he has locked up and plans to kill slowly. The right couple would have been General Yin and Anna May, coming to an understanding of each other and living happily ever after. However, Barbara enters his throne/bedroom to plead with him for the life of the poor slavegirl. This is an emergency, and she didn't have time to dress. She's wearing her satin nightgown that flows like a bridal train down the stairs of the dais. He's sitting enthroned, and she kneels at his feet to beg him. Her face comes up to his knee. She asks him for mercy while holding back tears, an actress's trick that gets to the viewer more than her weeping outright. He denies her pleas. The tears well up and up, and spill. She lifts her face to his face, her lips trembling, eyes, cheeks, and lips moist, her head almost touching a knee of his spread legs, which are draped with the silk of his smoking robe. They don't touch each other, but they tantalize and agonize nearer and nearer. Smoky snakes of incense entwine them. But she's a woman of God. She says, crying softly, looking up, looking down, pulsating, daring to teach this general, 'It's good to do something when there is no advantage to you, not even gratitude.' He has no morals; as we were taught from grammar school, life is cheap in Asia. Listening, he moves closer, she moves closer. Two-shots of their heads nearing. He slides past her lips, and gives her a hug. She allows it, her motivation being that she feels sorry for him. They hug, and they part. 'I will think over what you have said,' he says. She rushes back to her room, where she takes off her satin nightgown and puts on one of those spangly mermaid-skin evening dresses. She has to try another plea in a different outfit. The general could've looked down, as the camera does, and seen pretty far down her décolletage. She's wet with tears again. This time he touches her. He wipes her eyes and cheeks with a silk hanky. More tears well and fall. He wipes her off again, and again. The audience is catching thrills. Are they going to make out? Are the tails of that silk handkerchief tickling her neck and the tops of her tits? Are his lips going to land on her lips in an inter-racial kiss? Will her heavy head come to rest in his crotch? And he peel off her mermaid skin and carry her to the canopy bed? Which has all along been a large part of the ravishing decor. Will its lush curtains open for them, and close, and two masculine feet and two feminine feet thrash out, his on top of hers, and their four feet kick and stiffen? I saw that once in a Hong Kong movie; he was a demigod and she was a mortal. The wedding bed was in a garden among the flowers and under the sky. The bed was like a chamber or a stage, you could live in there. The actor who played the demigod had Star Quality, not just good-looking-for-a-Chinese—a thin straight nose, eyes which beheld his lover's ways so that from then on she's wonderful, even when she's alone, because watched from the sky whatever she does and wherever she goes. Whatever she asks, he answers, 'Forever.' But back to Barbara Stanwyck and General Yin. Are they going to get it on? Or neck or what? He picks up his teacup and drinks, and quietly leans back in his throne. And dies. He has poisoned himself before he can defile her. The name of that movie was *The Bitter Tea of General Yin*. They named him that to castrate us. General Yin instead of General Yang, get it? Again the chinaman made into a woman."

"No, no," said Charley Bogard Shaw. "That's Yen. *The Bitter Tea of General* Yen."

"Yen Shmen," said Wittman. "That movie was a death-wish that Confucius and Lin Yutang take poison as co-operatively as Socrates."

Stepgrandfather Lincoln Fong raised his hand. You had to let the old guy talk, and once started, take over. "Yes, Ah Goong," said good Wittman.

Mr. Fong stood, waited for attention, and addressed each dignitary, "President Ah Sing"—that is, Grand Opening Ah Sing—"Mr. Chairman" —that's Wittman—"ladies and gentlemen, Lin Tse Hsü was General Commissioner of Canton Against Narcotics. He stopped the opium from coming in for five months. He arrested two thousand Chinese dealers. He executed addicts. Nine out of ten Cantonese were addicted to opium. He wrote to Queen Victoria, held meetings with the British and American Tobacco Company, and led a raid on a factory, confiscated the shit, and detained the British manufacturers for seven weeks. There are paintings of Lin burying opium in trenches half a football field long and seventy-five feet wide and seven feet deep. The Queen fired Lin from his office, and sent her navy to enforce opium sales. Your grandmothers and grandfathers, using Cho Cho's tactic, chained sixty junks across the Boca Tigris. Ten thousand of our Cantonese relatives fought with hoes, pitchforks, and two hundred new guns. They dumped opium into Canton Harbor like the Boston Tea Party. The British broke through into the Pearl River Delta and up the Yangtze to the rest of China. The famous joke of the nineteenth century: the West brought three lights—Fiat Lux, Standard Oil, and the British and American Tobacco Company. Why China went communist was to build an economy that does not run on opium."

"Thank you, Ah Goong," said Wittman. "Let's give Mr. Lincoln Fong a big hand." PoPo's old man took his bows and sat down. Please, don't another competitive old fut get up, and another, orating through all the wars, war after war, won and lost. "I'm doing dope no more, no, sir. Lest our grandparents dumped Brit shit in vain. We don't need dope because we're naturally high. We come from a race of opium heads. Nine out of ten— wow!—of our immediate ancestors were stoned heads. We're naturally hip. Trippiness is in our genes and blood. In fact, we need kung fu for coming down to Earth, and kung fu is all we need for flight. I'm quitting cigarettes too. Ah Goong, you have given me the political strength to take a stand against the American Tobacco Company." Wittman turned his pack upside down, and strewed cigarettes amongst the hair.

"The Delta they're blowing us out of nowadays is the San Joaquin Delta. The footage of John Wayne beating his way through the hordes on Blood River, they shot on the San Joaquin River. They keep celebrating that they won the Opium Wars. All we do in the movies is die. I watch for you, Charley; your face appears, but before I can barely admire you, they've shot you dead. Our actors have careers of getting killed and playing dead bodies. You're targets for James Bond to blow to pieces. Did you know that J.F.K.'s favorite *reading* is James Bond *books?* The books are worse than the movies. Have you read one? You should, and dig what the President gets off on. He has ideas for what you can do for your country, and empire. There are these 'Chigroes'—what you get when you crossbreed a Chinese and a Negro—mule men with flat noses and cho cho lips and little eyes and yellow-black skin. They're avid to be killer-slaves. 'Chigroes.' It makes my mouth sick to say that out loud. You actresses have got to refuse to play pearl divers in love with James Bond. You have to get together with Odd Job. That's where the love story ought to be. That's not funny. A face as big as Odd Job's should star on the Cinerama screen for the audience to fall in love with, for girls to kiss, for the nation to cherish, for me to learn how to hold my face. Take seven pictures of a face, take twelve, twenty of any face, hold it up there, you will fall in love with it. Mako got his face up there, filling the screen with shades of oak and gold, this-color wongsky skin, and these eyes, and this nose, and his cho cho lips. What should be done with a face in close-up is to behold and adore it. They skin Mako alive. They peel him alive. He's skinned by his fellow Chinese. Hearing their voices making vulture-like sounds of an inhuman language, and watching Mako's screaming face, you imagine the skinning. You don't see it on camera. Where's my banana? Here, I'll show you, like so—peeling yellow skin. A strip, another yellow strip. And Mako is screaming, 'AAaaa! AaaAAagh! AAaaaaiyaaa!' His solo screams fill the sound track. 'AaaaaAAAaah! Aaaaaieeeeee!' We've been watching his face directly, then we watch it through the crosshairs of Steve McQueen's rifle. The audience wants to kill him so badly. We're in an agony of mercy to shoot him out of his pain. Steve McQueen, to whom he has been a faithful sidekick, does him the favor. Bang! Here's what they really think of their little buddy. Squanto and Tonto and Li'l Beaver. They have skinned and shot their loyal little tagalong buddy. Die, Hop Sing, Wing Ding, Chop Chop, Charlie Two Shoes, Tan Sing. Skin that cute li'l Sherpa. Like the banana he is! And no Pocahontas to save him. She's busy sticking her neck out for John Smith."

Wittman held the banana in his fist so the peelings flapped out like two arms and two wings. "Mako got nominated Best Supporting Actor for his role as the banana. He didn't win the Oscar but. None of us gets an Oscar except James Wong Howe—for the cinematography on *Hud*. You guys have got to get your asses out from behind the camera. You're the most all-around talents in Hollywood, but they don't give Oscars for what you do best. There ought to be an Oscar for the One Actor Best at Playing a Horde. You run around and around the camera and back and forth across the set. Clutch guts, twitch, spazz out—the bullets hit here and here—fall like trip-wire ankles, roll downhill, dead with face up to the sky and camera. The director sends you back in there for the second-wave attack. 'I was killed already in the last scene,' says the conscientious supernumerary. 'That's all right,' says the director: 'Nobody can tell you apart.' I accept this Oscar for Most Reincarnations." Again and again, we're shot, stabbed, kicked, socked, skinned, machine-gunned, blown up. But not kissed. Nancy Kwan and France Nuyen and Nobu McCarthy kiss white boys. The likes of you and me are unstomachable. The only hands we get to hold are our own up our sleeves. Charlie Chan doesn't kiss And Keye Luke doesn't kiss. And Richard Look doesn't kiss. We've got to kiss and fuck and breed in the streets."

Poor Wittman Ah Sing, Ah Star. It's going to get worse. He could spend the rest of his life advocating our stardom. When the *Planet of the Apes* series begins, the Asian American actors will say, "Here's our chance. You can look like anything under those ape costumes." But the roles will go to those who have to wear brown contact lenses. Pat Suzuki, after singing so well in *Flower Drum Song*, will play an ape-girl in *Skullduggery*; she roots in the dirt and grunts and squeals, and points, jumping up and down. And John Lone will play the title role in *Iceman*, a grunting, gesturing Neanderthal; his forehead is built up, his jaw juts prognathously, you won't recognize a Chinese-American of any kind under there. And when he gets to show his face in *Year of the Dragon*, John Lone, who has the most classic face amongst us, will have to have it broken on camera, and his eyes beaten shut. The last third of the movie his expressions are indecipherably covered with blood. He begs to be killed, and his co-star cradles his head, then pointblank shoots it off. The U.S. will lose the war in Viet Nam; then the Asian faces large on the screen will be shot, blown up, decapitated, bloodied, mutilated. No more tasteful off-camera deaths. We're going to have a President who has favorite movies rather than favorite books. The British actor who will bring back Fu Manchu claims not to be a racist because he doles money to the boat people. The actress who plays the dragon lady says that if you people picketing the set want movies from your p.o.v., "make your own movies." She doesn't understand that her movies are our movies, and that those horde-like picketers are her fellow SAG members.

"Thank you," said Wittman, eating the banana, no waste. "You feed the artist—thank you." He dropped the peel among the hair and cigarettes. "If there were Oscars for Improvisation and for Directing Oneself, you guys would sweep them. You made four hundred films about some kind of Chinese, whose roles were barely scripted. Maydene Lam and Richard Look and Keye Luke, all of you, you sized up the scene, and invented the dialogue with appropriate dialects and business. You keep giving your name to the character you're playing. Whenever the name on the left in the credits is the same as the name on the right, you aren't getting credit for acting. You just be the oriental you are. They think you behave oriental without having to act. 'Just say something Chinese,' says the director, throwing you into the movie. 'Do something Chinese.'

"Which gives me an idea. You have the set-up to do some sabotage. Go ahead, take whatever stereotype part. They ask you to do Chinese shtick, make free to say whatever you want. True things. Pass messages. 'Eat shit, James Bond. Kiss my yellow ass.' 'Fuck off, John Wayne. I love Joang Fu.'

'Ban the Bomb.' 'C.I.A. out of Southeast Asia.' Gwan's grandchildren—take over the movies.

"And say who we are. You say our name enough, make them stop asking, 'Are you Chinese or Japanese?' That is a straightman's line, asking for it. Where's our knockout comeback putdown punchline? Who *are* we? Where's our name that shows that we aren't from anywhere but America? We're so out of it. It's our fault they call us gook and chinky chinaman. We've been here all this time, before Columbus, and haven't named ourselves. Look at the Blacks beautifully defining themselves. 'Black' is perfect. But we can't be 'Yellows.' 'Me? I'm Yellow.' 'I'm a Gold. We're Golds.' Nah, too evocative of tight-fisted Chang. Red's our color. But the red-hot communists have appropriated red. Even Fruit of Islam, though too fruity like Fruit of the Loom, is catchier than anything we've got. The image of a black bulge in the jockey shorts scares the daylights out of the ofay. We want a name like that, not some anthropological sociological name. American of Chinese extraction—bucktoof ethnick. A.J.A. is good—sharp, accurate, symmetrical. The long version sounds good too. Americans of Japanese Ancestry. Makes up for 'jap.' And the emphasis is right—'American,' the noun in front, and 'Japanese,' an adjective, behind. They had the advantage of Relocation Camp to make them think themselves up a name. We don't have like 'Americans of Chinese Ancestry.' Like 'A.C.A.' We are not named, and we're disappearing already. We want a name we can take out in the street and on any occasion. We can't go by what we call ourselves when we're among ourselves. Chinese and Hans and Tangs are other people of other times and another place. We can't go to the passport office and say, 'I'm a Han Ngun,' or 'I'm a Tang Ngun.' I'll bet that Tang Ngun are gone anymore even from that red Asiatic country on the opposite side of the planet. Try telling the census taker, 'I'm a Good Native Papers Boy.'

"For a moment a hundred years ago, we were China Men. After all, the other people in the new world were Englishmen and Frenchmen and Dutchmen. But they changed themselves into Americans, and wouldn't let us change into Americans. And they slurred 'China Man.' 'Chinaman,' they said dactylically. One of the actresses who is giving me a bad time—I'm forsaking her—said, 'Is China Man like china doll? Like fragile?' Here I'm trying to give us a Sierra-climbing name, a tree-riding name, a train-building name, and she said, 'You're fragile like china?' She's a Mississippi Delta Chinese, and says 'fragile' like 'honey chile.' 'China Man' makes echoes of another word.

"Once and for all: I am not oriental. An oriental is antipodal. I am a human being standing right here on land which I belong to and which belongs to me. I am not an oriental antipode.

"Without a born-and-belong-in-the-U.S.A. name, they can't praise us correctly. There's a favorable review here of our 'Sino-American' theater. When the U.S. doesn't recognize a foreign communist country, that's Sino-American. There is no such *person* as a Sino-American."

"They used to call us Celestials," said PoPo, "because at one time they glorified us so."

"But you never called yourself a Celestial, did you?" said Wittman. "They called you Celestial hoping that you'd go to heaven rather than stay in America. You called yourselves Wah Q and Gum Sahn Hock and Gum Sahn How."

PoPo said, "Gum Sahn Po. Gum Sahn Lo Po Nigh. Sahm Yup Po. Say Yup Po." The old fut names for Gold Mountain Ladies made people laugh.

Wittman said, "Sojourners no more but. Immigration got fooled already. You not be Overseas Chinese. You be here. You're here to stay. I am deeply, indigenously here. And my mother and father are indigenous, and most of my grandparents and great-grandparents, indigenous. Native Sons and Daughters of the Golden State. Which was a name our ancestors made up to counteract those racists, the Native Sons and Daughters of the Golden West. We want a name somewhat like that but shorter and more than California, the entire U.S.A.—ours.

"They get us so wrong. 'Sun Ch'üan, the king of Wu, played by an American. . . .' Of course, he's an American. As opposed to what? We're all of us Americans here. Why single out the white guy? How come I didn't get 'an American' after my name? How come no 'American' in apposition with my parents and my grandma? An all-American cast here. No un-American activity going on. Not us.

"When I hear you call yourselves 'Chinese,' I take you to mean American-understood, but too lazy to say it. You do mean 'Chinese' as short for 'Chinese-American,' don't you? We mustn't call ourselves 'Chinese' among those who are ready to send us back to where they think we came from. But 'Chinese-American' takes too long. Nobody says or hears past the first part. And 'Chinese-American' is inaccurate—as if we could have two countries. We need to take the hyphen out—'Chinese American.' 'American,' the noun, and 'Chinese,' the adjective. From now on: 'Chinese Americans.' However. Not okay yet. 'Chinese hyphen American' sounds exactly the same as 'Chinese no hyphen American.' No revolution takes place in the mouth or in the ear.

"I've got to tell you about this experiment I volunteered for in college. I answered an ad for 'Chinese-Americans' to take a test for fifty bucks an hour, more per hour than I've ever made—but hazard pay. So we Chinese-hyphenated-schizoid-dichotomous-Americans were gathered in this lab, which was a classroom. The shrink or lab assistant asked us to fold a piece of paper in half and write 'Chinese' at the top of one half and 'American' at the top of the other. Then he read off a list of words. Like 'Daring.' 'Reticent.' 'Laughter.' 'Fearful.' 'Easygoing.' 'Conscientious.' 'Direct.' 'Devious.' 'Affectionate.' 'Standoffish.' 'Adventurous.' 'Cautious.' 'Insouciant.' 'Painstaking.' 'Open.' 'Closed.' 'Generous.' 'Austere.' 'Expressive.' 'Inexpressive.' 'Playful.' 'Studious.' 'Athletic.' 'Industrious.' 'Extroverted.' 'Introverted.' 'Subtle.' 'Outgoing.' We were to write each word either in the left-hand column or the right-hand column. I should have torn up my paper, and other people's papers, stopped the test. But I went along. Working from the inside, I gave the Chinese side 'Daring' and 'Laughter' and 'Spontaneous' and 'Easygoing,' some Star Quality items. But my bold answers were deviated away in the standard deviation. The American side got all the fun traits. It's scientifically factual truth now—I have a stripe down my back. Here, let me take off my shirt. Check out the yellow side, and the American side. I'm not the same after they experimented on me. I have aftereffects—acid flashbacks. I got imprinted. They treated me no better than any lab animal, who doesn't get the journals nor invited to the conferences that announce the findings. I happened to pick up the weekly science section of the newspaper, and saw a double-decker headline: 'Oriental Frosh Stay Virgins Longest / Caucasian Boys Get Most Sex Soonest.' When I thought they were testing my smarts, élan vital and spelling, they were checking out my virginity. There was this other test where they squeezed my Achilles tendons with calipers. I was to rate the pain from discomfort to unbearable, which level I never reached. I thought it was a pain tolerance test, but maybe they were testing for inscrutability. I'm not making this up. I tell you, there's a lot of Nazi shit going on in the laboratories. Don't fall into their castrating hands. Even if you don't go off into longterm or side effects physically or chemically, you're fucked philosophically. I'm never going to know what my straight head would have thought unaltered. I'm off, like the roosters you hear crow any time of day or night that you walk past the labs. No more lab gigs.

"I *am* this tall. I didn't get this tall by being experimented on by scientists trying to find the secret of height. They're looking for a time hormone in the pituitary gland; maybe the chronons are up there. Speeding them up (or slowing them down) may fool the body into growing more. They're taking unused time from the brains of cadavers and injecting it into the brains of short little orientals. You Sansei kids, stop going to height doctors to fuck with your hypothalamus. How many inches anyway between short and tall? Two. Three. Not many. The price of size—your mind. Don't be a generation of height freaks.

"It has to do with looks, doesn't it? They use 'American' interchangeably with 'white.' The clean-cut all-American look. This hairless body—I mean, this chest is unhairy; plenty hairy elsewhere—is cleaner than most. I bathe, I dress up; all I get is soo mun and sah chun.

"Which is not translated 'Star Quality.' Do you see it? Is my Star Quality showing nakedly yet? I've been trying to acquire it through education, attitude, right words, right work. Don't trust the movies, that stars are born. In a democracy, Star Quality can be achieved. And it can be conferred; I can love anybody. I'm learning to kiss everyone equally. Do you want to learn too? There's this theater game we play for warming up. Everybody goes around the circle and kisses everybody else. I judge who gets the title —Best Kisser in All the Land. The kissing contest is too good to keep backstage. Ladies and gentlemen, do I have some volunteers for free kisses? Step right up. That beautiful girl over there, Nanci, holds the title of Best Kisser and all the rights, duties, obligations, and privileges pertaining thereto. She'll participate. Now do I have some volunteers? Here's your chance. Come on up and take the championship away from her. Old futs too, come on, come on. I'll hug and kiss you myself. Nah, nah, nah, just kidding, la. I don't dig that shit either. But I challenge you old futs. You've been scolding me too much for the flagrancies of hugging and kissing going on in this play. You need to be taught a lesson, accusing me of affection. I'm going to unbrainwash you from believing anymore that we're a people who don't kiss and don't hug."

Led by PoPo, quite a few old futs stepped right on up. Nanci and Taña volunteered, the show-offs, and Sunny and Lance, good at parties, fielded a contingent—"We're game."—including Caucasians who had tuned out during the racial business.

To help everybody over shyness, Wittman went first. He kissed his wife, and got ready to kiss this girl he'd had a crush on, an obsession for, wanted but can't have, quite a few girls of the unattainable type, and a girl that was always making him puzzle over her physicality, and his mother, and his grandmother. Test his rule: Kiss the one you love for as many seconds—five six seven eight—as you kiss anyone you can't stand, an ugly girl the same hardness you kiss a pretty one. Equality in food, jobs, and amount of loving. He touched a rough complexion, pores all wrecked by too much stage make-up, hot lights and late hours, and liked the feel of zits on his finger-tips. A man of principle kisses everybody as though they're the same beauti-ful. Everybody was getting the same kiss off of him. This girl he was trying to forget put her hand on his face and her other hand on his naked, feeling chest, maneuvering. Is this going to be a cheek smack, or are we going to land on the lips? They kissed mouth to mouth, she turning aside, impercep-tible to onlookers but felt by him, her move away from him. All he had to do was prolong that kiss, pull her to him for half a second too long, and it would slide into another meaning. He put his hands on her waist, and tickled her. He pounced on the next girl, and tickled her in the armpits. And somebody ambushed him from behind, Taña tickling him. Wittman laughed. Whereby his community shouted out a title for him—Most Laughable.

To cheers and comments, each man went around and kissed each of the ladies, and each lady kissed all the men. Because everybody excelled at kiss-ing, Wittman gave all of them titles—Most Juicy Kisser, Most Sincere, Best Technique, Most Succulent, Most Experienced, Most Passionate, Mr. and Miss Congeniality, Most Promising, Most Style, Coolest, Hottest, the One Who Causes the Most Dreams, Most Motherly (not won by Ruby Long Legs), Most Sisterly, Most Brotherly, Most Troublemaker, Most Suave, Most Dangerous. Those whom Wittman didn't personally kiss, he dubbed-thee by observation.

So these champion kissers were practicing a custom of a country they were intuiting. If ever it happens that the Government lets us take vacations to China, we're going to find: everywhere friends and relatives who will embrace us in welcome. Everywhere demonstrative customs of affection—holding hands, sitting in laps, pats and strokes on heads and backs, arms around waists, fingers and cheeks touching cheeks. It has to be that way. Chinese live crowded, don't have enough chairs, or space on the sofa, so sit close and all sleep together in the one bed at inns and at home. In a land where words are pictures and have tones, there's music everywhere all the time, and a party going on. Whenever they need affection during the labor of the day or the insomnia of the night, why, they betake themselves pub-licly, and the crowds receive them with camaraderie and food. The whole country—on all its streets—is an outdoor café. Commadres and compadres are always around for some talk, a card game, and a midnight snack. A bil-lion communalists eating and discussing. They're never lonely. Men are brothers holding hands, and women hold hands, and mothers and fathers kiss children. We see evidence of their practices here: The day people from that country step off the boat, or off the plane, they walk up and down Grant Avenue holding hands with one another, or arm in arm, or one's arm around the other's neck and the other's arm around the waist, walking and talking close face-to-face. You have to look fast. The next time you see them, they're walking apart. They've learned not to go about so queer. They have come to a lonely country, where men get killed for holding hands. Well, let them start a new country where such opposite creatures as a man and a woman might go about the streets holding each other's hand in friendship.

Given heart by a loving community, Wittman confided to them his marriage. "While off guard, I got married, she married me. I have a wife to support. I'm having a bad time of it. I've been looking for a job. The other day I was at an interview, and trying not to smoke, I set my socks on fire. I had my foot over my knee like this. I was rubbing up the fuzz on my new socks. Gotta match? My face and your ass. I mean your ass and my face. I mean, nevermind. The next thing I knew, I'd lit my match on the bottom of my shoe, and touched it to my sock, like so. Whoosh. Flambé. Flaming foot of fire. Flash fire." As he talked, Wittman did what he was saying, and for a moment looked like Prince Na Zhen, the malicious baby, who runs on wheels of fire. Fire rushed around his ankle and leg. The kids yelled for an encore. The mothers yelled at him for burning himself. "I'm all right. It doesn't hurt. I'm okay. See? My ankle's fine. Flame out so fast, it didn't burn through. I didn't feel a thing. The interviewer probably thought he was seeing things. No, I can't do fire socks again. You can only do it once per sock. This other sock I fired up already. I didn't get the job.

"I applied at the insurance company where my wife works. Don't worry, I knew better than to use her as a reference. Does anyone know why it is that at certain jobs such as insurance and teaching, they won't hire husband and wife? Family fights and family sex in front of the customers? I dressed straight-arrow. I treated the receptionist like she's boss. I applied myself, and filled out the forms without wedging any wisecracks or opinions into the answer spaces. I'm trying to be a Young Affordable, like you; then I'll buy my own shoes and new socks. I borrowed these shoes from the costume shop. They're too big for me." He lifted his foot over his knee. The shoe, too heavy, kept going, pulling him over with it. "I took an arithmetic test in these shoes. I matched rows of long numbers with other rows of long numbers, digit for digit same. For example, is 68759312 exactly the same or not the same as 68759312? I did not add, did not subtract, just read horizontally and vertically. What for I went to college? I did pretty well, got everything right. And this personnel guy says to me, 'You people are good at figures, aren't you?' I can't think of how to answer right off. I should take that as a compliment? It's within his realm of *in*surance to recognize in me one of a tribe of born mathematicals, like Japanese? I say, 'Who, me? Not me, man. I come from the group with no sense of direction. I'm more the artistic type. What do you have in the creative line?' I didn't get a callback.

"At a corporation that I don't know what they actually produce, I told the interviewer about having organized a sales campaign before. And he says, 'Made fifty cents on the dollar?' I think I heard right. I say, 'What you say?' He says, 'Made a dollar out of fifty cents.' I let him have it on the immorality of profits. 'I'm against profits,' I say; 'I won't work for a corporation that profits from making shit. And if you're making something worthwhile, you should be giving it away.'

"What they always ask is, 'Why do you want to join our firm, Mr. Ah— Ah Sing?' They don't understand, I don't want to. I have to. And I don't join; I rule. But the most they'll let me do is the filing. How I answer, I say, 'I be-leaf in high high finance. I be-leaf in credit. Lend money; get interesting. Smallkidtime, I like bang money like Scrooge McDuck. I also likee bad Beagle Boys—follow map and dig under city into fault. No, not San Andreas Fault. Bang fault. Safu.' I was up for teller—I'm pretty smart— passed typing, passed adding machine—but when they call the tellers 'our girls,' I can tell they're not about to hire me.

"I'm unfit for office work. I'm facing up to that. And I can't write sales anymore. It fucks me up bad to sell anything to anybody. I have no attitude against blue collar, just so long as they make fruit cocktail instead of bombs, but I hate to lie that I'm not too overeducated. At this hiring hall for Fruitvale, guess what the guy says to me? He says, 'Do you have your green card?' My skin turning browner, my back getting wet, my moustache drooping, I say the truth, 'I don't have to show you no steenking green card.' And I don't, don't have to show it, and don't have one. I get so fucking offended.

"Unemployed and looking, my task is to spook out prejudice. They'll say any kind of thing to the unemployed. In Angel tradition, let me pass on to you the trick question they're asking: 'What would you say your weak point is?' They ask in a terribly understanding manner, but don't you confide dick. You tell them you have no weak point. Zip. 'None that I can think of,' you say. 'Weak point?' you say. 'What you mean weak point? I only have strong points.' They get you to inform on yourself, then write you up, 'Hates business,' 'Can't add,' 'Shy with customers.'

"My caseworker at the Employment Office, that is, the Office of Human Development—he's right over there—give him a hand—stand up —take a bow—Mr. Leroy Sanchez—advised me to get a haircut, and sent me to this shopping-news office on the Peninsula. On the bus, I thought out the power that would be mine peacemongering the shoppers with an aboveground grass-roots press. I'd be practicing right politics among locals who buy and sell. A radical can't accuse me, 'Poet, aussi, get your ass street-ward,' that is, aux barricades et rues of Burlingame. I'd already be out on the block. Dig: the shopping news taking a stand on zoning—zoning can change society—re-seating the draft board and ex-locating the recruiting office. We'll sponsor contests with trips to Russia and Cuba and China for exchange workers and exchange soldiers. They will feel possessive of the Alameda shipyards, and can't bear to bomb them. We'll join one another's Friends of the Library and League of Women Voters and Audubon Society and food co-op and Sierra Club and S.P.C.A. and SANE and cornea bank. We exchange families and pets and recipes and civil servants. Like Leadership Day in high school, we hand over the running of the Government and everything to them, and vice versa. We do one another's work and keep up one another's social invitations. Sister cities conduct the foreign policy. Pretty soon we'll be all miscegenated and intermarried, we'll be patriotic to more than one place. By the time I got off the bus, I wanted the gig a lot. I was on time for my appointment. I gave my plan for world peace to the editor. I hope he appropriates my ideas. And you appropriate them too. Please. He asked, 'How old are you?' They think we look young. I told him nicely that I wasn't a short and young Chinese boy. He didn't hire me. I'll make my own shopping news. I'm passing the hat. Will you please put some money in it toward offset printing of my shopping news?"

As you may imagine, when Wittman promised a love story, but it was turning into a between-gigs story, he was losing some audience. He didn't try to stop them. Go ahead, leave. He did notice when this one and that one cut out. It's all right. Go. Go. Squeeze out between the knees and the chairbacks. (There are two types of audience members when they're excuse-me-leaving-excuse-me—some turn their ass and some their genitals toward the faces in a row.) They love fight scenes; they love firecrackers. But during a soliloquy when a human being is thinking out how to live, everybody walks about, goes to the can, eats, visits. O audience. For those who stayed with him, those with hungry ears but nobody has read to them since bedtime stories, he kept on talking. Those kind people were putting money and red envelopes into the hat.

"Readers will be able to pick up my shopping news for free. I'm going to give ideas on how to live on barely anything. From experiments in living, I know that three thousand dollars a year is plenty enough to live on and to sock some away as back-up for eventualities, and for projects such as this play. Our editorial policy will be that Congress has to pass Walter Reuther's plan for a guaranteed annual minimum living wage for United Auto Workers and everybody—three thousand dollars, which will bring every American up to the official poverty level. A married couple could pool their money—six thousand dollars. Two couples—twelve thousand dollars, a ten-percent down payment on a hundred and twenty thousand dollars worth of communal land. Life is possible.

"I want to run an information exchange on how to live like a China Man. Whenever you buy a newspaper, whenever you spend a dime for a pay toilet, you leave the door of the dispenser or the can open—don't slam it—for the next guy on voluntary poverty who comes along. I've found a route of newspaper dispensers where somebody's being regularly thoughtful of me. I hardly buy anything. I use the bathroom at Pam Pam's without being a customer, and they're okay about it. Lately I order pizza, and leave an unbitten wedge for some hungry person to grab ahead of the busboy. Do the same with club sandwiches. I'm going to make a listing of cafés where you may sit for a long time over one cup of coffee, and they don't say, 'There's a dead one at table eleven.' Sticks and stones. Just be sure to tip the waitress extra well. The Christian Science Reading Room is a private club for yourself alone, no other readers ever in there. Old St. Mary's has a reading room too, and the church part is open day and night seven days a week; in the middle of the night when you're freaking out, it's a quiet dark place to come down, sniffing the India Imports smells. Sometime in our lives, everyone ought to live on just what nature and society leave for us. Loquats dropping off the park trees bid us who know they're not poisonous, 'Eat me. Eat me.' To live on leavings, we find out just how inhabitable this planet, this country is. I pick up stuff off the street that I don't even need. I have to think up uses for what's there. If you sit on the seawall at Baker Beach or Aquatic Park for quite some time, you'll see the shoes and socks that nobody is coming back for. You'll not be wearing a drowned man's shoes; he went out into the water or walked along the shore and lost his landmarks. If they're still there after your own long walk, they're yours.

Take them or the tide will. Of course, later, you will lose those shoes, and the watch that was inside one of them; there's a losing karma to things that you find. Like there's a stealing karma to hot stuff. When a Chinatown coot gets his unregistered gun stolen from under his pillow, and another old coot gives him his, that gun gets stolen too. My free shopping news will help every human being survive as an artist. If you hadn't helped me put on this show, I was going to drop Xeroxed copies of scripts into Goodwill bins. Painters can use the Salvation Army thrift shop for a gallery. Shoppers who buy art there would also buy playscripts, and read them and perform them.

"Among the ads about the price of bananas and birthday clowns and other odd jobs, I plan to keep running my idea for an anti-war ritual: Cut off the trigger finger instead of circumcision for all the boy babies, and all the girl babies too. Chop. I'll volunteer to have mine done first. On the other hand, the people who love shooting, they'll use their toes, they'll use their noses. It's more difficult to make peace than war. You take war away from human beings, you have to surrogate them with projects that haven't been thought up yet. Workers at weapons factories could keep their jobs making missiles but out of papier-mâché, and install them in the landscape for admiration. They're launchable. We let ourselves go at long last, drop them on Russia and Cuba, and invite them to drop theirs on us.

"You didn't come to the theater on your night offu to think about jobs and war; you came to be entertained. For my last bit, I'll tell you about marriage. I was learning to live poor—for one only. Then I got married. But. I have mixed feelings about that. About her. I may be getting a divorce. I have a marital problem. I married my second-best girl. I like her. She started the marital problem. She said that she's not in love with me. 'I'm not in love with you, Wittman,' is how she put it. I answered, 'Well, I'm not in love with you either, but. It's okay.' If I were in love with her, or vice versa, we should go to a shrink. Shrink the *romance* out of us. She—my wife—said, 'We haven't been romantic about each other. I never fantasized about you.' And I said, 'That's good. I don't want anybody fantasizing about anybody.' And she said, 'Out there somewhere is the soul chick you're going to fall in love with and leave me for. She's waiting for you, and you're waiting for her. The prosaic things you do, Wittman, will be interesting in her eyes. You'll become brave showing off for her. You better start regretting our marriage now so you won't regret everything when you're old, and it's too late.' One of the things I like best about my wife, she'll face a bad trip head on.

"I am sometimes somewhat in love with her. But it's not fate or magic.

There's a specialness about her that is photographable. She has an expression on her face like she's appreciating whomever she's looking at. All she has to do is regard me, behold me like that, and I won't be able to leave her. She's listening; I hope she doesn't get self-conscious on me; I hope she isn't acting. The way her top lip upcurves with a dip in the center—she can't act that. She can't make mean lips. She smiles sideways. Quite a few movie stars have a sideways smile and beholding eyes, and we fans want them to keep reacting like that—to us, to everything. And she's got long blonde hair. I wouldn't mind a shrink immunizing me to it. I don't like being taken in by movie-star eyes and movie-star hair and movie-star lips.

"She admitted to me how she got this guy. Before she met me. On a rainy night, she went with her girlfriend and this guy into a coffeeshop. He held the umbrella and the door for this other girl to go ahead; he went in next. Water poured off the umbrella onto the girl in back, that is, her, my wife. He had made his choice. She said to herself, 'I'm going to get him.' At the next party, she let her hair down all clean and dry, a-tumble and curly, cascades of it down her back and shoulders, parted to the side, the way bad girls part hair, for a hank to fall over one eye and have to be seductively pushed back. That guy didn't have a chance. He was mesmerized in love, and the only thing changed about her was her hair. She's told me her magic. I've seen her with her hair wet and in a rubber band and in curlers. I'm not taken in. I'm not under her blonde power.

"She's not Chinese, I'll admit, but those girls are all out with white guys. What am I to do, huh? I don't want a Hong Kong wife marrying me for a green card. I've been testing my wife out. There was this sofa game in *Life* magazine a long time ago, where the guy sits at one end of the sofa and the girl at the other. They look into each other's eyes. In the next frame, they move closer together. 'Irresistibly,' said the caption, they meet in the middle. In the last frame, they're in each other's arms, kissing. A time clock at the corners of the pictures marked off minutes and seconds. There were three test couples in a series of long photographs. I've wondered, what happens if you mix the couples up, or pair strangers at random? My wife and I tried it. She can resist forever. She kept talking; she recited love poems; she read. So I read back to her Thomas Hardy, where Sergeant Troy says, 'Probably some one man on an average falls in love with each ordinary woman. She can marry him; he is content, and leads a useful life. Such a woman as you a hundred men always covet—your eyes will bewitch scores on scores into an unavailing fancy for you—you can only marry one of that many. . . . The rest may try to get over their passion with more or less success. But all these men will be saddened. And not only those ninety-nine men, but the ninety-nine women they might have married are saddened with them. There's my tale.' 'We don't want to be part of a system like that,' I told her. We're going to prove that any two random people can get together and learn to care for each other. I'm against magic; I go into despair over things happening that skip causation. The superior man loves anyone he sets his mind to. Otherwise, we're fucked.

"From the day that I made my explanations to my wife, she hasn't cleaned the apartment. I noticed before long that we'd gone through the dishes. Some of them have turned into ashtrays. I can trace the mess beginning at when I took my Hardyesque stand against romance. There are coffee cups all over the place with mold growing out of them. I can hear the dregs festering and bubbling. Her cups are especially disgusting because she uses cream. But black coffee grows mold too. Even non-dairy coffee creamer grows mold. Coffee must be nutritious, it can cultivate that much life. You have to watch where you step or sit. You kick aside newspapers, and the coffee cups underneath spill coins of mold that blend with the rug. All the doorknobs have towels and coats on them. I don't know where so much stuff comes from. It doesn't belong to me. It probably used to be in the drawers and closets, and she isn't putting it back. The place smells of cat piss and cat shit. My sense of smell is shot from smoking, but the cat is getting through to my nose. She got this S.P.C.A. cat and made it into a flealess indoor cat. The vet de-fleaed it the same day the fumigator came. The cat never goes outdoors again. She didn't have a cat when I married her. She does clean out the cat box and refill the kitty litter. But that fucking disoriented cat's been shitting in the clothes and newspapers. You don't want to step or sit for the cat turds.

"At meals, we clear off two spots at the table for her setting and my setting. The centerpiece is growing—rib bones from Emil Villa's Hickory Pit, a broken wineglass and candlewax and shrimp shells from an October candlelight dinner, plates from our last evening of clean dishes, movie popcorn boxes and used paper plates. I eat amongst mementos of other breakfasts, other suppers, naked lunches.

"The water standing in the kitchen sink started out as a soak for the pots and pans. Some are soaking in the bathtub too, and the skillet is in the living room from when we ate out of it. She can't wash dishes anymore because you can't run clean water without delving your arm through the scum and knives to unclog the drain. I wish, were I to flip the dispose-all on, a rotation would vortically twirl the room including the cat, and grind everything down and away.

"To be honest, one of my wife's attractions is that she's got a coin-operated washer and dryer in the garage. She did some laundry the other day; she picked her clothes out of the piles, and washed them, and ironed them. She does outfits to go to work in. I tossed in a pair of my skivvies, which didn't come back. As long as she's running a wash, she could do an item of another person's, right? I don't give her a full load. It's not as if she has to get depressed at the laundromat." Wittman put on his shirt; *he* didn't have the habit of dropping dirty clothes on top of piles of newspapers and banana peels and hair and cigarettes.

"We've been running all over the apartment churning up the newspapers and cat shit, yelling at each other, looking for a shoe and car fare and the phone. The off-the-hook noise is driving me nuts. I fell down slipping on a phonograph record under newspaper. She's always late for work because she can't find her car keys, or the house keys. They'll fire her, then the two of us on Unemployment, she can stay home and clean up. I was almost late myself tonight. The keys to the place were in the toaster oven. I don't know how they got there. Like the gravity has been acting up. She does cook. She's been standing at the stove and eating over the saucepan. If I want any, I have to eat her leftovers. We're leaving the front door unlocked, which the bags of garbage and the bags of groceries are shoving against. Anybody who would want to do some thieving in there, clean us out. Please. The ironing board unfolded out of the wall and dropped across the doorway.

"In the bathroom, I drape my washcloth on the rim of the sink, flat and neat, and she puts hers on top of it. Mine never dries. It took me days to detect that the mildew I was smelling was coming off of me. The newspapers for reading on the john get wet and print the tiles black. The black in the shower stall is an alga, and a strain of red alga is growing too.

"On Wednesdays, she says, 'Tonight's garbage night.' She knows the schedule. On her way to her car for work, she could pick up a bag of garbage and beat the scavengers to the cans. I've never believed the stereotype that Caucasians are dirty, but. Her place wasn't a dumpyard when I first went over there. Cleaned up for visitors, I guess. Good thing I haven't given up my own apartment until she learns better habits. The broom is missing. We need to hose the place out, or burn it down—a good fire—and start over. She isn't house-proud. I won't ask her to clean up. Our conversation has got to transcend garbage and laundry and cat shit. I don't want to live for garbage night. Domesticity is fucked. I am in a state of fucked domesticity. I am trying for a marriage of convenience, which you would think would make life convenient at least.

"Each of us announces to the other which room he's walking to. 'Well, I think I'll watch t.v. while I eat this t.v. dinner.' 'I'm going to read in the bathroom.' We don't want to lose track of each other's whereabouts. Things sure don't feel like they're about to end up in sex again. Yet how am I going to leave her? I ought to go out the door with my laundrybag and my toothbrush, and keep walking." He held his thumb and forefinger in a downward ring, as if holding his toothbrush by a suitcase-type handle.

"I had thought that one advantage of marrying a white chick would be that she'd say, 'I love you,' easily and often. It's part of their culture. They say 'I love you' like 'Hi, there,' nothing to it, to any friend, neighbor, family member, husband. You know how verbal they are. No skin off their pointy noses to say 'I love you.' But all I'm getting is, 'I'm not in love with you, Wittman.'

"The marriage is about two months old. I know what will happen next. I'm going to stay married to her; we're going to grow old. At our deathbed scene, whoever's not too gone to talk—she, I hope—will say at last, 'I love you.' I'll hear her. (The ears are the last to go.) And I'll think, Do you mean *in* love with me? Have you now or at any time in our life together ever loved me? Did you finally fall in love with me for a few moments during our long marriage? And since she has E.S.P. on me, she'll answer, 'Sure. Do you love me back? If you love me back, nod or blink.' I'll die suspicious and being suspected of loving and loving back. I'll nod, I'll blink. So I lied.

"Taña, if you're listening in the wings, you're free to leave if you want to leave me. But I'll always love you unromantically. I'll clean up the place, I get the hint. You don't have to be the housewife. I'll do one-half of the housewife stuff. But you can't call me your wife. You don't have to be the wife either. See how much I love you? Unromantically but."

Out of all that mess of talk, people heard "I love you" and "I'll always love you" and that about dying and still loving after a lifelong marriage. They took Wittman to mean that he was announcing his marriage to Taña, and doing so with a new clever wedding ritual of his own making. His community and family applauded. They congratulated him. They pushed and pulled the shy bride on stage, and shot pictures of her and of the couple. They hugged the groom, and kissed the bride. They teased them into kissing each other. More cameras flashed and popped. They threw rice. They congratulated their parents and grandparents. Their parents congratulated one another. Friends were carrying tables of food through the doors, and spreading a cast party and wedding banquet. And more firecrackers went off. And champagne corks popped. To Wittman and Taña—long life, happy marriage, many children. Taña and Wittman Ah Sing were stars in a lavish, generous wedding celebration. To drums and horns, the dragons and lions were dancing again, a bunny-hopping conga line that danced out of the house and into the street. Wittman's community was blessing him, whether he liked it or not.

And he was having a good time. He still had choices of action, more maybe. If he wanted to drop out and hide out, he had heard of the tunnel that goes under a hill between the old Army Presidio and the Marina for a subway never built. And somewhere in Fresno, there's an underground garden of fifty rooms. And he himself had been beneath the Merced Theater in Los Angeles. He had memories of dug-out dressing rooms that were part of an underground city where Chinese Americans lived and did business after the L.A. Massacre, nineteen killed. He and other draft dodgers could hide in such places until the war was over. But better yet, now that he had Taña—she could be the paper-wife escort who will run him across the U.S.-Canada border at Niagara Falls. He had made up his mind: he will not go to Viet Nam or to any war. He had staged the War of the Three Kingdoms as heroically as he could, which made him start to understand: The three brothers and Cho Cho were masters of war; they had worked out strategies and justifications for war so brilliantly that their policies and their tactics are used today, even by governments with nuclear-powered weapons. And they *lost*. The clanging and banging fooled us, but now we know— they lost. Studying the mightiest war epic of all time, Wittman changed— beeen!—into a pacifist. Dear American monkey, don't be afraid. Here, let us tweak your ear, and kiss your other ear.

THANKS   To friends whose stories inspire my stories:

EARLL KINGSTON   for the railroad reader of the West, the man with the addictive
   sperm, the Osaka Stock Exchange, and more.
JAMES HONG   for his role in *The Barretts of Wimpole Street*.
JOHN CRONIN   for the man whose Dear John letter falls out of the *P.D.R.*
JAMES D. HOUSTON   for the fool-for-literature's reading list from *West Coast
   Fiction*, Bantam Books, Inc., 1979.
MARGARET MITCHELL DUKORE   for "I'd rather be dead than boring," from
   A Novel Called Heritage, Simon and Schuster, 1982.
SUSIE QUINN GANIGAN and DUSTY on the train.
BRITT PYLAND   for his arrangements of postcards at the airport.
VICTORIA NELSON   for her recall of *The Saragossa Manuscript*.
STEPHEN SUMIDA   for the four-act play, which is his novel-in-progress about being
   lost in the archipelago and the return of the fox, and for his luaus.
PHYLLIS H. THOMPSON   for the wisdom about vows from "Blue Flowers," a poem
   in *The Ghosts of Who We Were*, University of Illinois Press, 1986.
L. LEWIS STOUT   for the Electric Cassandra from *Trolling in America*, a screenplay.
AURORA PUTSY HONG   for how to tell left from right.
GARY AND MOLLY MCCLURG WONG   for Gavino McWong.
JACK CHEN   for *his* Pear Garden in the West.
ROBERT WINKLEY   for his memory of the Sun Yat Sen Hallowe'en tradition.
JACK PRESLEY   for his contribution to R.N.A.-D.N.A.
RICHARD DI GRAZIA   for "the marriage of Death and Fun" from "The Witness," a
   poem, and for fire socks.
DENIS KELLY   for his dancing bouillon cube.
RHODA FEINBERG   for the papier-mâché missiles.
JOHN VEGLIA   for asking after that land where words are pictures and have tones.

To the John Simon Guggenheim Foundation and the M. Thelma McAndless
Distinguished Professor Chair in the Humanities at Eastern Michigan University for
generous financial support.

A NOTE ON THE TYPE

The text of this book was set in a digitized
version of Electra, a typeface designed by
W. A. Dwiggins (1880–1956). This face cannot be
classified as either modern or old style. It is not
based on any historical model; nor does it echo any
particular period or style. It avoids the extreme
contrasts between thick and thin elements that
mark most modern faces, and attempts to give a
feeling of fluidity, power, and speed.

Composed by New England Typographic Service,
Bloomfield, Connecticut

Printed and bound by The Haddon Craftsmen,
Scranton, Pennsylvania

Typography and binding design by
Dorothy Schmiderer Baker